THE PRINCE'S CINDERELLA DOC

LOUISA HEATON

PREGNANT BY THE PLAYBOY SURGEON

LUCY RYDER

MILLS & BOON

First Published in Great Britain 2019
by Mills & Boon, an imprint of HarperCollins*Publishers*
1 London Bridge Street, London, SE1 9GF

The Prince's Cinderella Doc © 2019 by Louisa Heaton

Pregnant by the Playboy Surgeon © 2019 by Bev Riley

ISBN: 978-0-263-26967-3

MIX
Paper from
responsible sources
FSC® C007454

FSC
www.fsc.org

This book is produced from independently certified FSC™ paper
to ensure responsible forest management.
For more information visit www.harpercollins.co.uk/green.

Printed and bound in Spain
by CPI, Barcelona

Louisa Heaton lives on Hayling Island, Hampshire, with her husband, four children and a small zoo. She has worked in various roles in the health industry—most recently four years as a Community First Responder, answering 999 calls. When not writing Louisa enjoys other creative pursuits, including reading, quilting and patchwork—usually instead of the things she *ought* to be doing!

With two beautiful daughters, **Lucy Ryder** has had to curb her adventurous spirit and settle down. But because she's easily bored by routine she's turned to writing as a creative outlet and to romances because—'What else is there other than chocolate?' Characterised by friends and family as a romantic cynic, Lucy can't write serious stuff to save her life. She loves creating characters who are funny, romantic and just a little cynical.

THE PRINCE'S
CINDERELLA DOC

LOUISA HEATON

MILLS & BOON

To Becca, with all my love.

You are the strongest young woman I know. xxx

CHAPTER ONE

FOR YEARS DR KRYSTIANA SZENAC had walked along the beach with her dog Bruno, allowing her gaze to fall upon the faraway façade of Il Palazzo Grande—the Grand Palace. It was like a fine jewel in the warm sunshine. A glittering building set atop a hill, with every window, every white wall, reflecting the light. She'd often wondered about what it would be like to live in such a place, but had never imagined for one moment that she would ever pass through the arched gates into the royal sanctuary where the King and his son the Crown Prince lived.

He didn't know it, but she felt a kinship with the Prince, and every time she thought about their connection—which was often—she would smile to herself, knowing it was ridiculous because he didn't even know she existed!

But he was about to.

Krystiana sucked in a breath as the large armoured car drove her through the gates and into the palace grounds. She gazed out of the window, feeling like a silly little tourist as she took in the guards in their dark blue uniforms and the white sashes that crossed their chests, the flower displays—perfectly tended, not a weed in place—and the architecture: solid white walls rising high, the crenelated roof with the billowing flag of the royal family and the circular towers in each corner.

It had all the hallmarks of the castle it had once been, even down to the other guards she saw at the top of each tower, ever watchful, even though there had been no threat to Isla Tamoura for hundreds of years. It was pomp and circumstance for the tourists who flocked to the island in their droves, keen to explore this jewel off Italy's south-eastern coast.

Did Crown Prince Matteo feel safe behind these walls? She couldn't see why he wouldn't. All the barriers… All the guards… Security was high. She'd already had her bags searched before she was even allowed in the car. A rugged, dark-suited secret service agent had frisked her down too—the most bodily contact she'd had in years.

It had made her feel uncomfortable, but she'd bitten her lip until it was done and then smiled politely at the agent as he'd opened the car door for her. *'Grazie.'*

The agent hadn't said much. He'd had that mysterious, moody, steely exterior down perfectly, getting into the car and saying into his phone in Italian, 'I have the parcel. Delivering in fifteen minutes—that's fifteen minutes.'

She'd raised her eyebrows, having never been referred to as a parcel before. She'd been called a lot of other things in her life, but never a *parcel*.

The car purred its way through another set of arches and then came to rest outside a columned terrace. The agent got out, adjusted the buttons on the front of his dark suit and looked about him before opening her door.

Krystiana stepped out, her nerves getting the better of her at last, and wished she'd had something to eat before leaving home. Just something that would have settled her stomach. But there'd been almost no time to prepare. The call had come in unexpectedly. She was needed immediately. There had just been time to pack a bag for an overnight stay. To call her neighbour and ask her to feed and walk Bruno.

A day of living in the palace! It was almost a dream. That a woman like her—a woman who had been raised initially in Krakow, Poland—should find herself hobnobbing with royalty.

Well, it wasn't exactly hobnobbing. It was work. Standing in for the royal doctor to run the Crown Prince through his yearly physical. She'd been chosen because she shared a clinic with Dr Bonetti, the King's private physician, and had already had her background checked. That was what happened when your colleague was the King's doctor. There could be no chance of any impropriety connected with the royals.

They'd already had enough excitement, after all.

A red carpet led from the car up to the white stone steps and into the palace proper.

On wobbly legs she ascended the stairs, aware that the agent was following along behind her. She assumed someone else would bring her bag. As she neared the top of the steps and saw the opulent interior of the palace she felt her pulse quicken, and her mouth went as dry as the Dune Dorate—the Golden Dunes.

She tried her hardest to appear nonchalant as she walked across the marble floor towards a man dressed like a butler, who had the rigid stature of an old soldier.

'Dr Szenac, welcome to the Grand Palace. It is a pleasure to welcome you to these halls. My name is Sergio and I shall be your attendant whilst you are here. Have you been to the palace before?'

She shook her head, her long golden plait swinging at her back. 'No. It's my first time.'

'Oh! Well, please don't let it be your last. I'm reliably

informed that the public tours are very entertaining and informative, if you wish to know anything of its history.'

She'd never been one to study history. History should stay in the past, where it belonged. Not be dragged back into the present at every opportunity. She could appreciate beautiful architecture, and respect the amount of time a building had stood in place, but she was far more interested in the people who lived in it now.

'Thank you. I might do that one day.'

Sergio led her up a curved stairwell, adorned with portraiture of Kings and Queens of the past. She could see the familiar glossy black hair and beautiful blue eyes of the Romano family in most of them. Occasionally there was a portrait of someone who had married into the family, including the one she stood in front of now: Queen Marianna, sadly passed.

'She was beautiful, wasn't she?' asked Sergio.

'Most definitely.'

'And not just in looks. She had a very kind heart. It broke her when her son was taken. She died never knowing of his safe return.'

Krystiana nodded. It was tragic. Crown Prince Matteo's kidnapping had been a story she had followed with bated breath, praying for his safe release. It had been a couple of years ago now, but still, she knew in her heart that it would never be forgotten by those involved.

'The Prince must have been devastated when he got home to discover his mother had died?'

Sergio nodded sadly. 'They were very close. Ah, here are your quarters.'

He stopped in front of a set of double doors and swung them open wide, and once again she tried to appear unaffected by the riches within, simply nodding and smiling.

'Thank you, Sergio. These look wonderful. I'm sure I'll be very comfortable.'

'Your initial appointment with the Prince is at three this afternoon. Take time to settle in. Pull this red sash—' he indicated a brocade sash that hung by the white marble fireplace '—if you want anything and I'll be with you momentarily.'

'Thank you.'

'A servant will bring up your bag. Are there any refreshments I can get you? A drink, perhaps?'

She *was* thirsty, and now that some of her nerves were settling she felt that maybe she could eat. 'Some coffee would be wonderful. And some water? Maybe a bite to eat? I had to come here in rather a rush and I'm afraid I didn't get a chance to dine.'

'I'll have a selection of food brought up to you immediately. Do you have any allergies or food preferences?'

'No.'

He bowed. 'Then I will be back shortly. Welcome to the Grand Palace, Doctor.' And he departed, closing the doors behind him.

Krystiana spun around, headed straight over to the doors in the far wall and flung them back, allowing in the bright sunshine, the freedom of the outdoors, as she stepped out onto a large terrace and breathed in the scent of bougainvillea, jasmine and columbine.

An array of flowers grew in small ornamental pots, framed by clipped firs in taller blue pots. A table and six chairs were sheltered by a large umbrella. Below her were the private royal gardens and she took a moment to take in the sight. They were simply gorgeous: a low maze with a water feature at its centre—a stone horse crashing through stone waves—an ornamental garden, a lily pond, a mosaic. Little paths ran here and there—one down to a grotto, another through a set of rose arches to a circular bench and a bust.

Someone had poured a lot of heart and soul into this garden. She wondered who. Some gardener? A series of them? Each of them adding something new during their term, perhaps?

Beyond the palace walls she saw olive groves, small terracotta-coloured churches, roadside shrines and undulating hillsides that shimmered with heat from the overhead sun. It was something she could paint. She often turned to creativity when she was stressed. She'd never had such a view before—she *had* to sketch it before she left.

Not that I could ever forget this.

The view had a timeless quality. She almost felt she could stand there all day admiring it. But reality beckoned, and so she turned to observe her rooms more carefully. It was the most sumptuous suite—all white marble and silver accents. A large bed occupied the centre of the bedroom, with pristine white sheets and a gold counterpane. There was a desk and chair in the living room, a comfortable pair of sofas in palest cornflower-blue and vases of fresh flowers on almost every surface. A door in the corner of the bedroom led to an en-suite bathroom, with a sunken bath in the centre, a walk-in shower, a toilet and bidet and a huge assortment of toiletries in a room that was all mirrors.

Briefly, she wondered about the poor maids who had to clean it each day, buffing it to a shine, because not a single surface had a fingerprint or a smudge on it anywhere.

But what would you expect in a palace?

The opulence was meant to make her feel good. Treasured and important. But Krystiana had always preferred simplicity and rustic touches. Wooden bowls, plain knives and forks for her food. Simple cloth mats beneath her plate. Watercolours. Plain whitewashed walls—the minimalist look, with stone and driftwood she'd collected from the beach where she walked each day, barefoot, her trousers rolled up as she paddled in the water.

All of this was nice. Amazing, in fact. But it wasn't real.

She felt like Alice through the looking glass, looking at a world she didn't quite understand. But she was keen to know more.

Crown Prince Matteo Romano shook the hand of the cultural attaché from Portugal and bade him a safe journey home. He was looking forward to the future visit he would take to Lisbon, to see for himself the amazing artwork said to be displayed in Galleria 111. The attaché had done a fine job of convincing him the place was worth fitting in to his schedule, especially as he was such a fan of the surrealist painter António Dacosta, the work of whom the gallery had confirmed they had a huge stock.

As soon as the attaché had left, Matteo let out a breath and relaxed for a moment. He was almost done with his schedule for today. A few brief moments alone, and then he would meet the new doctor who had been brought in due to Dr Bonetti's family emergency.

He hoped everything was all right with the man's family. He'd known Dr Bonetti for years, and had met his wife and children. They'd all dined together on occasion and he thought very well of them all. He envied the doctor his happy marriage and his smiling children. They all seemed so *together*. So…*content*.

None of them had the stresses that were placed upon *his* shoulders. Who could understand the burden of being a prince, a future king, without having lived in his shoes?

He reached for the coffee that Sergio had brought in earlier, along with the news that the stand-in doctor had arrived and was settling in. The drink was cooler than he'd like—his meeting with the Portuguese attaché had gone on longer than he'd expected—but he continued to drink it until it was finished. Then, needing the freshness of the outdoors and the calm that viewing the gardens gave him, he stepped out of the terrace doors onto the balcony to gaze down into the palace gardens.

As always, he felt serenity begin to settle in his soul and he closed his eyes and breathed in the warm, fragrant air. *Perfezionare.* Perfect. His hands came to rest on the rich stone balustrade and for a moment he just stood there, centring himself. Grounding himself.

Behind him there was the gentle sound of Sergio clearing his throat. 'Dr Krystiana Szenac, sir.'

'*Grazie*, Sergio.'

He turned and there she was. Dressed in a black knee-length skirt and an emerald-green blouse, her blonde hair flowing over her shoulder in a long plait. A hint of make-up and an amazing smile.

She curtsied. 'Your Highness.'

'Dr Szenac. It's a pleasure.' He stepped forward to shake her hand. 'I appreciate you coming at short notice and hope our pulling you from your schedule hasn't disrupted your life too much.'

'No. Not at all. I was able to make new arrangements. When your country calls, you answer.'

He smiled. 'Indeed. I take it your journey was uneventful?'

'It was wonderful, thank you.'

'And Dr Bonetti?'

'His wife has been taken into emergency surgery, but I'm afraid that's all I know.'

Emergency surgery? That didn't sound good.

'Let us hope she pulls through. Alexis Bonetti is a strong woman—I'm sure her constitution will hold her in good stead.'

She nodded. 'I hope so.'

'May I offer you a refreshment before we settle down?'

'I'm fine, thank you. Sergio had some coffee brought to my room.'

'Excellent.'

He stared at her for a moment more and then indicated that maybe they should sit down at one of the tables on the sun terrace. He pulled out a chair for her, and she smiled her thanks at him as she sat down.

He sat opposite. 'Well, I'll try not to keep you here too long. I just need my yearly physical to be carried out. Dr Bonetti usually does the deed, but this year it will be down to you—if that's all right?'

'Absolutely.'

'He usually runs a barrage of tests—I'm sure there's a list somewhere. And then, if I'm all okay, he signs me off for another year.'

'I know what to do—don't worry. He emailed me your file, with a list of assessments I need to put you through and the paperwork that needs filling out.' Dr Szenac smiled. 'According to your file you're in very good health, and your last couple of physicals had you back at full health after your...' she looked uncomfortable '...blip.'

'My *kidnapping*. Yes. Well... Two years in a cave, will do that to any man.'

She nodded. 'Yes. My apologies for bringing it up.'

'Not at all. My therapist says it's good to talk about it. The more often the better.'

She smiled her thanks.

He didn't want her to feel uncomfortable, so he tried to change the subject. 'You're originally from Poland?'

'Yes. Krakow.'

'I've never been there. What's it like?'

'I don't know. I haven't been there for years. I just remember the grey and the cold.'

He saw her shiver and it intrigued him that she could still feel it, all these years later, just *thinking* about it.

'When did you move here?'

'When my mother died. My father was…away, and I had no one else except for my Aunt Carolina, who lives here.'

'On Isla Tamoura?'

'Yes.'

'Well, I'm very glad you're here.' He smiled.

She nodded. 'Yes. Me too.'

CHAPTER TWO

WHEN KRYSTIANA WOKE the next morning, the first thing she did was reach over and turn off her night-light. It was an automatic thing—something she hardly noticed doing—but today when she did so she stared at it for a moment, wondering if Crown Prince Matteo had one too.

For two years he'd been stuck in a cave. Was he now afraid of the dark?

Throwing off the bedcovers, she got up and threw open the double doors to the sun terrace. The fragrant air poured in and she closed her eyes for a moment as the warm rays from the sun caressed her skin. This was what she loved about living here. The warmth. The colour. The heat. The beauty of this treasured isle.

How fortunate that her aunt lived here. It had been exactly what she had needed after her experience at the hands of her father—to leave such an ugly existence behind and come to a place that only had beauty at its core. There had been a new language to learn, but wonderful, loving, passionate people to support her. New friends. A new life. Isla Tamoura had given her a new beginning, a new hope, and she loved it here so much.

Krystiana took a quick shower and braided her long hair into its usual plait, donned a summery dress and sat down to eat the breakfast that had been brought in on a tray. She was used to eating breakfast alone. She quite enjoyed it. But this time, before her day started, she grabbed her pad and pencils and began sketching the view from her balcony. This afternoon she would be going home again, so there was no time to spare.

Her sketch was vague. Outlines and shapes. She would fill in the colour later, allowing her imagination to take flight. She took a couple of quick photos using her phone.

She almost lost track of time, and when she did glance at her watch she saw there were only a few minutes until nine o clock—her scheduled time to give the Prince his yearly physical. She left her pad and pencil on the bed, finished her orange juice and then pulled the sash to call Sergio. She wasn't sure exactly where in the palace the examination would take place.

Sergio arrived, looking as perfectly presented as always. 'Good morning, Dr Szenac. I hope you slept well?'

'Very well, Sergio, thank you. I have my appointment with His Highness Prince Matteo, to start his physical, but I'm not sure where I have to go.'

He nodded. 'I believe you are expected in the private gym. Dr Bonetti always carries out the yearly check-ups there.'

'Thank you.' She'd had no idea the palace had its own gym—but, then again, why wouldn't it? Matteo and his family could hardly pop out to the local leisure centre if they wanted to lift a few weights, could they?

Sergio led her through the palace, down long tapestry-filled hallways, past vast vases so big she could have climbed inside and not been seen even standing upright. They passed a coat of arms, a suit of armour, and fireplaces filled with flowers, until he brought her to a set of double doors.

'The gym, Dr Szenac. All of Dr Bonetti's equipment has been laid out for you, and the computer has been set up for you to enter the results of each test for the record.'

'Thank you—that's very kind.'

'The computer isn't likely to be difficult, but if you do have any queries we have an IT expert on hand.'

'That's marvellous.'

Sergio smiled and opened the doors.

The gym was filled with all types of equipment—treadmills, stair-masters, weight machines, free-standing weights, workout equipment, yoga mats. Anything and everything seemed to be here, and one wall was made of glass that revealed a room beyond filled with a full-length swimming pool.

Pretty impressive!

But she didn't have time to linger. The Prince would be here at any moment and she wanted to be prepared.

She was running her eye over what she needed to achieve today, reminding herself of the assessments, when she became aware of a presence behind her.

'Dr Szenac.'

She turned and bowed slightly. 'Your Highness.'

'I'm ready, if you are?'

Smiling, she nodded. 'Absolutely. Ready to begin with the basics? I'll need to do blood pressure, pulse and SATs.'

'Perfect.'

'All right. Take a seat.'

She began to set up her equipment—the pulse oximeter that she'd place on his finger to measure not only his pulse but the oxygen levels in his blood, and the arm cuff around his upper arm that would measure his blood pressure.

His basic measurements were perfect. Exactly what she'd expected them to be.

'Okay, now I need to check your height and weight.'

'I don't think I've shrunk.'

She smiled. 'Glad to hear it.'

Again, his weight was perfect for his height.

'Now I'd like to set you up for a treadmill test. I'll need to attach you to a breathing tube, so we can measure oxygen intake, heart-rate and lung capacity whilst you run up a slight incline for three minutes.'

He nodded. 'Can I warm up first?'

'By all means.'

She looked at his previous measurements and typed them into the computer, aware that Matteo was stripping off behind her and beginning to stretch.

When she turned around she noted that he was in excellent physical shape. Clearly he used the gym often to keep fit. His muscle tone was almost beautiful. His figure was sculpted, without being overly worked. It seemed almost wrong to look at him and admire him like that. Not least because he was a prince.

'Right, I need to attach these electrodes, if that's okay?'

Does my voice sound weird?

He stood still whilst she attached the electrodes to his chest and body, trying her hardest not to make eye contact, then attached the wires that hooked him up to the machine for a reading. She fastened a breathing mask around his nose and mouth, and suddenly there was that eye contact thing.

She could feel herself blushing. 'Okay... For the first minute I want you just to walk at a steady pace and then, when I tell you, I'm going to increase the speed and I want you to jog.'

'All right.'

'Ready?'

He gave her a thumbs-up and she started the treadmill and the EKG monitor that would read his heart's electrical activity. The machine began printing out on a paper roll and she watched it steadily, keeping a careful eye out for any issues, but it all looked fine.

She glanced up at him as he ran with a steady pace, his body like a well-oiled machine as he tackled the jog easily. His oxygen intake was perfect; his heart-rate was elevated, but not too much.

When the three minutes were over she switched everything off and then laid a hand on his wrist to check his pulse. She felt it pounding away beneath her fingertips and kept count, then made a note of the result.

'You're doing brilliantly.'

He pulled off the mask. 'Good to know.'

'You work out a lot?'

'Can't you tell?' He raised an eyebrow.

'Well, I…er…yes… You look very…er…'

He laughed. 'I meant can't you tell from my results?'

She flushed even redder and laughed with him. 'Oh, I see.' She nodded. 'Yes!'

'I try to do thirty minutes every other day, alternating with the pool. Lifting weights. Half an hour of cardio…'

'You do more than me.'

'It's easier for me. My life is scheduled to the minute, so I know when I can fit things in to get everything done.'

She was curious. 'Is that a perk or a drawback?' she asked. She wasn't sure she'd want to be so regimentally scheduled each day. What about free time? What about spontaneity?

'It depends on the day.' He laughed again, wiping his face with a towel.

'And today?'

He shrugged. 'Well, I have this, and then I get to spend some time with my daughter.'

'Princess Alexandra? She's beautiful. How old is she now?'

'Five.'

'You must be very proud of her.'

'I am. But I don't get to spoil her as often as I would like.'

Of course not. She didn't live with him. The Princess lived with her mother, at her family's private estate.

'That must be hard for you?'

He stared into her eyes. 'You have no idea.'

Oh, but I do, she thought. *I know how hard it is being away from those you love. I know only too well.*

She blinked rapidly and turned away, forcing her mind back to the assessment. 'Next test.'

'I'm all yours.' He did a mock bow.

Krystiana smiled and then indicated that he should move to the next machine.

They were just about finished with their testing when the doors to the gym opened and in walked Sergio, looking grave. It was the most solemn Matteo had ever seen him.

He finished towelling himself down and raised an eyebrow. 'Sergio? What is it?'

'I have some unfortunate news for Dr Szenac, sir.'

She looked up from her notes and frowned. Was it about Dr Bonetti's wife?

'I'm afraid there's been an accident at your villa. A drunk driver tried to take the corner near your abode too fast and ploughed into your home. I'm afraid your living area and bedroom have been almost destroyed, and the property is not safe for you to reside in just yet.'

Matteo was shocked and looked to Dr Szenac. 'I'm so sorry!'

Her face was almost white. 'Is the driver all right?'

He was impressed at how her concern was immediately for the driver.

'I believe he got away quite lightly, all things considered. He's being treated by the medics now.'

'Okay. Good. That's good.' She turned away, her thoughts in a distant place. 'Oh, my God. What about Bruno?'

'Bruno?'

'My dog. He's a rescue.'

'I believe your neighbour was out on a walk with him at the time,' Sergio replied.

'Oh, thank goodness!'

She sank down into a chair, her legs obviously trembling, and put her head in her hands. Matteo felt for her. Was her home ruined?

'You must stay here with us. Until everything is fixed.'

She looked up, tears in her eyes. 'I couldn't possibly do that.'

'Nonsense! It's done. Sergio, could you arrange for Dr Szenac's clothes and anything she needs to be brought to her quarters here in the palace? Including her dog, who I'm sure will bring her great comfort. We're going to have a guest for a while.'

'I don't know what to say…' she said, beginning to cry.

He smiled. 'Say yes.'

She looked at him for a long moment and he saw gratitude. 'Then, yes. Thank you. Yes.'

He nodded. 'Sergio? Make it happen.'

'I'm so lucky I was here when it happened, she said later. Otherwise I might have been injured!'

'Well, you were here, and that's all that matters.'

'But—'

'No buts. There's no point in wondering about what *might* have happened. You just need to worry about what *is* happening.' He smiled. 'I learned that in therapy. Look at me—spreading the knowledge.'

She smiled as she stroked Bruno's fur. They'd had a joyous reunion when Sergio had returned with her dog, her clothes, her computer and some rather startling photographs of the damage to her villa.

'That's going to take weeks to repair,' she'd said.

'Let me take care of that,' Matteo had offered.

'I couldn't possibly let you do that! It will cost a fortune!'

'Are you insured?'

'Yes.'

'Then don't worry about it. Let me do something good for you. You were kind enough to step in at the last minute and help me out when I needed a doctor—let me step in and help you out when you need a...'

'A builder?' She'd laughed.

He'd smiled back. 'A knight in shining armour. Didn't you see my suit of armour downstairs? It's very polished.'

So of course she'd thanked him profusely, feeling so terribly grateful for all that he was doing to help her out.

'I appreciate that. I really do.'

'Nonsense. It's what friends do.'

And she'd smiled. *Were they friends?* 'Thank you.'

Matteo had invited her to dine with him that evening.

'You can bring Bruno. If he's lucky we might be able to feed him titbits under the table.'

'He'll never want to leave this place if you do that.'

And now they sat on his sun terrace, awaiting their

meal, staring out across the gardens below and watching the sun slowly set.

'By the way, I don't know if you've heard but Dr Bonetti's wife has pulled through. She's in a stable condition and expected to go home soon. He phoned from the hospital. Let my secretary know.'

'That's excellent news! Wow. So good to have such great news after earlier. And the driver who hit my home? Do we know about him?'

'Already home. And already charged by the police for drink driving. He's to attend court in a few days' time.'

'If it was an accident I'm sure he's very sorry.'

Matteo sipped his water. 'Unfortunately, from what I've discovered, the man is a known drunk. He's already had his licence taken from him and the car wasn't even his. It was his son's and he'd "borrowed" it.'

'Oh.'

'We'll get him into a programme.'

'We?' She raised an eyebrow.

'My pack of royal enforcers,' he said with a straight face, knowing there was no such pack at all.

'Enforcers?'

He laughed. 'I'm sorry. I don't really have enforcers. I was just… Look, he needs help. Someone will go and visit him and make sure he enrols into a programme that will get him the help he needs. Before he kills someone next time.'

'Maybe I could go and see him myself?'

'Is that wise? You're emotionally involved.'

'Which is why he might listen to me. Meeting the actual victim of his crime might make more of an impact.'

'Was hitting your wall not enough?' He cocked his head to one side. 'How do you know so much about crime and victimology?'

She looked down and away from him then, and he realised there was a story there. Something she wasn't willing to share.

'I'm sorry—you don't have to answer that.'

She laughed. 'Don't therapists suggest that talking is good for the soul?'

He nodded. 'They do. But only when you're ready. *Are* you ready?'

'I don't know.'

He sipped his drink. 'You'll know when it's the right time. And, more importantly, if it's the right person to talk to. You don't really know me, so I quite understand.'

She stared back at him. Consideringly. Her eyes were cool. 'I think you'd understand more than most.'

He considered this. Intrigued. 'Oh?'

She paused. Looked uncertain. And then he saw it in her face. The determination to push forward and just say it.

'I was six years old. And I was taken.'

'Taken?' His blood almost froze, despite the warmth of the sun.

'My father buried me in a hole in the ground.'

CHAPTER THREE

SHE STARED AT HIM, trying to gauge his reaction. 'Surprised?'

The Crown Prince opened his mouth as if to say something, but no words came out. He was truly stupefied. Shocked. His mind raced over the fact that she'd been kidnapped too.

'Of course I am! Your *father* did this?'

'He planned it. It wasn't a spur-of-the-moment thing. My parents had split up and had a bitter custody battle over me. Their divorce was not amicable.'

'That must have been upsetting for you.'

A nod. 'Yes. My mother was awarded full custody, but my father got to see me once a month. Just for one day. This particular weekend he told me we were going to play a game in the woods, where he worked as a gamekeeper. I was going to help him snare rabbits.'

Matteo listened intently, his face showing how appalled he was that something like this had happened to her.

'We went deep into the woods. It was dark and damp and there almost wasn't any light...the trees were so thick.'

'Were you scared?'

'Not to start with. I was comfortable being in nature.

I'd played in those woods. I was with my father. I thought I was safe. And then he showed me a bunker he'd made.'

'A bunker…? What was it like?'

'Not very big. Maybe the size of a single bed? The walls were lined with wood. Old pallets, I think. He told me we were going to play a game, and that to play I had to get inside the bunker and wait whilst he went and chased rabbits towards it. He told me the roof would open easily. That I'd be able to push it open and the rabbits would jump into the dark for me to play with.'

'Mio Dio…'

'Once he put the roof down I heard a padlock click. He said *"Przepraszam"*—I'm sorry—and then he left me.'

She took a sip of water, reliving that moment once again in her mind, hearing her father's footsteps as he walked away and how it felt for her tiny fists to beat against the solid roof above her head, lined with soil.

'He would come back when he could, to bring me food and water. I tried to escape, but…he was stronger than me. Once he brought a book and a candle, so I had light to read.'

'How long were you underground?'

'Six weeks.'

He looked sick. 'How did you escape?'

'I was found. My father had reported me missing, of course. Said I'd disappeared when he'd left me outside a shop. After a few weeks the police began to suspect him and followed him into the woods. Dogs found me. I'll always remember hearing them come closer, their barks echoing above me. I began to scream. I screamed so much I had no voice for three days.'

'And your father?'

She swallowed hard. 'He's in prison now.'

He nodded. 'Do you visit him?'

Why did he not know about this? She worked with his father's doctor! How come none of this had shown in her background searches?

Because she'd been a child. The records would be sealed.

'No. I've never gone back to Poland.'

'Do you think you should?'

Her head tilted to one side as she assessed him. 'Have you ever visited your captors in jail?'

Matteo thought for a moment, then smiled, caught out. 'Fair point. But my captors were strangers—yours was your father. You must have loved him?'

'I did. But not any more. It's not the same.'

'And…' He cleared his throat and took a sip of water. 'Do you have any flashbacks? Any issues from your captivity?'

'Not really. Apart from needing a night-light.'

'That's understandable.' He looked out at the broad expanse of rich orange-pink sky, cloudless and still.

'So, Your Highness, as you can see we are both injured birds.'

'I guess we are. But we're resilient and we'll both fly again.'

She looked uncertain. 'I hope I already am flying.'

He nodded. 'You are. Believe it.'

She smiled back, thankful for his understanding and support. Who'd have thought it? That she'd be sharing her story with the Crown Prince?

How many times had she gazed at these palace walls, wanting to let him know that she understood what he had gone through? How many times had she considered writing him a letter but decided against it? Assuming that he wouldn't actually see it, and that it would be dealt with by a private secretary.

They were probably the only two people on this island who shared such an experience. It bonded them. And here she was. Sitting across from him, watching the sunset, sharing with him her darkest nightmare.

'You're a good man, Your Highness.'

He smiled back at her, his blue eyes twinkling. 'Call me Matteo.'

She nodded. 'Krystiana.'

She lay on her bed, staring at the ceiling. Had she been a fool to blurt it out like that? She'd never told anyone here about what had happened. Only her Aunt Carolina knew—no one else. Until today, anyway. She hadn't even told Dr Bonetti, and he was her partner in the medical practice they ran in the town of Ventura.

But sitting opposite Matteo like that, being that close to him, she had wanted him to know. It was as simple as that. Being kidnapped was such a unique experience, and she'd needed him to know that she understood it. That she'd been through it, too.

He'd been so kind.

'Thank you, Krystiana. For sharing that with me,' he had said. 'It must have taken great courage to share something so...personal.'

She'd pushed her *tagliatelli* around her plate, biting her bottom lip. Trying to work out why she'd told him everything. Was she being selfish?

'I've kept it inside for so long… It felt good to get it out. I guess I knew you'd understand.'

She'd looked up, expecting to see sympathy or pity on his face, but he hadn't looked at her that way at all.

'Other people don't. Not truly,' he'd said. 'They couldn't.'

'No.' She'd sipped her water.

'I don't want you to feel bad for telling me. I can see it on your face that you're uncomfortable now.'

She'd smiled wryly at his perceptiveness. Was she an open book? Could he read her? Was she so obvious? Or was it that only he could see, because he'd been through the same thing?

She'd given a short laugh. 'I'm normally so private. I keep myself to myself. My best friend doesn't even know. There's no alcohol in this water, right?' she tried to joke.

Matteo had nodded. 'I'm honoured you shared it with me.'

Krystiana continued to stare at the bedroom ceiling. So different from the one in her villa. Back home she had a ceiling fan in the centre of the roof; here she had a chandelier, reflecting the brightness from her night-light around the room.

Her conversation with Matteo hadn't been uncomfortable because she'd shared her story with him—it had become uncomfortable because she hadn't realised what sharing it might make her *feel*. She'd entrusted him with something of herself and she didn't like it. Okay, it was only a small piece of her past, but still... If she'd told him that, what else might she say?

She felt as if she'd given him some of her power and that felt wrong. It was an unexpected emotion.

She got little sleep that night, and when she did finally wake in the morning she vowed to herself that maybe it would be a good idea to stay away from the Crown Prince for a while, He had a busy life, anyway—she probably wouldn't see him any more, and she would have to leave the palace to go to work each day at her practice and see her real patients.

She'd told him about her kidnapping because she'd

often thought he would be intrigued to know, but that was as far as it went. That was all. Their lives were separate.

It was as if she was just renting a room and he was her extraordinary new landlord.

A car was waiting to take her to work. A sleek, black armoured vehicle, with its engine idling and one of those dark-suited Secret Service guys behind the wheel.

Krystiana trotted down the steps, ready for work, but also ready to drive past her old home and see the wreckage for herself first. She was anxious, her belly full of a twisting apprehension so that she hadn't been able to manage any breakfast and had only had a single cup of coffee.

'Come on, Bruno! Hurry up!' Her dog, a middle-aged pooch of indeterminate breed, with the character of a grumpy geriatric, ambled after her.

Sergio opened the car door for her. 'Have a good day, Dr Szenac.'

'*Grazie*, Sergio.' As she got into the car, she almost jumped out of her skin. 'Your Highness! What are *you* doing in here? I thought this was the car that was going to take me to work?'

He smiled. 'Matteo—remember? And good morning to you, too. I thought I would come with you to survey the damage to your house.'

'B-but…' she stuttered. 'Aren't you busy? Surely you have more important things to be getting on with? Like helping to run a country?'

'One of my citizens has had her home destroyed by a fool who should never have been on the road in the first place. I am doing my duty by attending the scene of the tragedy to see if there is anything I can do.' He leaned in. 'It's called being supportive—so accept that fact and close the door. Bruno!'

He patted his hands against his lap and her dog jumped in, up onto the car's expensive leather seats and smoothly onto the Prince's lap. He gave her a smile that was cunning and smooth, sliding his sunglasses down onto his face.

'Is that your disguise?' she asked.

'No. I have a baseball cap, too, and when we get to your villa both of us will have hard hats. The site manager will show us around.'

'They're working on it already?'

'From first light this morning.'

She pulled her legs in and Sergio shut the door behind her. 'That's impressive.'

'It's what I do.'

Krystiana smiled at him and then she laughed. He really was very kind. And going completely above and beyond anything she'd expected of him. Not that she *did* expect anything of him. He'd been her patient for one day. Now he wasn't. And, although he'd said they were friends, she wasn't sure how to negotiate that particular relationship.

She didn't have the best track record with men, and she hadn't been kidding when she'd told him she kept to herself. She'd only got one friend and that was Anna Scottolini, her next-door neighbour. She'd neglected to tell him that the best friend she'd mentioned was a senior citizen in her ninety-second year of life.

'You passed, by the way.'

'I'm sorry?'

'Your yearly physical. With flying colours. You're fit as a fiddle.'

'How fit *are* fiddles?'

She shrugged. 'Very, it would seem. Bruno! Don't be embarrassing!'

Bruno had decided the lap of the Prince was a very

good place to begin washing his nether regions and had set to with gusto. Feeling her cheeks flame red, she reached over to grab the dog and pull him onto the seat between them.

'Sit there. Good dog.'

Matteo smiled at her and she felt something stir within her. Whatever it was, it made her feel incredibly uncomfortable.

Matching him, she pulled her sunglasses from her handbag and slid them over her face and turned to look out of the window.

If I don't look at him, I won't think about him. Yeah. Like that's going to work!

Krystiana's villa sat atop a small hill on the road into Ventura—or out of it, depending upon which way you were going. When Matteo stepped out of the vehicle in a simple white shirt and dark trousers, and donned his baseball cap and sunglasses, he could see the palace far in the distance, shining like a pearl. White and glittering.

He wondered briefly, now he knew exactly where she lived, if he would be able to spot her home from the palace walls?

Because of course he would always think of her now. No matter what happened in the future, he would feel a kinship with this woman at his side because of what they'd both been through. After she'd told him what had happened he'd initially been shocked, but drawn in by her story. So similar and yet so different from his own.

Six weeks underground. Alone and in the dark.

Kindred spirits. That was what they were. So he was glad he'd made her the offer to stay at the palace whilst her home was worked on, and he did want to see the damage for himself—but had it only been that? Concern for one

of his citizens? Concern for someone he'd like to think
of as a friend? Or something more?

He felt at ease when he was with her. There was something relaxing about her. But that in turn worried him,
simply because it *was* so easy to be with her. He could
be himself—and he hadn't been himself for a very long
time. It was confusing and alarming, because what did it
mean? For so long now he'd held himself apart from everyone. Ever since he'd returned home. And yet he'd spent
one day with her and had discovered that...

He turned to look at her house. At the metal fencing
around the perimeter and the crumpled mess beyond it.
Because that was what it was. A crumpled mess of brick
and rubble, mortar and plaster, glass and wood. He'd seen
something similar when he'd once gone to help during the
aftershocks of an earthquake the island had experienced
a few years back.

*Thank goodness she hadn't been inside when it had
happened. If Dr Bonetti's wife hadn't been ill he'd have
done his physical as usual and Krystiana would have
been at home.*

Fate? He didn't believe in that any more.

Pure luck? Maybe...

A man in a high-vis vest and a yellow hard hat came
around the corner. He raised a hand and ambled slowly
over the loose rubble before coming to the metal fencing
and opening a panel. 'Your Highness.'

'Carlo?'

'*Si.*'

'This is Dr Szenac—she is the owner of this property.
Could you walk us through it? Let us know what's happening?'

Carlo nodded and led the way. The ground was uneven,

loose bricks and rubble everywhere, so Matteo turned to offer her his hand.

'I'm fine,' she said. 'Watch where you're going and I'll follow.'

He nodded. It was probably a good thing that she hadn't accepted his hand. After all, he was meant to be keeping his distance.

I really must work harder on that.

Her kitchen and bathroom looked untouched by the collision, but the rest of her downstairs rooms and to some degree the rooms above had pretty much collapsed down on top of each other. The vehicle that had smacked into the villa had been a large four-wheel drive, and the driver had been going at some speed. She'd expected to see a car-shaped hole in her wall, or something, but not this. This was…*shocking*. This was the home she had built up since moving out of Aunt Carolina's…

'I'm so sorry, Krystiana,' Matteo said as they surveyed the wreckage.

She didn't want to cry. She had done her make-up for work later. Now she was going to look like a panda.

One of her sofas seemed to be missing. Some framed photographs lay on the floor, their glass cracked and missing fragments. Bending down, she went to pick one up. The only picture she had of her mother. Her eyes welled up again and she began to sob, her hand clamped over her mouth as she tried to cry silently.

'Hey, come here…' Matteo pulled her towards him and she huddled against his chest, the photograph of her dead mother in her hands.

He was warm and comforting. Soothing. And although she wanted to remain there for ever she sniffed hard and pushed away from his chest, stepping out of his arms. She couldn't. No. It wasn't right.

'I'm fine. Really. Show me everything, Carlo.'

Carlo looked at Matteo for permission and she saw him give a terse nod.

She followed him around, listened as he gave complicated observations about lintels and weight-bearing walls and nodded, pretending she understood everything he said. They couldn't go upstairs. It hadn't been made safe yet, he said. But she'd got what she needed. The one thing that mattered. There'd been no way she was leaving her mother in the rubble. In the darkness. Like a piece of discarded litter.

'Thank you. You've been very informative.'

'How long should the work take?' asked Matteo.

'If we can get the supplies we need, four weeks minimum. But it may be longer than that.'

'Do what you can. Money is no object—do you understand me?'

'Yes, Your Highness.'

Matteo turned to her. 'I'll walk you back to the car.'

And he followed her through the building site that was now her home, occasionally putting the tips of his fingers on the small of her back, guiding her through.

When they reached the car, he sighed. 'Are you all right?'

'I'm fine.'

'Maybe you shouldn't return to work today?'

'I have to. I have my own patients *and* Dr Bonetti's. I can't let them down and I won't.'

'All right. I'll have the car drop you off and then pick you up again tonight.'

She shook her head. 'You don't have to. You have work too, remember?'

Matteo nodded. 'Yes. You're right. But it seems wrong leaving you when you're upset.'

'I'll be fine. We're strong, aren't we?'

He smiled. 'We're strong. Yes.' He glanced at the back seat of the car. 'Want me to take Bruno?'

'He sits in the office with me. Patients seem to like it.' She shrugged.

'Interesting medical student…'

'He has a passion for bones.'

It was a lame joke, but she was trying to make light of the situation. It had been a stressful twenty-four hours, but she'd been through worse.

Matteo smiled dutifully. 'I'll see you at home, then.'

Home.

She got into the car, waiting for him to slide in next to her. Bruno gave a wag of his tail and licked some dust off the back of her hand.

'Don't wait up.'

Krystiana spent the day treating patients, and for almost six hours barely gave a thought to her ruined home or her palatial sleepover. She treated an infected jellyfish sting, a child with chicken pox, two bad sunburns, a bad case of laryngitis, gout, completed a newborn baby's assessment, and checked a wound on the foot of a Type Two diabetic—all before lunch.

It felt good to get back to her normal routine, to see her patients' faces and to slide back into the routine of consulting and issuing prescriptions. There was a rhythm to it, a logic. Medicine was often a puzzle, with the patients the clues, and there was nothing she loved more than to solve the puzzle and heal the patient. Helping people was what she did best, and it made her feel good about herself that she could do so.

A therapist would no doubt say that it was down to her feeling so powerless and impotent when her father had kept her below ground. That the fact that she hadn't been able to help her mother when she died fired her soul now.

Maybe it was true. Who knew? Perhaps that was why she was so anxious to leave the palace? She'd done her thing. She'd helped out when Dr Bonetti hadn't been able to make it and now her part was over. She wasn't needed at the palace any more, but she had to stay there because she needed a place to sleep.

Or did she? Maybe Anna, her next-door neighbour and best friend, could put her up until the work on her house was done?

No. I can't ask her to do that. She's in her nineties! And besides, how would I pay for the repairs? I'm insured, but that would take ages, and Matteo is getting the work done quicker than I ever could.

It felt wrong. He was being so generous and she wasn't used to someone helping her like that. She was used to standing on her own two feet. Being independent.

She was mulling this over when her next patient arrived. Sofia De Laurentis. Sixteen years old and the daughter of a duke. A lot of her patients came from among the upper echelons of society, but class and prestige were not enough to keep away disease.

Sofia was Krystiana's last patient of the day, and she entered her consulting room looking nervous, fidgeting with her backpack.

'Hello, Sofia, what's brought you here today?'

Sofia couldn't meet her eyes. 'You can't tell anyone, but… I think I might be pregnant.'

Krystiana didn't react. 'All right. What makes you think that?'

'My period is late. A few weeks. And I feel weird.'

Krystiana took some details. The date of her last period and how long they usually lasted. 'Have you taken a pregnancy test?'

'I bought one. I had to go in disguise—can you believe that? There were two tests inside and I used them both.'

'Positive?'

Sofia nodded.

'And do you know who the father is?'

Another nod.

And then she asked the most important question as her patient was only sixteen. 'Did you consent?'

'Yes.'

She believed her. 'Okay. Let's get you up onto the bed.'

Krystiana felt her tummy, but it was still too early to feel the fundus—the top of the womb—above her pelvic area. She smiled, and helped pull Sofia back up into a sitting position.

'Take a seat.'

She prepared to take her blood pressure, wrapping the cuff around her arm.

'So, I can take a blood sample to confirm the pregnancy if you wish. Do you want to keep the baby?'

Sofia shook her head, her eyes welling up with tears. 'I don't know. My father will be furious.'

'You live with your father? What about your mother?'

'She died when I was young.'

Oh. Krystiana knew a little of that pain. She had been left with no parents at a young age, whereas this young girl still had her father.

'You have time to make a decision. You have options. You could keep the baby, or have it adopted. And of course you can also have an abortion. But *you* must be the one to make the decision—no one else can make it for you and no one can force you to make it. Do you understand?'

'Yes.'

'But, again, that's *your* decision.'

Sofia nodded. 'So what do I do now?'

'You think. The first trimester can sometimes be difficult, and not all pregnancies make it through. Take some time to think what you would like to do, and in the meantime I'll book you in with a midwife for a visit. If you'd like to tell your father in a safe environment then you can always do so here, with a member of staff or myself attending. Are you feeling sick at all?'

'A bit.'

'Try nibbling on something as often as you can. Hunger can trigger nausea. Have a biscuit or two at the side of your bed for first thing in the morning, before you get up. Nothing chocolatey—something plain. A ginger biscuit, or something like that.'

Sofia stood up. 'Thank you. You've been very understanding.'

'It's my job.'

When Sofia had left the room Krystiana sat for a moment and pondered her young patient. She had a difficult time ahead of her—a future that no one could predict just yet. And she felt in a similar situation, with her home in disarray. Her living area open to the stars.

She realised that she had always struggled in every area of her life. It was a state of affairs that she had become used to. Perhaps that was why the richness and opulence of the palace made her so uncomfortable? It hid the real world. It wasn't reality. It was a mirage.

Krystiana liked her minimalism. Her stone. Wood. Brick. She wasn't used to marble and crystal and silk. She wasn't used to servants and having things done for her. She enjoyed the simplicity of making her own breakfast. Chopping up fruit and adding it to a bowl of oats gave her pleasure. She liked looking after her own home. Polishing it. Sweeping the floors, cleaning her bathroom.

At the palace those sorts of chores were done by servants. And she didn't like the idea that someone else was having to pick up after her. It didn't feel right. It felt as if parts of her everyday life were being taken from her. And since moving to the island Krystiana had started relying on her gut feelings and instincts, because she'd realised rather swiftly that they were the only things she could trust.

She reached for the phone, intending to dial the palace and tell them not to send her a car because she was going to make her own way. But then she realised she didn't know the number, and that all her things—her clothes, her personal computer, everything she valued—were there. She had to go back. Maybe just for one more night? And then she would pack her things.

She wasn't Matteo's doctor any more. He didn't need her. She'd told him about their shared experience and she didn't need to share any more. Because she knew that if she did stay his friendship, his easy nature, would cause her to share more. But she couldn't do that. Because sharing with him would mean *trusting* him.

And she couldn't trust anyone ever again.

Visiting the building site that was Krystiana's home, Matteo had felt incredibly disturbed. One half of the villa looked fine, the other a total wreck. They had picked their way through the rubble, being careful not to stumble, and then Krystiana had found her mother's photograph.

Watching Krystiana crumble like that had opened his own scars. They had both lost their mothers. They both knew that kind of loss. His heart had gone out to her and before he'd been able to stop himself he had pulled her into his arms and held her tight.

He had wanted to make her feel better—wanted to let her know that she wasn't alone. That was all. But listening to her cry, feeling the wetness of her tears seeping through his shirt, he hadn't wanted to let her go.

Realising that had disturbed him. What was he doing? Getting involved in her life like this? Inviting her to stay? Offering to rebuild her home? Sheltering her not only with his house but with his arms, his embrace? He didn't need to be worrying about someone else like this. He did *not* need another emotional crisis in his life. He'd had more than enough to last a lifetime! Getting involved with others, caring for them, only caused him pain in the long run.

And then she'd stepped away from his arms and he'd felt relief. Relief that she was trying to be strong all by herself. It was a clear sign that she did not want to depend upon him and that was fine by him. He didn't need anyone depending upon him personally like that. He knew he could never give anyone what they'd want from him. He'd vowed never to love again, so if he couldn't care for someone like that what was the point? He'd been humiliated once.

He'd felt some of the pressure he'd been putting on himself dissipate. But of course then he'd felt guilty for acting so selfishly. Princes were not meant to be selfish. They were not meant to look out only for themselves, but to look out for their people. And wasn't Krystiana one of his people?

After the car had dropped her off at work he had returned to the palace to carry out his duties. He'd had a pile of reports that needed to be read and signed off, and he'd also needed to meet with his secretary to discuss his schedule for the next few months.

He had a busy time coming up. His father, the King,

was going to abdicate within the year—on his seventieth birthday. These next few months would be a whirlwind of appointments, visits, public walkabouts and royal duties. Everybody wanted to see the man who would soon be King.

But as he'd sat at his desk he hadn't been able to concentrate. All he'd been able to think about was Krystiana. How displaced she was. The disruption in her life and what he could do to make it better.

He'd ended up pacing the floors and constantly checking his watch. She'd finish at six p.m. and then the car would bring her home.

He knew he needed to sort his head. Clear it. He knew he needed to create more distance between them. He couldn't let her in past his defences. The risk simply wasn't worth it.

He'd already lost his mother, his wife, and almost his child. That was too much loss for one person to deal with. Letting someone in, letting them get close, was dangerous. Matters of the heart were terrifying in how vulnerable they could make a man. They were a weakness. One that those guerrillas had used with impunity, making him think that his wife and child had been killed.

He would let Sergio deal with Krystiana from now on. He didn't think she would be upset by that. Hadn't she been the one to push him away in the villa?

He was only doing what they both wanted.

So why did he feel disturbed by it?

Krystiana came back to the palace after work and hoped that she would be able to get to her quarters without being seen. If she did meet Matteo she would be politeness personified, but she would tell him that she was tired, that she needed to take a shower or a long bath and then she would be going to bed. It was best all round if she left him to get on with being the future King and she got on with being a doctor. She'd helped him out for one day—that was all. She had told him about her past and that was it. It didn't need to go any further than that.

He was a very nice man—kind, considerate and clearly compassionate. Plus, he had the warmest blue eyes she had ever seen. The type of eyes, framed in dark lashes, that invited confidences. She knew without a shadow of a doubt that if she spent any more time in his company, as his friend, she would grow attached to a man who couldn't possibly remain in her life. They were on two separate paths.

He was Crown Prince. She was a medic. And those two things did not have any future unity.

Krystiana hurried to her quarters, closing the doors behind her and walking straight over to her bed. Sitting down on the mattress, she pulled her mother's photograph from her bag, dusted it off with her fingers and placed it on the bedside cabinet, staring at it for a brief moment.

If only you could see me now, she thought. *Living in a palace in Italy.*

It was far removed from where they had lived in Kraków. What would her mother say?

He's handsome. Is he single?

She smiled at her mother's imagined voice and, raising her fingers to her lips, kissed them and pressed her fingertips to her mother's photo. *'Tęsknię za toba,'* she said. *I miss you.*

A knock at the door had her wiping her eyes and sniffing before she called out 'Come in!'

Sergio walked into the room. 'Good evening, Dr Szenac. His Majesty King Alberto has invited you to join him and his family for this evening's meal.'

'Oh, that's very nice of him but I'm rather tired. It's been a stressful day and I'd really like to just turn in—maybe have a tray brought to my room, if that's okay?'

Sergio nodded. 'I understand.' He turned and made to go, but then stopped, as if changing his mind. 'It would not be wise to turn down the King's invitation, Dr Szenac. I believe this very morning he approved the finance for the renovation of your villa and he wishes to meet with you. I fear he would not take kindly if you did not come.'

Of course. It wasn't just Matteo paying to fix her home. It was coming out of the royal family's purse. To live in their home, to take their money and then not even show her face at dinner would be incredibly rude.

She glanced down at Bruno, who had settled into his doggie bed and was chewing on his toy.

'Right. I understand. Please tell the King that I will be happy to join him and his family at dinner. What time should I be ready?'

'Dinner is at seven.'

'Perfect. Thank you.'

'The dress code is smart casual.'

She wasn't worried about the dress code. She was worried that they would sit her opposite Matteo and she would end up looking into those deep blue eyes of his all evening.

He didn't always eat dinner with his father. They both led such busy lives, on such different schedules, it was rare for both of them to be home at the same time. But his father had just come back from a short break in Africa and wanted to catch up with his son before a tour around Europe took him away again.

It was a good thing they both enjoyed travelling and meeting new people.

'It was a great shame to be informed about Dr Bonetti's wife. I hear that she has pulled through?' his father asked.

'Yes. My advisor tells me that earlier today she was moved off the critical care unit and on to a ward.'

'That's excellent. I must send them a token of my affection. Remind me to tell my secretary.'

Matteo smiled. 'I will.'

And that was when the doors to the dining room were opened by Sergio.

'Ah! This must be our new guest. Dr Szenac!' The King got to his feet. 'Welcome! I'm so pleased to meet you, though it is such a shame it has to be under such difficult circumstances. How is your home looking?'

Matteo watched his father greet Krystiana, kissing both her cheeks and smiling broadly. Krystiana looked tired, but her eyes were sparkling still.

She curtsied. 'Your Majesty. Thank you. The work has begun, so hopefully I won't have to impose upon you and your family for too long.'

'Nonsense! Our home is your home. We wouldn't have it any other way. Please—take a seat.'

Sergio held out a chair for her and she settled into it—directly opposite Matteo.

He smiled at her. 'How was work today?'

'Interesting. Though it always is. You never know who's going to walk through the door.'

'Keeps you on your toes!' his father said.

She nodded.

Sergio filled her glass with water and laid a napkin over her lap. 'Can I get you a drink, Dr Szenac?'

'I'm fine, thank you, Sergio.'

'We must introduce you to everyone. You know who I am, and my son, but on your right is my sister Beatrice, and opposite her is her husband Edoardo. They're here on a flying visit from Florence.'

Krystiana smiled at them both. 'I'm very pleased to meet you.'

Matteo could see that she was nervous. Surrounded by royalty. Hemmed in by titles. A king, a prince, a duke and a duchess. She was blushing, her face suffused with a rich pink colour in both cheeks, as she struggled to make eye contact with anyone. He hated seeing her looking so uncomfortable.

Knowing how badly her day had started, he decided to rescue her. 'How's Bruno doing with the change in his home-life?'

She looked up at him, grateful. 'He's adapting very well. Almost as if he always suspected he was meant for palace life. I think he likes having servants.'

He laughed, enjoying her smile.

'And how are *you* adapting to being back in palace life, Matteo?' asked his Aunt Beatrice. 'It must be such a relief for you to get back to normal?'

He nodded. 'It is, but I expected it to be different... getting home.'

'How do you mean?'

Beatrice looked extremely interested, but then again she would be. He hadn't seen her since before his kidnapping, and he hadn't had much chance to talk to his father's side of the family about what had happened.

'When you're in that situation, held captive, what keeps you going is the thought of returning home. Of getting back. Of everything being all right again.'

'But...?'

'But it's not that way at all. You feel like you've been held captive in time, and that although everyone else has moved on you're still in the same place. You want to process what has happened, but it's difficult.'

'Your father tells me you had some *therapy* afterwards?' She said it as if therapy was a bad word.

'Yes.' He looked at Krystiana and smiled. She would know what that meant. 'I still am.'

'Really?'

'I've found it to be helpful.'

Beatrice raised a perfectly drawn-on eyebrow, but didn't ask any more.

He shared a look with Krystiana. 'There are some… after-effects you don't expect.'

'Like what?' asked Edoardo, sitting back as the first course arrived and the servants laid steaming bowls of soup in front of them all.

'Bad dreams. And being enclosed in any small space is a little unnerving now. Being afraid of the dark.'

Krystiana looked up at him. He knew. Knew that she was the same. That she had the same fear as him. And suddenly he didn't want to be at this dinner any more, surrounded by the others. He wanted to be somewhere talking to *her*. Asking her about how she dealt with the same things. Whether she'd beat the fears or still struggled with them.

'And, of course, there was all that business with Mara,' said Beatrice, with a snide tone to her voice. 'I always said she wasn't the one for you.'

Yes, well… 'She was my best friend, Aunt Bee.'

'So she should have waited for you.'

'She was alone and afraid.'

He tried to stand up for his ex-wife, despite his feelings. He knew what she'd gone through. They'd talked about it many times, and as far as he could see she'd done what any person would. The humiliation he'd felt, expecting to come home to a wife when in fact she was actually his ex-wife, had been his to work through.

His aunt sniffed and dabbed at her lips with her napkin. 'Well, so were *you*, I'd imagine.'

'She had no idea if I was alive or dead. She was trying to raise a baby, all alone, and she was grief-stricken and needed comfort.'

'So she turned to Philippe? An old boyfriend?'

'He was there for her when I couldn't be. Come on, Aunt Bee. You know Mara and I weren't a true love-match. We had an arranged marriage. I would never have stood in the way of her finding her true love.'

'She'd just had your *child*!' Beatrice was clearly appalled by Mara's behaviour.

'That's enough, Bee,' said his father, bringing order to the table. 'I do apologise, Dr Szenac. We are a passionate family and often our get-togethers can be a little…heated.'

She smiled at him. 'That's all right. Please don't apologise. I'm sure it's the same in any family.'

'I'm grateful for your understanding. Is your family like this?'

Matteo saw her take a sip of soup, her hand trembling, and knew it would be difficult for her to answer. Her mother was dead. Her father was in prison.

'I have only my Aunt Carolina, and though we love each other very much we do have our moments.'

His father guffawed. 'So we are normal, then?'

Krystiana laughed, too. 'Yes, you are.'

Edoardo leaned over. 'You're a doctor, I believe?'

'Yes. I have a practice in Ventura, which I share with the royal physician, Dr Bonetti.'

'Ah, yes. I think someone told me that earlier…before you came. Are you married, Doctor?'

She blushed. 'No.'

'Planning on it?'

She shook her head. 'No.'

'Why ever not?' interrupted Beatrice.

Krystiana looked uncomfortable. Again. Matteo understood that his family could be a bit much. They were inherently nosy and thought they were the authority on most subjects.

He interjected for her. 'Marriage isn't the be-all and end-all of life, Aunt Bee. Plenty of people remain happily single.'

'But what's the point of *being* here, then?'

Krystiana looked at him in a panic. 'How did you and Mara meet?' she asked, clearly wanting to divert the topic of conversation away from herself.

'We were distant cousins and we had known each other since we were children.'

'You grew up together?'

He nodded. 'Her father is an earl. We were best friends. Went to school together. I loved hanging out with Mara—it seemed the most obvious thing that we should marry, and of course it strengthened the relationship between our families.'

'You had a happy marriage?'

Matteo shrugged. 'It seemed to be. We had our ups and downs, but all couples do. Our friendship was something that neither of us wanted to lose. And we haven't—despite what happened.' He flicked a look at his aunt, who clearly still disapproved.

'You weren't worried that marriage to one another would change your friendship?' Krystiana persisted.

'No. We knew we loved one another and had done for years. We didn't expect marriage to change that.'

She nodded. 'That's good. I'm glad you were happy together.'

He smiled, feeling they were in some kind of a conspiracy together. 'Me too.'

'And then you had a child together,' added Beatrice, raising her eyebrows as if she doubted the wisdom of that decision.

'Alexandra. She's beautiful, by the way, and I can't wait for you to meet her.' He directed his answer to Krystiana.

'I look forward to it.'

His face was stretching into a broad grin as he looked at her, and he was almost forgetting there were other people around the table. When he did remember, he looked at them to see they were looking at him rather strangely. He looked away and sipped at his wine.

He could remember the look on Mara's face when she'd told him that she was pregnant. She'd looked so happy! And he'd been thrilled too that he was about to be a father. But he'd known Mara wasn't the soul mate he'd always hoped for. Mara had always talked about having children, and about how she hoped to be a good mother to her baby. How she hoped to care for it herself as much as she could, and not let royal nannies get in the way and take over. They'd both had such dreams for their child, and it was disappointing that it hadn't worked out.

But he was pleased for Mara and the happiness that she had found with Philippe. He was pleased that, despite the kidnapping trauma, she had managed to move on with her life and find true joy with a man she loved. A proper love. Romantic love. Something he'd once yearned for but had now vowed to stay away from.

He'd been hurt by what had happened between him and Mara. But he couldn't imagine being in love with someone and losing them, the way his father had lost his mother, the love of his life.

If anything, he was a little envious of Mara. But he knew he wouldn't find anything like that for himself.

Couldn't find that for himself.

Because what if he lost it all again? It had hurt to let Mara go. To let another man help raise his child. And he'd seen the devastation romantic loss could cause.

He didn't ever want to go through that pain.

He'd had enough pain already.

Krystiana asked to be excused at the end of the meal, as she had a long day at the practice tomorrow, and Matteo offered to walk her back to her quarters. She was a little anxious about that, but figured it was only a short distance and she could hardly refuse him in front of his family.

And as they walked Matteo began to tell her more about his kidnapping.

'...and then they just came out of nowhere.'

'The people who took you?'

He nodded, those blue eyes of his now stormy and dark.

'Yes. They emerged from the side of the road, holding machine guns and wearing masks. I had to stop the car. Mara was in the back, pregnant, breathing heavily from her contractions.'

'I remember she was in labour. It was on the news.'

'They approached, threatened my men with guns to their heads and pulled me from the vehicle, binding my hands with rope and pulling a dark bag over my face.'

'You must have been terrified!'

'I was. I thought they might do something to Mara, too. That we might lose the baby. I remember struggling, trying to free myself, trying to do what I could to distract them from my wife and unborn child.'

'But they left Mara behind?'

'Yes. They were just after me. I was hit over the head with something. A rifle butt—maybe something else. I think I passed out and they dragged me to another vehicle.'

She shook her head in amazement. 'I don't know how I would have coped with that.'

'We drove for a long time. I tried to remember which way the vehicle turned—right or left—whether I could hear anything outside that might help—like trains or traffic, the sea…anything!'

'And did you?'

'No. We headed deep into the country and I was dragged into somewhere dark and cold.'

'The cave?'

'Yes. I was chained like an animal to a metal post and kept there, underground, for two years.'

Krystiana swallowed hard as they arrived at the door to her quarters. She was imagining it all too clearly. How it must have felt. The panic inside him. The loss of control. The helplessness. Being at someone else's mercy. She knew how that felt *exactly*.

'Two years… I thought six weeks was a long time.'

'You were just a child.'

'I know, but…'

He looked down at the floor. 'It makes you realise the resilience of the human spirit, doesn't it?'

She nodded, biting her lip. His story reminded her so much of her own, and she'd never had anyone who had been through something similar to talk to about this. The need to share with him was intense.

And that was exactly why she had to go into her room. She'd thought she'd said goodbye to all these memories. Had put all the pain in a box and stored it right at the back of her brain, where it couldn't hurt her any more. But being with him, listening to him talk about his own experiences, made her want to bring it back out again and pick over it. Analyse it. Try to make sense of it.

'Well, I have a long day of work tomorrow. I need to be up, bright and early.'

'Of course.' He nodded, then looked at her. 'How do you sleep?'

She looked into his eyes then, and knew she couldn't lie to him. 'With a night-light. You?'

He smiled, but it was filled with sadness and empathy. 'The same.'

Krystiana nodded. She should have known. She'd always been embarrassed about having one, and she'd never dreamt she would ever tell anyone about it—because why would she need to? No one would ever get that close. But telling him had been easy. *Easy.*

'Well, goodnight, Matteo. I hope you have pleasant dreams.'

'You too, Krystiana. You too.'

She woke early, disturbed by a dream in which she'd found herself back in that bunker, back in that hole in the ground, screaming for someone to find her, to save her, when suddenly the roof had opened. She'd shielded her eyes from the light as she saw someone kneel down and offer her a hand. When she took it, and when she was pulled from the earth, it was into Matteo's arms, and suddenly she'd found herself against his chest.

She'd woken with a start, her heart pounding.

Needing some fresh air before work, Krystiana stepped out into the morning sun and stopped in the gardens for a moment, just to breathe in the warm summer air, her eyes closed.

She'd expected to be alone. No one else awake but the servants, busily working away behind the scenes, but she suddenly felt a presence by her side.

She opened her eyes and saw Matteo. 'Morning.'

'Good morning. Couldn't sleep?'

She couldn't tell him about her dream. 'I just needed some fresh air. I've never enjoyed being cooped up inside.'

He looked out over the gardens. 'No. Nor me. Come on—let me show you everything.'

He walked her down a path that lay before her like something in an exquisite painting. Green hues of olive and emerald, fern and lime, pine and sage, were layered and interspersed with shots of fuchsia, gold, white and rose. Someone talented had landscaped these gardens, and as they walked past lily ponds and bubbling water features, fountains and grottos, she marvelled at all that she could see.

'This is a beautiful place. Are these gardens open to the public?'

'No. They're my own private project.'

She looked at him, amazed. '*You* designed them?'

He smiled. 'Designed them, helped build them, planted almost every seed.'

'But this is *years* of work!'

'I started young. I always had—what do they call it?— green fingers!'

She laughed. 'Yes! Wow. I had no idea. You must have missed it incredibly when you weren't here.'

'I knew they were in good hands. And the thought of them kept me going when I was captive.'

'The memory?'

'I kept imagining myself walking along the paths, lifting a flower to smell its scent. I tried to remember how I'd built it. Created it. In my head I lost myself here many times. But by losing myself here, I *kept* myself. If that makes any sense?'

She nodded. 'It does. It anchored you.'

'*Si.*'

He led her down a curving stepped path, bordered with bushes she couldn't name that were higher than her head, flowering with tiny blue and white flowers, until they emerged in a sun garden that had a sundial at its centre. The floor had been laid with coloured stones—a mosaic depicting a knight fending off a giant green dragon.

'You did this, too?'

'It came from a book I read as a child. The tale of St George and the Dragon. A story that fascinated me. This mosaic was a birthday gift from my mother when I was ten years old.'

'A whole mosaic? My mother used to buy me socks for *my* birthday.'

He smiled. 'Socks are useful. Was it cold in Poland?'

'Only in winter.'

'Was your birthday in the winter months?'

She laughed. 'No. July.'

She went over to look more closely at the sundial. It was made of a dark stone, slate in colour. But marbled with white. She had no idea what it actually was, but the dial itself was exquisite, with a hand casting a shadow to one side.

She checked her watch. 'It tells the correct time.'

'Of course.'

She looked around them, saw that the palace was hidden by trees and bushes. 'You could almost imagine the palace isn't there,' she said.

Matteo smiled.

'If I lived here permanently I'd want a reminder of this

at all times of the year, so that even in winter I'd know that spring was coming,' she said.

'Don't you know that anyway?'

'Yes, but…sometimes it takes a long time to get what you want. I'd want to capture this. This beauty.'

'You could take a photograph.'

She looked at him then. 'You know what? I can think of something better!'

He frowned. 'What is it?'

She smiled. 'Just you wait!'

'You want me to *paint*?' Matteo looked at Krystiana, doubtful.

He could plant a flowerbed, landscape a garden, and would eventually rule a kingdom, but to paint a picture? With his fingers? He wasn't a child…

But something about Krystiana's smile made him willing to give it a go. There was something about her. Something compelling. But for the life of him he couldn't work out what it was.

She was lit up from the inside at the thought of painting, and she'd had a servant at the palace fetch her painting equipment from her room. There were easels and palettes, and paints in acrylic and watercolour in all the colours of the rainbow.

'Remind me again why we're not using brushes?'

'Because this is much more fun. Touch the canvas as you create. Be at one with your picture. I want you to paint the garden. Not just what you see, but what it makes you *feel* as you look at it. I want you to try and use colour to feed your emotions into the work.'

'How do I do *that*?'

'Don't think about it too much. Go by instinct—it's what I do.'

He looked at the blank white canvas. 'I feel ridiculous.'

'Forget I'm here.'

'Are you going to be watching me?'

'No, I've got to go to work. But I would love to see your painting when I get back.'

He looked at her doubtfully, but then he closed his eyes for a moment, enjoying the soft breeze over his face, the warmth of the sun upon his skin, and tried to think about how this garden made him feel.

Before he knew it the soft, warm, fragrant breeze of the garden had awakened his senses. And he began.

Krystiana watched him for a moment, mesmerised by the tentative smile appearing on Matteo's handsome face, and when she realised that she was watching *him* more than she was watching the painting, she quietly slipped away.

CHAPTER FOUR

PRINCESS ALEXANDRA ROMANO was a dainty little thing and cute as a button. With her father's features, she had the cutest large blue eyes, framed by thick, long, dark eyelashes and the sweetest smile.

Her father carried her on his hip. 'Alex—meet Krystiana.'

Krystiana gave her a little wave. 'Hello, Alex. You didn't come to meet me from work, Matteo. I'm sure you have plenty of other things to be doing.'

'We were out for a walk. I saw the car pull up and thought I'd introduce you two.'

Behind her, Bruno jumped out of the car and Alex squealed with delight. 'Doggy!'

Matteo put her down so that she could give Bruno a cuddle. He happily rolled over onto his back, tongue lolling.

'I can't compete with a dog!'

'Can any of us?' She smiled at him, then reached into the back seat to grab her bag.

'How was work today?'

'Good. You?'

'Good. I finished my painting, by the way. I'm not sure you'll think it's Picasso, but…it's done.'

'Maybe you could show me later?'

He nodded. 'Sure. Alex? Come on, now, sweetheart. We must go.'

'But I want to play with the puppy!'

Krystiana smiled at her. 'I'm sure Bruno would love it if Alex took him into the garden. I've got some bags if he misbehaves.' She pulled from her handbag a small pouch filled with blue plastic bags.

Matteo took it. 'Thanks. Maybe you could join us later? Collect Bruno before my darling daughter wears him out completely.'

'Sure. I've got some work to do on my computer first.'

'Okay. I'll see you later.'

She nodded, anxious to be away. She'd spent the day worrying about their time in the garden that morning. About how pulled towards him she often felt. Was she a moth? Or was she the flame? Either way, allowing herself to get close to Matteo was dangerous. He was a very attractive man and he was far too easy to talk to, far too easy to care about.

She knew she would fall deeply if she allowed herself. It was a fatal flaw. She was too trusting. And she simply couldn't allow that. She wanted to love and be loved, but she was scared of it. All the people that she had loved had been lost. And the one person who should have loved her the most had hurt her irreparably.

Love did something to people. It twisted them in ways they did not expect and there was no guaranteeing who it might happen to. She didn't want to take any risks with her heart.

'I'll see you later.' He picked up Bruno's lead, and with his daughter began walking the dog away from her.

And that's how easy it is, she thought. *For you to be discarded. For people to move on and leave you behind.*

Her father had loved her so much he had tried to hide

her underground, but now that he was in prison did he ever try to contact her?

No.

Some love! And that from the man who should have loved her the most.

Krystiana did not need to be loved so little or so much that someone wanted to ensnare her. Or lie to her, convincing themselves that what she didn't know wouldn't hurt her. Because they'd be wrong.

A relationship with an aunt and a dog was as far as she would go. Matteo could be a friend, an acquaintance, and nothing more.

Matteo stood watching his daughter play in her sandbox outside. She had such joy in her face as she scooped sand, trying to make herself a sandcastle and then arranging her carved wooden dinosaurs into position, as if they were protecting it.

Alex made all her own sound effects, too. 'Grr…' she said, and made roaring noises as she stomped them around the base of the castle.

He couldn't help but feel his heart swell with his love for her. She was just so perfect. He and Mara might not have been perfect, but their little girl was. As long as she was in his life, then nothing else mattered. She was all he needed and his whole heart was hers. There would never be anyone else and that was okay. She was the most honest person he knew. An open book. He didn't have to worry about Alex breaking his heart. At least, he hoped not.

He knelt down, suddenly feeling the need to be close to her. He smiled—because how could he not when he was with his beautiful daughter?

'Are you building a castle? Or a palace?

'A palace.'

'Ah, I see. Like this one?'

Matteo settled down onto his knees and continued to watch his daughter play. He was so proud of her. Of the way she'd grown so big and strong without his help or influence in her early years. He was so sad that he'd missed them, but he knew that Mara had not let their daughter forget him. His ex and her new love had raised Alex wonderfully. And even though Mara had left him, she'd never taken away his daughter.

Alberto, his father, wouldn't have stood and watched idly as Mara took away the future heir to the throne. And it saddened him that his own mother hadn't lived long enough to see her grandchild grow up. An undiagnosed brain aneurysm had ruptured one evening after she had gone to bed.

'She looks like you when she concentrates.'

He jumped at the voice and stood up, noticing Krystiana holding on to Bruno's lead.

'Krystiana. I thought you were still working?'

'I needed some fresh air. Being inside for a few hours always makes me feel this way. It's so beautiful out here, I'm amazed you ever go back indoors.'

He nodded. 'If I could spend my life out here then I would be a very happy man.'

Kneeling again, he began to build his own sandcastle and situated the dinosaurs around it. He created a small moat and made one of the dinosaurs fall into it. He made an 'ahh...' noise as it fell.

Alex chuckled.

He and Krystiana shared a smile and he felt something inside him—a warmth he hadn't felt before, something weird that made his heart pound—and he had to look away from her, focus on what was happening with Alex.

But he was totally aware of the very second that Krystiana left with Bruno. He momentarily stopped what he was doing and watched her go...

He knew it was late, but she was needed. *Now.*

Matteo banged on her door. 'Krystiana! Are you awake?'

There were some muffled sounds and then he heard her call out.

'I'm coming—hang on!'

He waited, aware of the clock ticking onwards and trying his best not to be impatient. When she finally opened the door he tried not to notice her delightful bed-head and sleepy blue eyes. Nor the fact that she wore a short white robe, tied at her waist, revealing very bare, shapely legs.

'A boat has sunk just off the coast, carrying Syrian refugees. There were families on board. Children. A team has been assembled on the beach, and a rescue operation is underway, but as one of the few medics on the island—'

He didn't need to say any more. The tiredness was instantly gone from her face and instead it was filled with a determination.

'Give me two minutes!'

She ran barefoot across her quarters to the bedroom and yanked open the wardrobe, grabbing a pair of jeans, a soft tee shirt and a jacket, and pulled everything on over her pyjamas. At the bottom of her wardrobe, was a bag that she grabbed, and in much less than the two minutes she'd asked for she was ready to go.

'What do you know so far?'

The royal car raced the team of helpers down towards the beach, where an impromptu camp had been set up to appraise and assess the refugees as they were rescued and brought to shore.

Overhead lights had already been erected, lighting up the coastline, revealing the massive operation already at work. To one side was a tent with a white flag with a red cross on it, and it was to this that she raced.

Matteo had leapt out of the vehicle when they'd arrived and headed straight across the sand towards a small motorised boat that was waiting to take him out to assist with the rescue. It was such a small island, but she was aware that the royal family had helped out in a crisis before. It made them more beloved of their people, showing that they didn't just sit behind the protective walls of their palace but that they got their hands dirty and helped out whenever there was a problem.

Years ago there'd been a small earthquake in Italy, but the tremors and aftershocks had affected Isla Tamoura, bringing down buildings and trapping people in the rubble. Alberto and his son had gone to help there—she could remember seeing it on the news.

She had to assume he knew what he was doing now and that he was in safe hands. Right now she had patients who were wet and cold and in danger of hypothermia.

Krystiana entered the tent and was thrilled to see Dr Bonetti already there, assessing a bedraggled patient. Giving him a quick nod of greeting, she got to work to check on patients of her own.

A woman sat in front of her, huddled in a blanket, shivering. Her eyes were wide and terrified.

She gave the woman a reassuring smile and showed her the stethoscope. 'I'm a doctor. Krystiana. What's your name?'

'R-Roshan.'

'Roshan? I need to listen to your heartbeat, okay?' She patted at her own chest and her patient nodded.

Her chest sounded fine. Her heart-rate was a little fast,

but she put that down to the situation. Slowly she tried to communicate with Roshan, explain the examinations she needed to carry out. Blood pressure. Temperature. Pulse. Oxygen saturations. She moved more slowly than she would have liked, but it was important not to frighten this woman any more than she already was.

Her body had been under huge amounts of stress, but all she found was that Roshan was soaked through, a little dehydrated and also very hungry.

As the examination went on Roshan began to cry, saying things in Arabic that Krystiana didn't understand. She seemed to be asking her about something. Pleading. Her words were a cacophony of sounds. What could it be?

Krystiana could only imagine how scared she was. So far away from her home. A place she'd had to flee from for whatever reason. Was her life in danger? What had she offered the captain of the boat in exchange for her passage? Had she given him everything she had? All her money?

It made her sick to think about it.

She gave Roshan an extra blanket, and was just about to check on another patient when Matteo came barging through the tent entrance, a soaked child in his arms.

Roshan cried out and threw off her blanket. *'Qamar!'* she screamed.

Krystiana pointed at an empty cot. 'Over here.'

She watched as Matteo carried the child over and carefully laid him on the bed.

'He's not gained consciousness since we picked him out of the water but he's breathing. I noticed a lump on the back of his head.'

'Ask Dr Bonetti for warm IV fluids. He'll show you where they are. And fetch some more blankets.'

Matteo raced off to do her bidding whilst she examined Qamar and tried to gain venous access.

He was indeed unconscious, but breathing at a steady rate. The lump on the back of his skull indicated that something had hit him hard, knocking him out, though thankfully she couldn't feel any fracture, or a break to the skin that would need stitching.

She peeled him out of his wet clothes—Roshan helping when she realised what Krystiana was doing—and then covered him with the blankets that Matteo brought over.

'I have the IV.'

'I've inserted a cannula—let's get him hooked up.'

'What can I do to help?' he asked.

'Look after Roshan for me. I think she might be his mother.'

She got in the cannula and started the warm IV running. Then she checked to make sure he had no other visible wounds or any broken bones. She checked his heart-rate and it was steady and sure, but he was thin and bony and she didn't know how strong he was. She'd be happier getting him to a major hospital, where they could give his head a scan to make sure there were no brain bleeds or contusions.

She looked over at Matteo, who was doing his best to communicate with Roshan. His clothes were soaked from carrying Qamar, but he wasn't complaining. She was so grateful to him. For getting involved like this. She could see that he was doing a wonderful job with Roshan, who now sat beside the bed of her son, clutching her prayer beads and dabbing at her eyes with a tissue.

'*Shukraan! Shukraan...*' she said to them both.

Krystiana looked at Matteo. 'What does that mean?'

'I don't know. Perhaps she's saying thank you?'

'Maybe. Are there any more?'

'The boats are going to stay out in the bay for a few more hours, but it looks like we got everybody.'

'How many people in total were on that boat?'

'So far, twelve.'

Twelve people in the water.

Dr Bonetti came over to greet Matteo and thank him for his assistance.

'What's the status of the other patients?'

Dr Bonetti looked grave. 'Mild hypothermia in some cases. A couple are a little malnourished, but that can be easily sorted out over the next few weeks. One had a dislocated shoulder that I've re-sited. We did lose one, though.'

'Who?' Krystiana asked.

'An old man. The coldness of the water was too much for his heart.'

She felt awful at the news. What these people must have gone through—trying to find freedom, doing everything they could, even something that was dangerous, to try and achieve it. What must it have been like for them, travelling on that boat, all huddled together without enough rations to go around?

Had Roshan given up her share of fresh water so that her son would survive the journey? Parents did that, didn't they? Loved their children so much they would gladly give up their own lives if it meant their child survived. That was what they were meant to do, anyway, if the situation arose. She'd like to think she would do the same thing.

'What's going to happen to them?'

'We'll keep them here overnight. Make sure everyone is stable. And then they'll have to be transferred to hospital—'

Matteo frowned. 'They'll have to go on another boat?'

'We have a shuttle boat that can take them. We've used it before—they'll make it there safely.'

Matteo frowned. 'A shuttle boat? I have a ship they could use. It would be larger and more comfortable. Faster, too. I imagine they won't want to spend much time on the water again.'

Krystiana looked up at him. 'That's very kind of you.'

'It's the least I can do. I'm just ashamed it's not more.'

She smiled at him, her gaze dropping to his wet shirt. 'You must be freezing. Here—take a blanket.' She offered him one of the warm blankets from the pile and draped it around his shoulders.

He looked down at her as she did so. 'Thank you.'

Krystiana looked up into his blue eyes and fireworks went off in her belly. Those hypnotic eyes of his…those thick dark eyelashes… His soft, full lips…

Blinking rapidly, she cleared her throat and looked away. 'Well, I must get on. Neuro obs and…stuff.'

Matteo also looked awkward. He nodded. 'Of course. I'll go and make arrangements for the ship to escort these people tomorrow.'

She nodded and turned away, feeling the skin on her face flaming with a heat that she'd never experienced before, her heart pounding, her mouth dry.

What on earth was happening?

And why did she feel like this?

CHAPTER FIVE

SHE DIDN'T SLEEP much that night when she got back to the palace. Her mind was a whirlpool of thoughts.

I'm attracted to Matteo.

It had to be that. She knew what the first flames of attraction felt like and what she'd felt hadn't been flames but a raging fire, out of control.

There'd been another man once. When she'd been at university. Adamo… She'd studied with him and he'd been nice. They'd gone out on a few dates—dinner, dancing—and he'd had the ability to make her laugh.

She'd begun to think she'd found the one. Something that had started as a slow burn had quickly become a flame. She'd fallen in love with him and, determined to be the one who took control of everything, had asked him to marry her.

And that was when her world had come crashing down around her ears again. Because he'd said no. He couldn't marry her. He was already married! Krystiana, to him, had been nothing but a fling.

It had made her feel used and stupid and ashamed. She had let her attraction to him roar out of control as she'd sought the happiness she felt she deserved, but she'd been a fool!

It had taken weeks for her to sleep again, to think

straight again. It had been as if she'd been thrown back in time to when nothing made sense and she'd hated that—because she'd always kept herself safe by controlling everything in her life.

After what had happened with her father—and then Adamo, who had humiliated her—she had vowed to herself never to give her power away again. Never to give her heart to anyone. Because those who had your heart had the power to hurt you and she'd been through enough.

But this thing with Matteo...she didn't feel she had a choice. It felt like something that was happening without her having a hand on the steering wheel. She was in a car and it was careening out of control, down a sheer mountainside, and the brakes weren't working.

How could she stop it?

I could leave. I could rent a place. Nothing is stopping me. And that would be my choice, then, wouldn't it?

That seemed a good idea, and it was still a good idea after breakfast, when there came a knocking at her door. Hoping and praying that it wasn't Matteo, she opened it to see a woman she didn't know holding the hand of Princess Alex, his daughter.

She beamed a smile at the little girl and crouched down to her level. 'Hello, Alex! What are you doing here?'

'I'm going horse-riding!'

'Horse-riding? That sounds fun. I've never done that—aren't you lucky?'

'One day, darling, Krystiana, you will ride a pony of your own.'

She tried to ignore the voice of her father in her head.

'Could you come? Bruno, too?'

She thought about it. She could. After the hullaballoo of last night's rescue she needed something nice and settling. It was the weekend, she didn't have work today or tomorrow, and she really liked Alex. Perhaps it could be the last thing she did before she packed her things and left?

'All right. But I'm going to leave Bruno here. I'm not sure how he is around horses and I don't want there to be an accident. Is that all right?'

Alex nodded. 'Come on, then! We're going *now*!'

'I'll meet you there. I just need to change.'

Alex and the woman who was clearly her nanny nodded and headed off, whilst Krystiana checked her wardrobe for the right gear. What did people wear to ride horses? She hoped she'd get a gentle one. She'd hate to be stuck on the back of a galloping horse she couldn't stop...

She'd had enough of that kind of terror already.

Krystiana reached up her hand to stroke the mane of a beautiful grey horse. 'She's gorgeous!'

'Her name is Matilde.'

She jumped, not having expected to hear Matteo's voice. She'd thought it would just be Alex and her nanny. Maybe a groomsman, but no one else.

'Matteo...'

He smiled at her and patted the horse on its neck. 'She's a gentle beast and she will look after you.'

'Good. I'll need that. I haven't ridden before.'

He looked surprised. 'No? Then I'm glad you agreed to come along. Everyone should ride a horse at least once. Horses spark a passion that often consumes.'

Horses weren't the only thing that sparked a passion... She'd lain await all night thinking of him.

'Well, I could hardly turn down a princess, could I? And give up the opportunity of a lifetime?' She'd always wanted to ride a horse.

He laughed. 'No one can turn her down! Once she turns that smile upon you, you're lost.'

She knew the feeling.

'And the dark horse? Is he yours?'

He smiled. 'Galileo? *Si*. A very proud beast.' He could see the uncertainty in her face. Her anticipation. 'Nervous?'

'Yes. A lot.'

'Do you trust me?'

How could she answer that? To say anything but *yes* would be rude. 'Sure.'

'Don't worry. I'll lead Matilde with a guide rope and Sofia will guide Alex's pony. We're only going for a gentle walk through the orchard. No galloping.'

He smiled to reassure her.

'Alex, *mio cara*, let's get you up in that saddle.' He lifted his daughter up onto the horse's back, making sure she was secure and steady before letting go. 'Your helmet is on tight?'

'*Si*, Papà.'

Krystiana looked uncertain. 'I may need help getting up on this beast. How do you do it without falling off the other side?'

Matteo smiled at her. He held Matilde's reins firmly and showed Krystiana how to put her foot into the stirrup and hoist herself into the saddle.

She did it quickly, not wanting him to have to hold her around the waist or touch her bottom, because if he touched her anywhere below the belt line she feared for her heart-rate.

He mounted his own steed.

'Are we all ready?'

The two women nodded.

'Alexandra?'

His daughter nodded, her eyes on her horse's neck.

He made a small noise of encouragement to his horse and used his stirrups to urge the animal into a walk. The other three followed behind as he led them into the orchard.

The sun shone down on them from above, warming her bare arms and feeling good. As she adjusted to the horse's gait Krystiana found herself relaxing somewhat, beginning to enjoy the adventure.

It was everything she'd hoped it would be. The horse's motion was almost a rocking movement, hypnotic in its rhythm, and with the warmth of the sun and the beautiful orchard all around them she felt herself wanting to just relax and drift off—especially as she'd lost a lot of sleep last night.

It was such a strange world, she thought. That one moment she could be attending refugees on a beach, and the next moment be horse-riding. What were Roshan and Qamar doing now? And the others? Were they already in hospital? Were they feeling better?

Matteo led the parade of horses down a steep slope and along a small grassy path that would take them into the main thicket of trees.

As they moved along she listened to the birds singing, and then she heard the steady trickle of water and smiled when he led them towards a small babbling brook. Picture-perfect.

They stopped for a moment, and the horses sniffed at the water but chose to nibble on the tall grass alongside it.

'Is everyone all right?' asked Matteo.

Krystiana nodded—as did Sofia, the nanny.

'*Si*, Papà,' said Alex.

He smiled and urged the horses onward.

* * *

He'd not known Krystiana would be horse-riding with him and Alex. He'd thought it was just going to be himself, the nanny and his daughter. It had been a surprise to see her standing there at the stables, in figure-hugging jeans and a checked shirt. All she needed was a Stetson and she would look like a proper cowgirl.

Her long hair was in its usual plait. He'd spent the entire night, tossing and turning in bed, wondering what her hair would look like spread out over a pillow.

That moment they'd shared in the refugee tent had been...*electric*. He'd felt it. He'd noticed that she felt it too, but luckily she'd done something to avoid it.

He didn't need the complication of another relationship. He'd married his best friend and hadn't made that work—what hope would there be for anyone else? Plus, he couldn't contemplate the *idea* of another relationship. If you loved someone, you lost them, and the pain of that was too much.

His father was a different man since losing Matteo's mother, and when he himself had come home to find his mother dead and that his wife had moved on and begun a new relationship, he'd decided there and then that the only person he would ever love again would be his daughter.

He wasn't looking for love. Or a fling. His position dictated that a fling would be very bad news indeed. The Crown Prince of Isla Tamoura did *not* use women in such a way. He had standards. And morals.

Any deeper relationship was a no-go, so...

But seeing her here this morning had fired his blood once again, and he was glad that she was a novice with horses—it meant that he could lead without having to look at her or make eye contact, and everyone seemed quite content to just ride along and view the scenery in peace and quiet.

Not that his mind was peaceful. Or quiet. It was coming up with a million and one thoughts about Krystiana that he kept trying to push away.

I am not risking my heart again. No way.

The kidnapping, and then coming home to find his marriage over, his mother dead, were three huge stresses he'd already had to cope with, and there was his coronation coming up at the end of the year…

He just wanted to relax whilst he had the chance. He did not need the added complication of a forbidden crush. Because that was what it would be. They'd shared an experience. They'd both been glad to find someone else who knew how that felt—that was all.

A mind trick. The body playing games.

He knew he was stronger than that. He'd spent two years wondering if this was the day he was going to die and carrying on anyway. If he could get through *that*, then he could get through *this*.

A few more weeks and she'd be gone from his life. Any future physicals would be conducted by Dr Bonetti, and if he retired he would ask another doctor to take over that particular duty.

He could resist his feelings for a few more weeks.

CHAPTER SIX

'SHE'S BEAUTIFUL…' WHISPERED MARA.

Matteo looked over at his ex-wife, who lay on their daughter's bed as she went off to sleep. 'She is.'

Mara smiled. 'I wasn't talking about Alex. Though she is *very* beautiful, of course. I meant the woman I saw you with.'

He decided to play ignorant. He didn't need his wife playing games. 'You've already met Sofia. You hired her.'

'The *doctor*, Matteo.'

He raised an eyebrow. 'Krystiana? She's just staying here until her place gets fixed.'

'Is that all?'

He picked up the book they'd been reading to Alex and quietly slid it back onto his daughter's bookshelf. 'Of course that's all.'

'Are you sure, Matteo?'

He raised an eyebrow. 'Yes.'

'*Krystiana?* Not Dr Szenac?'

'We're friends. You call friends by their first name. Remember, Mara? We're friends—it's what *we* do.'

She nodded. 'Of course! Of course that's what friends do. I'm just not sure I've ever seen *friends* look at each other the way you two do.'

'I barely know her.'

'You barely know her or you're friends?'

His ex-wife slowly got off the bed, hoping their daughter wouldn't wake. They both crept from the room and Mara pulled the door almost closed as they headed into the next room.

Matteo handed his ex-wife the glass of wine she'd started earlier. 'Please don't, Mara.'

She stared him down. 'Don't what?'

'Don't try to matchmake.'

'I'm not! But I *am* asking you to be careful.'

'You're hinting. Just because you're all loved up, and you feel guilty about giving up on me, it does not mean I'm your responsibility.'

'I'm not trying to fix you up, Matteo. I'm asking you to think carefully about what you're doing.'

He shook his head at her, amused. 'Nothing's happened.'

She smiled. 'Keep it that way—or you're going to hurt a lot of people.'

The next day Krystiana found herself standing outside her villa with Aunt Carolina, who had agreed to meet her there. Some progress had been made. A lot of the loose rubble had been cleared and the first-floor ceiling had been propped up by scaffolding and made secure, whilst a lot of the loose brickwork had been hacked back, so that the hole in her wall had become almost twice the size. Inside, her furniture looked forlorn and strange, open to the elements, but she thanked her lucky stars that there'd been no rain and therefore no water damage.

'Carlo!' She waved to the foreman and he waved back, jumping down from a digger that was removing debris to another part of the site. 'How is everything going?'

'It's going as well as can be expected. My team are working hard and at all hours round the clock.'

'Are we still looking at a few weeks' work?'

'Three...four weeks, maybe. As long as there are no more surprises.'

'You've had surprises?'

He smiled. 'Not yet.' He turned to look at her aunt and she realised she hadn't introduced them. She did so.

'Buongiorno.'

She noticed the interested smile on Carlo's face as he looked at her aunt, and saw that Aunt Carolina was smiling back.

'You're working hard all day, every day? Seven days a week?' Carolina asked.

'Si.'

'Perhaps I should bring you and your crew some food? Some drinks?'

'That would be very kind of you—thank you. We lose a lot of time on lunch breaks, going to find food to eat, so that would help us work faster.'

Carolina beamed. 'Well, I'd like to think I was helping...'

Krystiana looked from one to the other and found herself smiling. Who'd have thought it? Carolina and Carlo? Her aunt had lived alone ever since her divorce, years ago, and had always said that men were more trouble than they were worth.

Clearly she was having a change of heart!

'Come on. We need to get going or we'll be late for lunch ourselves.' Krystiana interrupted.

'Of course. I'll see you later, Carlo.'

Carolina waved as she walked away with her niece back to their car.

Once inside, Krystiana turned to her. 'Well, *you've* changed your tune!'

'He was a very nice man!'

'They all are. To begin with. You tell me that all the time.'

'Maybe so—but being alone isn't all it's cracked up to be. You have to give someone a chance to prove you wrong.'

Did she? Her father had proved her *right*. Those who had your heart could hurt you the most. As Adamo had. Did she have to give Matteo a chance? He seemed nice and kind. He seemed a good, strong, caring man. But what if that was just his public persona? What if he was someone else entirely?

The smile on her aunt's face put doubt into her mind for the next couple of hours, and she found herself wondering, as she was being driven back to the palace, whether she'd been too harsh in her decision-making and ought to give Matteo the opportunity to show her that he was not going to break her heart.

Perhaps if they went out once or twice, and the excitement of something new died down and the fear dissipated somewhat, she'd discover that they didn't have much in common anyway—so what was she worried about?

It could hardly become anything, anyway. He was a prince! He wouldn't enter a relationship lightly, either.

When she got back to her quarters she stared at the suitcase in the bottom of her wardrobe and decided she would leave it there just a little bit longer.

CHAPTER SEVEN

MATTEO HAD INVITED her to dinner in his quarters. He wasn't sure whether he should have or not, but he'd figured, *What the hell?* He was a grown man, they were both adults and they were friends. It wasn't as if he didn't have any self-control. He liked her. He could spend time with her. But that was all it would be.

It wouldn't be a late night. She was bound to be busy, would no doubt have some work to do in her quarters, and he'd only just said goodbye to Mara and Alex, who had gone back to their own private estate in Ventura. There was a load of work for him to catch up on.

He knew he might be playing with fire, but he also knew he couldn't spend the next few weeks jumping out of his skin every time he had to spend time with Krystiana. Best to have a couple of hours in her company and cool the heck down. Okay, so she had beautiful eyes and a nice smile. She was kind and generous and easy to be with…

I'm not exactly talking myself out of this, am I?

He put on some dark trousers and a white shirt. Simple elegance. Something he could feel relaxed in. He didn't want to look as if he was trying to impress her. Because he wasn't. But any gentleman showed respect for the woman he was with by dressing nicely for her.

Krystiana arrived on the dot of seven, her gentle knock

at the door signalling her arrival. His heart hammered in his throat and he paused before answering the door, but then he took a deep, steadying breath and swung it open.

And there she stood, looking gorgeous and summery in a blue wraparound dress, that long plait of hers over one shoulder.

'Hi. Come on in!' He stepped back.

'Thanks.' As she stepped in he automatically leaned forward to drop a kiss upon her cheek. He held his breath as he pressed his face close to hers, and his heart almost leapt from his throat as his lips pressed against her skin. She smelt of flowers and soap and something he couldn't quite put his finger on. Whatever it was, it was delicious.

And then he was pulling away and he could breathe again.

She'd flushed a beautiful pink in her cheeks and, clearly trying to distract him from it, she pointed. 'What's that? The painting you promised to show me?'

He nodded at the canvas on the easel, draped with a cover, smiling, but looking apprehensive. 'I'm no Da Vinci, but, yes. Here you go. What do you think?'

He pulled the cover off with a flourish so that she could see it.

An explosion of colour leapt out and he watched her face carefully as she picked up the canvas to consider it properly. Clearly he was new to painting, but he had tried hard and his use of colour was good for an amateur. Even if he said so himself. He'd enjoyed doing it and considered doing so again.

No, he wasn't Da Vinci, or Picasso, or any other famous painter. But it was definitely a Romano. Rich in texture and colour, a riot of green interspersed with cobalt blue, scarlet red and sunshine-yellow. A vast blue sky clear of clouds sat overhead, and he'd even attempted the mosaic floor, using his fingertips for each tile.

'Matteo, it's marvellous!'

'Thank you.' He was pleased that she liked it—he took pleasure from *her* pleasure.

'Are you sure you did this? It's beautiful! You've done a wonderful job for your first time.'

'Imagine what I'd be like with practice.' He smiled.

She looked at him, her smile uncertain.

'Yes! Yes, I imagine you would be brilliant!' She laid the canvas back upon the easel and admired it better by stepping back. 'You've captured the very essence of the garden. Full of life and joy. This will keep you going in the winter months when there's less in bloom.'

And suddenly he knew something. 'I'd like you to have it.'

'Me?'

He nodded. 'I can look at the real thing every day. You'll be going home soon and I'd like to think you will remember your visit.'

It saddened him to think of her leaving. She was a kindred spirit. Someone who had experienced the same thing as he and that was important. Who else would understand what he had gone through?

But it was more than that shared experience. There was a naturalness about Krystiana. Something about her that spoke to him. And it was confusing and worrying and exciting in different ways. But that was the whole point of tonight. To show that he could deal with that and not act on it. Krystiana could never be more than his friend, and that was the thing that he needed to remember more than anything else.

Besides, princes could not be with commoners. It was against the law of his country. So...that was that. As Mara had tried to forewarn him. And it was a *good* thing, because it kept him safe. She was out of bounds and men like him did not have flings. The media would have a field-day if he did. But thankfully his heart was boxed away. To all intents and purposes it was still in that mountain cave and he had to leave it there.

'I'm honoured. Thank you.'

He smiled, and being caught in her gaze once again was exhilarating. Everything else faded away and all he saw was her. He blinked and stepped back, indicating they should go further out onto the terrace, where the views were impeccable in the late evening light.

'Would you like to take a seat? Sergio will be here momentarily with the first course.'

'What are we having?'

A dash of attraction with a hint of lust and a heavy dose of desire.

'I told him to surprise us. I'm sure he won't let us down. He has quite the palate.'

'Really?'

'His family own a winery. Up in the Auriga Hills.'

Good. That's better. Talk about Sergio. The most unromantic topic you can think of. Wine and grapes and feet squishing grapes in age-old barrels. Sergio's feet. Yes, now, there's an image.

'I didn't know that.'

'I'm sure he'd love to show you around one day.'

'Have you ever been?'

'Yes. A few years ago now, though. Before I was kidnapped.'

She nodded. 'How do you feel about it now?'

He didn't mind talking to her about that, either. 'Sometimes it's like a dream. Like it never really happened to me. Other times it's like a nightmare and I remember everything. How about you?'

'Well, it's been a lot longer for me since it happened. But I understand what you mean. I tried to make sense of it once, by going to the place where it had happened. I thought if I confronted it then it wouldn't have any power over me.'

'What was that like?'

'Strange. The landowner agreed to walk me out to the spot where my father had created the bunker. He was very sweet to me. Very kind. Asking after my well-being, wanting to know that I was all right. He even apologised to me for not knowing. For not realising that I was out there. And then he pointed at a dip in the ground. It just looked so normal and inconsequential. No different from the rest of it. And yet in my mind it had held such power. The hole had been filled in, and scrub and mulch covered it over, but I stared at it, trying to imagine myself in such a small hole, shivering in the cold, clutching a book for comfort.'

He could imagine it all too easily. 'Did you have nightmares before?'

'Every night.'

'And going to the place…did that help get rid of them?'

'It did. I saw it was just a place that meant nothing any more. It wasn't the bunker that had harmed me—it was my father. That takes longer to get over. Someone close hurting you. But, yes, it was a good thing for me to do. It exorcised the ghosts that lingered. Gave me closure.'

'How so?'

She glanced at him. But thankfully not for too long. Her eyes were like welcoming pools he wanted to stay in.

'I think it's because it was the place I wanted to escape from so much. A place I told myself I would never again go near. I'd built it up into this huge thing. So that place…

it haunted me. By returning I showed that I was stronger. I proved to myself that *I* was in control.'

Matteo nodded. He understood. And he was in awe of her bravery and courage.

'You could go back too, you know. I believe in you. If you could get through two years in that place, then you can get through anything.'

'I don't have to go back. I've thought about it, but the bad dreams are only occasional and my therapist has been helping me a lot…sorting through my feelings.'

'Good. Talking therapy works really well. I'm glad you're getting a lot from it.'

He nodded. 'I am.'

At that moment Sergio arrived, carrying a tray, and laid down a small bowl in front of each of them. 'Butternut squash risotto,' he intoned. 'Do enjoy your meal.'

'Do you think being held hostage made you a different person?' she asked after a while.

'I'm still me.'

'Of course—but are you a stronger you now?'

'I'd like to think so. I've been given a different perspective on life. On trauma and struggle and just wanting to survive. I'd like to think I have taken that and learned from it, so that I can be a strong king when I take the throne.'

'You'll make an *excellent* king,' she said emphatically.

He was pleased at her confidence in him. It was something he shared. 'Thank you. I shall certainly try my very best.'

She nodded. 'I've no doubt. What other royal opens up his palace to a homeless woman? Helps search for survivors under earthquake rubble? Goes out to rescue asylum seekers? You're not afraid to get your hands dirty.

You care. You're compassionate. You'll make an excellent monarch.'

She clearly meant every word. He was truly touched by her confidence in him. 'Thank you. That means a lot to me.'

She stared back and he found himself caught in her gaze. What *was* it about her that did this to him?

'Eat your risotto before it gets cold.'

She nodded, smiled and picked up her fork.

She imagined, as he spoke, what it might be like to be with him. Who wouldn't? He was a prince. Handsome and charming. A presence with an overwhelming masculinity that made itself known whenever she was with him. He was a good listener, a caring and thoughtful person, and she could see that he liked people.

He was always courteous and considerate to the servants in his employ, chatting to everyone the same way, no matter whether they were another member of the royal family or a gardener. She could appreciate his kindness, his heart, and his concern for his people and the future he might bring them. Clearly being King was something he took seriously.

But her body responded to him in ways she did not want. Her heart fluttered with excitement every time she saw him and she yearned for something more than what they had. But that was just her being foolish. A remnant from a previous time in which she'd trusted people.

'How do you see your life changing when you become King?' she asked, genuinely interested.

He shrugged. 'I imagine it will be pretty much the same. Just my title will be different. I'll be expected to attend more events. To do more touring, perhaps.'

'Isn't it hard for you to be away from your family?'

'It can be. The kidnapping made me see how important family is. Material things—possessions—those don't matter at all. It's people who count. Being with the ones you love. Leaving them hurts me, but it gets easier each time I do so.'

He ate a mouthful of their next course—a rich lasagne, oozing with béchamel sauce.

'What about you? You left your childhood home and moved to another country. Don't you ever miss Poland?'

'Sometimes. But I'm not so sure it's the country I miss as much as the people I knew there. Friends I made at school. The therapist I saw who became a good friend. My school teachers.'

'You enjoyed school?'

She smiled. 'I did. Very much so. I even thought I'd become a teacher when I was little—I loved it that much.'

'What made you become a doctor?'

'My mother dying the way she did. Hit by a bus. When I got to the hospital and saw how they were trying to save her, I...' Her mouth dried up and she had to take a sip of water. 'I felt in the way. I wanted to help too, but there was nothing I could do but cower in a corner. It wasn't until much later—after I'd moved to Isla Tamoura—that I decided I would never feel that helpless again and so I trained as a doctor.'

'You had focus?'

'Yes. It helped me a lot. Knowing I was working towards something.'

'I feel the same.'

'How so?'

'I grew up knowing I would become King one day. They train you for it, you know. Special lessons in law and etiquette and the history of tradition. They school you in politics and languages and even body language.'

She laughed. 'Really?'

'Really.' He smiled. 'I've always wanted to be a good king. As good as my father and loved by my people. But I've always known I don't want to be just a title behind the palace walls. I want to be involved—I want to get right down at the grass roots and know people. Be an active king who achieves things and is not just a figurehead. I want to be seen doing worthwhile work, not just waving at crowds from behind bullet-proof glass. Being a man of the people means a lot to me, and I intend to get it right. The kidnapping showed me just how much people matter, and if I can help them then I will.'

'Like housing homeless doctors?'

Matteo smiled. 'Exactly.'

She ate another mouthful of food, contemplating her next question.

'What?' he said.

She looked up at him.

'I can tell you want to ask me something.'

Krystiana dabbed at her mouth with a napkin. Then sipped her water. 'Do you ever get lonely?'

He looked straight back at her, considering her question. 'Do *you*?'

'I asked first.'

Matteo sat back. 'There's an element of being a royal that makes you lonely. People put you on a pedestal— they think you're above them so they don't try to reach you. They just admire you from afar. I'd like to think that I'm accessible to everyone, but... I have my father and my daughter. And my extended family, like Beatrice and Edoardo.'

'That's not what I meant.'

'What *did* you mean?'

'Do you miss being married?'

'My marriage to Mara was never a true love-match. Not romantic love, anyway. We were best friends and we still are, despite what happened. I haven't lost her. What about you? Do you ever see yourself settling down?'

She shook her head. 'No. No way.'

'Why not?'

How to answer? Krystiana looked out across the terrace, past the gardens and deep into the countryside, where the setting sun was making everything look hazy and dark. Should she tell him about Adamo? *No.* That was a whole embarrassing situation she never wanted to be in again.

'I don't think I'm capable of giving myself wholeheartedly to anyone. Not any more.'

'Why not?'

'Because I'd have to trust them, and that would make me vulnerable, and I promised myself I would never be made to feel vulnerable ever again.'

She stared back at him as if daring him to challenge her. To argue with her. Perhaps to laugh at her silly fears.

But he didn't do any of that.

He simply nodded in understanding. 'Okay. Good enough.'

'Well, thank you for inviting me to dine with you. I've had a wonderful time.'

Matteo nodded. 'It was my pleasure.'

They stood together by the doors, awkwardly trying to work out how to say goodnight to each other.

He felt that the right thing to do would be to kiss her on the cheek as he said goodbye, but when he'd done that earlier he'd inhaled her scent of soap and flowery meadows and felt a surge of hormones flood his system with arousal and attraction. If he did it again he simply wouldn't get to sleep tonight, and he'd already spent enough sleepless nights lately.

'It will be my turn to entertain you next.'

'I'll look forward to it.'

'All right. Well…goodnight, Matteo.'

'Goodnight, Krystiana.'

He hesitated, and reason told him it would be impolite just to walk away, strange to shake her hand and downright rude to do nothing at all. *Friends* kissed each other goodnight—and they were friends, weren't they?

Leaning in, he kissed one cheek, then the other, trying his hardest not to breathe in her delicious scent.

That would be wrong.

For him *and* for her.

It was just attraction. Nothing more. He couldn't be with her. Nor did he want to be. Being with Krystiana would mean falling hard for her and he wouldn't let that happen. He lived his life in the public eye. She'd be scrutinised down to her every blood cell by the press. And hadn't she just told him that she would never be vulnerable again? Nor trust anyone? Plus she'd already said that she didn't want to get into a relationship anyway, so…

Being in the public eye made you vulnerable. Being in a relationship made you vulnerable. It laid you out bare and then fate would tear you to pieces. Life was cruel and impossible to win. He wouldn't even try to put either of them through that.

But he knew he was attracted to her. She was so easy to talk to. He felt relaxed when he was with her. His true self. He could tell her things that he would never tell anyone else…

He shook his head vehemently as he closed his door. Nothing could come of it. No matter how much his body cried out for the intimacy of hers.

He could fight instinct. He could fight attraction.

And what would be the point in getting involved with someone he knew was not suitable? Falling for Krystiana would *destroy* him. He knew it. She was the type of woman he would fall hard for and he didn't want to be laid open to hurt again. Or humiliation when it all went wrong. And why wouldn't it? Everything else had.

Her life was going in one direction and his in another. They were in a fake bubble right now, and it wasn't sustainable.

Matteo turned and walked straight into his bathroom. He needed a cold shower.

Krystiana smiled at Mara, who sat opposite her in a splendid pure white tailored dress. The dress showed off Mara's sylph-like figure, all long limbs and elegance and grace. They'd met in the corridor of the palace as Mara had dropped off Alex and they'd come for a coffee in the royal gardens.

'What was it like for *you* when Matteo was taken?'

Krystiana was intrigued. She wanted to know what it had been like for those left behind. She was thinking specifically of her own mother, as they'd never had much time to talk about it before she died.

Mara let out a slow sigh. 'It was very difficult. No one knew what had happened to him and I feared the worst. Especially as I'd seen their treatment of him when he was taken. They hit him over the head with a rifle. The sound it made will haunt my dreams for ever.'

'Didn't you have guards? A convoy of any kind?'

'Yes, of course. But they took out the lead car and then surrounded us with armed men. And there'd been a new guard riding with us, who was actually one of them, and he had his gun at Matteo's head. They had no choice but to back down.'

'And then what happened?'

'Then he was gone. I screamed. I cried. I had to get into the front of the car to use the emergency radio. I was still contracting. Still in labour. It seemed an age before help arrived.'

'You gave birth *alone*?' Krystiana could hardly imagine that. At least her mother hadn't seen her being treated roughly. Had never seen inside the hole in the ground. Had not had to go through something like childbirth afterwards.

'My mother came, and my sister. They were able to get to the hospital in time.'

'And it was an easy birth?'

'My blood pressure was high, but the doctors felt that was because of what had happened. The trauma of Matteo's kidnapping. The violence. I delivered in Theatre—just in case it became an emergency and they needed Alex out quick.'

'You must have been frightened?'

'Very.'

'Alex was all right?'

'Yes.' Mara smiled. 'She was beautiful.'

'She still is.' Krystiana smiled too. 'Is Alexandra the name you both chose?'

'It was one of Matteo's choices. I'd not been sure about it, but with him gone like that... I had to choose it. And now I love it. It suits her perfectly.'

'You had no doubt that he'd return?'

'At the beginning? None at all. But when time kept passing. Days into weeks. Weeks into months. A year... I began losing hope. I wanted my child to have her father.'

'That must have been hard for you.'

What had her mother felt as each day passed? Each week? A month? Had she feared her daughter dead?

Mara nodded. 'It was. To lose my best friend, the father of my child… I felt incredibly alone. But I was expected to carry on. Be a representative of the royal family. Appear brave in the face of the *paparazzi*. It became too much, and I began to lean on an old family friend.'

'Philippe?'

She nodded. 'I know a lot of people hate me for it. For moving on. But when you're so alone…your heart cries out for comfort.'

Krystiana considered that. The need to be held *was* a powerful one. To be listened to. *Heard*. When was the last time someone had given her a long hug? When had she last snuggled against someone? Bruno didn't count. He was a dog. But perhaps she felt she could do it with Bruno because dogs loved unconditionally? Dogs didn't trick you, or let you down, or bury you in a miserable hole.

And as she gazed at Mara she wondered. Wondered how she could seem so content, so happy, knowing that life could be unfair and take your loved ones away from you so quickly?

'You and Philippe are happy?'

She smiled. Beamed, in fact. 'Very.'

'I'm glad for you. That you found Philippe.'

Mara nodded her thanks.

CHAPTER EIGHT

'OUCH!' KRYSTIANA WHIPPED her hand from the rose bush, shaking it madly to take away the pain. One of the thorns must have pricked her as she'd knelt down to smell the scent of the misty blue bloom.

The rose was called Blue Moon. Her favourite. Her mother had grown Blue Moons in her small patch of garden, and as Krystiana had wandered through the gardens that gave Matteo peace she had hoped to find some for herself. Spotting the familiar bloom had drawn her to it, and she had reached for it without thinking.

'Are you all right?'

She spun to see Matteo coming towards her. He looked very handsome today. Dark linen trousers and a white shirt, the sleeves turned up to the elbow.

She glanced at her finger and saw a small drop of blood forming. 'I'm fine. I just caught myself on the thorns.'

'Let me see.'

She shook her head, backing away. 'No, it's all right. I—'

But he had her hand in his, examining it carefully, his touch gentle, yet commanding.

She had to stand there, breathing shallowly, trying not to stare at him as he looked at her hand. She did not want this. Did not *need* this. His proximity. His tenderness in looking out for her.

'Really, it's all right.' She insisted.

'You're bleeding.' He reached into his pocket and withdrew a white handkerchief.

'It'll stain…' She tried to protest, but he wrapped it around her finger anyway. She sagged, feeling him apply pressure. She also winced.

'Does it hurt?'

She shrugged. 'I don't know. Maybe a little.'

'Perhaps you have a thorn in it?' He removed the handkerchief for a closer look, but it was hard to see as blood kept coming.

She really wanted her hand back. Having him being this attentive to her was really playing with her mind.

'I've got tweezers in my bathroom. I'll check later.'

She yanked her hand free from his and gave him a brief smile, trying to appear grateful when in reality, she felt anything but. No. She *was* grateful. But that was just one of the many things she was feeling.

'What are you doing out here? I thought you had a meeting?'

In fact that was the reason she had come out here in the first place. She knew it was his sanctuary, but she'd known he was meant to be busy and she'd needed space to breathe and think.

'It got cancelled.'

'Oh.' She bit her lip, trying to think of something to say. 'You didn't want to go and see Alex instead?'

'She's napping. I'm planning to spend some time with her when she wakes up. I came out to find you because I thought you might like to hear about what happened with Roshan, Qamar and the others.'

She was very interested. 'Oh, yes?'

'They made it safely to the hospital. Qamar regained consciousness quite quickly and his dehydration issues and malnutrition are being thoroughly taken care of by a specialist team of dieticians.'

That was wonderful news. 'I'm glad. What will happen next for them?'

'They'll be found homes, once the doctors give them the okay to leave, and I've put out a few feelers with the authorities to see what we can do—maybe get them some work, places in schools, that kind of thing.'

She smiled. He was so good. So generous. Selfless. She liked that about him. 'That's fantastic. I hope they find the peace that they deserve.'

'Me too.'

'And you? What are you going to do today, now you're free?'

'We're going to go swimming in the pool.'

'Oh, that's nice.'

He smiled. 'Well, I don't get to go to public pools, and I love swimming. Mostly in the sea, but the pool will do. You should come too.'

Krystiana in a pool? In a swimsuit? With Matteo, who'd be wearing nothing but shorts? That was a little too intimate for her liking.

'I...er...think I'll pass.'

'Come with us. It will be fun.'

'Not for me, it won't.' It was out before she could censor it.

He frowned. 'Why not?'

A million excuses ran through her head and she considered them all. But her hatred of lying convinced her to tell him the truth. If he knew, then he would leave it alone and not force the issue.

'I can't swim.'

'What?' He looked at her incredulously.

'I can't swim. I never learned.'

'You had no one to teach you?'

'No.'

She felt her cheeks flush. After her kidnapping she had been too busy with her head stuck in books, and swimming had seemed a luxury that she didn't want to pursue. What would have been the point? She never intended going near water, except to maybe admire it. She never wanted to go in it.

Yes, she now lived on an island, surrounded by water, and after seeing what had happened to those refugees they'd rescued perhaps she ought to, but...

Matteo beamed and his smile melted her heart.

'Then I will teach you.'

'No.'

'Come on. You'll thank me for it.'

'No, I... I don't even have a costume!'

'We'll buy you some.'

'No, honestly, Matteo, it's fine—'

'I won't take no for an answer.'

She could see in his eyes how much he wanted to help her learn to swim. How much he wanted to give something back to her. How excited he was by the idea.

She thought of her pale, pasty body next to his tanned, glowing sun god look and cringed inside. It would be embarrassing, wouldn't it? And spending some downtime with him would only add to the feelings she was already having. She couldn't let that happen.

How on earth am I going to get out of this?

He had to admit to himself that he hadn't quite thought this through—offering to teach Krystiana to swim. He'd just blurted out the invite. It had seemed the right idea at the time and he hadn't been able to get past the knowledge that she didn't know how to. Swimming was something he had always done, and he found a freedom in the water that couldn't be found elsewhere. It was soothing. Good for the mind. And he wanted to share that with her, knowing that she had been through the same kind of trauma as he.

As she entered the pool house, looking nervous, wearing a thin robe, he saw her long, elegant legs and got a flash of intensity through his body. There was something about her. So innocent. So vulnerable. So alone. He could connect with those feelings. He'd felt the need to surround her and protect her this afternoon in the garden, when she'd hurt herself. When he'd seen her bleeding. He'd felt his heart pound and blood rush through his veins.

Okay, it had only been a small puncture wound, but it had been enough to awaken his protective side. He'd wanted to keep the world out so that he could help her, and then, up close to her, holding her hand, inhaling the scent of her, looking into her warm blue eyes it had made his senses go wild—into overdrive—and he had not wanted to let go.

When she'd pulled away he'd seen it in her eyes that she felt something too, and that knowledge had made him stop. She didn't want to get involved with anyone. Nor did he.

He had to back off. To stay away from her. But something kept him there. The need to teach her something. To enjoy the time they had left before their lives reclaimed them. There'd been that look on her face...one that he couldn't resist...and then she had told him she couldn't swim. She lived on an island! And he didn't want her to go without helping her in some small way.

Getting to the pool before anyone else, he'd pounded out a couple of lengths already, hoping that by doing so he would exhaust his body enough not to react to hers. Because he was aware of just how much he did react to her physically, and being in the pool would be a lot more intimate than dinner on the balcony.

He pulled himself from the water and went over to meet her. 'Hi. Thank you for joining me.'

She looked uncertainly at him, then at the surrounding pool. 'Where's Alex?'

'She'll be here soon. I thought you might appreciate some time one-to-one before she gets here. No one likes to see a five-year-old swim better than them.'

'Oh, that's thoughtful. Thank you.'

'Soon you'll be splashing around like the rest of us.'

'I don't imagine you splash much.'

He smiled and ran his hands over his hair to keep it from his face. 'Maybe not.' He laughed.

'So…' She gazed at the pool, at the way the water rippled, reflecting against the walls and the ceiling. 'How do we make a start?'

He looked at her, feeling his blood surge at the thought and trying to control it. 'You take off the robe.'

She looked at him uncertainly. Hesitant. Torn between wanting to spend this time with him and being afraid of what time with him like this might do.

He was a majestic, gorgeous hunk of man, who seemed oblivious to the effect he was having on her. Which was a good thing—because imagine how embarrassing that might be?

She felt shy about taking off her robe. He might assess her body. Krystiana knew she wasn't considered *unattractive*, but that didn't mean she oozed confidence. She still had her doubts and her insecurities, and being in just a swimsuit would make her feel terribly exposed. Vulnerable. And that feeling was something she tried to avoid.

'Would you mind turning around?'

'Of course not.' He turned his back on her so that she could slip off the robe, and for a brief moment she just stood there and gazed at the broad expanse of his bronzed back. At the width of his shoulders and down to his narrow waist, to the swimming trunks that showed a wonderfully toned backside, and then the long, muscly thighs, darkened by fine hair.

Would he chance a look at her?

No. He's not like that.

Krystiana quickly tugged off the robe and slipped into the pool.

He turned when he heard her moving in the water and slipped in next to her. 'All right?'

She nodded. The water had felt cold at first, but now she was in she realised it was perfect.

'How do you feel about putting your face in the water?'

She looked at its rippling surface. 'I won't be able to see anything.'

He nodded, understanding her fear. 'I have goggles.' He reached over to the steps behind him, where a pair hung. 'Best to wet your hair first, before you put them on.'

She nodded, dipping her head back until the full length of her braid was dripping.

'Here.'

He stepped towards her and she had to suck in a breath as he stood close, helping her with the goggles. They were a bit loose, so he tightened them for her. She was just inches away from his marvellous masculine form and she didn't know where to look. Or to put her hands. He was wearing almost nothing.

'I must look silly.' She blushed.

'You look perfect. So, do you want to try putting your face underwater now? Take a breath and then just lower yourself down for a moment and see what it's like.'

'Okay.' She sucked in a couple of deep breaths before pinching her nose and lowering herself beneath the water's surface.

The world sounded strange from underneath. Muffled and weird. She could see Matteo's ripped abs and long legs, his feet standing sure on the bottom of the pool. She took a quick glance at his shorts, at the line of hair from his belly button that disappeared beneath the fabric.

She stood up again with a rush.

'How was that?'

'Fine.' She lifted the goggles onto her forehead and laughed, blushing. 'It was good!'

He smiled back, clearly enjoying her success. '*Fantastic*. I'll get you a float.'

She watched as he easily heaved his form from the pool, the water rushing down his body, and fetched her a blue square of solid foam from the side before he hopped back in.

'Right—now you're going to try to glide.'

'Glide?'

'You're going to hold this float in front of you. Arms nice and straight, face in the water. And with your feet you're going to push off from the wall and see how far you can glide across the pool.'

That sounded simple enough. 'Okay…'

'Deep breath, face down, then push.'

'Sounds like you want me to give birth.'

He smiled, clearly following her line of thought. To give birth you had to be pregnant, and to be pregnant you had to have had *sex*.

She felt tingles inside. Her belly was fluttering and

she was beginning to realise that she was *enjoying* this. Something she'd been dreading since he'd suggested it.

Sucking in a breath, she held the float in front of her, put her face down and pushed off the wall behind her. She surged forward, gliding swiftly and surely through the water until her breath ran out, and then she stood up suddenly, gasping for air. 'I did it!'

'You did! You're a natural! Do it again. But this time kick with your feet as you're gliding.'

'Okay.'

She made her way back to the side of the pool and carried out his instructions, and this time she made it almost halfway across.

'I'm doing it! Did you see?'

'I did! Try it again.'

She did it over and over again, kicking her way all the way across the pool, occasionally lifting her head for a gasp of air, until she reached the other side.

'Teach me something else!'

'Okay. Let's try it without the float.'

'Without?' She wasn't too sure about that. How would she stay on top of the water?

'Yes. Watch me.'

She watched him dip under the water and push off from the wall, and smiled in relief as his body naturally drifted up and glided across the surface, before he stood once again to look at her.

He brushed his wet hair back from his face. 'Easy—see?'

'Easy for *you*, maybe.'

'Have faith, Krystiana. See if you can swim out this far to me.'

He was just over the halfway mark. Technically, it wasn't that far, and she knew that with the goggles she'd be able to see under water just how far away he was. He could be with her in a second if it went wrong.

'I'm trusting you to catch me if I start to drown.'

'You won't drown. You can do this.'

'Okay.'

She adjusted her goggles once again, then sucked in a deep breath and tried to do what she'd seen Matteo do. Head under, push off the wall, kick with her feet, hands out in front of her... Under the water, she could see him. His reassuring torso, his hands out in front of him, ready to reach for her when she got close.

And she made it!

Grabbing his hands and feeling him pull her towards him, she got to her feet, laughing and beaming with joy. 'I did it! Did you see me?'

'You were great!'

He was holding her close. Her hands lay wet and warm upon his chest. And suddenly she realised she was staring into his eyes, and he into hers. Their bodies were touching and she gazed up at his lips, studded with water droplets, and realised, intensely, that she wanted to kiss them so very much.

The realisation hit her with the force of a wave and she glanced up at his eyes to gauge what he was thinking. She thought she saw the same desire in his gaze, too.

The desire, *the need*, to kiss him was just so strong, and as they closed the gap between them, inching ever closer, infinitesimally, she felt her heart pound and the blood roar around her body as if in triumph.

He'll hurt you. Everybody hurts you.

She silenced the voice. Not wanting to hear it. Not in this moment. Not right now. All she wanted right now was...

His lips touched hers and she sank against him, feeling her body come alive. Every nerve-ending was sending sparks. Her heart was pounding with exhilaration at the feel of him beneath her hands as she pulled her even closer.

Nothing else mattered there and then. To be swept away like this was indescribable. The real world dissolved. Fears were silenced. And the hot, sultry desire that she'd tamped down for so long was given free rein.

'Krystiana?'

Matteo's voice called to her as she hurried to her quarters, her hair still dripping.

She turned. 'Yes?'

Stop blushing. Why am I blushing? Oh, yes, I just kissed a prince!

'I forgot to say, what with…' His cheeks reddened and he looked uncomfortable. 'My father has invited you to the ball tonight.'

Her heart sank. 'Ball?'

'It happens every year.'

'Oh.'

She didn't have any outfit suitable for a ball. But how to get out of it without upsetting anyone? Events were moving far too swiftly for her right now. That kiss in the pool had been madness!

'I…er…don't have anything suitable to wear for a ball.'

'I'll get some dresses sent to your rooms for you to try.'

'Erm…'

'Or Mara might have something you could borrow?'

She nodded. 'Okay.'

'Excellent. I'll see you later, then?'

She watched him walk away, wondering just what the hell she was doing…

CHAPTER NINE

MATTEO SAT SWIRLING the wine around in his glass, mesmerised by its movement and colour, though not yet having touched a drop. He just needed to do something with his hands—anything, really—to keep his mind off that moment in the pool with Krystiana.

I kissed her.

She'd emerged from the water, smiling, laughing, so pleased with her progress, and she'd lifted her goggles onto her forehead and beamed at him—a smile that had gone straight to his heart and made it beat like a jackhammer against his ribs. And something—something he hadn't been able to fight—had taken over his common sense and all reason and logic and he'd somehow convinced himself that just one kiss would be okay!

Hah!

He'd fought against it. They'd only known each other for such a short time, and he'd been determined since returning from his kidnapping not to get involved with anyone. Was he so weak? That all it took was a nice smile and a long braid and a shared experience to make his resolve crumble?

He thought over their time together, looking for clues. When had he first begun to succumb to her charms? But he couldn't see the exact moment. He couldn't discern it at all and that frustrated him.

Krystiana had looked at him in shock afterwards. Had quickly waded away from him, clambered up the pool steps, apologising all the way.

No matter what had happened, he'd not wanted things to be awkward between them. He'd wanted to put it right. So he'd chased after her and *asked her to the ball*—as if his mouth had been operating on a different system to his brain.

It hadn't been his place to invite her, and he hadn't meant to ask, but he hadn't been able to bear her running from him like that. He'd wanted to apologise, to put things right, but when she'd turned to face him the invitation had popped out instead.

Matteo pulled the cord that would summon Sergio, and when his servant arrived he asked him to fetch him a canvas and paints. Sergio bowed and disappeared, returning about thirty minutes later with the equipment he needed. Painting the garden had felt good before. Freeing. It had eased his mind and he needed that right now.

He set up the easel out on the sun terrace and thought about how he felt inside. And then, using his fingers, as he had before, he began to daub the surface of the canvas with paint.

He was so carried away with what he was doing he almost didn't hear the footsteps behind him, and he started somewhat when Sergio spoke.

'Dr Szenac, Your Majesty.'

Matteo turned, shocked to see her standing there, but he smiled, glad to see her. Glad that she didn't seem to have been made uncomfortable by what had happened.

'You caught me. I thought I'd try this thing again.'

She smiled back, but it was brief. Fleeting.

'That's good. That you're getting something from it. Those colours look great, but you were great with them last time, so...'

He could sense she had something to say. 'Are you all right?'

'I'm going to leave.'

His heart thudded painfully and the smile dropped from his face. 'What? Why? Because of what happened in the pool? I'm sorry if I've made you uncomfortable, I—'

'I'm going to a hotel. I need to take back control of my life, Matteo. It's slipping away from me here.'

He didn't know what to say. Had he caused this? By kissing her? She had to know that it had been an accident. That it wouldn't happen again.

But those words weren't said. He couldn't. It wasn't as if he was going to beg her to stay. Princes didn't beg. He had to respect her decision, and it was probably best in the long run anyway. Neither of them needed to get involved.

He felt the need to preserve his dignity and he lifted his chin. 'When will you go?'

'Tomorrow morning. I just thought it polite to let you know. As you were so kind as to let me into your home.'

'It was the right thing...' There was more he wanted to say but he was struck dumb, the words caught in his throat. He couldn't say any of them out loud. The one person who soothed his soul, who made him feel he could genuinely smile again, was going because he'd screwed up?

'It's for the best. For both of us, I think,' she said.

He agreed. It was for the best. But he didn't feel ready. He'd thought he'd still got weeks left with her. Weeks in which they would talk and develop their friendship. In which to get her out of his system. But for her to leave now, so abruptly… Because he'd overstepped a line he'd never intended to cross…

This was why he didn't get involved with people any more. Relationships got complicated.

'I'll always consider you my friend, Krystiana. I hope our…moment hasn't jeopardised that.'

She shook her head. 'It hasn't. I've always felt connected to you and I think I always will. It's been an honour to know you.'

He nodded.

She seemed to want to say something more, but no more words were forthcoming. Was she struggling to speak as much as he? Did she want him to fight for her to stay? Or just to let her go? *What do I want?*

She nodded a goodbye and walked away.

Matteo swore to himself, his anger and frustration rising. He turned back to his painting, looked at the happy colours, the swirls of green and yellow. His palette lay off to one side and he dipped his hand in black and swept his hand across the canvas. The black cut a swathe through the light—sorrow darkening the joy.

And he stared at it until his anger abated.

'Which one do you want to try first?' Mara spread her hand out at the array of dresses she'd hung up on the rail she had prepped for Krystiana. 'I think the blue would really bring out your eyes.'

Krystiana was in no mood for any colour bringing out anything. Least of all her eyes. She didn't want anyone to notice her. Didn't want anyone to see the sadness that was in her soul.

'What about the black one?'

Mara looked at her as if she was crazy. 'The black one?

No, no, *no*, Krystiana! The black is too safe. It's wrong for you. How about the red?'

No. Red would be too much. Everybody would look at her.

'What about that one?'

Mara hefted it from the rail. 'This one? I think this one will look lovely on you. Try it on!'

Krystiana took it, draping the pale grey silk over her arm and going into the bedroom to try it.

The grey was perfect. Almost silver, but not quite. Sleeveless and with a sweetheart neckline. It was understated. The kind of dress that wouldn't make her stand out. And despite it having been designed for Mara, who was sylph-like in build, it fitted Krystiana perfectly, moulding her curves.

She twisted and turned in front of the mirror, admiring it but telling herself to not get too excited. Tonight, she would hug the wall, a glass of wine in her hand, which she probably wouldn't drink, and after an hour or so she would slip away, unnoticed.

She was sad that she had made the decision to leave, but it was for the best. Matteo was getting too close. Getting under her skin. And she didn't know what to do with that!

She'd kissed him in the pool.

She could feel her attraction for him growing and it hurt. Pained her that she could do nothing about it because it wouldn't be right. Getting involved with a man like him... Losing control... Giving him power over her...

If she went into a relationship with a powerful man like him she'd lose. Her heart and her soul. She'd be open and out of control. That short kiss had shown her how out of control she had become in such a small amount of time.

One kiss and already she'd knocked down the walls keeping him out.

He belonged to his people, not her, and if she tried to be with him in any way the media would want to know who she was. They would begin to dig into her background and her life—her history would be revealed to all.

No one on Isla Tamoura except for Aunt Carolina and Matteo knew about her past, and that was how she wanted it to stay. She had built a new life here. People didn't look at her with the knowledge of her past in their eyes. She wasn't pitied. She wasn't asked about it and that was the way she wanted it.

'How does it look?' Mara called from the other room. 'I hope you're going to show me.'

Krystiana pulled open the door and stepped out, smiling at Mara's obvious glee. 'What do you think? Does it look all right?'

Mara gazed at her in awe. *'È bellissimo!'*

'It's not too much?'

'No! You look breathtaking.'

Krystiana gazed down at the gown and bit her lip, reconsidering. She didn't want to look 'breathtaking'. At all.

'No, no! Don't look like that. You're wearing it. I've even got a clutch to match it. And shoes. What size are you?'

Krystiana told her.

'Perfect! You'll be the belle of the ball!'

'I don't want to be the belle. I'm not a guest of honour—just a friend, that's all.'

'Oh, come, now. That's *not* all!'

She frowned. 'What do you mean?'

'You like him, yes?'

Krystiana blushed madly. She couldn't tell Mara! Mara had once been his *wife*!

'Not like that.'

Mara raised an eyebrow. 'I wish I could believe you.'

'There's nothing between us. In fact, I'm leaving tomorrow.'

'You're leaving?' Mara looked shocked.

'Tomorrow morning. I have to.'

Mara nodded. 'Maybe that's wise...'

Krystiana turned away and began to unzip the dress. Even Mara could see that she and Matteo would be a bad thing.

Mara laid a hand upon her arm, stilling her. 'I know it will hurt you to leave.'

'It's the best thing for both of us.'

Mara nodded her head solemnly. 'It's a pity, but I admire you for being so sensible.'

'I'm not being sensible. I don't know *what* I'm being.'

'What do you feel for him?'

Krystiana blinked. Unsure how to answer. 'I like him. Maybe too much,' she said.

Mara nodded. 'He's easy to like. Easy to love.'

Krystiana stared at her. 'I don't *love* him, Mara.'

That was just ridiculous!

She'd read somewhere that when you felt attracted to someone you could blame your medial prefrontal cortex, because that was the part of the brain that was responsible for any *love at first sight* activity. The inferior temporal cortex reacted to visual stimuli, the orbitofrontal cortex reacted emotionally, the anterior cingulate cortex caused physiological responses and the right insula dictated arousal.

Basically, it meant that most of your brain was going overboard, so no wonder you couldn't think straight!

But as she got ready in her room, trying to sort out

her hair and make-up for this, her last evening at the palace, she tried to tell herself that she was doing the right thing—even though she strongly suspected her thoughts and decisions were based on her emotional responses.

She liked Matteo. More than she should. So getting away from him was the obvious solution. Besides, he probably wouldn't want to speak to her much tonight, anyway. She'd clearly shocked him when she'd told him she was leaving, so perhaps tonight would be okay? They could avoid each other all evening.

She put in her diamond drop earrings and stood in front of the mirror, checking her reflection. The grey dress was actually very beautiful. Understated and classic. It was a pity it was on loan, because she loved it very much.

Krystiana checked her watch. Nearly time to go.

Why do I feel so nervous?

There was a tentative knock at her door and, suspecting it was Sergio, she went and opened it. Only it wasn't Sergio at all.

It was Matteo.

Her heart leapt into her throat when she saw him standing there in dinner jacket and black bow tie. He looked gorgeous! She almost took a step back. Not sure why he was here.

'I've come to escort you to the ball. On your last night here with you as our guest it seemed right. No hard feelings?'

'Oh. Right. Okay.'

'We're okay?'

She nodded. 'Absolutely. I can't thank you enough for all that you've done for me.'

Matteo gave her a short smile. 'You look *bellissimo*. Truly.'

She flushed at the compliment. 'Thank you. So do you.'

He held out his arm for her to slip her hand through, and they walked arm in arm down the palace corridors.

For a few moments she felt quite awkward, being with him. She'd not expected him to come to her door, but he was most certainly a gentleman and clearly he didn't want an unescorted lady arriving at the ball. He was wearing some kind of scent that was playing havoc with her olfactory senses, so she tried a bit of mouth-breathing to try and calm them down.

'How many people are going to be there?'

'A few hundred.'

A few *hundred*…

'Where is the ball being held?'

'In the White Room.'

'I don't think I've been there.'

'We use it only for the most special of occasions.'

She nodded, walking alongside him, trying not to think that this might be the last time they'd be together. Trying not to think of how much she liked him. How much he might think that she was running away. Because she didn't like to think that she was.

'Will Mara and Alex be there? So I can say goodbye?'

'Of course.'

'Great. That's…great.' She didn't *feel* great. She felt sad. But she had to do the right thing.

A few hundred.

He stopped suddenly. 'I think I should leave you here. If we arrived together it would send out the wrong message.'

'Maybe you're right.'

She was wrong for him. He was trying to tell her that. The kiss in the pool had been a blip on both their parts. They couldn't be anything more. It had just been physical.

She nodded. 'I'd rather everyone assumed I was just a normal guest. Nothing to do with you.'

Which I'm not.

He removed his arm from hers and straightened his jacket. 'And of course I'd hate to throw you to the wolves. The press,' he explained.

'Exactly. I'd rather stay out of the papers.' Though that was the least of her worries. She'd rather stay as far away from him as she could because she just didn't trust her physical reactions to him.

He smiled ruefully. 'You promise not to leave without saying goodbye?'

'I promise,' she said, hating every word, knowing that deep in her heart she longed to be in his arms and held by him, pressed close, cherished and adored. Their kiss in the pool might have been the biggest mistake she'd ever made, but it had felt so good! And that was why it was so confusing.

'I don't want you to leave without a chance to...'

She got sucked into the hypnotic gaze of his eyes. 'Chance to what?'

She saw the hesitation in his eyes. The fight within him. And then he was stepping close.

He reached up to stroke the side of her face. 'I feel like I know who you are. And that I'll never meet anyone else like you again. I'm not sure I want to lose you.'

Krystiana sucked in a breath, trying to steady her racing heart. 'I...'

'You feel it, too.'

'Matteo...'

And suddenly his mouth was on hers.

She closed her eyes in ecstasy. Giving herself one more moment of bliss. A single moment in which she'd allow herself to take what he could give.

Her hands lay upon his chest and she could feel his heart pounding, the muscles beneath his skin, the way he wrapped himself around her as he pulled her closer still.

Her logical mind was screaming at her to stop, but she couldn't. She silenced the voice. No, that was wrong. The voice disappeared. Because all she wanted to experience was the feeling of his lips upon hers. Her body pressed against his. The fire building in her soul. The heat that was searing her skin, making every nerve-ending electric.

She'd never felt this before. Never been like this with anyone before. Not like this. There'd been awkward fumbles and kisses from guys she'd not felt such attraction for, and with Adamo it had been good, but with Matteo it was a fierce thing—a force that powered through her like a hurricane. Unstoppable and unrelenting.

As the kiss deepened and her tongue entwined with his she groaned in delight, cradling his face in her hands, feeling the soft bristles of his beard beneath her skin. She knew she wanted more. Oh, so much more... But...

They broke apart and stared at each other, both surprised, both overwhelmed by what had just happened. Stunned.

Her fear at what would happen when she had to leave had just been made worse! Kissing him had just made it a lot harder.

Why am I doing this to myself? What on earth is going on?

Krystiana looked up and down the palace corridors but no one was around. This was just between her and Matteo.

'I'm sorry. We...er...shouldn't have done that.'

'No.'

'But we keep doing it.'

'Yes.'

'Why? Why would we punish ourselves like this?' She was almost in tears. Could hear it in her voice.

He took a step back. 'I'm sorry. I don't mean to. It's just that when I'm with you…'

'What?' She needed to know what was driving him. What was causing him to keep kissing her. Because then it might make sense to her why she kept kissing *him*.

He frowned and took a step towards her, his gaze dropping to her mouth before he looked back up at her eyes.

'I'll see you in the ballroom.'

The White Room was exactly that. White walls and ceiling. A white marble floor. Columns thick as tree trunks like silver birches, pulling the gaze upwards towards numerous crystal chandeliers. Huge gold vases held swathes of white lilies, roses and jasmine.

As she descended the steps towards the milling crowds, accepting a flute of champagne from a server, Krystiana hoped she could lose herself in the crowd. Even if she *did* feel there was a huge neon arrow above her head, lit up with the message *I just kissed your prince!*

She felt torn. And exhilarated. Confused and trapped. Could the whole world see the imprint of his lips on hers? Was it written all over her face? Heat and lust and secrets?

I should have known better!

She was muddled in her thinking. Being with Matteo stopped her brain from working properly. She really felt something for him, and it wasn't just attraction—it was something more than that. Krystiana had never wanted to be with a guy as much as she wanted to be with him. She had never felt more attracted to someone in her life.

This was new territory for her! Uncharted, dangerous territory, with someone who was forbidden!

Or was he?

Now that she'd kissed him, now that she'd tasted a little of what he had to offer, a new voice was suggesting that maybe she should enjoy it. Maybe it was all right. Maybe, just maybe, he *was* the man for her…

Perhaps that was why it was so confusing—because she was fighting something that she should just accept. But how would she know for sure? How would she know she was safe giving him her heart? It had never worked before when she had done that. She couldn't think of one relationship in her life that worked well. Well, except for with Dr Bonetti. They loved one another. But they were from the same world.

Krystiana took a sip of her champagne, intending only to take a small swallow, but downing the whole thing in one. Surprised, she passed her empty glass to another server and took another full glass, determined to go slower with this one.

If two people were attracted to one another then why shouldn't they make something of it? Why shouldn't they act on their attraction? They were grown adults. They could make their own decisions.

He'd been through the same things as her. The same scares, the same terrors, the same fears. He knew how she felt and she him. Where would she find *that* again?

Sighing, she sipped her champagne, stopping only to turn at the fanfare of trumpets as an official announced the entry of His Majesty King Alberto and his son, Crown Prince Matteo.

She stared up at him from her place in the crowd and could see the certainty and assuredness on Matteo's face, trapped within a practised smile. She saw the way his gaze coasted all around him, oozing authority and power as he descended the steps into the room, and how he stayed a few steps behind his father, honouring royal etiquette.

She glanced at Alberto. The King she'd met just once. A tall, proud man, he was greeting a long line of people, smiling and shaking hands. He looked a little more drawn than before. A bit grey... He carried a heavy weight upon his shoulders—perhaps it was that?

He was soon to abdicate. And happily, by all accounts. Krystiana had no doubt that Matteo would make a fabulous king. He was strong and steady. Overflowing with charitable, selfless acts that his people adored him for.

As do I.

Matteo would make an excellent leader for his country. All that he had been through had only served to make him stronger.

The King got to the end of his long line of meet-and-greet people and stepped up to a white podium which was adorned with the Romano royal coat of arms—a gold shield, with a sword at its centre, flanked by a lion on one side and a unicorn on the other, both rearing up as if honouring the sword.

The room went quiet.

The King looked about him, waiting for his moment. The ultimate public speaker. 'Ladies and gentlemen of the court, nothing makes me happier than to see you all here—though my happiness is tinged with a little sadness that this will be the final ball I will host as King. But my successor is one you all know, love and respect, and I know that he will follow the honour, tradition and heritage of this fine land. My only son—Matteo.'

The crowd clapped, smiling broadly.

'We all know his story. For those of us left behind it was an unsettling time. We were cast adrift, uncertain, unknowing. We tried what we could to ensure his safe return, but each time—as you know—the guerrillas who held him proved not to be reputable people and they kept him from us. Matteo did not get to see the birth of his daughter. He did not get to see her early years or experience the joy that we did as she began to sit up, then crawl, then walk. Nor did he hear her first word, but I'm sure he was very pleased to hear it was "Papà".'

He smiled at his son, who stood proudly by his side.

'But we did get him back, and he has proved his strength and fortitude. Returning strong and unhurt by his time away, for which we are very grateful. Tonight I would like to name this ball in his honour, and also to announce some incredible news.'

The crowd inched forward, eager to hear it.

Behind the King, Krystiana saw Matteo's smile falter somewhat as he turned his gaze to his father. Clearly Matteo did not know what the King was about to say.

'It has been decided that in anticipation of Matteo taking the throne next year, he will go on a six-week tour of the kingdom of Tamoura, visiting every major city and every urban centre, meeting the people and showing the world that no one can beat down the strength and courage that my son has. He will be a *strong* king! A king committed to the welfare of his people. Hopefully, he will meet as many of them as he can. His full itinerary will be posted tomorrow at the royal court and the tour will begin in one week's time!'

Matteo's smile broadened, as if he'd already known this would be the King's proclamation, but she knew better. She could see the surprise in his eyes.

He didn't know about this.

She was shocked, too. He was leaving the palace. Perhaps it was a good thing that she was packing up tomorrow, because if she'd stayed her heart would have been broken anyway. He would be leaving on a tour of the isle. No doubt with a jam-packed itinerary. He would be returning to the world where he lived and she… She would be returning to hers. She had patients. He had subjects.

The bubble was popping. She'd always known that it would. She would have popped it herself tomorrow. This would push him. Prepare him for kingship. It would be a good thing for him. Good for her, too. Because if he was leaving in just one week, then she could leave knowing that his mind would not be on her departure, but on his travelling arrangements.

You see? We never would have had a chance. I was right to stop this.

She tried to make herself feel happy about that, but she was struggling.

The King stepped back to hold out a hand to his son and Matteo stepped forward to take it. As he clasped his son's hand and pulled him into a hug the crowd began to cheer and applaud.

But their cries of joy quickly changed to cries of shock as King Alberto slumped in his son's arms, his face pale and sweaty, and Matteo had to lower him gently to the ground…

'Call for an ambulance!'

Matteo couldn't believe that this was happening. What was wrong with his father?

Holding his father fast, he stared at his slack face. 'Papà, hang on—don't you die on me!'

Behind him, he heard a commotion as someone pushed their way through the crowd and he heard her voice.

'Excuse me! Excuse me—please, make way…'

And then there she was. Krystiana. Kneeling down on the floor beside his father, a pool of grey silk around her as she assessed the situation, her fingers at his neck, assessing for a pulse.

'Okay, he's breathing—that's good.' She quickly unbuttoned the King's jacket and laid her ear against his chest and listened. 'Does someone have a watch? With a second hand?'

A man Matteo didn't know offered one and he passed it to Krystiana, who kept her gaze on it as she listened to the King's chest once again.

'He has tachycardia.'

Matteo frowned. 'What?'

'A fast heartbeat. Too fast. We need to get him to hospital, where they can give him some drugs or a shock to bring it back down.'

Servants arrived in droves to usher the guests into another room so that the paramedics could come in, get the King on a trolley and attach electrodes to his chest to monitor his heartbeat. It was one hundred and fifty-two beats per minute.

'Papà, you're going to be all right.'

The King took his son's hand in his. 'I'm okay…'

The paramedics looked to Matteo. 'Are you coming in the ambulance?'

He nodded. 'Yes. So is she.' He pointed at Krystiana, who looked shocked to be included.

'Then, let's go!'

Matteo and Krystiana followed the paramedics down the long palatial corridors and out to the ambulance. Thankfully their arrival had been through the rear gates, so hopefully there wouldn't be too much about this in the press the next day. Besides, it was just a fast heartbeat. He wasn't having a heart attack or anything. They'd get him sorted out at the hospital.

As they got on board Krystiana looked at the ECG tracing. 'It looks like he has atrial fibrillation.'

'What does that mean?' Matteo asked, needing to know everything that was going on.

'It's the upper chambers of the heart. The atria. They're creating irregular impulses that are rapid and uncoordinated.'

'What does that mean for my father?'

She shrugged. 'It could be a temporary thing and stop on its own, but he might need assistance to stop it.'

'How?'

'Drugs. A shock to the heart.'

'An electric shock? But why now? What's caused it?'

'I don't know, Matteo. I don't know your father's health history. Does he have high blood pressure?'

'I don't think so. He hasn't mentioned anything.'

'Heart disease?'

'No. Papà, how do you feel?'

'Like something is trying to jump out of my chest.'

'Are you in pain?'

'No, it just feels...*weird*.'

'We're nearly there. Hang on.'

He felt Krystiana lay a reassuring hand upon his shoulder.

The paramedics kept on observing the trace, monitoring his father's blood pressure and pulse rate, and Krystiana had placed an oxygen mask over the King's face, murmuring to him to try and control his breathing, to remain as calm as he could. Before he knew what was happening they were pulling up at the private entrance the royals used at the hospital.

They wheeled his father in and got him hooked up to another heart machine as the paramedics relayed what had happened to the attending physician.

The doctor told the King that they would give him a

beta-blocker to try and get his heart-rate below ninety beats per minute.

'You might feel some tiredness, and your hands and feet may get cold. We'll monitor your blood pressure continuously and see how you get on.'

'*Grazie.*'

'You must just rest for a while.'

'*Si.*'

Matteo had expected more action. This was his father's *heart*! Could he die?

'Why aren't you doing more?' he asked the doctor.

'We're doing what we can. We have to see if the medication will bring down the heart-rate.'

'And if it doesn't? How long do we leave it?'

'Matteo, give them time,' Krystiana said, her voice soothing and calm.

He glanced at her, saw the concern on her face and knew instinctively that she was right. They didn't need him interfering and asking too many questions or getting in the way. This was their territory. They were the ones who knew best.

'Matteo...?' His father held out his hand to him.

'*Si*, Papà?'

'I think I might have to hand over to you earlier than suspected.' He smiled, his eyes sad.

What? No! That wasn't what Matteo wanted to hear. Become King? *No.* His father still had years left in him. Didn't he?

'No, you won't. This is just a blip, Papà. You'll be back home tomorrow—just you wait and see.'

'No, I fear not. There may be some things I have kept from you...'

Matteo frowned.

'Dr Szenac? Would you mind if I spoke to my son alone?' his father asked.

Krystiana nodded and stood up. 'Of course. Take all the time you need.' And she stepped out of the private room, closing the door quietly behind her.

Matteo turned back to his father, apprehension and fear filling his heart. 'What is it?'

'I wasn't sure when would be the best time to tell you… but…when you were away I got ill. The cardio doctors believed it was stress brought on by your kidnapping.'

Cardio. The heart. An ice-cold lump settled in his stomach.

'What happened?'

'I had a heart attack.'

He stood up in shock. *'What?'*

'It was minor, Matteo, but I needed bypass surgery. You see this scar line?'

Matteo frowned as he stared at his father's chest. His father was quite hairy, and he almost couldn't see it. The scar that ran from just below the dip in his throat down to the bottom of the sternum.

'Why didn't you tell me?'

His father shrugged. 'I was always going to abdicate when I turned seventy—you know that. When you were taken I had no idea where you were. My only son. My only child. The stress of everything… The day you were returned to us was the greatest in my entire life! For a moment, I thought Alexandra would have to take the throne!'

He tried to laugh. But it fell flat in the small room.

Matteo stared at the scar. A mark that showed his father to be frailer than he'd realised. Not the invincible, strong man he'd believed him to be but human, just like the rest of them.

'You should have told me. How did you manage to keep this from me?'

'I swore everyone to secrecy. Why upset you? You had just come home, learned that your mother was dead and your marriage was over! I couldn't tell you about this, too! I was protecting you, believing I would last until your coronation anyway. Honestly, I thought you would never have to find out. And I'm sorry that you have.'

Above his father's head, the machine beeped out the fast heartbeat. The drugs didn't seem to be working. Matteo felt doubt and fear. He couldn't lose his father.

'*Ti amo*, Papà.'

'I love you, too. Now, let me rest awhile.'

'All right. I'll just be outside—but buzz if you need *anything*. Okay?'

'I will. Go now.'

He kissed his father on the cheek and left the room. As soon as he saw Krystiana all the emotion he had been feeling came to the fore and he felt tears burning his eyes. He went straight into her outstretched arms.

Being held by her, being close to her, made him feel comforted. She was warm and loving and he knew that she cared for him. She *had* to. Ever since that kiss they'd shared… It hadn't been one-sided. She'd responded too. And now she was the one to comfort him, to make him feel safe. He'd always felt safe with her, and *safe* was a good thing after two years of never knowing if you'd get to see tomorrow's sunrise.

She sat him down. 'Are you all right?'

He told her everything his father had said about his prior heart condition. The heart attack. The bypass.

She sat listening, nodding occasionally. 'That makes sense. Fibrillation like that can often be caused if there's a prior heart condition.'

'Will he be all right, do you think?'

'It's a long time since I worked on a cardiac ward, Matteo. I'd hate to say the wrong thing. But what we *do* know is that he's in the safest place he can be. Where his heart-rate will be continually monitored.'

'When should the drugs take effect? The rate was still high.'

'They should have worked by now, really. He might need shocking. They might give him amiodarone... I'm not sure.'

He took her hand in his. 'I'm glad you're here.'

She smiled back uncertainly. 'I'll stay for as long as you need me.'

He was glad to hear it. His foundations had been rocked and he needed an anchor. He didn't know what it was that was flooding through him, these feelings for her—feelings that he'd never expected to have again. But the thought of losing her whilst his father teetered on the edge of an abyss... *No.* It would be too much.

He reached forward to stroke the side of her face. 'Thank you. There's something about you, Krystiana... I don't know what it is, but...'

She was looking deeply into his eyes, their souls connecting. 'Don't say any more.'

He nodded. 'Thank you.'

He narrowed the distance between them and felt his lips connect with hers. He'd craved her ever since he'd last kissed her, but that kiss had been different. This one was gentle and slow, savouring every moment, every movement. She tasted of champagne, and her honeyed scent stimulated his senses into overdrive. He wanted so much more...

He barely knew what was happening in his world right now. But he was looking for comfort.

* * *

Matteo's father was sitting upright in his bed, looking nervous. The doctors had placed pads on his chest and were going to try and shock his rhythm back to normality.

'Will it hurt?'

'Yes, but not for long. And if it works you'll feel much better almost instantly.'

'Good. All right. Go ahead.'

He laid his head back and the doctor pressed a button that lowered the pillow end of the bed. He had to be flat for this.

Once he was lying flat, the doctor looked about him. 'Charging…stand clear…*shocking.*'

King Alberto's body flinched violently and then he groaned, relaxing back onto the sheets.

Krystiana looked at the heart monitor, but his heart-rate remained high. She felt for the King. This couldn't be good at all.

'Charging. Stand clear. *Shocking.*'

Again the King's body went into violent spasm and then collapsed again, but this time the heart-rate began to drop and finally went down to eighty-four beats per minute.

The cardio doctor smiled at Matteo. 'We have sinus rhythm.'

Matteo reached for his father's hand. 'It's done, Papà, you're going to be okay.'

Alberto smiled wearily at his son. *'Grazie a Dio!'*

'We'll keep monitoring your father overnight, but if he maintains his rhythm I see no reason why he can't be up and about tomorrow.'

The cardio doctor shook Matteo's hand, smiled at Krystiana and then left the room.

Krystiana sat down in the chair opposite Matteo and

smiled, happy for him and his father. She knew how much he needed his dad. Knew that connection. She missed her own—or she missed the father she'd *believed* she'd had before he took her. That father—pre-kidnapping—had been someone she'd idolised.

Afterwards…after all she'd been through…their relationship had been spoiled. She'd had no father to come home to. And every time she'd turned on the television she'd seen her father's face. Every time she'd opened a newspaper there had seemed to be a new story about him and his 'unstable mind-set', according to ex-girlfriends and old enemies who had all earned a few *zloty* selling their stories.

When she'd gone back to school everyone had treated her differently. Even the teachers. All she'd wanted was normality. To be treated as she had always been treated. But all the kids had suddenly wanted to be her friend. To be invited back to her house so they could examine the home that had once belonged to Piotr Szenac.

Even her own mother had begun acting strangely, and she'd felt a distance between them. A distance that had puzzled her—because surely her mother had wanted her back? She'd fought for custody of Krystiana.

And then she'd died. Less than a year after Krystiana had come home Nikola Szenac had been hit by a bus. Krystiana had been fetched from her school lessons to be told by the headmistress. And then she'd been alone in the world, struggling to understand all that had happened, until Aunt Carolina had reached out to save her.

And now here she sat, an orphaned girl from Poland, beside the bed of the King of Isla Tamoura.

'We should get something to eat. It's late.' Matteo stood up and kissed his father's cheek. 'Is there anything you want me to bring tomorrow?'

Alberto smiled. 'Some decent pyjamas would be good. These hospital gowns are a bit itchy.'

'Nonsense! I'm sure they are the finest cotton.'

'Hmm... You're not wearing one, though, are you?'

'Fair point. Goodnight, Papà. Krystiana and I will be back in the morning.'

Alberto turned to look at her curiously. 'I must thank you, Dr Szenac, for saving my life.'

She shook her head. 'I didn't do anything. Not really.'

'You looked after me *and* my son. I am grateful you were with us.'

She smiled. He was a good old man. A good father. 'I'm glad you're feeling better, Your Majesty.'

'Call me Alberto.'

She blushed. That didn't seem right. He was the King of Isla Tamoura! Calling him by his first name was intimate. For friends and family. She wasn't family—so did he consider her a friend?

'Thank you, Your Majesty.'

He smiled. 'Go and get some sleep. It's been a long day.'

'It has. Yes. You too—sleep well.'

'I'm sure I will. Now you go and do the same.'

CHAPTER TEN

ONCE THEY WERE back in the palace Matteo couldn't help but pull her close, savouring the feel of her in his arms. He'd nearly lost his father. But she was still here and he needed her closeness and comfort.

'You were my rock tonight. I don't know how I would have got through it without you.'

'You'd have survived. You'd have had no choice.'

'I guess not.' He looked at her and stroked her hair. It was so soft.

'You need to get some sleep,' she said.

'Are you prescribing that?'

She smiled. 'I am.'

'Perhaps you could help me sleep tonight?' he asked, with intent.

She knew exactly what he meant. But was he suggesting it for the right reasons?

Laughing, she pushed him away, pretending that she had misunderstood. 'I could prescribe you a sleeping tablet.'

'You're not my doctor, though.'

She smiled. 'No. I'm not. All right, why don't you have a mug of warm milk? A warm bath?'

He considered both options. 'I've never enjoyed warm milk, and I take a shower first thing in the morning.' He raised an eyebrow. 'There is another way that you could help me sleep…'

Krystiana could only imagine how wonderful that might be, but someone had to be sensible here. 'And what would that be?'

'You could come with me to my quarters and make sure I get into bed on time?'

She tilted her head to one side, considering it. Trying her hardest not to laugh.

Oh, she wanted to. She could feel her body saying *yes*. 'Perhaps.'

'You could lie in my arms and stroke my hair until I fall asleep.'

She smiled. 'I could.'

'There are many things we could do. I keep fighting this…but I want you in my arms so much, you have no idea.'

She had a very clear idea. She could feel his arousal pressed against her.

He kissed her lips. Then her neck, trailing his mouth delicately down the long, smooth stretch of skin, drinking up her little moan of pleasure. 'I hear that orgasm is a wonderful precursor to a good night's sleep…'

He heard her throaty chuckle and raised his head to look into her eyes, a dreamy smile upon his face.

'Prolactin levels *do* make men sleepy. As does oxytocin and vasopressin—all produced by the brain after sex.'

'I love it when you talk dirty to me.'

She laughed, but then her face grew serious. 'You know, wanting sex is a classic response after someone has experienced the shock of feeling their mortality.'

He raised an eyebrow. 'Is that right?'

'Yes. People want to prove they're vital. What better

way of cheating death than to do the very thing that creates life?'

He cocked his head to one side. 'Is that a bad response?'

'Not necessarily. But a woman likes to know that her man wants her because he wants *her* and no other reason— not just because he wants to prove how full of life he is.'

He looked her directly in the eye, so that she was not mistaken. 'I want to be with *you*. Because you've been driving me wild for days and I've not been able to do anything about it. Because I've been fighting it. Telling myself it was the wrong thing to do. But right now I'm not sure I believe any of that. What happened tonight proves that life is short. I want your lips, your kisses, your arms around me. I want your body pressed into mine and to hell with everything else! I might have had a shock tonight, but that shock has taught me that life is meant to be lived—and why should we deny ourselves what we want in life more than anything?'

She smiled.

The press of her curves against his body was almost driving him insane! To hell with tradition and law and being careful! He'd done that for so long, and since coming back from the mountains he had kept a tight control on so much of his feelings and emotions. But he couldn't do that with her. She changed him. Made him want. And need.

And right now he needed her in his arms and in his bed.

She kissed him on the lips. 'Then I'm yours.'

What the hell am I doing?

Acting recklessly. Giving in to her temptations. Not thinking.

Despite everything—despite the fact that he could have anyone he wanted—he wanted *her*, and that knowledge was strangely exciting and powerful. It gave her a thrill. Her heart pounded and her blood hummed with an inner energy that she couldn't explain when she was with him.

As she slipped out of the grey dress lent to her by Mara she looked at herself in the bathroom mirror and wondered briefly who this woman was. She felt as if so much had changed since she had come here.

Krystiana removed her earrings, her necklace, slipped her feet out of her heels and removed the last of her underwear. On the back of the bathroom door was a robe and she pulled it on, checking her reflection.

I'm ready.

Sucking in a deep breath, she opened the bathroom door and leaned against the doorjamb as she gazed at Matteo, who stood waiting for her beside his bed.

'Are we sure about this?'

'Do we have to be?' he asked, before making his way over to her, his hands cupping her face and pulling her lips towards his once more…

'Good morning.'

'Buongiorno!'

She kissed him, inhaling his lovely male scent of soap and sandalwood. 'Any news from the hospital?'

'He had a restful night.'

'That's great!' she said, even though she knew that the quicker King Alberto recovered, the faster everything would change, throwing them into turmoil once again. But that was for later. For a time she wasn't ready to think about.

He must have seen the hesitation in her features. 'What's wrong?'

'Nothing. Honestly, I'm happy for your father.'

'But?'

'But nothing.' How could she tell him? It was incredibly selfish! What did she want? For his father to be ill a lot longer?

He smiled and pulled her close for a kiss.

It was heaven. Being kissed by him. Being held by him. In his arms she just felt so...*adored.* It was an addictive state, and Krystiana knew all about addictions, having looked after many addicts in her time. They constantly craved that high. That feel-good moment when every worry and concern just melted away because they were in a state of bliss. She could understand it a little more, experiencing this. The high she got being with him.

'Are you going to the hospital this morning?'

'I thought we could go after breakfast?'

'You want me to come with you?'

'I'm taking Alex to see her grandfather. Mara's staying here, as she has a business meeting, and I thought Alex might cheer him up.'

She nodded. Alex brightened everyone's lives. She was such a cutie. And she would grow up to be a stunner, she had no doubt. If Krystiana was going to get to know Matteo, perhaps she ought to get to know his daughter better, too?

'All right. But are you sure you need me in the way? It seems like a family moment.'

He took her hand and squeezed it. 'I want you with me. Now, let's eat. Out on the terrace—it's a wonderful morning.'

Sergio—who appeared to be totally unruffled to find her in Matteo's bedchamber this morning—served them dark, strong espresso, sour cherry *crostatas*, custard-filled *ciambellas* and some *strudel di mele*, alongside a selection of fresh fruits and juices.

'I can feel myself putting on the pounds just looking at this.' Krystiana smiled.

Matteo smiled back at her and reached for her hand, bringing the back of it to his sugared lips and kissing it. 'Eat.'

Mara brought Alex to them, greeting Matteo by kissing both his cheeks and doing the same to Krystiana.

'Give your father all the best from me and tell him I'll be in this afternoon.'

'I will.'

Matteo crouched down to look at his daughter, who smiled at him from behind her mother's legs, holding a bedraggled teddy.

'Hey, Alex! Are you ready to come with me and see Nonno?'

Alex nodded. Smiling, Matteo reached out for her hand and then scooped her up into his arms.

'*Saluta tua madre.*'

Alex gave her mother a smile and Mara bent down for a kiss. 'You be good for your father.'

Alex nodded, hugging her teddy.

Mara smiled too, and then her eyes narrowed with amusement as she looked at the two of them. 'Something's changed…'

Matteo smiled. 'Just pleased to be with my daughter again, in the knowledge that my father will be back pounding the hallways before we know it.'

'Okay…' But Mara seemed to suspect there was something else. She looked at Krystiana and seemed to come to some conclusion. She raised an eyebrow. 'You're *happy.*'

He laughed. 'Is that so wrong?'

Mara smiled 'Being happy? No. Not at all. Remember to say hi to your father for me.'

'I will.'

She kissed her daughter and walked away.

Today was going to be a *good* day. He was going to see his father and then, when he got back, he was going to think about what was happening between him and Krystiana.

It was all moving so fast. And he had done something he'd told himself not to do. He'd given in to his physical desires and slept with her, and it had been wonderful, mind-blowing, and everything he'd suspected it would be. But where did it leave them? It could never be serious between them. That was against the law—they couldn't marry. And he'd never thought he'd be the type to have a fling, so...

Whatever happened, he wanted to do the right thing. He didn't want to upset Krystiana. He didn't want to confuse Alex about who was in her life and who wasn't. And nor did he want to cause pain to himself.

He strongly suspected he might do that anyway. Either way, whatever it was that they had could not continue for any length of time. The time would come when it would have to end.

The question was, could he end it without hurting her?

Matteo and Alex walked hand in hand into King Alberto's room, Krystiana following dutifully behind.

'Papà! How are you?' Matteo kissed his father on both cheeks.

'Much better, today, Matteo. Now! Do I see a tiny little princess who needs a big hug from her *nonno*?'

He reached out for Alex and the little girl let go of her father's hand and jumped up into Alberto's grasp.

'Careful, Papà. You're meant to be resting.'

'Holding my granddaughter will do me *good*, Matteo.' Alberto kissed Alex and gave her a little tickle, and her wonderful bright laughter filled the room. 'Oh, and Dr Szenac! You are here, too! Hello! How is my son behaving himself without me there to keep an eye on him?'

Krystiana smiled. 'He's being good.'

'I'm glad to hear it. Though I'm surprised to see you here today. You doctors just can't stay away! You're like vultures!' he said with a laugh.

Krystiana felt her heart pound with nerves as Alberto sat Alex on the bed and passed her a small wrapped gift. 'Here, I got you something. Open it!'

Alex tore through the paper and beamed when she saw a book covered in bright animals. She lay back against her grandfather and began to turn the pages.

'Alex, what do you say to Nonno?'

'Grazie.' Alex smiled shyly at her grandfather.

'Good girl.' Matteo ruffled her hair, smiling at the cute response. 'How on earth did you get her a present?' he asked his father. 'I thought you were on bed rest?'

'One of the perks of being a king, Matteo, and I needn't tell you, is that I have servants to do my bidding.'

His son smiled. 'Ah... Have the doctors been in to see you yet?'

Alberto nodded. 'Yes. They've checked me out and told me I need to take it easy. Take it *easy*? I run a country, I told them. That's no easy feat.'

Matteo smiled. 'And you do it very well. If I'm half the King that you are then I will consider myself to be lucky.'

'Well, you're going to get the chance earlier than you suspected.'

Krystiana felt her heart miss a beat. Matteo? King? That was *very* different from just having a romance with a prince.

Matteo frowned. 'What? No. You're as fit as a fiddle.'

'That's just it, Matteo. I'm *not*. I wish I were—I do. I know you need more time to get used to the idea, but you've had a whole lifetime waiting for this day. I'd hoped that a grand tour of Tamoura would be a gradual introduction to your new duties, but I'm having to face facts. My heart has given me a second warning now. If I want to be around to see this beautiful little one grow up and walk down the aisle one day, then I've got to take a step back earlier than I expected.'

Matteo glanced at Krystiana. 'What does that mean?'

'I'm going to abdicate *now*. The press have been notified already, and told that it's my recommendation that you are crowned as soon as it is possible.'

Matteo shook his head. 'Papà, *no*!'

Alberto reached out to take his hand. 'Matteo... No one *ever* feels ready. Do you think I was? Do you think I knew what I was doing when the crown was placed on my head? No. But it's how you act when it is. How you learn and grow to become the man you need to be to carry the country forward.'

'But...'

Matteo seemed lost for words, and almost on the verge of having to sit down. Instead he reached out for Krystiana's hand and squeezed it, not noticing the King's raised eyebrows as he did so, nor his questioning look at Krystiana.

'You still have months left before you said you'd abdicate. Take that time—a final farewell to the people. I—'

Alberto held up his hand for silence, his face stony. 'I was a new father when I took the throne. You were three weeks old. I was sleep-deprived, stressed and worn out. I'd just finished a world tour, had a new baby son... Life *happens*, Matteo. There will never be a perfect time. Dr

Szenac, *you* seem to know my son well. You think he's ready, do you not?'

Krystiana swallowed, her mouth suddenly dry. She looked at Matteo, knowing he wanted her to say something that would support Alberto's carrying on for a bit longer. But she couldn't. She had to answer the King honestly.

'He's more than ready.'

Alberto smiled. 'You see? Everyone else knows you can do it.'

Matteo would make a great king. He was kind and caring, considerate and thoughtful. Yes, he had been through a great ordeal, but it had only served to make him stronger. More resolute.

But what did that mean for *them*? She had *slept* with him!

Alberto smiled. 'You will take the throne, Matteo.'

She saw Matteo glance at her with uncertainty, and in that glance so many things were conveyed. Doubt. Fear. Hesitation.

They were at the beginning of a relationship that could be something amazing. But she had no idea of how it was to be with someone like him! He was a *prince*. About to become a *king*. And she was just a normal girl from Poland. A doctor.

This acceleration of events was terrifying. What *was* she to him? Would it become serious? Was it casual? Would she be discarded and left behind?

'Are we going to talk about what happened today?' Matteo threw his jacket to one side as he walked into his quarters, Krystiana following slowly behind.

'Okay…'

'My father wants me to become King! I thought I had

more time. I thought that…' he turned to look at her, saw the concern on her face '…that *we* had time.'

'We do. Don't we?'

'If my father has already alerted the press, then the focus of the whole country will be upon me. And also on *you.*'

She remembered what media attention felt like. It had been awful. Terrifying at times. But she had survived it. 'They would only be focused on me if we were together.'

He stopped pacing to face her. 'I guess that's the big question, isn't it?'

She gave a single nod. 'It is. What *am* I to you, Matteo?'

It was a terrifying question to ask. It would put him on the spot. But it was an answer she needed to hear, because she needed to know. Needed to prepare herself for whatever onslaught was coming.

'Honestly? I don't know.'

That wasn't good. A small part of her had wanted him to say she was his everything. That he couldn't get enough of her. That he couldn't bear to be without her. But he wasn't saying any of those things.

'I don't want to hurt you. I know that. This situation is complex and extreme, and I can't assume that you'd want to be a part of this mad world that I live in.'

She said nothing. No, she didn't want to be hurt either. But she had a feeling she would be.

Krystiana sank down into a chair. 'Perhaps us being together is a bad idea? I get the feeling your father would not approve.'

Matteo looked down and away, as if he was weary.

'You're going to become *King*, Matteo. Sooner than you thought. Perhaps you and I ought to back off from one another for a while until all of that is done?'

Part of her thought that if they did back away from one another they would each have breathing space. This all seemed to be moving so fast! He was going to wear the crown! Perhaps with time apart he would begin to see that they weren't best suited, and by then she would have prepared herself for the inevitable and her heart would not be as broken as she suspected it might be.

Matteo sighed. 'You might be right.'

She'd suggested it, but it was still a shock that he accepted it so readily. Perhaps he'd meant more to her than she to him?

Krystiana swallowed, her mouth dry, trying her hardest to stop the tears from burning the backs of her eyes, trying to be brave. They'd had one great night and it had been the most amazing night of her life. And to wake this morning, in his arms… She couldn't remember ever feeling so happy. But she'd always suspected that if they were to have any type of relationship it would be a brief one, and now it was looking more than likely that that was true.

It didn't make it any easier to know that he could happily discard her so quickly.

After Krystiana had gone Matteo stepped out onto his sun terrace and looked out over the hillsides. He knew he had to give them both space, but in his heart of hearts he also knew that, if he was being honest, nothing could ever have come from their relationship. He'd been an absolute fool to allow his desire and his lust for her to overcome every iota of common sense and logic he possessed!

His father had announced to the press that he was abdicating and that his son would be crowned King as soon as it was possible. The media was in a frenzy, as was to be expected, and he… He was apprehensive.

He should be thinking of his country. How the small

kingdom of Isla Tamoura needed him to be a strong leader. And yet all he could think of was Krystiana.

Things had happened between them so quickly. And he suspected he knew why. They could both connect on something that not many people got to experience— thankfully. Their kidnapping. He couldn't imagine what it must have been like to have been taken by her own father. He tried to imagine his father doing such a thing. Locking him into a hole in the ground. His mind just couldn't compute it. Krystiana's father must have been so desperate after he lost his custody battle... He knew how crazy *he'd* almost gone, thinking he would never see his own child.

Krystiana had told him, hadn't she? That she didn't want a proper relationship. That she couldn't foresee having one. So really maybe he was doing her a favour? She didn't want this either!

His pathetic attempt to convince himself that he was doing this for *her* made him feel slightly ill.

He got up and began to pace once again—back and forth, back and forth. He caught a glimpse of his reflection in the mirror and stopped to stare at himself, trying to work out when it was that he had changed from being a man determined never to get involved with anyone again into a man who had barely been able to keep his emotions and desires in check around Krystiana.

He'd never wanted to feel loss again and yet he'd got involved with a woman he knew he could never have!

How on earth had he ever allowed it to happen?

She found herself standing outside Mara's office, holding the grey dress she'd borrowed draped over one arm. She knocked.

Mara opened her door. 'Krystiana! Come on in!' She stepped back to allow her entrance.

'I thought I'd better bring back your dress. It's been cleaned. I think one of the servants spirited it away when I was at the hospital this morning.'

Mara smiled, taking the dress from her. 'Thank you. But you could have kept it, you know?'

Krystiana shook her head. 'Oh, no! It must have cost a fortune. I couldn't do that.'

Mara gazed at her for a moment, obviously sensing her nerves and anxiety. 'What's wrong? Come on—sit down. Tell me what's going on.'

And suddenly the tears were falling. She couldn't help it. It was almost as if Mara's empathy and kindness had just opened up the dam and it had all come pouring out.

Mara, bless her, sat next to her with an arm around her shoulders. Just being there. Just waiting for when she was ready to talk.

'Matteo and I...' Krystiana sniffed, dabbing at her eyes with the tissue that Mara offered her. 'We've been...er...' How to say it? This was his ex-wife! But she was also his best friend, so...

'You've been...courting?'

She knew? 'Not really. Not *dating*, as such. Just... I'm not sure how it happened, really, but...'

Mara waited.

'We slept together.' She felt awful telling Mara this.

'And now it's complicated?'

Krystiana nodded. 'It always was.'

'I understand. Matteo and I, even though we knew our future, were caught up in an extraordinary situation. And now the man that you...you have feelings for is about to be King, and that's not a normal thing at all for anyone to have to face.'

'No one would approve of us.'

'You don't know that.'

Krystiana didn't have to think for too long. 'I do. Matteo held my hand in front of his father and I could see he wasn't pleased about it.'

'The world is complicated, Krystiana. Nothing is always simple or as it seems. Sometimes all you can do is go with what your heart tells you.'

'It's telling me so many things.'

'Then perhaps you should ask it a question? How would you feel never to have Matteo in your life ever again?'

She couldn't imagine what that would be like. To only see him on the television… In the newspapers… Online… 'It would be awful.'

Mara smiled. 'But you would survive it?'

'I've already survived so much. Had my heart broken too many times. I'm not sure I want to go through that again.'

'Sometimes we have no choice about our battles.'

Krystiana smiled ruefully. 'You sound like you're trying to tell me to prepare myself. That there is no future for us.'

Mara looked away. 'I like you, Krystiana. I think you and Matteo could be amazing together. You'd make each other happy.'

'But…?'

'But if you want to be with him then you need to talk to him.'

'About what?'

Mara smiled. 'About everything.'

CHAPTER ELEVEN

MATTEO OPENED THE door to his quarters to see Krystiana standing there, looking apprehensive and nervous. Smiling, he welcomed her in, dropping a kiss on her cheek. She looked so beautiful, her eyes bright and kind, her smile full and wide. He felt his heart lift at seeing her, even though he felt depressed.

'Hi,' he said.

'Hi. I wonder if you have a minute to talk?'

'Sure. Can I get you a drink?'

'No, it's all right. I just want to say this whilst I have the nerve to and then I'll go.'

Oh. That didn't sound good. But, then again, she was smiling—so what did that mean? Had she made a decision?

'I'm all ears.'

'Yes.'

He narrowed his eyes. 'Yes…?'

She laughed. 'Yes! To you. To *us*. One of us has to say it! I want us to try to be together. Despite all that's going on, despite you becoming King, and despite other people's disapproval—when there is any, which I'm expecting there to be. I'm just a doctor, after all, and—'

'Hang on—let me get this straight. You want us to be a…a couple?'

His heart soared. Not for one moment had he thought she would come to such a conclusion, but she had, and it was wonderful, and despite all his fears he wanted this one moment when he did something for *him*. Because his life was about to spiral madly out of control when he became King. He knew he was throwing caution to the wind, despite the rules, but surely he could worry about those at a later time?

'Come here.' He pulled her into his arms, his lips meeting hers, and he kissed her as he'd never kissed her before!

He knew what this had cost her. He knew how terrified she must have been to say it. And it felt *so right*. This was the woman he'd been waiting for his entire life. She was perfect. Intelligent, kind, loving, beautiful. And she understood him. Understood more than anyone else ever could. Because she'd been through it, too.

And when his father had collapsed he'd felt *safe*, knowing she was with him. He'd felt loved, knowing that she was thinking about *him*, that he was thinking about *her*.

She was his strength. His heart. His life. And though he was worried about what the future might entail for them, his fear was not as strong as his love. His need. That was a bridge they could cross later. Surely there was a way?

'I love you so much, Krystiana Szenac!'

She smiled back. 'And I love *you*!'

They kissed. Unable to get enough of each other. He had no doubt that he would have taken her to his bed right there and then, if he'd been able to, but he had people coming. Delegates. Business meetings.

'Let's celebrate! Just you and me. Away from here. I could get us reservations at Jacaranda. Very discreet.'

'Go out with you in public?' Her face was flushed with excitement and nerves and apprehension.

He nodded. 'We need to get away from this place. Just be *us*.'

Krystiana nodded and gave him a quick kiss before she headed back to the door. 'Dress code?'

He gave it some thought. 'You'd look beautiful in anything.'

She laughed. '*Formal* would have done nicely.'

'Formal, it is.'

'Right. Then I'm off to get ready.'

He checked his watch. 'It's two-thirty in the afternoon.'

'A girl needs time to look her best, Matteo.'

'You're already perfect.'

She smiled and blew him a kiss. 'Good answer. But I'm still going to have a bath and do my hair.'

She began to close the doors behind her.

'Wait!' he called, sliding over to the door in his socks, skidding to a halt in front of her. 'One last kiss?'

She pressed her mouth to his and he savoured the taste of her.

'Not the last, Matteo. But the first of *many*.'

She'd needed to be brave many times in her life, but going to see Matteo and admitting what she wanted, to be in a relationship with him, was probably one of the bravest things she had ever done. She had put herself *out there*. As if she was on a precipice and he had the ability to knock her off, to send her crashing to her doom.

She'd given him that power and he hadn't let her down at all. Her gut instinct had been *right*! He wanted to be with her as much as she wanted to be with him!

And she was quickly learning that one of the advantages of living in a palace was that there seemed to be a hairdresser, stylist and make-up artist always on site. Apparently Giulia was there mostly for Mara and Alex's sake, but she was thrilled to get her hands on someone new and decide what to do with her.

'Your hair is just *bellissimo*! Thick and long.' Giulia was running her fingers through it, admiring it, trying it this way, then that. 'I think we need a messy up-do. Like this—see? But if we leave these strands here and here we can make tiny plaits and twist them through... like this. *Si?*'

Krystiana had never done more than put her hair in a thick plait. 'Whatever you think is right will be fine.'

'We can tousle it, tease it, and if we are careful we can use jewelled slides here and there. Let me do it and I'll show you—I promise you'll love it.'

'Okay.'

'And what were you thinking for make-up?' Giulia looked at her carefully in the mirror. 'Such expressive eyes... You need more than mascara on those. How about a deep, dark smoky eye? A nude lip? Earrings to match the jewels in your hair?'

Krystiana frowned. 'You're the expert. How long will all that take?'

'A couple of hours. We have plenty of time and then we can take a look at your wardrobe.'

'My wardrobe...?'

She didn't really have much in there. It wasn't as if she had loads to choose from. She'd mostly got ordinary work clothes with her. Suits... Dresses fit for being in her practice office—not a romantic soirée.

'Some things have been sent over for you.'

She turned in her seat. 'Oh? From whom?'

'The Crown Prince.'

'Matteo?'

'Well, he had a little help from me. I went shopping at his request.'

'When?'

'When you first arrived at the palace. He wasn't sure how much we would be able to rescue from your home, so he sent me out to fetch you a range of outfits.'

'Oh. But you don't know my sizes.'

'Stylists can *tell*. Just by looking. Trust me—I have picked you out some wonderful things.'

Krystiana smiled at her reflection as Giulia set to work with her hair. She quite liked it that he'd wanted to get some clothes for her, and she wasn't at all upset that he might have been a bit presumptuous in assuming that she was staying.

If he hadn't done it then she'd be knocking on Mara's door again, raiding *her* wardrobe! And there was something wrong about wearing the clothes of a man's ex-wife to make him fall for her! She was looking forward to searching through the boxes and bags that were now on the bed to see what there was.

She'd never been treated in such a way! Had always been careful with money, even though her job paid well. Growing up in a household where her mother had scrimped and saved every *zloty* had clearly rubbed off on her.

With her hair looking exquisite and her face made up by the talented Giulia, who could do things with a blender brush that Krystiana had no idea how to replicate, she set to going through the new outfits.

There were trouser suits and tailored dresses, flowing skirts and perfect heels. Linen trousers…even a couple of swimsuits! But in the end they both agreed that a duck-egg-blue dress, that skimmed over her hips and flared out just above the knee would be perfect.

Krystiana tried it on, twirling and twisting in front of

the full-length mirror to check how it looked. 'This is so pretty, Giulia! Did you choose it?'

'Matteo chose this one. He said it would match your eyes and it does.'

Krystiana smiled. 'Good. Then I shall definitely wear it. Are we all done?'

Giulia tapped her lips as she assessed her. 'It needs one more thing… Here.' And she pulled from one of the bags a small box, cracking it open for Krystiana to see the jewelled bracelet inside.

It glittered and caught the light and it was the most beautiful thing she had ever seen. 'Oh, my word! He bought me *that*?'

'Yes.'

'It must have cost a fortune! I can't wear that! I'll be afraid of losing it all night.'

'It has a safety chain. Try it.'

Giulia clipped it around her wrist and she felt the weight of it on her arm. Just enough to notice. If it *did* fall off she would know instantly.

'So… I'm ready?'

'Yes, you are. I'll gather my things together and then I'll go.'

'Thank you, Giulia. You're a miracle-worker!'

'It was my pleasure. Have a good night.'

There was a gentle knock at her door and Krystiana opened it.

Matteo stood there, looking handsome in a smart suit, his white shirt crisp and clean, open at the collar. He looked like a handsome spy, set to seduce.

'You look…' He looked her up and down, his eyes appreciative. 'Amazing!'

She blushed. 'Thank you! So do you.'

'May I escort you down to the car?'

He held out his arm and she slipped hers through it, smiling. 'Thank you! You may.'

Together they walked through the palace corridors, past various members of staff going about their duties. They all looked up and smiled at the two of them and Krystiana felt admired and adored. Clearly they were a handsome couple.

In the car, they were driven slowly through the grounds of the palace and out through the gates, then down towards the bustling capital city of Ventura. Before she knew it they were pulling up outside a smart restaurant, set back from the road. Either side of the doors were railings behind which had gathered a bunch of people with cameras.

She felt her heart begin to race. 'Are they paparazzi?'

'Looks like it.'

'How did they know we were coming here?'

'I don't know. Someone must have let something slip. Shall we go back? We don't have to go out there.'

Her heart was racing and she felt a little clammy. Back in the palace she'd been sheltered from this, and though she knew she'd agreed to this, now that the moment was here it still felt a little…frightening.

'Just stay by my side—all right?' she said.

He nodded. 'Keep your eyes on me. When we're out of the vehicle we'll give them one moment when we stand together, give a quick smile, and then we'll be indoors. I promise you they can't see inside, and they can't step through the door. We'll have privacy for our meal. All right?'

She nodded, not sure she could speak.

'Okay. Deep breath and then one, two, three…'

Matteo opened the car door and suddenly a barrage of flashing lights assaulted her, blinding her slightly. She could hear clicks and whirrs and felt the flashes blinding her, leaving imprints on her retinas. She had to fight the urge to hold her hand in front of her face and run inside.

Instead, she gripped his arm, feeding on his sure strength and composure, and when she looked up at him he was smiling down at her with such ease that she couldn't help but smile back. And then they gave the press what they wanted. A quick pose. A quick smile. A small wave and then they were inside the restaurant.

She let out a heavy breath and looked to Matteo with relief. He was smiling at her and he kissed her gently on the lips. 'You did great.'

'It all happened so fast.'

'We all learn how to work the press. Give them enough to keep them fed and watered, but always leave them hanging on for more. And always be polite.'

'It almost feels like a game.'

'It is. They're all in competition with one another for the best shot, the best photo, the best smile. Because that's what sells.'

'I guess tomorrow everyone will know who I am?'

He nodded. 'They won't know for sure, though. It will all be speculation.'

So he can deny us later?

She hated it that the thought flittered through her brain, and she dismissed it. If he'd not wanted anyone to know about them then he would have ordered the driver to bring them here. He wouldn't have got out of the car with her. She was just being ridiculous and nervous because she was putting herself out there, on the line. Of course she could trust him.

The maître d' met them and escorted them to a small private booth at the back of the restaurant. A piano played softly in the background, and she quickly realised it wasn't being piped through speakers but was an actual pianist sitting at the instrument.

Candles lit the restaurant, alongside wall sconces and chandeliers, creating an intimate mood, and she sat at the table, suddenly feeling hungry. The nerves from facing the press had emptied her stomach.

A server draped her serviette over her lap and poured water into their glasses. 'Would you like to see the menu?'

'Thank you,' she said.

The server bowed and presented them each with a leather-bound menu. 'The special today is venison, which has been marinated in juniper, served with a parsnip *velouté* and a wild mushroom sauce.'

'Thank you,' she said again, and smiled shyly at the server and watched him walk away. 'This place is beautiful.'

'It's a favourite of mine. The chef is very good.'

She smiled. 'Did you come here with Mara?' she asked. She didn't want to think that this was where Matteo had brought *all* the women he'd wanted to impress in his past.

'No. I didn't. I only found this place after Mara and I had split.'

She smiled shyly. Thankful.

'So, what do you fancy?'

Krystiana beamed and reached across the table to take his hand. 'You.'

'Tell me what you were like as a little boy.'

She couldn't imagine what he must have been like. *Her* only recollections of growing up in Poland seemed to be around her own kidnapping, and then afterwards moving to Isla Tamoura. Adapting to a new way of life and thinking how strange it was. Surely his childhood had been a lot more sturdy.

He smiled. 'My father would tell you that I got into all types of mischief.'

'And what would *you* tell me?'

Matteo laughed. 'That he was right! There was this one time he was having an official meeting. Very important. Children not allowed. I can remember being fascinated about why all these important-looking people were allowed into this room and I wasn't! Was there some treasure there they were all looking at? Were they eating fabulous food? Did they have great computer games? I felt sure I was missing out on something, so I crept in and hid behind a drape at the back of my father's chair. I listened and listened, absolutely sure that I'd hear something secret or amazing. But they were droning on about olive yields and crop rotations and it was the most boring thing I'd ever heard—so I thought I'd liven things up.'

'What did you do?'

'I jumped out from behind the curtain and made the loudest and best dinosaur noise that I could possibly make.'

She laughed, imagining it. 'What happened?'

'My father turned in his seat and gave me *"the look"*. I knew then I was in trouble. I was escorted out, and about an hour later he came and told me off—said that as punishment I had to help the gardener for the afternoon.'

'Wow.'

'And of course you know how *that* turned out. I ended up designing nearly all of it.'

'It sounds like you were a very happy young boy.'

'I was. I *was* lucky.' He looked at her. 'How about you? There must be something from your childhood that's a good memory?'

She had to think about it. But then she remembered. 'My father once promised me a pony. He said that one day that I would have the best pony in the world! He got me a poster for my room, and a small cuddly toy that was a horse, but he said that one day I'd ride a pony that was all mine. I never got to do it, but I remember how hard he tried to give me what I wanted. He wasn't always a bad man.'

'Matilde could be yours.'

She looked at him. Was he serious? 'What…?'

'She could! You on Matilde, myself on Galileo—we could have many happy rides together.'

'You see a future for us, then?' she asked, her heart beating merrily. She was testing him gently. Needing the reassurance of his words.

He sipped his water. 'Of course.'

Later, Matteo walked her back to her rooms in the palace. Once inside the doors of his family home she had pulled off her heels, and she padded barefoot through the corridors, her head leaning against his arm.

She'd had such a wonderful evening with him. Listening to his stories and tales, laughing at his anecdotes, of which he had many, and just enjoying listening to him speak.

She realised just how long it had been since she'd been able to do that. Her whole adult life had been filled with patients—sitting and listening, assessing, analysing, looking for clues to their physical or mental state, considering diagnoses, selecting help methods and suggesting therapies and strategies they could use to get better.

But tonight she had just *enjoyed*. And she had told him a few tales of her own. Not having to be guarded about what she said, knowing that he would enjoy whatever it was and really listen to it.

She'd felt so good with him. So natural. And as she'd

looked into his eyes over the table, as they'd eaten delicious food that had tasted as good as it looked, she'd just known that she could fall for this man hugely. If she hadn't already.

At her door, she turned to face him, pulling him towards her for a kiss. His lips on hers felt magical. This truly was blissful! To have such joy and happiness after all that they had both gone through. It almost felt as if it were a dream. And to think she had nearly denied herself such happiness…

'I want you to stay with me tonight,' she said boldly, looking deep into his eyes, telling him with her gaze exactly what she wanted.

He kissed her again, and then she took his hand and led him inside…

'Could you undo the zip?'

Krystiana turned away from him, to present him with her back. He gazed at the soft slope of her shoulders, at the gentle curls of honey hair at the nape of her neck and at the long zip that trailed the length of her spine. He took hold of the zipper and slowly lowered it, leaning in to kiss her soft skin as he did so.

She leaned back against him, gasping softly as his lips trailed feather touches and his hands slipped under the dress at each shoulder and slid the fabric to the floor.

Turning again, she faced him with a smile and he took in everything about her. The softness of her skin, the gentle swell of her breasts, her narrow waist, the feminine curve of her lips.

'You're so beautiful,' he whispered, reaching for her mouth with his own, sliding his hands down her sides, curving them over her buttocks and pulling her against him. Against his hardness. Wanting her to know how much he wanted her.

'*Matteo!*' She gasped his name as his hands cupped her breasts, and then again as his tongue found her nipples, delicately licking and teasing each tip. He worked lower, down to her belly, hooking his thumbs under her panties and slowly, slowly pulling them down.

He wanted to lose himself in her, but a loud voice in the back of his mind was yelling at him, telling him that this was *wrong*. That nothing could come of it. He would have to let her go and he was being a terrible man—keeping up the façade that everything was fine. Soon he would have to tell her the truth, and that would tear her apart. He didn't want to be just another man who would break her heart, so he kept putting it off and putting it off—and now look at where they were.

She thought they were making love.

But he knew he was saying goodbye.

She woke in his arms. A lazy smile was upon her face. Her body was still tingling, comforted by the feel of Matteo spooning her from behind.

Last night had been everything she had ever dreamed of, and she knew that out in the wider world the people of Isla Tamoura would be waking up to newspaper reports of the coronation and the Crown Prince's new beau. They would have the rest of their lives to enjoy each other. They'd made it official last night, with that public appearance. Now everyone would know.

Briefly she wondered if she ought to call the practice and make arrangements for her patients to be taken on by Dr Bonetti for a short while. Later on she could decide about when she'd return. It had been so long since she'd taken any time off she felt sure Dr Bonetti wouldn't mind, and she'd just covered for him, so…

There's plenty of time before I have to do that, though.

Getting out of bed, she pulled on her robe and opened up the double doors that led outside, closing her eyes to the wonderful warmth of the early-morning sun.

This would be her life from now on. This wonder. This joy. Living in the palace with the man of her dreams, the love of her life. Yes, she knew she loved him. Everything would be different now.

She glanced back at Matteo, still blissfully asleep in her bed, his face relaxed, and realised they'd both got through the night without a night-light. It was as if the love they had between them was what they needed to be strong enough to fight off the fears that plagued them.

Was that all it took? A loving pair of arms?

Whatever it was, she didn't mind. She was happy. And in love. Probably for the first time in her life. She had fallen for him deeply.

His eyes blinked open and as soon as he saw her he smiled. '*Buongiorno.*'

'*Buongiorno.*'

'You're up already.'

'Ready to face the world!'

He groaned. 'No. Not yet. Let's just stay here and pretend the rest of the world doesn't exist. Come back to bed.'

She smiled coyly at him and padded back towards him, disrobing and falling into his arms, feeling his lips on hers and delightful sensations rippling through her once again.

'Aren't you tired?'

'Of this? *Never.*'

Krystiana laughed. 'Don't you have to go to the hospital this morning?'

Matteo groaned and rolled over to check his watch,

blinking at the time. 'Yes. Of course. You're right. Five minutes…then I'll get dressed.'

'Five minutes?' She bit her lip and looked at him questioningly.

He laughed, unable to help himself. 'I can do a lot in five minutes.'

And then he disappeared under the bed sheet and she felt his mouth trail down her skin, lower and lower, until she gasped with surprise and delight.

She'd wanted to capture the moment of Alex playing in Matteo's beloved flower garden. She'd thought it would be a wonderful gift for him. So as Alex frolicked amongst the blooms, trying to catch butterflies with a gauzy net, Krystiana stood back, splashing colour onto canvas.

She'd show him when he got back from seeing his father! He would love it. It would be unique. It would be put in pride of place in his quarters. The lush greens of all the foliage, the spots of gold, bronze, cherry-red, fuchsia-pink and lapis-blue flowers, and amongst it all a beautiful little girl, her long ebony locks flowing behind her, her net held high, ready to swoop.

'Look at me, Krissy—look!'

She was so beautiful, Matteo's daughter, and it was important to Krystiana that they got along. She wanted to create a happy painting. Made with love.

Just as she was adding the finishing touches she felt a prickle on the back of her neck. The sensation of being watched.

She turned to see who it might be.

It was Matteo. Up on his sun terrace, looking down at them. He was far enough away not to be able to see the painting, but there was something about his stance that made her think he was upset.

She put down her brushes and wiped her hands on a soft cloth. 'Alex? Let the painting dry, won't you? Don't touch it. I'm just going to see if your father is all right.'

Her first thought was that maybe something had happened with his father. Had King Alberto deteriorated? Perhaps he'd had a heart attack in the night?

Oh, please don't let him be dead!

She hated to think of Matteo being hurt in such a way. Going through the loss of his last remaining parent...

The thought made her steps slow, and for a moment she stopped still completely, just to breathe. To gather herself—strengthen herself for whatever revelation was about to come. It had to be something bad, didn't it? Otherwise Matteo would have come down to see her in the gardens with Alex.

Everything had been going so well since last night. They'd both finally found happiness. Was the beginning of their love going to be marred by death? She sincerely hoped not...

Krystiana didn't knock as she entered his quarters. She knew he would still be out on the sun terrace and he was—standing with his back to her, ramrod-straight. There was a sternness to the set of his shoulders, to the upright nature of his posture—as if he was holding himself so as not to break.

'Matteo?'

He didn't answer her. Or turn around. And that alarmed her. She walked to his side so that she could see his face. It was cold and stony. Like a statue.

She reached out to touch his hand with hers. 'Matteo? Are you all right? What's happened?'

He said nothing for a while, then he blinked and squeezed her fingers tightly, before responding, 'I went to see my father.'

She felt as if a cold, dead lump was weighting down her stomach. 'Is he all right?'

'Fine. Well, health-wise, he is. The doctors think he can come home.'

She felt a wave of relief surge over her. 'But that's *great* news!'

He nodded. 'It is.'

'So…why aren't you happy? You look…stressed.'

And that was when she noticed that in his other hand he held a small glass of whisky. He lifted it to his mouth and sank the drink in one gulp. Wasn't it a little early for hard liquor?

'Matteo? You're scaring me. Tell me what's going on. *Now.*'

He turned to look at her and she could see that he had been crying. His eyes were red and puffy.

'My father saw the newspapers this morning. He was not pleased that he had to learn about us through a third party.'

She sucked in a breath. 'Okay…' That was acceptable. They should apologise for that. King Alberto should have been told by them. They'd got that bit wrong. 'Does he not like me?'

'He does. But…' He glanced at his glass and saw that it was empty. Scowling, he placed it down on the balcony edge. 'He reminded me of a certain unpalatable truth.'

She blinked, not understanding. 'What truth?'

Matteo turned away, as if unable to look her in the eyes. And that scared her.

'The law of my country states that those first in line to the throne can only marry another of royal blood.'

What? No. That couldn't be right!

But the more she thought about what that meant, the

more she knew something like this had always been going to happen. It had all been going too well.

The tears escaped. Trickling down her cheeks. 'Royal blood?'

He could only marry a princess? Or a duchess? Something like that? Well, she wasn't either of those things! She was just a girl from Poland who'd once lived in a giant block of flats. A girl from a poor family whose father had hunted rabbit and pigeon to feed his family meat. A girl who had fled to this island seeking a better life than the one she'd had to leave behind.

They were worlds apart. The only way she'd have royal blood would be if she stole it from someone and kept it in a small vial!

'This is ridiculous! It's got to be wrong!'

'It's not wrong. It's an archaic law of my land and has been for hundreds of years.'

Her eyes widened as her brain scrambled to find some way out of this. 'But if we didn't know, surely it isn't our fault?'

He turned and walked over to the liquor cabinet. Without a word he refilled his glass and knocked back the whisky again, his gaze downcast to the floor.

And suddenly she knew. She tried to make him look at her. 'You *did* know. You knew and yet you slept with me anyway. You made me think that we could be together! How could you? How could you treat me like this? Like a…a plaything. A toy! What did you think I was? Some kind of casual fling?'

'Krystiana—'

But she didn't want to hear it. She'd told him she'd been hurt before, and how much it would cost her to trust someone again, and what had he done? He'd lied. He'd kept secrets. He'd used her. For his own gratification!

He was worse than Adamo.

Overcome with tears and humiliation, she fled from his room.

Matteo winced as his door slammed behind her and felt sick to his stomach. The visit with his father had been a lost battle before he'd even entered the room—and now this. Surely there must have been another way he could have done this? Another way he could have gently explained how they could never be more than what they were now.

But his father had forced his hand. He had told him that he needed to tell her the truth or that he, Alberto himself, would have the royal chamberlain inform her of the rules by the end of the day. Tell her that she would have to give up her claim on the King's son because he could never be hers.

'Why are you doing this?' he'd asked his father.

'I'm trying to stop it before either of you get hurt.'

But it was already too late. His father didn't know the depth of his feelings for Krystiana. Or hers for him. And he hated it that he had trampled all over her heart with his dirty shoes.

But, hell, she'd not wanted a relationship either—so what the hell was *she* doing, allowing them to get into such a situation? He'd thought they'd both be safe. Neither of them had wanted it and yet somehow, in some way, they had been unable to stay away from each other.

And now he was faced with another loss. Another heartbreak. Was he doomed to suffer? He should never have got involved, he told himself once again, as he slammed his hand against the wall in frustration and upset, and he would never allow himself to get into a situation like this ever again.

His heart would be off-limits.

Access granted only to his daughter.

Krystiana refused to pack the clothes that had been bought for her. Or the jewellery. Or any of the gifts she'd been given during her time in the palace. If she took any of it all it would do, when she got home, would be to remind her of what might have been, and her heart was instinctively telling her that if she wanted to get over this then she had to leave it all behind. Then she could almost pretend that it had never happened. Like she had when she'd left Krakow. All she'd taken with her then had been some clothes in a small suitcase and a solitary doll with only one arm.

She'd seen plenty of patients in her time who had used denial as an effective tool to pretend that bad stuff hadn't happened. And right now she thought it was a damned good strategy! Though she'd suggested that they might do better by facing the bad stuff, so that they could heal, right now she wanted to wholeheartedly embrace the concept.

Angrily she went from drawer to drawer, grabbing her clothes roughly and shoving them into her suitcase, throwing in her shoes. She didn't even bother to wrap her paints and spare canvases separately.

Who cares if I get paint over everything?

She didn't. Her heart had been broken the instant she'd realised that Matteo had lied to her, and she knew she couldn't stay a moment longer. She couldn't believe the mess she had got herself into!

I fought against this attraction. I should have listened to myself.

If she had, then none of this would have happened and she'd already be out of here. She should never have stayed for that ball. She should have gone.

But it had been impossible. Her desire for him had

been plain fact. There'd been no way to walk away from her love. Her soul mate. The man she'd seen herself with all the way into the future.

How gullible she must have seemed for him to use her like that, knowing how she'd been treated in the past. He'd known what it had taken for her to open to him like that, to put herself out there, and he'd—

She cried out loud as pain ripped through her chest and hiccupped her way through her final packing. Bruno sat in the corner, his head tilted as he watched her frantic movements, trying to work out what was going on.

His father must have delighted in forcing Matteo to tell her the truth. Or perhaps she should *thank* the King? She'd seen it in his face, that time Matteo had clutched Krystiana's hand for support in the hospital. The way his eyes had narrowed… She should have questioned it then.

Behind her, the doors to her apartment opened.

'You're leaving?'

Mara stared at her, her face a mask of shock and concern.

Krystiana wiped at her eyes, determined to stop crying once and for all! 'I have no choice!'

'There must be something you can do…'

'There isn't, so…' She turned to Mara and pulled her towards her for a hug. 'Thank you for being my friend here. It could have been awkward between us, but you made it so easy. Thank you.'

Mara hugged her back. 'Are you kidding me? It's so obvious that what you and Matteo have is real. You look at each other the way Philippe and I do.'

Krystiana sniffed. 'It was never real. Matteo *knew* I couldn't be with him.'

Mara looked away.

Krystiana stared at her. 'You did too?' she asked with incredulity.

'I'm sorry. But I couldn't be the one to tell you. To break your heart.'

Krystiana slammed down the clips on her suitcase. 'A heads-up might have been nice!'

'I tried! I told you to talk to him!'

But she didn't want to hear any more. Did *everyone* lie? 'I've got to go. Say goodbye to Alex for me?'

'Where are you going?'

She shrugged. 'A hotel somewhere? A bed and breakfast?' She looked at Bruno. 'One that takes dogs…'

'Will I ever see you again?'

'Do you read the *Lancet*?' Krystiana smiled, trying to crack a joke in the midst of her trauma.

'No.'

'Then I guess not.'

'I'll talk to Matteo.'

'There's no point. I wouldn't have any more to do with him if he was the last man alive.'

'Krystiana, please! Promise me you'll wait here until I get back?'

She nodded, knowing she was going to break her promise. But what did she owe Mara, if anything? Mara had been complicit in this lie, too. Mara whom she'd thought was a friend.

After Matteo's ex-wife had left Krystiana took one last look around the place and then left, trailing her little suitcase behind her.

'Come on, Bruno. Let's go.'

CHAPTER TWELVE

SHE'D NOT BEEN lying when she'd told Mara she'd stay at a hotel or a bed and breakfast. She just hadn't said it would be in Rome.

Isla Tamoura was not a place she could be right now. Everyone would know her—know her face. She wouldn't be able to find refuge at work either. People would show up just to gawp at her and ask questions. To see the royal fool. She needed to go somewhere no one would find her.

She'd dropped Bruno off at her aunt's place. Thankfully she'd been out, so she'd left her aunt a note on the counter. Bruno would be fine with her—she knew that.

At the airport, the first thing she spotted was her face on the front of a newspaper. She was standing next to Matteo outside the restaurant last night. Smiling. Looking nervous, but happy.

Feeling sick, she fumbled in her handbag for a pair of large sunglasses and let her long hair down loose. She didn't want anyone spotting her. Didn't want anyone recognising who she was.

She sneaked into the women's toilet and splashed her face with cold water, staring at her reflection, trying to equate the drawn-looking woman in the mirror with the one who had just this very morning woken up in the arms of the man she loved. A woman who had believed that her worst problem at the time was whether she'd have time for a quick shower before breakfast.

How was she here? Why had he lied? When he knew that the truth was the most important thing he could have told her?

Sliding the sunglasses back onto her face, she headed out of the bathroom and went to the customer service desk.

'Are there any flights to Rome soon?' she asked the perfectly groomed woman behind the desk.

The woman, whose name tag read *Leonora*, tapped at her keyboard, reading the screen in front of her. 'Yes, ma'am, there's a flight at three this afternoon.'

'Any seats available?'

'Yes, ma'am. Window and aisle.'

'Okay. Who do I need to see to book that?'

Leonora told her where to go, and before she knew it Krystiana had a plane ticket and had checked her luggage. Only an hour until her flight time. What to do to pass the time?

She saw a coffee shop and felt the need for a huge slug of caffeine, and maybe some restorative chocolate, despite the feeling in her stomach.

She sat down at a small table, trying not to be noticed. Opposite her, a man sat with a woman whom she supposed to be his wife. They were discussing her picture on the front page of the newspaper. Wondering whether they were serious? Whether they were in love?

She tried to sink down in her seat, hoping no one would notice her.

I should have bought a paper to hide behind.

She looked about her and saw a discarded one on the

table next to her. She picked it up and shook it open, hiding her face from the crowds.

One hour to go and she could be out of here!

Matteo stared at the empty apartment. 'She's really gone.' He felt guilty. Angry. It had all come crashing down around his ears so quickly. Such intense happiness, contentment and love, and now this.

He was feeling empty. Stunned.

Heartbroken.

The thought that he might never see her again almost crushed him into inertia. It was like being back in that cave, wondering if he'd ever see his loved ones again?

Mara laid a friendly hand upon his arm, her face filled with sympathy. 'She told me she'd wait.'

'She didn't want to get involved with me. *Told* me she didn't want a relationship. That she didn't want to be that vulnerable.'

'She loved you, though. You can't help who you fall in love with.'

'Like you and Philippe?' It was a cheap shot, and it was out of his bitter mouth before he could reel it back in. He was hurting and wanted to lash out, but he should never have lashed out at his best friend. 'I'm sorry. Forget that.'

'No, you're right. I gave up on you. I left you behind.'

'You thought I was dead. It's hardly the same.'

'But I still must have hurt you.'

'I thought I'd never love again. I was determined that no one, anywhere, would open me up to loss. Ever.'

'Krystiana left because she couldn't be with you in the way that she needed.'

'She left because I *lied*. I hurt her. Whatever must she think of me?'

'She'll be okay. She's strong.'

'She shouldn't *have* to be okay. Shouldn't have to be strong. She deserved the truth, but I never told her any of it because I knew how deep I was already in!' He'd never felt so frustrated in all his life. 'I thought I could bury my head in the sand. I thought I could find a way around it.'

'I'm sorry, Matteo.'

'I need to speak with my father.'

'He's resting. He needs to take it easy. You can't go in there, all guns blazing.'

'So what do I do?'

'I don't know. Maybe you should just accept the fact that you got this wrong?'

Matteo sank onto the end of the bed. 'In the worst way possible…'

'You don't know that for sure.'

He looked at her with resignation. 'Yes, I do.'

On arrival in Rome, Krystiana headed straight to the nearest information desk and looked for hotel and bed and breakfast listings. She didn't want anywhere in the main city, but something on the periphery. Somewhere a bit more remote.

She found a perfect place called the Catalina that belonged to an elderly couple. Their bed and breakfast was on the outskirts of Rome, in Lazio, and her bedroom windows looked out over the countryside that formed part of the Riserva Naturale di Decima-Malafede. A nature reserve that was meant to host a population of wild boar.

After the hustle and bustle of life in the palace and work in Ventura, it felt good to be looking out at trees and grassland. Anything that didn't remind her of life at the palace was absolutely fine by her.

She checked in under a made-up name, wearing the floppy sunhat she'd bought in duty-free and the large sunglasses that covered half her face. And then she sat in her room, dwelling on all that had passed.

Krystiana was doing what she always did in times of trauma—she was painting. Her room was beginning to fill with some pretty dark canvases now that she'd been here a week. It stank of paint and turpentine. She hadn't eaten much and seemed to be existing on coffee. Espresso.

She refused to do anything else. Hadn't turned on the television or read the news. She didn't want to hear anything about what might be happening on Isla Tamoura. Didn't want to think about Matteo in his garden, or playing with Alex, or eating breakfast on his sun terrace. To wonder whether he was being groomed to meet up with women who were more *suitable*. With *royal* blood. As opposed to the normal red stuff that ran in *her* veins.

He hadn't tried to contact her—which she was pleased about. It was what they both needed. No contact. Otherwise it might be too painful.

I've been a fool!

She'd spent her entire life telling herself that she was worth something. That she wasn't damaged goods and that she deserved the truth. And even though she'd thought she'd found it in Matteo, clearly she'd been wrong. He'd been forced to reveal his lies. The way Adamo had. Her mind reeled as to how she could have been so misled. She'd believed so much that he felt the same about her.

He was a good actor. Perhaps it was something they taught young royals on Isla Tamoura. Always to seem confident and believable. There were all those speeches they had to make—that had to be part of it, didn't it? Because being a good, strong king was something he wanted to present himself as. He was practised.

I never stood a chance.

And now, just as she'd known she couldn't dig her way out of that hole in the ground when she was six, she knew that the situation she was in was just as futile. It was almost a special skill she'd developed—acknowledging when something was a hopeless case—and there were only two things you could do when you had no power at all: accept it, or suffer trying to fight back.

She'd had enough suffering in her life. And though she knew it was going to hurt, walking away from the man she loved, she knew she had no choice. She was resigning herself to the fact that she'd been right. People were weak and they let you down. Love saved no one.

She hoped she would learn something from this experience. Learn that she could only ever depend upon herself, as she'd always suspected. That at the end of the day, no matter how many people you had around you, it was down to you and you alone to survive.

'What about Katherine? She seemed very interested in you.'

Alberto sat across the breakfast table from Matteo, who was nonchalantly tearing pastries apart, but only nibbling tiny parts of them.

He sighed. 'She was very nice. Clever conversation...'

'And *pretty*!' His father laughed. 'She would provide you with some beautiful children.'

Matteo smiled. 'I already have a beautiful child.'

'Your coronation is in one month. Are you going to be ascending the throne with a fiancée?'

'I don't think so, Papà. A relationship takes time to build. I can't make a decision like that after only spending one evening with someone.'

'Of course not. But it would be nice for the country to

have another happy celebration to look forward to after the coronation.'

Was that all that mattered? All that *should* matter? His *country*? What of his own life? Did that not matter at all any more? 'I won't be marrying anyone, Papà. I dined with Katherine because she was a guest here. No other reason. Not because the country needs a pick-me-up. I've already sacrificed so much—don't ask me for any more.'

Alberto held up his hands in supplication. 'Fair enough. I won't push. Now, are you bringing me my granddaughter later today? I haven't seen Alexandra for an age.'

'She'll be here later. Mara is bringing her over with Philippe.'

'He's a good man for her.'

'Yes, he is. Better than I ever was.'

His father looked at him, considering him. 'And…the doctor? You haven't heard from her?'

'No.'

Matteo did his best not to think of her too much. It hurt. It was too painful when he considered what he had done. It had never been her fault. It had always been his. He'd known the rules from the beginning and he'd thought he could do his own thing anyway.

'Good. You need to move on. More important things are coming up.'

He nodded. But he knew he would *never* forget her. How could he?

'You've got your robe fitting today, yes?'

The coronation robes needed adjusting for Matteo's broad form. 'Yes.'

'I might come along. It's been a long time since I saw those robes. My own coronation, in fact. That was a great day. Great memories. It'll be the same for you.'

'I'm sure it will.'

'You're sure you're all right? You seem very…*absent*.'

'Fine.'

'You'd tell me if there was something bothering you?'

'Of course!'

'Good. I'd hate to think you were keeping something from me, like before.'

'We never *kept* it from you, Papà. It was something new for both of us. We were trying to work it out for ourselves first.'

The King nodded as he hauled himself up from the table and then surprised his son by saying, 'Dr Szenac did seem a very nice woman. I'm sorry I had to force your hand, but I had to do it before you got in too deep. I couldn't bear the idea that you were going to get hurt further down the road, and neither was it very fair to her, when *you* knew the situation. I was surprised at you, son.'

Matteo stared at his father. 'We were already in too deep. We got hurt anyway.'

'I know what it's like to lose a loved one, Matteo. When I lost your mother, I…' He shook his head, clearing away the thought. 'Anyway, I did what I thought was best. For you. I only want the best for you.'

'*She* was the best, Papà. And I ruined it.'

Alberto nodded. 'I'm sorry.'

And he left his son sitting at the breakfast table, surrounded by a litter of pastry crumbs.

She'd been spending a lot of time in the nature reserve. It was just so peaceful out there and she'd managed to complete quite a few new paintings—including one of a sunset over the lake that had been astoundingly beautiful.

Decima-Malafede had been a comfort to her torn and broken soul, but after she'd packed the last of her canvases, checking out her room for one last time, Krystiana went downstairs, hugged the proprietors of the bed and breakfast, who had become good friends, and bade them goodbye.

It was time to go home.

Aunt Carolina had called with the news that repairs to her villa were complete and it was liveable again.

The news had been a nice surprise, but she'd felt a wave of sadness wash over her. Matteo had done that for her. Sorted out the villa. She'd kind of imagined, not too long ago, that they would both drive back there in one of the palace cars and look around the rebuild together. She'd briefly imagined putting the place up for sale, seeing as her new life was going to be based in the Grand Palace, the House of Romano.

None of that was to be. *What a fool!*

But she couldn't stay here, hiding away from life. Enough time had passed for her to be able to return, and hopefully the media would have moved on. Surely Matteo would have told them their relationship was over?

'They might still try to talk to you. Get the inside story on Matteo,' Aunt Carolina had warned.

But how could she stay away? She needed to return to work, and she needed, more than anything, to find her old routine. Her routine had kept her safe and secure. Unknown and unloved. That was the best way.

Handing over her key, she gave the owners a sad smile, thanked them for their care, their consideration and their silence, and then she walked out through the front door.

Wondering just what she might be walking back to.

Her villa felt strange. Hers, but not quite hers. Maybe because Bruno wasn't with her? She needed to collect him.

Krystiana set her bags down and slumped onto the sofa, feeling apprehensive at being back. There'd been no press on her doorstep. Had they given up? Figured she was gone? She hoped so.

With nothing better to do, she reached for the remote and switched on the television. As it came to life she heard the voice of the newscaster mentioning that the Crown Prince of Isla Tamoura was now King Matteo Romano, after his coronation earlier that day.

No wonder there aren't any press at my door.

She stared at the images of him on the throne, red ermine-trimmed robes around him, as he held the sceptre and orb, a crown of gold and jewels upon his head.

He looked very regal. And handsome.

She sucked in a sudden breath, the loss almost too much to bear.

She didn't know how to feel. Her heart was breaking so painfully. How was it still so raw?

She grabbed the remote and turned off the television, trying to wipe the images from her brain as she began to cry, holding a cushion in front of her as if its very presence might somehow cushion the force of the pain racing through her once again.

It was like a thorn in her side. A pain twisting deep in her heart.

He'd moved on.

Without her.

Clearly he had accepted the duty he was meant for and she wanted to be happy for him. But…

It hurt. More than she'd believed possible.

Krystiana cried herself to sleep, still holding the cushion like a shield.

'You thought I wouldn't find out?'

'Find out what?' Matteo sipped calmly from his espresso.

'Don't be coy with me, Matteo. You *know* what I'm

talking about! The law that now allows you to marry a commoner!'

Matteo wiped his mouth with a napkin as he shook his head. He'd thought about this a lot. Thought about what was right. And what he knew was this—he loved Krystiana. He would never find such a connection again. His entire happiness had been destroyed by a law that was archaic and out of date, and he'd been determined that his first order of business as King was to get it changed.

His entire life had been empty since she'd left and his heart had *ached*. He had fought against himself more than anyone else, in deciding to do this. Nothing might come of it—she might never forgive him—but he had to try.

'You want me to be a king who leads his country into the future, yes?' he said now.

'Of course!'

'Well, in that case I take it upon myself to change a few things. Make this a new, modern monarchy. We need to move with the times if we want our people to relate to us and respect us.'

'Are you going after her?'

Matteo stared at his father. Wasn't it obvious?

'Yes. If she'll have me.'

He expected his father to rant and rave, to argue that a king should never debase himself by begging for a woman's affections, but surprisingly he did not.

Instead, his voice was low and gentle. 'She means this much to you?'

'I love her and I've been miserable without her here. Couldn't you tell?'

His father nodded. 'Yes. I could.'

'You lost Mamma years ago. But if you could have a chance to get her back wouldn't you take it?'

His father stared at him, his eyes softening, welling up with tears. 'Yes.'

'Well, then… Would you deny me the love of my life? Knowing how it feels to be lost without her?'

'No. I would not deny you. You must love her very much to have done this.'

'I do.'

He stepped forward to clasp his son and pat him on the back. 'Then you have my blessing.'

Matteo was surprised. 'Really?'

'I've seen how you've been since she's been gone, and quite frankly you're almost back to how you were after you first came home after the kidnapping. You have no life in you. No joy. The only time I see you happy is when you are with Alex. I wasn't the right king to challenge the rules, but you *are*. Like you say—it's the future.'

'Thank you,' he said, feeling emotional. 'That means more than I can say.'

'Do you think you can bring her back?'

'I don't know. But it was never about the law keeping us apart. It was about me not telling her the truth. I'll need her to put her trust in me and I'm not sure if she will.'

'Well, call me when you know for sure.'

'I will. Thank you, Papà.'

'Good luck, son.'

CHAPTER THIRTEEN

AFTER A LONG day at work—and it had been a *long* day—there was nothing Krystiana loved more than to walk along the beach, barefoot, watching Bruno frolic in the sea. There was peace out here, freedom. *Anonymity.*

She'd spent the last few weeks fielding questions from her patients, trying to move them back to the topic of themselves rather than her and her fleeting romance with their King. It had been hard denying that there was anything going on, and every time someone questioned her about it it was like being stabbed in the heart again as she told them that, no, she and the King were not together. That it had simply been a friendly meal together and the press had misconstrued it.

It was exhausting, quite frankly—so much so that she was even considering moving elsewhere. Maybe starting her own medical practice…perhaps in Rome or Florence? Somewhere far away from here.

But she'd already fled from one home. She didn't want to have to flee another. She loved this island so much.

Bruno yapped with happiness as he brought her over a ball he'd found and dropped it at her feet. She picked it up and threw it as far as she could, smiling as he chased after it. She couldn't take him away from this, either.

She looked out to sea, watching a white yacht in the

distance. It looked so calm and peaceful. So pretty. Almost worth painting.

But she didn't have her easel or paints. It was just herself and her dog.

And that's all it's ever going to be.

Matteo's anxiety levels soared once he got into the car that would take him to Krystiana's villa. He knew she was back. He'd been notified the second she came back, her ID having flagged up a special program in the airport.

When his secretary had told him he'd had to fight the urge to go after her straight away, knowing there was no point in doing so until the new law had been passed. He wanted to present it as a *fait accompli.*

He'd missed her so much, and when he'd learnt that she had flown to Rome he'd wondered if she was ever going to come back. But she had, and he had taken some comfort in knowing that she was back on the island. He had stood each evening on his balcony, looking out towards where he knew her villa was, imagining that she was looking at the palace on the hill so far away...

It was a romantic notion, he knew, and probably a bit silly, but it was because he was heartsick, missing her like crazy. He knew that once he saw her again he would be able to tell her everything he had been doing. He would apologise profusely and hopefully—*hopefully*—she would take him back.

But she might not. He'd hurt her—he knew that—and she might not want to risk that again. Plus there'd be the whole thing of being back in the public eye again. He'd already ordered the press to stay away from her villa and her place of work, to give her some chance of returning to normal. He'd even taken one newspaper to court, taken legal action against them harassing her, and thankfully they'd obeyed the order.

Everyone missed her. Mara wanted her back. Alex talked about her. Well, mostly it was about Bruno, but still…

As the sleek, dark vehicle pulled to a halt outside her refurbished villa he felt the butterflies in his stomach all launch into flight at once. His heart pounded, his mouth and throat went very dry, and it took him a few moments to get out of the car. When he did, his legs felt as if they would go out from under him.

He was met with a flashback of what the place had looked like after the crash. The debris, the rubble… The accident that had caused their love to happen.

It was weird how life worked. If there'd been no accident she wouldn't have stayed at the palace and he wouldn't have got to know her, to fall in love with her.

He glanced at the windows. Had she seen him yet?

Straightening his jacket, he walked up to the door and knocked, his heart hammering, sweat beading his armpits.

There was no answer. So he knocked again.

A silver-haired head popped up over the fence next door. 'Hello? Are you after Krystiana? Oh, my God! It's *you*!' The head disappeared as the woman next door curtsied. 'Your Majesty!'

'Has she gone out?'

'She doesn't get back until late these days.'

'Where is she? Work?'

'No, no. She goes down to the beach with the dog.'

He turned to look down at the long sweep of golden sand far in the distance. 'That beach?'

'I guess so. I'm not sure.'

'Thank you. What's your name?'

'Anna.'

'Thank you, Anna. I would be grateful if you didn't mention this visit to anyone just yet.'

'Of course not.' She made a zipping motion across her lips and smiled.

He smiled his thanks. A reprieve. A moment or two in which he could gather himself some more.

He got back into the car and gave the order to his driver. 'Take me to the beach.'

'Yes, sir.' And the driver fired the engine.

Sitting on the sand, looking out to sea, as she often did, she thought about all that had happened in her life to bring her to this spot. The quirks of fate. The actions of others and how they could impact on your own life and the choices you had to make.

If she'd not been part of Dr Bonetti's practice... If her Aunt Carolina had lived somewhere else... If her parents hadn't divorced...

No wonder she wanted as much control over her own life as she could get.

She was sitting there, drizzling sand through her fingers, when she felt a prickling on the back of her neck. As if she was being watched.

Krystiana turned around...curious, cautious...her heartbeat increasing slightly, searching for a pair of eyes, hoping to brush it off as a flight of fancy, or that perhaps it was just another dogwalker, or a fisherman come down to the coast.

But it wasn't a dogwalker or a fisherman.

It was a king.

Matteo stood tall and proud, his dark form silhouetted against the sun as he walked across the sand directly towards her. She scrambled to her feet, dusting off the sand from her clothes, her heart thudding away like a jackhammer.

Why was he here? After all this time?

What was left for them to say to each other?

Far behind him, blocking access to the beach, were security guards so they could have privacy. She saw their dark-suited forms, the sun glancing off their sunglasses.

She fought the need to run towards him, to fall into his arms. But her love for him had almost broken her so she held firm, letting him come to *her*. If he was here to make an apology, then he could do all the work.

He looked as handsome as ever. Maybe even more so. Was he taller? Or was it just a different bearing he had? That somehow becoming King had changed him?

'*Buonasera*, Matteo.'

'*Dobyr wieczór*, Krystiana.'

She was surprised to hear her own language. 'You learned Polish?'

'A little.'

'That's good.' She sucked in a huge breath. 'What brings you here?'

'I came to ask for your forgiveness.'

Forgiveness?

Krystiana's heart almost leapt from her chest. 'Why?'

'Because I love you and I can't live without you.'

Her cheeks flushed with heat at his words. Words she'd longed to hear him say, but words that put daggers into her heart. Why was he doing this? They couldn't be together! It was torture.

She looked down and away. 'Let's not go through this again.'

'I want you to come back with me, Krystiana,' he said.

No! Please don't say that to me! I can't go through this heartbreak!

'Matteo, no—'

'I changed the law.'

She looked up at him, shocked, her heart thudding. 'What?'

'I changed the law about kings not being allowed to marry who they wish. And even if it had been impossible for me to change it I would have come and fetched you anyway. We could have lived in sin.' He smiled.

She stared at him, open-mouthed. Surely he was joking? He'd changed something that had been practically written in stone since his country had begun writing its history? For *her*?

But it didn't matter what he'd done. The law wasn't the point. His lying to her was what had been the fault.

'But…'

'I'm sorry. So, so sorry! For hurting you. For making you think that I had lied to you.'

'You did.'

'But I didn't mean to! I was confused. Torn by everything that I was feeling for you. I kept trying to fight it, but I couldn't, and before I knew what was happening we were getting serious and—'

'Are you blaming *me* for this?'

'No! Absolutely not! You're blameless. I tried to make it feel as if it was your fault, but no, it was all mine. I knew what it would do to you and yet I still did it. I should have thought about how much you needed me to show you that I could be trusted, that I could be relied upon and I can be all those things! Because I'm thinking more clearly now than I have in my entire life!' He paused to gather himself again. 'I love you and I want to show the world that, and I want you to see that I also acted from a place of fear. Something I found hard to admit to myself. I'm a king. I was a prince. I never thought I'd want anyone ever again after my kidnapping and then you walked into my life. I tried to fight it. I did. I think you did, too. But something kept pulling us together and I'd already been through so much, I thought to myself that I could allow myself this brief moment of happiness and to hell with the consequences! I thought we could deal with them later.'

'Until your hand was forced.'

He nodded. 'I don't expect you to forgive me. Or to trust me. Not at first. But I am begging you and I will get on my hands and knees to ask you to give me the chance, again, to show you who I really am.'

'Who are you?' she asked, her voice almost trembling.

'A man who loves you. Who wants to marry you and keep you in my life for ever, until death do us part.'

It was everything she wanted to hear. And she wanted to trust him, so much!

'Your father hates me, we—'

'My father doesn't hate you. He was trying to protect me from getting hurt further down the line. Not realising how much we were already in love! But now he knows and he has given us his blessing.'

She was in shock. Not sure what to say. 'He has?'

'Yes. I'm sorry, Krystiana. Sorry I wasn't strong enough to do this in the first place. To have fought for you. But I couldn't do anything to change the law until I became King myself. Then I could put forward a new decree. These things take time, needing approval from my parliament, all that nonsense, and I couldn't tell you what I was doing, because I didn't want to give you false hope if I failed.'

He stepped forward, tucked a windblown tress of hair behind her ear. 'There could never be anyone else but you. It's always been you, Krystiana. Let me show you the truth of my love. The truth of my heart. That you can put your life and your heart into my hands and I will keep them safe. That I will cherish you and adore you for evermore.' And he made to kiss her.

She thought for just a moment. Hesitated, but then she closed her eyes in ecstasy as his lips touched hers and somehow, before she knew it, her arms were around his neck and she was pulling him close, revelling in being with him, kissing him, holding him, once again.

He had changed the law for her. And he was trying so hard to explain why he had acted the way that he had. And she could forgive him for that, because she'd known he'd been just as confused as she.

They could be together! She melted into the kiss, sinking against him.

'Are you sure you want me?' she asked him breathlessly. 'I'm complicated and I have faults and I get mad quickly and I—'

He smiled, laughing. 'I do.' And then he let her go, so that he could get down on one knee.

Reaching into his pocket, he pulled out a small red box, something that he had bought a long time ago, but had never had the chance to use. Opening it, he revealed a beautiful diamond solitaire ring, that winked and glittered in the low evening sun. Bruno dropped his ball, as if sensing the moment and came to sit by Matteo's side, looking questioningly at them both.

'Krystiana Szenac. You brought light into my life. Gave me hope where there was none and I cannot live without you. I love you so much! Will you do me the honour of becoming my Queen?'

Krystiana gasped, laughing.

He was looking up at her, smiling, hope in his eyes and she knew instantly where she wanted to be.

At his side.

'Yes! I will!' She held out her hand so that he could slide on the ring and it fitted perfectly! She gazed at it in awe, then she pulled him to his feet and kissed him.

The beach melted away, her sorrow melted away. Perhaps happiness did eventually come to those that waited?

She'd never thought so much joy could come from so much heartbreak.

Never thought that that amount of joy, could ever be hers.

EPILOGUE

'IS THIS ALL RIGHT?' Krystiana tried to speak without breaking her smile as she gave her newly learned royal wave from the car touring through Tamoura.

Matteo glanced at her and smiled. 'It's perfect. As are you.'

They were travelling in a convoy of security, in front and behind of their car were mounted soldiers in their finery, the horses' hooves clip-clopping along the roads as Matteo and Krystiana and Alex were driven through streets filled with adoring, cheering crowds.

In front of them, Alex waved madly from a window, enjoying being the centre of attention, but after a mile or so of doing the same thing, the little girl got a bit bored and she sat beside Krystiana and laid a hand on her stepmother's barely swollen belly.

'When is the baby coming?' she asked. 'Today?'

Krystiana smiled at her stepdaughter and stroked her cheek lovingly. 'Not today, darling. Many more sleeps before the baby arrives.'

Alex sat back in her seat. 'I want a girl.'

'Do you? We'll have to wait and see. It could be a boy *or* a girl. Now, wave, *mio caro*. The people want to see you.'

She smiled at Matteo and clutched his hand with her

own, squeezing it tightly. It had been almost two years since Matteo had arrived on that beach to ask for her hand in marriage and since then so much had happened. So much had changed!

They'd got married in a beautiful cathedral, with the ceremony nationally televised. They'd honeymooned in the Caribbean, and when they'd returned home to begin their royal duties together Krystiana had discovered that she was pregnant with his child.

And life as *Queen* was everything she had hoped it would be. She wasn't just a figurehead. She wasn't just her husband's wife. She was a pioneer, bringing her work and experience to the forefront, opening up clinics and bringing awareness for those who had been abused, held hostage or kept as slaves. The press loved her and she made sure she used every public opportunity that she could to help those that were less fortunate.

She was still doing good.

Still helping.

And her heart was filled with love and hope for the future.

She wasn't alone any more.

The darkness and the fear were gone.

And love and light filled her heart every day.

* * * * *

PREGNANT BY THE PLAYBOY SURGEON

LUCY RYDER

MILLS & BOON

To anyone who's ever faced heartbreak and triumphed, this one's for you.

CHAPTER ONE

ER PHYSICIAN DR. DANIELLE STEVENS crossed the parking lot toward the employees' entrance of St. Mary's hospital in downtown Vancouver with the sneaky feeling that her life had been cursed. If she didn't know better she would swear it was Friday the thirteenth and the universe was having fun at her expense.

She'd woken to rain—not exactly an unusual occurrence in Vancouver—and then discovered her shower was on the fritz and the water pipes were making alarming noises. Of course that meant she'd have to forgo her showers until she got someone to check it out. If that hadn't been bad enough, she'd been out of coffee because she'd forgotten to stop at the supermarket and stock up on the basics. Basics like coffee, peanut butter, cheese curls and hair conditioner. Which meant not only was she caffeine-deprived, she was also starving and having a hair day from hell.

Then she'd found an unwelcome gift—a half-chewed bird missing its head—courtesy of her neighbor Hilda Frauenbach's cat Axel.

Yuck.

And, because her car was *still* in the workshop, she'd had to hotfoot it ten blocks in the pouring rain.

Good times.

Good times that were bound to continue rolling because although today might not be the thirteenth, it *was* Friday. And Friday nights in the ER could only be described as the second level of hell, because by the end of the work week any good sense people might have decreased in direct proportion to the amount of alcohol they consumed.

Trying to ignore the sneaky feeling that her life was unraveling, Dani felt her hip vibrate and paused to dig her phone out of her shoulder bag.

Thinking it was her mechanic, with yet another lame excuse as to why her car hadn't been fixed, she swiped irritably at the screen only to discover a Facebook notification inviting her to check on what Richard Ashford-Hall the Turd—oops, the Third—was doing in Cabo Mexico.

She took great pleasure in deleting the notification with a decisive jab. "No," she told the screen firmly, ignoring the sick, shaky feeling she usually got when Richard's name was mentioned. "I do *not* want to see what that sick, cheating rat-fink bastard is up to now, thank you very much."

And frankly, she had even less interest in seeing with whom he was doing it. She just hoped the woman knew what she was getting herself into.

She hadn't but that chapter in her life was closed.

Thank God.

She just wished people would stop reminding her of how stupid, naïve and trusting she'd been—or how fabulous her life could have been if she'd been prepared to stay married to a serial liar, a habitual cheater and an all-round spoilt man-brat.

She shivered as memories of her marriage assailed her. She'd rather be living on a houseboat that was falling to pieces with questionable plumbing, eating peanut butter and cheese curls for the rest of eternity than be back in the vipers' pit that was the Ashford-Hall family.

Heck, she'd rather be dealing with Axel's unsuspecting gifts than having to deal with spoilt, entitled rich boys and their creepy friends.

Noticing there was a voice message from the mechanic, Dani accessed it, grimacing when, "Hey, Sweetness!" emerged loudly. She quickly turned down the volume before someone overheard. "Listen, it's about your car. Are you sure you don't want me to contact a friend who can give you a good deal on a trade-in for this wreck? I'm sure we could work out some kind of payment arrangement," he said.

His voice was heavy with insinuation that made her skin crawl—*double yuck*—and reminded her of the men belonging to the super-elite club her ex had belonged to.

"Besides, there's a whole bunch of frayed wires that I'm having a hard time identifying and there's more rust here than an old tug boat. Call me. *Anytime*."

Annoyed, she called the mechanic back and got the workshop's answering machine because the work week had already ended. *Damn*.

"This is Danielle Stevens," she said firmly. "Negative on the trade-in and the intro to your friend."

She was pretty sure the guy had illegal contacts, and she had no intention of acquiring stolen property. She might want to do things as cheaply as possible but buying a hot car wasn't one of them.

"Just fix my car!" she yelled. About to disconnect, she added a better late than never "please," because her mom had taught her that people tended not to respond positively to rudeness.

Drawing in a lungful of air, she held it for a couple of seconds before slowly expelling it along with her irritation.

There. Look at her being all Zen and going with the flow.

Okay, so maybe she wasn't going with the flow so much as dealing. Besides, it wasn't like dealing was anything new. So she was going to be without her car again this weekend? No big deal. It just meant she'd be walking the gazillion blocks to the marina after her shift. She'd done that before and survived too. It had been in her student days but she was still young, right—if thirty could be called young—and she was pretty sure a six-hundred-mile walk was good for her.

Besides, hadn't she noticed just yesterday that her jeans were getting a little tight? This way she could get that much-needed exercise she was always promising herself without having to give up peanut butter or cheese curls.

It would be good for her. Great, even. Unlike the two years she'd spent as Mrs. Ashford-Hall. Two years she could never get back. Two years—make that three—she would give anything to erase from her memory.

Muttering about the questionable heritage of the entire male race—car mechanics, landlords and ex-husbands especially—she stepped out from behind a line of parked cars just as an SUV roared past, hooting at her, the dumb woman not looking where she was going, and drenching her with a lovely mix of dirt, rainwater and God knew what else in the process.

She gave a gasping shriek and lurched backward, arms windmilling frantically as she stumbled over the uneven surface of the road. The next instant she collided with the bumper behind her and went down like a felled cypress.

Knocked from her hand, her phone went one way and her shoulder bag the other, spilling its contents across the asphalt.

Stunned, and spluttering with shock at finding herself

sprawled in the road, Dani closed her eyes for a dozen rapid heartbeats, wondering what the hell she'd done to deserve this day. She felt movement in the air around her and opened her eyes to see a pair of concerned moss-green eyes looking down at her from about a foot away.

Whoa. Where did he come from?

Pretty sure she wasn't dead, she blinked up into a face so ruggedly beautiful it might easily have graced the silver screen—or her most private fantasies if she hadn't been taking a kind of permanent hiatus from the entire male race.

Even so… She couldn't prevent her fascinated gaze from taking in a high, broad forehead surrounded by thick dark glossy hair, high cheekbones, strong nose, square jaw and a firm, masculine mouth perfectly framed by a couple-hours-past-five-o'clock shadow.

The stubble gave his square jaw a toughness that suggested he was Alpha to the bone and didn't care who knew it. For a split second she had an overwhelming urge to reach out and trace his sculpted mouth, maybe feel that rough, obvious sign of masculinity…but that would just be the shock talking.

Her fingers tingled, as though she'd given in to the impulse to touch his jaw, and it took another couple of beats to realize he was talking.

"You okay?"

The rough tones slid across her senses like a mini-orgasm and she froze as unwelcome tingles spread to places deep inside her that had been dead for three long years. She looked down, expecting to see her clothes melted right off her body or maybe steam rising from the soaked fabric because he was hotness personified.

Panic immediately gripped her throat at the realization. *Oh, no*, she instructed herself firmly. *Absolutely no tingling for anything with a Y-chromosome. You're done with the whole male race, remember?*

Done. Finished. *Finito.*

"Ma'am, did you hit your head?"

Ma'am? Seriously? Since when was she a "ma'am" to a hot guy? She wasn't *that* old and, looking at the fine laugh lines at the corners of his eyes, she was pretty sure she was a good bit younger than he was.

Realizing that she was staring up at him like an idiot, she opened her mouth to say *I'm fine,* because that was her mantra, and was mortified when a rasp emerged instead. It looked as if her breath had been knocked out along with her remaining brain cells.

Desperate to regain her dignity, she shoved dripping hair out of her eyes and sat up, biting her lip to prevent a moan from emerging when pain radiated out from her hip and elbow.

Before she could stand, he dropped a large warm hand on her shoulder—probably to stop her from throwing herself at him, because she could totally see that happening to him.

With other women, she amended hastily. *Not her.* Nope, she was made of much sterner stuff and she'd given up on his species.

"Stay there a moment," he ordered but he needn't have bothered.

She'd spent her entire marriage being ordered around and she was done taking orders from anyone not responsible for her salary. Besides, she was sitting in a cold puddle of rainwater that was soaking into her jeans and sweater, finding its way into some pretty uncomfortable places.

"Um…" Great—now she was speechless. "I don't think so," she muttered, scrambling to her feet and wincing as a host of places hurt. Chief among them her pride.

It was then she realized that he was holding her shoulder bag in one large tanned hand and gathering up its scattered contents. He should have looked ridiculous but the feminine accessory just made him appear more masculine, if that was possible.

Balanced effortlessly on the balls of his feet, he reached for an unopened box of tampons and had her groaning in embarrassment—although she had no idea why. She was a doctor, for heaven's sake, and it wasn't as if it had burst open, scattering tampons all over Vancouver.

Sunglasses followed, and when he picked up the latest Janet Evanovich novel that she'd bought a couple days ago instead of groceries, he paused, turning to the back so he could read the blurb.

She tried to grab it but he held it out of reach until he'd finished. "Two hot guys?" he queried curiously, as though *she* was the crazy fictional character hooked on a hot cop and an even hotter bounty hunter.

Rolling her eyes, she grabbed the book, her bag and began stuffing everything inside. What she didn't see was her phone or her wallet, which made her panic because it held her last twenty dollars in change. Dani glanced around to find her rescuer holding the battered leather wallet and checking out her hospital ID badge—the one with the picture where she looked like a complete psycho—tilting his head as he studied the photo.

He looked amused, damn him.

With a sound that resembled a panicked squawk, she snatched it from him and stuffed it into the depths of her bag, ignoring the grin and the one arched brow that filled her with irritated envy because she'd have *killed* to have had that talent during her marriage. A talent that conveyed a whole host of emotions from disbelief and skepticism to outright condescension.

His was filled with a masculine amusement that threatened to derail her thought processes.

Out of the corner of her eye she finally spied her phone, and had to get down on all fours and really stretch to retrieve it from under a nearby car. With it finally in her hand she turned—in time to catch him staring at her backside.

She must have made a sound of protest—okay, more of a protesting squawk—because his teeth flashed as his green gaze slowly rose up the front of her dirty, soaked sweater to linger on her mouth before lifting to her eyes.

And, wow. Look at that, she thought with horror as her nipples tightened into painful little points of arousal. Seemed her body wasn't dead after all.

"I'm taking a break from anything with a Y-chromosome," she blurted out, and wanted to crawl back under the car when his low chuckle slid across her senses like rough velvet, sending goose bumps skittering across her skin.

Heat rose up her neck into her cheeks and she gave in to the urge to cover her face in the guise of shoving her hair off her face. *Oh God.* What the heck was wrong with her mouth today?

"Good to know," he drawled. "Though it does explain the expiration date."

Huh? Peeking through her fingers, she found him holding up a square foil package that looked suspiciously like…*a condom*? Her eyes widened and she backed away from it as though it might bite.

"Um… I…uh," she stuttered, looking around frantically for an escape route while fighting a hysterical laugh—because she hadn't needed one of those in so long she probably wouldn't know what to do with it. "That's not…" She shook her head desperately and backed away. "Nope. *Definitely* not m-mine."

She scrubbed both hands down her face and moaned in embarrassment when he bent his knees to peer straight into her eyes. *God. He was even hotter up close.*

"You sure you're okay? You took a pretty hard fall."

She was absolutely *not* going to discuss her graceless tumble, her sore bottom or anything else. "I'm fine, really," she said quickly, desperately wishing it was true, desperately wishing she could just disappear. Because it was bad enough that anyone had witnessed the embarrassing incident. That it was the hottest guy in the Northern hemisphere just proved her theory that the universe was out to get her.

"What about this?" he asked, holding up the unopened condom.

She nearly choked. "I…um…you keep it," she finished in a breathless rush.

"Thanks," he said wryly. "But what if *you* need it?"

She pressed her lips together and shook her head frantically. "I won't," she assured him hurriedly. "I'm taking a break, remember?"

His mouth curled in a half-grin that was filled with wicked trouble as he reached out to tuck a wet curl behind her ear. "So you said."

The move was so unexpected that she stilled, feeling the rough pads of his fingers brush the sensitive skin of her ear. Unexpected because it sent a bunch of pleasurable sensations skittering across her skin. And unexpected because…because she couldn't remember the last time a man had touched her; the last time she'd actually *wanted* a man to touch her.

And she suddenly did. With frightening need.

Ack!

That it was happening now with a complete stranger was more than a little unnerving.

She licked her lips and shifted nervously.

"Just out of curiosity…" Hot Guy murmured.

He was clearly oblivious to the melting going on inside her head…and, fine, in her thighs too. Melting that left her dizzy and a little too turned on for comfort.

"Does that mean you're currently into women, then?" He looked intrigued, as if he was picturing her kissing another woman when she'd been picturing kissing him.

"What?" Her mouth dropped open and the dizziness vanished. *"No!"* she practically yelped, knocking his hand aside and backing up a couple of steps. "Not that there's anything wrong with that but no, I am not into… *Sheesh!*" Rolling her eyes, she blew out an exasperated breath. "You are such a…a *guy*!"

"Guilty," he murmured, eyes wicked. "But I'm glad."

"Glad?"

"That Sweet 'n Sassy isn't batting for the other team."

Slapping a hand over her eyes, she blurted out, "Oh, my God!" She wished the ground would open up and swallow her. "Please, *please*, stop talking." She gave a laughing groan and pointed a finger in his direction. "And forget you heard that. In fact, forget the last ten minutes altogether because… Oh, *great*," she muttered, catching sight of a couple of co-workers at the entrance, gesturing at her to hurry up and pointing at their watches. "Gotta go."

She was about to step into the road when she was brought up short against a warm, hard—extremely hard—chest as a car whooshed past. "Careful," he murmured in her ear and for the second time in ten minutes Dani experienced that full-body shiver.

Yeah, Dani, she lectured herself silently as her knees wobbled. *Great advice.* She'd be wise to heed it.

Fortunately it gave her the impetus she needed to mutter an apology and limp across the road toward the employee entrance. Safely on the other side, she felt inexplicably drawn to look over her shoulder—only to find him watching her retreat, a small baffled smile curving that incredibly sexy mouth. As though he couldn't believe what he'd just experienced.

"Thank you," she called out, ignoring the niggling feeling in her gut that she was walking away from something good. Something exciting and…terrifying.

His mouth curved. "Any time."

She paused again, unsure why she couldn't seem to walk away, because she was pretty sure she should be running.

For long seconds they eyed each other across the wet road, until he finally gave a low laugh and asked in a rough, deep voice that slid into places she hadn't known were lonely, "Are you sure you won't reconsider your embargo?"

Was she?

"Nope," she said firmly, shaking her head with jerky exaggerated movements that should convince him—or was that her? So for good measure she added; "I most definitely will *not*."

Liar. You so would.

He was silent for a long beat, his gaze searching, before finally nodding. "My loss," he said and dug his keys out of his pocket. "See you around, sweet thing."

The sentiment that just fifteen minutes ago had made her want to gag filled her with a warm pleasure that no doubt came from hitting her head. Then her brain finally caught up and she gave herself a mental head-slap.

He hadn't meant anything by that parting shot, she told herself as she reluctantly turned away. Men flirted all the time. It was a kind of pastime…like drinking beer, burping and cheating. Besides, she had enough problems without adding a tall, sexy stranger with a kind streak to her things to obsess about.

The most pressing thing, she decided as she hobbled up the ramp, being that she was late for her shift and looked as if she'd been moonlighting as a mud wrestler.

Dylan St. James found himself smiling as he headed toward his Jeep. There hadn't been a whole lot to smile about lately but the hot little mess he'd just walked away from had done what no one else had in far too long. She'd taken him out of his head and made him smile—laugh, even—which was a miracle considering everything that had happened in the last two years.

He'd lost his grandfather after a long, protracted battle with esophageal cancer and a friend to a climbing accident—all in the space of two months. Reeling from the double whammy, he'd accepted a temporary commission on a West African Mercy Ship, thinking the change would help him deal.

He'd immersed himself in doing what he loved: helping people—kids especially—get to live relatively normal lives with his skill as an orthopedic reconstruction surgeon. Helping those who usually didn't have access to modern medical care.

He'd met some great people and had fallen into a casual relationship with an on-board coordinator—a relationship that had been more about propinquity and convenience than any deeper feelings, on his part at least. It didn't say much for him but he'd thought they were friends with on-again, off-again benefits—right up until Simone had dropped her bombshell…she was pregnant.

Yeah. Big shock that, considering that they'd lately been

more off than on and he'd never had unprotected sex. *Ever.*
Still, that hadn't been the worst of it, because although
he'd been willing to face up to his responsibility—without
getting married to someone he didn't have deep feelings
for—she'd had other ideas.

Ideas that had emerged one night when he'd finished
surgery earlier than expected and headed over to the mess
hall for dinner, inadvertently overhearing Simone and an
Australian nurse discussing him—or rather his family's
money. Simone had been bragging that she'd managed to
catch herself a rich Canadian doctor—her sole reason for
working in such God-forsaken countries on a boat that
didn't even have a swimming pool.

As if that was important on a hospital ship.

He'd been about to reveal himself when he'd heard
something even more enlightening—that the baby she
was trying to pass off as his belonged to a Mercy Ship
colleague. A *married* colleague.

To say she'd been shocked when she'd looked up and
seen him standing there was an understatement. There'd
been tears, pleas, threats and hysterics but in the end he
had been done. He'd finished his contract and come home.

She wasn't the first woman who'd thrown herself at
him after learning that his family owned the largest ship-
building company in the Pacific Rim and she probably
wouldn't be the last. He'd just have to be more careful, that
was all. Besides, he wasn't interested in marrying someone he couldn't see himself growing old with.

Not that he was against marriage. He wasn't. But
he hadn't found a woman who wanted *him* rather than
what his family's money could do for her. Hadn't found
a woman with whom he could build the kind of relationship his parents and grandparents had.

He sometimes wondered if he ever would.

Arriving at his Jeep, he keyed open the door and slid inside. About to shove his key into the ignition, he realized he was still holding the condom. Tossing it into his console, he chuckled at the horrified embarrassment on the woman's face and her insistence that it wasn't hers.

Now, *there* was a feisty little bundle of contradictions, he thought, picturing her huge gray eyes as she'd blurted out that she was taking a break from anything with a Y-chromosome, stirring up all kinds of mixed emotions he hadn't been ready to feel.

Shaking his head at himself, Dylan cranked up the engine. Reversing out of the parking bay, he drove toward the exit, feeling much more cheerful than when he'd landed a few hours ago. He had a few days to catch up with his family and then he'd be back in the saddle at St. Mary's as a consultant.

And if the thought of seeing a certain hot little doctor again made him smile with anticipation he chalked it up to the long flight, three days without much sleep and eight months of celibacy.

CHAPTER TWO

DYLAN FELL BACK into the hospital routine as if he'd only been gone for a week. His old partner, Steve Randall, had been so delighted to have him back that he'd cleared his calendar and headed for the South Pacific, leaving Dylan to handle any upcoming surgeries that couldn't be postponed.

Although he'd have liked to say he was too busy to think about the sweet little brunette from the parking lot, it was kind of disconcerting to discover that he was as susceptible as the next guy to a pair of soft gray eyes and a sweet sassy smile.

He was thirty-five, for God's sake. A surgeon. He'd been dating for twenty years; having sex for almost that long, and he'd never—not once—thought about a woman during surgery.

That was until he'd looked into the smoky eyes of an irresistible brunette as he'd reached for the scattered contents of her purse.

Not only had she invaded his dreams but the Zen-like calm he usually adopted in the OR as well. It had to stop. Distraction was costly—especially in his profession. With Steve off in Bora Bora he didn't have time to take a lunch break, let alone think about a woman determined to stick to her man embargo.

He wondered what had happened to leave her so wary and mistrustful of men. And if he experienced an inexplicable urge to find the guy who'd done it and pound him into the ground it was only because he had two sisters and would do the same to any guy who messed with them.

Yeah, he assured himself, he was feeling protective in an entirely *fraternal* way. It certainly wasn't because his ego had taken a little beating. Besides, he knew next to nothing about her other than the fact she worked at St. Mary's. Even if he'd wanted to prove to himself that he'd imagined the entire incident, St. Mary's was a large hospital. She could work anywhere, and he didn't have the time—or the inclination, he assured himself—to hunt down a woman who wasn't interested.

It was just as well that she'd turned him down because he wasn't looking for anything more than the occasional good time with an attractive woman who knew the score. And since she hadn't seemed like the "occasional" type, or even a "good-time" girl, he would forget all about her and focus on cementing his professional reputation.

With back-to-back appointments and two solid days of surgery, by the Thursday evening of the following week Dylan was ready to call it a day. He grabbed his leather jacket and turned off the lights as he walked through the darkened waiting room. It was after eight and he had plans to meet up with a couple of kayaking friends at a sports bar near the marina. He hadn't seen them since his return and was eager to get back on the water.

He dug in his pocket for his Jeep keys and was about to lock the door behind him when his cell phone rang. A quick glance at the caller ID had him smiling. "Hi, Mom, what's wrong?"

His mother's light, familiar laugh floated through the phone. "Nothing's *wrong*, darling. I'm just calling to find out how my favorite son is doing on his first week back and to invite him to dinner."

"Mom, I'm your *only* son."

"Still my favorite," she teased. "But don't tell your sisters."

Dylan chuckled, because he'd heard his mother tell his sisters the same thing. "I'd love dinner, Mom but I'm on call. It'll take too long to get back from West Vancouver if there's an emergency."

"That's the beauty of my plan, darling," said Vivian St. James smugly. "We're having dinner at the Regis with the Hendersons. You remember Fred and Daphne, don't you?"

For some reason his mother's overly bright, chatty tone put Dylan's senses on alert. He grimaced when her next words confirmed his suspicions.

"Well, their daughter Abigail is back from Europe, and we can all have a wonderful dinner tog—"

And there it was. "Mom," he interrupted gently. "Don't."

There was a short pause, then a bewildered, "Don't what, darling?"

Dylan sighed. "You're trying to set me up again."

"Don't be silly!"

His mother gave a laughing snort but Dylan could tell that he'd hit the nail on the head. His mother was trying to get him a date in the hopes that it would lead to the altar. She wanted grandchildren before she died—which was ridiculous because she wasn't yet sixty.

"Even if that's true, young man," she said in her "mom voice"—the one that said he was being deliberately unco-operative. "And I'm not saying it is, you need to get out and meet people. Women."

"Mom, I meet women every day. Besides, I *have* met someone," he heard himself say.

And then he wanted to slap himself upside the head for giving his mother false hope. Vivian would hound him until she met the mythical woman herself. He loved his mother fiercely but if she thought one of her brood needed a helping nudge in the right direction she wasn't above using both hands.

"You have?"

Oh, hell. His mother sounded so delighted at the prospect that her son was dating again after his friend's death. She thought all her children were amazing and wouldn't be able to resist meddling.

"That's wonderful, darling. Where did you meet and when can I meet her?"

No pressure there, St. James, he thought with amused exasperation. "Who says it's a her?"

There was a moment's stunned silence on the other end of the phone and Dylan could picture his mother's expression.

Then Vivian snorted. "Dylan Thomas St. James!" She chuckled. "There's nothing wrong with being gay but I know you're only trying to wind me up. So, when can I meet her?"

Fortunately he was saved from replying when his phone beeped an incoming call. *Talk about being saved by the beep.*

"Just a sec, Mom. I've got a call coming in." With a flick of his hand he accessed the call. "St. James."

"This is Rona Sheppard from the ER," a brisk voice said. "Are you still in the building?"

"I am," he said, shrugging out of his leather jacket and reaching for his lab coat because any call that included the words *Are you still in the building?* meant he wouldn't be going anywhere for a while. "What's up?"

"A young child with a traumatic arm injury," the supervisor said briskly. "ETA three minutes—vitals shaky."

"I'll be right down," he said before disconnecting, his mind already flying ahead to the case.

He was about to shove his phone in his pocket when he remembered his mother.

"Mom," he said, returning to his call. "I'm sorry but I won't make dinner tonight." He didn't say he'd been headed to Harry's on the marina anyway—mostly to prevent the lecture he knew would follow about the kind of women who hung out in sports bars.

"Oh, darn." Vivian sighed. "I've been giddy with happiness since you got back."

She very obviously *didn't* say she was disappointed that he wouldn't meet their friends' daughter but Dylan could read between the lines.

"Is it something bad?"

"I don't know yet but it's a little kid."

"Oh, darling, I know how much you hate these cases. Call me when you can."

He said goodbye and disconnected, taking the stairs instead of waiting for the elevator, because traumatic injuries were always bad. That it was a child made it that much more urgent.

Dylan had spent enough time in the ER to appreciate that when children were involved emotions ran high. It was one of the worst parts of working in trauma and he held a huge respect for the people who dealt with it on a daily basis.

Even as he hit the swing doors and headed down the hallway he could hear someone rapping out orders in a soft, feminine voice that sent skitters of recognition across his skin. From the rapid-fire instructions, he knew even before he approached the trauma bay that the patient had just arrived. Even more surprising was that right in the center of the chaos, directing proceedings, was the brunette from the parking lot.

The attending physician.

He didn't know why the sight of her so competently handling the emergency threw him but it did—enough that he paused at the entrance, his gut clenching in a combination of dread and anticipation.

The kid, probably no more than six or seven, looked so tiny and fragile on the bed that he felt his heart squeeze before he had a chance to take an emotional step back. These were the cases that ripped at him. And he'd feel it all the more deeply if his team wasn't successful in reattaching the severed limb.

The sight of the blood-soaked compression dressing instantly sucked him back to West Africa where he'd spent the past two years replanting limbs torn off in explosions and artillery fire or lopped off by *panga*-wielding soldiers. The young victims had been the hardest to deal with because often there had been no limbs to reattach, or necrosis and infection had already set in by the time they got to him.

It meant a lifetime of unnecessary pain, suffering and disability—if they survived—and it made him wonder what the hell it was all for.

Lost in horrific memories, he scarcely heard the attending ask, "Who's the ortho on duty? Has someone called?"

It was only when he heard his name that he was jolted back to reality.

"Rona said Dr. St. James is on his way."

Momentarily rattled by the abrupt shift from memories that were still far too fresh and vivid in his mind to the bright lights of the trauma bay, Dylan watched her frown and pull the stethoscope from around her neck.

"Isn't that the new guy everyone's swooning over?" she asked absently, fitting the scope in her ears and sliding the metal disc over the boy's chest. Without waiting for an answer, she addressed the second nurse. "Paula, we're going to need more blood before we can get him into surgery. Set up another bag and make sure we have enough on standby. Let's hope Hot New Guy's not just a pretty face. The last thing *this* little guy needs is to grow up without an arm."

Taking a deep breath, Dylan shoved the memories aside and stepped into the room as she turned to the monitor.

Removing the stethoscope, she impatiently slung it around her neck. "Dammit, where *is* he? Amy, call him again. We—"

"No need," he interrupted, his eyes already assessing the boy's condition as he reached out and pressed his fingers against the brachial artery above the boy's severed arm. It was slow and ragged, barely there.

Hyper-aware of her just two feet away, he knew the instant she recognized him by her audible inhalation. His peripheral vision caught the way her body stilled and he looked up into eyes wide with shocked recognition.

Holding her gaze, he kept his voice low and soothing. "What kind of injury do we have, Dr...? Uh... Stevens, is it?"

"I... I..." she stuttered.

Dylan didn't know whether to feel pleased or insulted that she appeared so rattled. The blond nurse must have also noticed her reaction because her gaze narrowed, bouncing between them as though she sensed the abrupt tension in the room.

"Dani?" the nurse said, not pausing in bagging the intubated child. "You okay?"

The words clearly jolted her and she abruptly blinked, going from in control to flustered in the blink of an eye. "He's…uh…he…um—" She frowned and firmed her soft mouth as she visibly pulled herself together. "He lost his arm an inch above the left epicondyle."

The nurses looked at her in surprise before sharing a significant look.

"I can see that," he said quietly, ignoring the silent exchange. "Did the EMTs say how it happened?"

A flush stained her cheeks and she grimaced before sucking in a steadying breath. In the blink of an eye she was once again the cool, collected physician. "Apparently a plate glass window fell on him," she reported briskly, with only the barest hint of a tremor.

"Is it a crush injury?"

"No," she clipped out. "Fairly clean. I…uh… I had to clamp the brachial artery to raise his pressure but I'm not sure how much longer he can wait for surgery."

She'd made the right call. He nodded to the cooler on a nearby trolley. "What's the condition of the arm?"

"I haven't had a chance to look but the EMT said it's intact."

He lifted the blood-soaked compression bandage and noticed that a clamp had been applied to the end of the artery. After a quick assessment of the splintered edges of the bone, he gave a short nod as he turned to head for the door.

"Take X-rays of both sections and bring him up as soon as he's ready. We'll be waiting."

On his way up to surgery, he punched in a number on his phone.

"Kate," he said, when the doctor answered on the third ring. "It's Dylan—how soon can you get to OR?"

"About twenty minutes to a half-hour, why?"

"I need your needlepoint skills for a replantation."

The older doctor gave a low laugh. "I'm not on call, Dylan."

"I know," he admitted. "But when a kid loses his arm you're my go-to vascular. I need you on my team."

He heard her suck in a sharp breath. "A kid? Please don't tell me it's a crush injury."

He pressed the button to call for the elevator. "It's not a crush injury. A sheet of plate glass lopped off his arm an inch above the elbow. There's some damage, obviously but it should be straightforward."

He heard her sigh. "All right—start without me. I'm on my way."

While he waited for the elevator, he paged the on-call vascular surgeon, as well as a plastic surgeon. Once the elevator arrived he stepped inside, his mind already on the procedure ahead rather than the woman he'd left in the ER.

There would be time enough later to think about his reaction to seeing her again—that one-two punch he'd taken to the chest when those startled gray eyes had locked with his. She'd looked stunned and flustered, as though she hadn't expected to see him again. And a bit dismayed—which she hadn't been quick enough to conceal.

He'd felt kind of stunned himself and it wasn't because one glance into those smoky eyes had dropped the bottom out of his gut. *What the hell had that been about?*

No, he assured himself, he'd just been surprised. Surprised at finding her directing proceedings without any trace of the charming clumsiness she'd displayed at their first meeting. Yep—just surprise at finding her without even trying, he told himself.

It couldn't possibly be that when he'd seen her something deep inside him had stilled and said, *There you are*.

Because that would be crazy when there wasn't a hint of insanity in his family tree.

When the elevator doors opened, Dani and the RN pushed the gurney out and rushed it down the hallway to Surgery. She'd left Amy behind in the ER, taking care of their little patient's distraught mother, who'd arrived just as they were getting into the elevator.

Seeing her baby lying almost lifeless on the large, adult-sized bed had been almost too much for pregnant Christine Nolan. Dani had told Amy to give her something to calm her down before they had two patients on their hands.

The instant they pushed the gurney through the swing doors an OR nurse grabbed the cooler. "Room Four," she rapped out briskly. "They're waiting."

They quickly maneuvered down the passage to where a scrub nurse was holding the doors open, and even as she released the gurney Dani found her gaze drawn, despite herself, to the team gathered around the wall screen, studying the X-rays she'd taken ten minutes earlier.

Or rather her gaze was drawn inexorably toward one team member in particular.

As though sensing her presence, he turned, his gaze locking unerringly on to her. She ignored the way her pulse leapt at the sight of him, standing head and shoulders above everyone else in the room. Already dressed in his surgical scrubs, gowned and bandanna-ed, Dr. Hot-and-Hunky looked as if he owned his universe.

And was ready to rock hers.

Her face burned with mortification at the memory of their last two encounters and she hoped she could keep from humiliating herself a third time. What must he be thinking? she wondered. First, that she was clumsy and blurted out whatever came into her head; and second that she'd heard that deep bedroom voice of his and everything in her had come to a screeching halt.

She'd looked up into moss-green eyes surrounded by long, dark lashes and her mind had gone blank as a slate. And then he'd asked her about the wound and she'd replied with something so inane even a second-year med student would have blinked.

She just hoped no one had noticed and cringed because she knew everyone *had*. Especially him. *Oh God*, she thought as a fresh wave of embarrassment crawled up the back of her neck. She'd stood there frozen as if she was a teenager again and had found herself face to face with the hottest bad boy in school.

Realizing she was *still* standing there, Dani spun away to make a quick escape. She was almost through the doors when his voice—deep and dark and sinful—reached her.

"Dr. Stevens?"

Tempted to ignore him, she shoved aside the primitive urge to run and turned slowly, giving herself time to school her expression. She was a thirty-year-old professional, she reminded herself. She sucked in a steadying breath, hoping he couldn't see her inner chaos and terrified because she'd never been any good at hiding her emotions.

She just hoped she could keep her mouth from blurting out embarrassing inanities. "Yes?"

His gaze swept over her face to linger on her mouth and for one horrifying instant she thought he would mention their first meeting or…or even worse…ask about her unprofessional behavior in the ER.

Actually, no. Worse would be that he somehow *knew* that her first impulse had been to check her hair and straighten her posture. Fortunately she'd done neither. *Unfortunately* she'd embarrassed herself and surprised her colleagues by staring at him as though he'd popped through a tear in the space time continuum dressed like a Roman centurion.

Heck, even *that* wouldn't have shocked her as much.

He lifted a hand and, startled, she jerked back a couple of steps until her back hit the wall, her eyes wide. Embarrassment crawled up the back of her neck when she realized he was just scratching his jaw.

Way to totally overreact there, Dani.

She hastily glanced around to see if anyone had seen that clumsy panicked retreat and nearly sagged with relief when she saw that no one was paying them any attention.

Get a damn grip, Dani.

Concern darkened his gaze. "You okay?"

"Of course," she managed coolly. "Just in a hurry to… uh…" She gestured behind her. "Get back to the ER."

After a short pause he nodded, his eyes dropping briefly to the pulse tapping out frantic Morse code in her throat. She had to battle an overwhelming urge to cover that revealing little sign of agitation.

"Anything I should know about the boy?"

His deep voice, pouring over her like a benediction, should have relaxed her but instead it ratcheted her tension up a hundred notches.

"Allergies, medical conditions, any medication that he's on?"

"Uh…no," she said, clearing her throat. "His name is Timothy Nolan and he's seven years old. His mother says he's a normal, active little boy who loves ice hockey and dinosaurs. He's a Canucks supporter."

A smile lit his ruggedly handsome features, stealing her breath and sending her pulse lurching around like a drunken sailor on shore leave. When her knees gave an alarming wobble, she snapped her spine straight.

Stop looking at his smile, she snarled silently. *Handsome guys who flash million-dollar smiles can't be trusted. So walk away, nice and calm.*

"Well, we'll have to see that he gets to play hockey someday."

Relief that he wasn't going to mention her recent lapses almost had her knees buckling again.

That's good, Dani. Focus on your patient and not on your queasy stomach and wobbly knees.

"You can replant?" It could simply be the adrenaline let-down that was making her shaky and hyper-aware.

"The X-rays look good," he said and though she understood what he wasn't saying, she pressed on, "So Timmy will be normal again?"

He sent her a pained look and sighed. "I'll give it my best shot but I'm not a miracle-worker."

"That's not what I hear," she clipped out, almost rudely and flushed when one eyebrow rose up his forehead at her snippy tone.

But she wasn't about to be intimidated—not like that day almost sixteen years ago when another bad boy had caught her fascinated stare and with a slow smile had propped his shoulder against her locker. Leveling her with a sleepy, knowing look, he'd drawled, "Think you can handle what I've got, little girl?" and roared with laughter when she'd turned tail and bolted.

She felt exactly like that now but managed to lock her

knees before they ignored the imperative from her brain to stand firm. She held his gaze a little defiantly.

His brow wrinkled, as though her behavior surprised him.

No more than it was surprising the hell out of her too.

After a short pause he repeated, "We'll do our best."

She gave a curt nod and had turned to go again when his voice called her softly.

"Dr. Stevens?" He waited until her gaze met his. "Don't believe everything you hear."

Dani got the feeling he was talking about more than just the hospital gossip that had him sleeping with more women than there were days in the month. And *that* was only since his return. Not only was she sure the rumors were grossly exaggerated but she hadn't received any creepy vibes from him.

Maybe not but you didn't get any creepy vibes from Richard either, a little voice of reason reminded her. *At least, not before the wedding. And look how that turned out.*

When she didn't respond, Dr. St. James sighed and looked as if he wanted to say something more. She braced herself, ignoring the way her pulse increased.

But then the anesthetist called his name and all he said was, "I have to go."

And look at that. She could feel the rush of disappointment that he hadn't…*what*? Pushed her up against the wall and put his hands and mouth all over her?

Sheesh, woman. Get a grip. This is a surgical suite. And maybe you could stop looking at his mouth and remember that you're on sabbatical from men. Remember why you've given them up.

She turned away abruptly, determined to leave with

her dignity intact but yet again his voice—a rough slide of velvet against her skin—stopped her in her tracks.

"Oh, and Dr. Stevens…?"

Awareness skated across her and she wanted more than anything to escape.

He waited until she looked back before drawling softly, "I'm *not* just a pretty face."

She was embarrassed that he'd heard what she'd said in the ER but pride stiffened her spine and had her lying smoothly. "I wouldn't know."

She relaxed, inordinately pleased that she could be cool and professional—or at least pretend to be—beneath that intense green gaze. His hypnotic eyes held her hostage for a moment longer, then he nodded brusquely and turned away.

Before the door swung shut behind her she could hear the steady beeping of the monitors over her thundering pulse and she said a quick prayer for little Timmy—and one for the steady hands of those he'd been placed in.

Once in the elevator, away from prying eyes—especially intense green ones that seemed to see right through her—she sagged against the wall and locked her knees to keep from sliding to the floor. Pressing a shaky hand to her even shakier belly, she gave a ragged moan and banged her head against the side of the elevator a couple times, hoping to knock a little sense into her head.

Oh. My. God. She couldn't believe it. The guy she'd brushed off, then spent way too much time thinking about, was a surgeon…*at the very same hospital where she worked.* Not only *that,* he was the very same Dr. Hot Stuff all the female personnel—married *and* unmarried— were drooling over. And if *that* didn't have alarm bells shrieking away in the back of her mind, nothing would.

Not interested, she told herself firmly. She'd barely survived a relationship with one rich, handsome and hotly in demand man and she had no intention of melting for another.

Nope. No way. No how. Absolutely no melting.

But she'd *dreamed* about him, she was forced to admit. The type of dreams a girl never shared with *anyone*—not even her best friend. The types of dreams that made her blush just thinking about them, because she hadn't had a sexy dream since she was a shy, awkward teenager mooning over hot bad boys.

She would rather step in front of a bus than have him suspect that she was like every other woman, swooning when he turned his green eyes her way, ramping up her hormones while every nerve-ending, every strand of DNA, perked up and did a Mexican wave.

Look at me! her nipples had yelled.

The elevator doors opened and she was hugely relieved that the hallway was empty and she could enjoy her little freak-out in private. Instead of heading for the ER, she ducked into the bathroom and barely resisted the urge to shove her entire head under the cold water tap and drown herself.

She splashed her hot face instead and when she caught sight of her flushed cheeks and bright eyes, paused to give herself a stern lecture. *No brooding over hot, sexy surgeons with green eyes*, she told her reflection firmly. *At least until you can behave like a mature professional.*

On second thought, she should just stay away from the entire species altogether. Besides, he had even more women throwing themselves at him than Richard Ashford-Hall III. She wasn't *ever* going to be one of a crowd again. She would never put herself in a position where she had to fight for any man's attention. It was too humiliating to discover that no matter what you did you'd just never measure up.

Besides, she was damaged goods, wasn't she? And no man, Richard had told her cruelly, wanted damaged goods. If she couldn't do what she'd been put on the earth for—provide him with an heir—she was no good to anyone.

CHAPTER THREE

DESPITE THE FREQUENTLY frustrating cases and long, exhausting hours, Dani loved the ER. She loved the adrenaline and the challenge of emergency medicine; of saving lives and solving puzzling symptoms before her patients were transferred to the right specialist.

She dealt with new cases, new patients, all the time, and though it made for an exciting profession, she sometimes missed knowing what had happened to the critical patients she'd treated—missed the relationship that developed between patient and healthcare professional.

Sometimes the people they revived in the ER didn't make it, and sometimes they went on to live long, happy lives—she liked to think because her knowledge, skill and training had made it possible. But it was cases like little Timothy Nolan that grabbed her and didn't let go. It became a necessity, driven by some deep inner need, for her to follow up.

So when she heard that he was finally out of surgery Dani took advantage of the usual Thursday night lull and headed for the elevators, pressing the button for the tenth floor when the doors swished open.

She wanted to see for herself that he was okay, that everything she'd done for him had been enough to save his arm. *That*, she admitted to herself, was always a worry.

That she'd done enough, done her best…when sometimes her best wasn't always enough.

But at least Timmy was healthy, and the hands he'd been passed on to skilled. The best, according to the grapevine in Vancouver. She didn't know if that was fact, or just the opinion of too many starry-eyed women.

It was after two-thirty a.m. when she headed down the passage toward Pediatric ICU, hearing the thin wail of a terrified child punching through the stillness. She spared a moment to think about the parents of that sick child and what they must be going through. And if she grieved the fact that she would never experience those highs and lows of parenthood for herself, she shoved it deep where it couldn't hurt.

It couldn't hurt as long as she didn't think about it. And she'd certainly become adept at ignoring things she couldn't change.

Something else she'd ignored was thinking about… *him*. Then she walked past the nurses' station and saw him, standing at the window of a small private room in the ICU. With his feet spread wide, one arm folded across his wide chest and the opposite elbow resting on his wrist, while long tanned fingers scratched his jaw, he looked big and tough and just a little bit dangerous.

Still dressed in black scrubs, the soft material stretched across the width of his shoulders, he might have been an intimidating figure if not for the dark strands of hair sticking up in places, as though he'd spent the night shoving his fingers through it.

The rasp of his fingers against the eight-hours-past-five-o'clock shadow had her steps faltering along with her pulse. Her breath caught and for one panicked moment she wanted to turn and bolt before he saw her. But then common sense reasserted itself. She was entitled to check on a patient who had gone through her trauma bay. Besides, now that she'd seen him she was prepared. She was fine. She was—

His head turned abruptly and she felt pinned to the spot by the force of that laser-sharp gaze. She froze, and for just a split second his expression remained closed, intense and just a little bit somber. Her pulse lurched for another reason altogether and she felt her gut clench.

Oh God, something had gone wrong.

Then he blinked and the intensity cleared. A gleam of…well, something she wasn't ready to identify, lightened his gaze.

Rubbing her chilled arms, she took those last dozen steps toward him. "You look tired," she said quietly, a little jitter sneaking through her when one dark brow arched.

"I do?"

"Tired…" She forced her gaze to search his. "But satisfied."

Feeling inordinately proud that she'd managed a coolly professional observation when she was feeling so self-conscious, she turned to look through the window to where a young couple stood huddled by the bed, their expressions filled with a desperate kind of love. Her gaze went unerringly to the boy's left arm, swathed from shoulder to wrist in bandages. The small fingers looked swollen but the color was pink enough for relief to relax her shoulders.

"It went well?"

He shoved his hands into the pockets of his scrubs pants and rocked back on his heels. "Yeah…" he murmured.

Out of the corner of her eye she saw him turn to look at her, and steeled herself against that perceptive probe that seemed to see everything she wanted to hide.

Keeping her attention locked on the little family of three and her expression bland, she challenged softly, "So…he'll be able to play for the Canucks one day?"

His laugh was a rough slide of velvet against nerve-endings scraped raw by the past, the late hour and the reluctant knowledge that she was attracted—completely against her will—to a man who made her ex seem like an unpopular loner.

The self-deprecating amusement in its deep sound had Dani's gaze jumping to his. He looked mildly disconcerted, as though she'd surprised him but that was probably just a trick of the light. Surgeons—especially the hot, hunky ones—tended to think they had a private line to God.

"You don't ask for much, do you?"

"Are you telling me the rumors are wrong and you *are* just a pretty face?"

The look he sent her was filled with an irritated kind of exasperation. "What did I tell you about listening to gossip, Dr. Stevens?" he demanded, taking her arm and steering her to the door. "And, for your information, men aren't…*pretty*."

No, she thought, that square jaw, the bold slash of his cheekbones and the high, broad forehead could hardly be called anything as frivolous as "pretty." He was too strong for that, too virile. But there was no doubt he was a ruggedly handsome man—a man with the kind of masculine sexuality that made women weak at the knees.

And in the head, she reminded herself.

He looked so pained that Dani would have grinned if she hadn't been blinking in surprise at finding herself expertly maneuvered out of Pediatric ICU toward the bank of elevators.

She stopped abruptly, wondering how it had happened. "What are you doing?"

He paused to grin down at her and she had to steel herself against the impulse to return it. *Dammit*, she thought, *he's sneaky.*

"I'm going to buy you dinner."

Her eyes narrowed in suspicion. "Dinner?"

The door opened behind them and a couple of nurses emerged, their curious gazes taking in the long fingers wrapped around her upper arm and the almost intimate familiarity of their bodies.

Fighting embarrassment, Dani edged away. The last thing she needed was to be linked even casually to Dr. Hot-and-Hunky.

He muttered a curse and dropped his hand as well as his voice, turning away even as he nodded at the women. "Yeah, you know… That meal you eat at the end of the day."

"It's three a.m.," she felt compelled to point out, ignoring the jitter in her belly.

His grin was lightning-fast. "Yeah, and I'm starving. So how about it? I know this great place in the West Wing that serves turkey sandwiches and hot coffee any time of the day or night. The atmosphere isn't the best but at least it'll be quiet this time of night."

And that was kind of the problem, she decided. The quiet intimacy of the twenty-four-hour bistro on the ground floor was a far cry from the bright cafeteria in the East Wing. Then there was being alone with him in a dim booth… Something that smacked of a date—something she'd avoided since her divorce.

"I'm on shift," she hedged, determined not to spend any more time in his company than was professionally necessary. "I just came up to see how Timmy was doing before heading back."

He punched the call button. "He's doing better than expected but only time will tell." He leaned against the wall and studied her with an unreadable gaze. "But then, you already know that."

She inclined her head in agreement, pretending he wasn't making her nervous. "So, how is the ER?" he asked, his eyes taking on a glint of amusement. As though he knew exactly what he was doing to her.

"Hopping," she replied, feeling her eyelashes flutter and cursing the faint heat climbing up her neck into her face. "Which is why I should hurry back."

His lips twitched and amusement gleamed in the gaze holding hers. "It's like a morgue down there, isn't it?"

Caught out in her lie, Dani rubbed her nose and contemplated lying again. The elevator arrived and she stepped inside. He followed, punching the ground-floor button before leaning back against the wall. When she avoided looking at him he chuckled, the sound low and deep in the confined space. Finally, she couldn't stand the suspense and sneaked a peek at him—which he caught. His brow arched, his eyes filling with amused knowledge of her prevarication.

She sighed. "How did you know?"

"I remember my ER rotation and…" He hitched a shoulder, the move straining the seams of his scrub top. "You're here. If it was hopping you would have waited until the end of your shift to check up on me. Make sure I know what I'm doing."

Unable to dispute his logic, Dani rolled her eyes and reminded him smartly, "I'm taking a break."

"From Y-chromosomes or from the ER?"

He gave a crooked smile that was entirely too casual

and appealing for her peace of mind. It left her jittery because... Dammit, she didn't know the *because*. And that was what worried her.

"It's just coffee and turkey sandwiches with a colleague," he said, following her out of the elevator when the doors swished open on the ground floor. "Besides, I thought you'd want to know how the surgery went."

Danielle Stevens looked at him out of the corner of her suspicious eye. He could practically see the wheels grinding away in her head and he bit back a smile. If he'd wanted to delay her departure, he couldn't have picked a better way.

She frowned. "You want to discuss your patient with me?"

"Your patient too," he reminded her cheerfully, telling himself that she wasn't really his type and wondering why he was suddenly so sure that she was. She wasn't beautiful—at least not in a classic way—and she wasn't sophisticated. But there was just something so... *appealing* about her that his gaze kept being drawn back despite himself.

She'd shoved the jumbled mass of her dark curls into a messy topknot that left tendrils escaping every which way. Her nails were short and round and though she wore no rings, her hands were long and elegant, as though they were meant to wear beautiful things. She wore no make-up except a swipe of mascara on those long, lush lashes as a careless nod to feminine vanity.

He dropped his eyes to her wide, unpainted mouth, with its full bottom lip and slightly longer upper lip, and wondered if it was as soft as it looked...if it tasted as sweet as he'd dreamed.

She shook her head. "Not anymore." A long curl swung

against her cheek and she brushed it aside with unconscious impatience. "Not once I sign off."

And then there was all that wary mistrust in her heavily fringed gray eyes when she looked at him, as though
she expected him to turn into a raging jerk. The women
he dated—his usual type, he admitted wryly—were confident, sophisticated women who knew the score. Women
who looked at him as if he was the next best thing to a
Tiffany bracelet, not as if she expected him to grow fangs
and snarl.

From the looks of Dr. Danielle Stevens, she didn't
know there *was* a score and would probably back away
from a sparkly bauble as though it might bite her...as
though *he* might bite her.

He had to admit that he was tempted to sink his teeth
into that wide, soft mouth. Just to taste, he assured himself, even though he knew he was lying.

He wanted more than a taste of Danielle Stevens.

She intrigued him, balancing a determined efficiency
with something soft and fragile. She was both tough and
gentle, sweet and tart. And beneath the smell of disinfec-
tant he detected the warm scent of woman with a trace
of cool freshness. It reminded him of a forest on a hot
day—cool, mysterious and more than a little intriguing.
It made him want to bury his face in her neck and breathe
it into his lungs, to see if she tasted as cool and fresh as
she smelled.

Which startled him. Because he couldn't ever remember wanting to smell a woman's neck before. Or at least
not with such...*need*. The thought surprised him, because
it had been a long time since he'd needed anything. Especially a woman.

He paused and pushed open the door to the bistro just
as her phone rang, and if he hadn't been studying her

with such brooding intensity he might have missed the odd expression that flitted across her face as she checked the screen.

Dylan swallowed a chuckle because although she'd frowned down at the caller ID she hadn't been entirely successful in masking her relief.

It was the second time a phone call had interrupted his plans for the night, he admitted ruefully but although he'd been relieved by the first, he couldn't help feeling just a little frustrated now the shoe was on the other foot. And did she *have* to look so damn eager to escape?

"I have to go," she said, using almost the exact words he'd used to his mother.

And without waiting for a response from him she turned and hurried away. Leaving him for the second time in less than a week to watch her walk away.

Realizing that he was watching the way her hips swayed—the sweet curve of her bottom in the shapeless scrubs and the long, slender legs eating up the distance—Dylan pressed his thumb and forefinger against his tired eyes and dragged air into his lungs.

It appeared he'd just discovered a weakness for sweet, sassy brunettes with sad gray eyes and a penchant for clumsiness.

Oh, yeah, he thought with a chuckle. Dylan St. James was a goner.

Dani pushed open the employees' door to find the city bathed in bright early-morning light. It had been a crazier than normal Friday night.

Aside from the rogues' gallery—drunk idiots who had been left to sleep off their stupidity—her most challenging case had been a middle-aged high society woman with a bunch of puzzling symptoms. It had turned out she'd unwittingly taken a cannabis overdose from helping herself to her nephew's marijuana cookies. And, while it had taken most of the night, a whole bunch of tests and a lot of frustration, it had been satisfying to discover that her instincts about it not being a brain tumor or a heart problem had been spot-on.

Recalling what the shift supervisor had said about the full moon, Dani turned in a circle to study the sky. Either Rona had been mistaken or it had dipped behind the mountains.

"Whatcha looking at?" ER resident Theo Anderson demanded as he and Amy descended the stairs. He looked up to scan the clear sky. "A bird? A plane? Or maybe a flying squirrel?"

"Isn't that supposed to be Superman?" she murmured, reaching up to pull the band from her hair and shake out the heavy, messy mass.

"Not in Vancouver," Theo said with a head-shake, slinging an arm around her shoulders. "But I can be your hero, if you like."

Laughing, Dani shoved him away. "I'm good." She gave in to a huge yawn, dreaming about hot food, hot coffee, a hot shower and her bed.

She wasn't dreaming about a hot man. *Nuh-uh. Nope.* Because they were the worst kind of trouble.

"No heroes required," she said, because she didn't need rescuing.

Okay, she *mostly* didn't need rescuing, she amended silently. Especially by someone who reminded her that she was a red-blooded woman.

Out of the corner of her eye she caught Amy studying her with a concerned frown. "You *do* know that not all guys are like your ex, don't you?"

Hiding a grimace, because the last thing she wanted

was to discuss her past on such a beautiful day, Dani watched Theo perform a magic trick for Wendy, a pediatric night nurse, and murmured, "I know that. Some of them are like Theo."

Amy snorted and pulled her sunglasses from her bag. "Okay, so I can totally see why you're off guys." Her smile faded. "But you can't hide forever, Dani. It's not healthy."

"I'm not hiding," Dani argued. "I just haven't met anyone who's tempted me, that's all."

Instantly an image of a tall surgeon with hot green eyes, a sexy mouth and big warm hands popped into her head, and suddenly she was experiencing the kind of shiver that made some women pull out their lip gloss and check their hair.

Fortunately she wasn't one of those women. Mentally crossing her fingers, because she wasn't *usually* one of those women, she said, "When the right guy comes along I'll go for it, I promise."

Yeah, like you did last week…and the other night?

Shut up, she told the voice, pushing out her bottom lip to blow an impatient breath.

"You thought Richard was Mr. Right," Amy pointed out with a logic that Dani would have liked to dispute but couldn't.

Okay, maybe she hadn't thought he was the *right* guy but she'd been embarrassingly geeky and inexperienced. He'd been the first guy to pay her any real attention and she'd been hugely flattered that someone as handsome and popular as Richard had been interested in *her*.

Probably the reason she'd fallen so fast and so hard.

"Maybe you should look for Mr. Wrong instead?" Amy suggested. "Get out of your head and have a little fun for a change."

Before she could respond, Theo called out, "We're heading for Harry's tonight. You two coming?"

Dani shook her head, glad of the opportunity to escape because once Amy got her teeth into something, she rarely let it go. "I've got a thing."

"A thing?" Amy demanded, her brow arched skeptically. "What thing?"

Yeah, Dani. What thing?

She shrugged helplessly, too tired to think up a legitimate excuse. "A *thing* thing."

Amy narrowed her eyes and pointed accusingly at Dani. "There—see. That's exactly what I'm talking about."

She blinked. "Huh?"

"You're allergic to fun."

Dani couldn't help feeling a little insulted as she stared at her friend. Was that how people saw her? "I'm fun," she argued. "I go out with you guys all the time—and wasn't it just last month that you had to stop me from dancing on the tables at The Gateway?"

"No, that was Wendy and Theo," Amy said dryly.

She grimaced. *Oh, right.*

"Dani," Amy said gently. "When was the last time you actually went on a *date* date? You know—with a guy you're attracted to?"

"I'm not ready to date."

Heck, she recalled with an inner wince, just the thought of having coffee and a sandwich with a colleague in a dim bistro had thrown her for a loop. She didn't want to know how she'd handle a *real* date.

Okay, so she *did* know. She'd panic and run—she winced again—like that geeky fourteen-year-old she'd once been. It was kind of embarrassing that she was still letting hot boys scare her.

Amy studied Dani with narrowed eyes. "Then maybe you can explain exactly what happened the other night with Dr. Hunky?"

Her belly clenched and then released but it was an effort to appear casual. "I don't know what you're talking about," Dani said absently, digging in her bag for her sunglasses. "I was expecting Steve Randall and I was… surprised. That's all."

Yeah, right. Shocked was a little closer to the truth.

"Hmm…" Amy said, with enough skepticism to have Dani, who was now pretending to look for her car keys, look up with a frown.

"What's that supposed to mean?" she demanded.

For a couple of seconds Amy looked conflicted, before she sighed. "I wasn't going to say anything," she began reluctantly. "But I heard that you and Dr. Hot Stuff were seen outside PICU the other night, looking pretty cozy."

Dani felt her jaw drop. "Wha—?" she spluttered, feeling her face heat. "Th—that's ridiculous. We were discussing Timmy Nolan and…" She spluttered. "I don't even *know* him."

Amy's answer was to raise her eyebrows. "Then why are you blushing?"

"Blu—? Of course I'm not blushing!" she yelped, her blush deepening at the sight of Amy's arched brows. "I'm annoyed that people haven't got anything better to do than gossip."

Amy snorted. "Annoyed? That a hot, sexy guy had his hands on you and was looking at your mouth?" One eyebrow rose up her forehead. "Yeah, I can totally see how you'd be *annoyed.*"

Dani's eyes widened and the base of her spine tingled. *He'd been looking at her mouth?*

At the expression on her face, Amy cracked up. "You

should see your face," she hooted, almost rubbing her hands together with glee. "You *so* have the hots for the big bad boy of Ortho."

With a dirty look, Dani pulled out her keys and stomped across the parking lot toward her car. She wasn't going to dignify that with an answer because there was no way she had the hots for anyone. Let alone the big bad— She stopped and snorted rudely.

Who the heck talked like that, anyway?

CHAPTER FOUR

DANI PARKED A couple of blocks from the marina so she could hit the supermarket. And, although she'd had every intention of walking right on by, before she knew it she was standing inside her favorite coffee shop, breathing in the heady scent of freshly brewed coffee and thinking she'd gone to heaven.

Owen Lawrence, the owner, looked up when Dani pressed her nose up against the display case and moaned. "Need a moment there, hon?"

Dragging her gaze away from the rows of freshly baked temptation, she laughed. "Hi, Owen. And, no—it's just been a *very* long night."

Jeez, had she just moaned?

Maybe Amy was right. Maybe she *did* need to get a life—especially since the closest thing she'd come to sex in years had been that full-body shiver she'd experienced when she'd walked into PICU the other night and seen a certain surgeon standing there, looking like the answer to someone's hot dream.

Not hers, of course. But someone's...

"Crazy night?"

She smothered a yawn. "You wouldn't believe *half* the stuff we get in the ER on Friday nights."

Pretending she wasn't coveting the decadent pastries,

Dani waited in line and casually glanced around at the patrons getting an early start to their weekend. An elderly couple sat nearby, holding hands and smiling, content to be in each other's company.

Before she could stop it, her mouth curved in an answering smile and if she felt a little pang, a little pinch right beside her heart. It wasn't that she was jealous. She was just... *Dammit*, she wanted that when she was their age too.

Heck, she wouldn't mind something like that at *her* age but she'd tried and it hadn't worked out. In fact it had left her with far more than a few emotional scars. Scars that ached now, at the sight of a young couple at the next table, laughing and fussing over a cooing baby in a stroller. Hidden physical scars that made having a perfect little family of her own just a pipe dream.

But that was okay, she told herself, ignoring the impulse to rub the ache where a child of her own would never grow. There were worse things than being unable to conceive. For one: being married to a man who believed he was entitled to jet-set off to exotic locations with models, actresses, friends... In fact any woman—single or married—who wasn't his wife.

Richard had been movie-star-handsome, romantic and attentive—right up until they'd married. Almost immediately he'd become demanding and critical of everything she said, the way she behaved and what she wore. Then had come the subtly cruel remarks and finally, after a year, the emotional abuse had turned into towering rages that often erupted into bouts of violence. She'd lived in a constant state of tension and hated to think how easily she'd been cowed.

Although he'd never actually hit her until that last so-called "business" weekend—the one that had ended not only her nightmare of a marriage but had caused her accident—he'd used his much larger size to intimidate. To literally push her around, grab her with hard, biting hands and knock her into things because he'd said he needed to knock sense into her.

She shuddered. She wouldn't *ever* live like that again. Maybe she was still a work in progress but she was never going to let a man crush her spirit along with her shaky confidence in herself as a woman.

She was older and wiser now, and she knew better than to be swayed by a pretty face and an expensive smile. Knew better than to think she was equipped to handle Prince Not-So-Charming.

Or sexy bad boys with hot green eyes that saw way too much.

Suppressing a shiver, Dani paid for her coffee and splurged on the biggest chocolate cream donut covered with chocolate ganache. Heading for the door, she took a huge bite of the sinful delight even before her foot hit the sidewalk.

She was so focused on stuffing her face with the melt-in-the-mouth donut and double-shot latte that she wasn't paying much attention to her surroundings—until two pre-teens on skateboards nearly knocked her off her feet.

"Watch it, lady!" they warned cheerfully, performing a perfect whatever before zipping off.

"*You* watch it," she yelled to their departing backs, before looking at where her half-eaten breakfast lay partly on the sidewalk and partly down the front of her scrubs. She was now wearing her coffee and a blob of chocolate cream.

"*Dammit*. I needed that."

With a sigh, she scrubbed at the stain with the paper napkin, mourning the loss of her coffee. Picking up the empty to-go cup and the rest of the donut, she tossed everything in the nearest trash bin and told herself it was just as well because she really *didn't* need the extra bazillion calories.

Muttering to herself, Dani turned to head for the supermarket—and walked into a wall of muscle and bone. The abrupt interruption of her forward momentum drew a startled squeak from her parted lips and she lurched backward, just as large hands closed over her upper arms to keep her from the same fate as her breakfast.

"Careful," a deep voice cautioned.

And when that smooth yet velvet-rough voice—that *familiar* velvet-rough voice—rumbled near her ear her head came up, the automatic apology dying in her throat. "Dr. St. J-James, what—what are you doing here?"

His eyes took a leisurely journey over her face, lingering on her mouth for a long moment before dropping to the coffee and chocolate stain on the front of her scrubs top.

"Since we keep meeting like this you should probably call me Dylan," he said, and chuckled, brushing one hand down her arm as he looked past her shoulder to the coffee shop behind her. "Apparently I'm doing the same as you." He tugged gently at the damp fabric. "Although wearing my coffee wasn't quite what I had in mind."

"I wasn't looking where I was going and some kids—" She saw amusement crinkle the corners of his eyes and abruptly pressed her lips together to stop herself from babbling.

"Yeah, I saw," he murmured.

The brush of his fingers, the closeness of his big hard body, had the breath backing up in her throat. It was a couple of seconds before she realized that her nipples had drawn into tight little buds of enthusiastic greeting.

His gaze slowly rose up her chest, paused at the frantic

pulse hammering against the delicate skin of her throat and then lifted to lock on to her eyes. The amusement had been replaced by a sizzling masculine heat that sent both panic and anticipation rolling across her skin.

Oh God. Oh God. Oh—

Realizing she was standing there, gaping at him, she said, "Um…" very intelligently, and then sucked in a steadying breath as she mentally scrambled to rein in her scattered wits. *Darn it*, what the heck *was* it about the guy that always caught her on the back foot, banished her IQ and reduced her to a stammering fourteen-year-old?

Whatever it was, she fumed, it was going to stop. *Right now.* All she had to do was remind him that she was still on the man wagon and—

"…breakfast?"

Dani blinked when she realized that he was talking and she'd totally missed it because she'd been gazing at his strong, tanned throat and wondering what it would feel like to press her lips there.

"Uh…excuse me?"

Amusement tugged at his mouth. One minute she was staring into smiling green eyes and the next, she felt her head go light, her knees buckle, just like all those swooning women who—

And then she was being thrust into a chair and her head shoved between her legs. The spots dancing in front of her eyes gradually faded and she became aware of his large, comforting presence beside her. The warm fingers on the back of her neck that kept her from sliding to the floor.

"I've never actually had someone fall at my feet before," he said chuckling, sounding just a little bit disgruntled.

She cracked open an eye to see him crouched beside her.

He dipped his head to catch her look. "I'm not so sure if it's a compliment."

All she could manage was a strangled laugh as heat and a mouth-watering masculine scent surrounded her, invading her lungs. He was close. *Too* darn close.

Her pulse gave an alarmed little blip and she jerked upright—or tried to—but his grip tightened.

"Take it easy," he murmured, his long fingers gentling to soothe the back of her head, to massage her neck and the tense spot between her shoulder blades.

Oh, that felt good.

"You fainted."

Fainted?

She shook her head in denial and opened her mouth to tell him she hadn't but a delicious heat had begun to invade her limbs, threatening to melt her bones. It occurred to her that if she didn't move soon she'd slide right off the chair into a puddle of yearning between his large, scuffed boots.

Oh, boy. Way to go on not embarrassing yourself.

She squeezed her eyes closed to dispel the swirling heat taking up residence in her belly, then sucked in a steadying breath before sitting up, stilling when she discovered him less than an inch away.

He'd recently shaved and the smell of soap and some manly scent—shaving gel…aftershave?—teased her nostrils. The shape of his mouth drew her gaze and she had the wildly inappropriate impulse to lean forward and lick it. The little flutter in her belly had her struggling to pull air into lungs that refused to work—probably because she was inhaling a heady mix of testosterone and male pheromones.

Long, tanned fingers cupped her jaw, sending a jolt

right through her. Her gaze jumped to his as he swept concerned eyes over her face.

"You have a little more color in your cheeks," he murmured, his thumb gently rubbing a line of heat across her cheekbone.

It sent a bunch of conflicting signals to the rest of her body: delicious tingles, nervous jitters and an insidious softening in places that hadn't softened for a man in nearly three years.

And if *that* didn't freak her out, the way his eyes darkened had her swallowing a panicked gasp and hastily retreating. She started to pull away.

"Don't tense up," he instructed.

He spoke in a deep, exasperated voice that had Dani opening her mouth to croak, "I'm f-fine," before wrapping her fingers around his wrist to push him away.

She couldn't think when he was touching her.

He resisted a moment before dropping his hand. He didn't, however, move back, and her belly gave a decidedly nervous little feminine quiver.

Oh, boy. Bad time to rediscover her hormones.

"When last did you eat?"

She blinked. "What?" *She* was thinking about sex and *he* was thinking about…food?

A bubble of hysterical laugher rose up her throat. It figured, she thought with a snort. Just figured that her body would come out of the deep freeze at the exact moment the man in front of her was focused on food.

"When last did you eat?"

She looked down at the coffee stain on the front of her scrubs and tried to think. "I…uh…" *Damn*, she thought, shoving her hair out of her eyes with shaking fingers. She couldn't concentrate with him so close. "Last night…yesterday…"

She shook her head impatiently and tried to stand but he casually shoved her back.

"I can't remember exactly. The ER was busy. *Dammit—* will you *move*?" she growled, embarrassed by the curious glances they were receiving. "I can't b-breathe with you so close and…" She lowered her voice. "People are staring."

"Let them stare," he said impatiently, rising smoothly to his feet. "Stay there while I get you something."

She made a sound deep in her throat—kind of an annoyed growl and distressed squeak—and tried to stand again but his hand dropped to her shoulder to keep her seated. She jerked her head up and opened her mouth to snap at him but he swiped a casual thumb across her bottom lip. The move surprised her—okay, shocked the hell out of her—rendering her mute as well as brainless.

"Stay there," he murmured. "Please."

It seemed she wasn't as immune as she'd thought— or wanted to be. Not if she was unable to ignore a man who looked at her with amused exasperation and banked heat. "Okay…"

His eyes took on a challenging gleam as he tugged gently on an errant curl that had escaped her topknot. When his fingers slid away they brushed her neck, sending a host of sensations scattering throughout her body. Her nerves jittered, causing something deep in her belly to pull taut. It was probably a good thing she was sitting down because her knees wobbled alarmingly.

She pressed a shaky hand to her hollow belly and groaned. Oh God, maybe she *was* hungry. Maybe she just needed food.

Yeah, you're hungry, all right, said the voice in her head, snickering rudely. *Hungry for sinful se—*

Nope, she was still quite comfortable on the wagon,

thank you very much. She had no intention—none whatsoever, she assured herself—of falling off for anyone.

Especially not a guy who wore his general hotness like a familiar well-loved T-shirt—one that stretched across his big shoulders, pulled taut over a wide muscular chest and fell loose around his abs and narrow waist before being tucked into low-slung jeans that were faded in strategic places and cupped some pretty cuppable places.

Her breath hitched and an unfamiliar burn took up residence in a place that had been empty for far too long. She shifted restlessly, because it made her uncomfortable and twitchy. And since being twitchy always made her irritable she decided it was probably way past time to hit the road.

Before the wagon rumbled on down the street without her.

Muttering to herself about the dangers of getting sucked into an Alpha man's orbit, she shoved back her chair—because the last thing she needed was nuclear blasts of testosterone and pheromones clouding her judgment and adding to her problems.

But before she could stand she caught a whiff of the sticky sweet scent of fresh donuts along with the aroma of hot vanilla bean latte and nearly moaned.

"Going somewhere?"

Looking up as Dr. St. James—*Dylan*—slid into the opposite chair, Dani's stomach lurched and rumbled simultaneously. She wasn't entirely certain if it was the sight of all that yumminess or the smell of coffee and donuts that had her subsiding back into the chair.

An eyebrow rose up his forehead as he slid a large to-go mug across the table. "Drink," he ordered. "And tell me why you were getting ready to ditch me again. You're starting to give me a complex."

Dani cursed her fair complexion that had heated guilt-ily at the mild censure in his voice. He sounded as though her reluctance had baffled or maybe hurt him. But, consid-ering that he had dozens of women vying for his attention, the idea that she could hurt his feelings was laughable.

"No, I wasn't," she lied. "I was… I was about to come and help you," she finished lamely. "And the only 'com-plex' thing about a man is his DNA. And even *that's* been decoded."

He laughed. "Uh-huh?"

Rolling her eyes, she spied the box he'd opened and was nudging across the table as though it contained a bomb.

A box of donuts? Jeez. That was about a gazillion cal-ories right there.

Her eyes narrowed accusingly because of course *he* didn't need to worry about whether his butt looked good in jeans. But, then again, he was the kind of man who'd look good in anything…and in nothing at all.

A shiver skated across her skin at the thought and she quickly looked away before he realized she'd just pictured him naked. He made a low, rough sound in the back of his throat and when she gave in to the need to look she saw he was studying her with that deeply intense gaze that seemed to see everything.

He inclined his head at the box, his eyes and his wicked grin daring her to give in to temptation.

She'd never been able to resist a challenge and, star-ing into his moss-green eyes, Dani felt tempted. *Really* tempted. For about a nanosecond. Because she had a feel-ing this sexy dare went beyond donuts and into the realms of her man embargo. No matter what she'd told Amy, she wasn't *nearly* ready to date and had a sneaky feeling she wouldn't *ever* be ready for a man like him.

He was too masculine, too sexy, too Alpha… Well,

frankly he was too *everything*. All the things that hit her every button…including her inner alarm.

Dragging her eyes away from the open box, she scowled. "I'm abstaining, remember?"

Hitching one shoulder, as though her resistance didn't bother him, he leaned forward and selected a chocolate cream ganache-glazed donut. And then, with his gaze on hers, he said casually, "I thought that was just from anything with a Y-chromosome," before sinking strong white teeth into the fried dough.

Her belly quivered and her tongue emerged to swipe across her bottom lip as she imagined licking glaze—*Oh God*—and chocolate cream off his lips.

She must have made a sound, because his eyes darkened and dropped to her mouth.

"No," she said a little primly, even as she squirmed on the seat, feeling turned on and jealous of a greasy pillow of fried dough. *Sheesh*. She clearly needed to date more if the sight of a guy enjoying a donut was making her both resentful of the attention he was giving it as well as aroused. "From *everything* that's bad for me."

He chuckled and nudged the box closer. "C'mon, live a little. You need to stabilize your blood sugar and…" He paused, looking far too innocent. "Isn't it your duty as a healthcare professional to think about my arteries by taking one or two off my hands?"

No looking at his hands, Dani ordered herself, and then promptly did…and shivered as she recalled how those broad-palmed, long-fingered hands had felt rubbing away her tension.

"Why?" she demanded skeptically. "Afraid they'll go straight to your butt and you'll have to buy new jeans?"

His gaze dropped to her front, as though he could see through the table and she barely restrained herself from squirming. His amused snort said he thought she was joking when she'd been serious as a heart attack.

"No," he drawled softly, his mouth curving wickedly as though he'd been thinking of *her* bottom. "And neither should you."

His eyes dared her, and one arched brow accused her of being a wimp. She returned it with a glare, secretly pleased that he thought she didn't need to worry about getting a big butt.

"So," she said, lifting her cup to blow on the hot liquid. "You want me to what…? Stay and help you empty the box?"

A self-deprecating smile tugged at his mouth. "I'll settle for feeding you before you pass out on me again. Not," he said, with a chuckle at her quick scowl, "that I object to getting my hands on you again but let's just say I find myself wanting to change your mind."

Ignoring the first part of his statement, she took a sip of latte to give herself a moment. "About…?"

His smirk grew. "You know what."

Dani's face bloomed with color as his meaning sank in. "I…um… I'm pretty sure that's not going to happen," she announced, rolling her eyes when he snorted.

Sheesh. Time to move the conversation into non-embarrassing territory.

"So…um…how's Timothy doing?"

He leaned back in the chair, looking relaxed and far too attractive so early in the morning—especially with her looking like week-old roadkill. His expression turned chiding and he looked just a little amused at her avoidance of a little harmless flirting.

"Remarkably well," he drawled. "Which you know since you visited him last night and then again this morning."

She frowned at this news that he was keeping tabs on

her but decided not to think about what it might mean. A smile bloomed at the memory of the little boy, almost bouncing off the walls with impatience. It was hard to believe he'd been at death's door just a couple days before.

"I did." She chuckled. "He wanted to know when Dr. Dylan was visiting, because apparently you'd promised to play catch with him."

"He's a cute kid," he said, his eyes taking on a little gleam she wanted to ignore. "And you're dodging the issue."

"What issue?" she asked politely, pretending to be clueless.

With a low laugh he shook his head at her and pushed the box closer. He took another bite of the donut he was still holding. "Go on," he urged, in a voice that was deep and sinful enough to tempt a nun to the dark side. "You know you want to."

And when she made a little distressed sound in the back of her throat because she was tempted—way too much and not just by the allure of fried dough—he snickered. *The jerk*.

"A little trans fat and a few empty calories once in a while won't hurt."

"Maybe not," she agreed. "But one always leads to two, and before you know it you've eaten the entire box and have to take up jogging to minimize the damage to your arteries…among other things."

"Are we talking about donuts or…?"

Her belly quivered at his implication but she ruthlessly squelched it. There would be no quivering. Not for him or anyone else. At least not until she had her life firmly in order.

"Yep," she said, making the *p* pop audibly. "Definitely donuts."

He chuckled, and with his eyes on hers stretched out his arm to hold the chocolate cream donut he'd just taken a bite of to her lips. "Why don't we share? That way you won't have to feel guilty."

And suddenly Dani wanted to step outside her safe, peaceful world. *Just once*, she told the voice in her head. Just once and then she'd go back to ignoring the way he made all the lonely little places inside her shiver with excitement.

Unable to look away, she leaned forward to sink her teeth into the sugary treat, very carefully avoiding taking a bite out of his finger too—which she was totally tempted to do.

Her taste buds instantly exploded and a vicious little tug deep in her belly drew her breasts tight, as though they were connected by some invisible thread. She must have made a sound, because his gaze rose slowly to hers, leaving a trail of fire streaking across her skin. The heat burning in the green depths had the breath backing up in her lungs.

She froze, her eyes widening. *Holy cow.* Whoever had said green eyes were hard and cold had never seen them catch fire. Her heart stuttered to a stop, because although she might not have seen it in a while there was no mistaking *that* look. The fact that it was focused on *her* had wild heat storming into her face.

Oh, no. No, no, *no*, she ordered herself frantically. No belly-clenching, knee-wobbling or heart-stuttering allowed. And if the alarming symptoms continued she'd head right back to the ER to order a full blood work-up... or maybe a neurological one.

She was far too smart to develop a...a *thing*—she wasn't going to call it an attraction—for Dylan St. James.

Wasn't she?

* * *

Without realizing he needed to, Dylan reached for her hand—and knew instantly that he'd made a tactical error when a jolt shot up his arm with a nasty little buzz. She must have felt it too, because her eyes widened and she gave a gasp of surprise.

Very interesting, he thought, narrowing his gaze on her startled expression. He'd heard about it, of course, but he'd never actually believed it existed. Nor had he ever experienced that sharp little zap of sexual heat.

Given the little bobble of shock that had nearly splashed hot liquid over the rim of her disposable cup, it appeared that neither had Danielle Stevens.

Eyes wide, wild color rushing beneath that soft skin, she jerked her hand free and quickly shoved it beneath the table to rub it against her thigh. Enjoying the sensations that little jolt had sent shooting up his arm, Dylan watched her struggle for composure, watched those wild fluctuations of color beneath her creamy skin.

Needing to put her at ease, he drew in a deep breath. "Danielle…" he began, pausing when she abruptly slapped her coffee cup onto the table and shoved back her chair.

"I…uh…oh, gosh, look at the time," she babbled, grabbing her shoulder bag as she lurched to her feet, almost toppling the chair in her haste.

He reached out to grab it before it crashed onto the floor and rose to his feet. She took a hasty step backwards, babbling out a garbled apology when she bumped into the table behind her.

"Look, don't g-get up," she stammered breathlessly as she edged away. "Enjoy your coffee and…and, thanks."

He started to follow her but she gave a little squeak of distress then turned and fled, leaving Dylan to watch in stunned surprise as she lurched her way between the tables to the door.

With a muttered and completely baffled curse, he followed. What the heck had he done to upset her? And she clearly *was* upset, because a woman didn't practically fall over herself trying to get away from a man for no reason.

He caught up with her a half-block from the coffee shop and grabbed her arm. "Dr. Stevens, wait—"

Wide-eyed, she spun around, wrapping her arms around her chest and curling her hands over her opposite elbows as though to protect herself from him. She was practically vibrating with tension.

Easily reading the wariness in her huge gray eyes, he slowly released her to shove his hands into his pockets. The last thing he wanted was to upset her—especially when his instincts were yelling at him to pull her close and not let go. He didn't think that would go down well.

"Hey…*hey*…" he crooned softly, cursing the caution in her storm-colored eyes and his own suddenly violent need. "It's okay." He gave her a crooked smile, hoping to draw one from her. "You can trust me. I'm a doctor."

The words had the desired effect, and with a muffled giggle she relaxed her shoulders. She drew in a deep breath and he watched her struggle to compose herself. He had to admire her grit, he told himself, because it was obvious that whatever—or *whoever*—had hurt her, they had done a really good job.

He hated thinking that some man had put his hands on her in anger but that was what all those little tells indicated. He'd grown up to respect women—his mother wouldn't have had it any other way—and to abhor bullies. A man who used physical violence on a woman or a child didn't deserve to be called a man.

"If that's the best you can do, Dr. St. James," she

drawled, shoving her hair off her face with a hand that trembled, "I'm going to start questioning the rumors about your supposed reputation as a playboy."

"What have I told you about listening to gossip, Danielle?" he chided gently, relief settling around him like a sigh when she rolled her eyes. And when her mouth curved into a tiny smile, lighting those mysterious eyes, he felt as if he'd won a huge victory.

"Dani."

He blinked. "Huh?"

"It's Dani. With an i."

He took in the perfect oval of her face, the gray eyes, wide and heavily lashed beneath the elegant arch of her brows, the smooth curve of her cheek, the delicate nose and wide mobile mouth with its longer upper lip and pillow-soft bottom lip.

Dani sounded too masculine—too androgynous—he decided, for such a feminine face.

"Danielle suits you better," he announced, enjoying the way her creamy skin took on a rosy hue, as though she wasn't used to compliments.

"It does not," she countered, with a spluttered laugh. "Danielle evokes images of a tall, elegantly sophisticated French woman draped in silk and reeking of expensive perfume. *So* not me."

"Oh, I don't know…" he mused, casually nudging her behind a large pillar out of pedestrian traffic. "I kind of think it suits you."

He found himself needing to touch her but was hesitant about spooking her into bolting again. Testing the waters, he reached out to tug at an errant curl lying against her pale neck and was pleased to note that, other than a quick shiver, she didn't retreat.

"Yeah, right," she snorted, looking down at her attire.

"Nothing says sophisticated elegance more eloquently than stained scrubs and battered running shoes." She lifted her head and arched her brow, still looking more like a Danielle than a Dani. "Be careful, Dr. St. James," she warned lightly. "Or people might think you've lost your touch."

Lost his mind, more likely, he thought with an inner chuckle. Out loud, he said, "Spend the day with me."

"Yes… No… I… *What?*"

She gaped at him as though he'd suggested something indecent, when the truth was he wasn't ready to let her go. Wasn't ready for her to disappear on him again; leave him fighting that baffling desire to pull her close and kiss her senseless.

He moved a fraction closer and dropped his voice. "Spend the day with me, Dani with an i," he murmured. "I promise to feed you something that won't stain your scrubs or end up on your thighs."

She rolled her eyes. "Dr. St. James, I—"

Her eyes clouded and he watched her inner struggle.

Just when he thought she'd accept, she gave a quick head-shake and said regretfully, "I'm sorry, I can't. I have plans for the weekend."

He was surprised by the strength of his disappointment. "Rain check?"

Looking undecided, she nibbled on her lip before lifting soft gray eyes to his. "Um…sure," she murmured. She turned away. Then, spinning around quickly, she said a little breathlessly, "And thanks."

Rocking back on his heels, Dylan folded his arms across his chest and tilted his head to one side. "For what?"

He liked that endearing confusion on her much more than the guarded look or the haunted expression she sometimes wore when she didn't think anyone was paying attention. And he wanted to, Dylan admitted with surprise. He wanted to pay attention to her. Wanted to watch her eyes darken, to catch the quick sexy hitch of her breath, the husky laugh that burst out of her almost as though that small bubble of humor couldn't be contained. And he wanted to pay more than a little attention to that soft, full unpainted mouth.

It was as though she could read his thoughts. Her gaze flittered away from his before sliding back. A faint blush stained the high, elegant cheekbones. "For rescuing me." She laughed a little self-deprecatingly. *"Again."*

"Any time."

She took another step backward and halted, shifting awkwardly. Dylan couldn't help feeling smug that she was just as confused as he was by whatever it was growing between them, even if she *was* fighting it tooth and nail.

She fiddled with the strap of her shoulder bag and turned away, nearly colliding with a couple strolling along the sidewalk toward them. "Oops, sorry…" she said, blowing out a shaky huff of laughter. "So, I'll see you around?"

He nodded and watched her nibble on that full bottom lip, wanting her to stay so badly he could taste it—wanting to test how that lip felt against his; wanting to make it soften and open even as all those sweet curves softened against him.

"You know where to find me," he called out, watching the impatient twitch of her hips as she hurried off.

He didn't know how long he stood there with a loopy grin on his face, staring at the last place he'd seen her, until an elderly couple paused with looks of concern on their lined faces.

"You okay there, son?" the old man asked when Dylan blinked them into focus.

He lifted a hand to rub the back of his neck and wondered what the heck had just happened. He felt...*poleaxed*.

"Yeah," he sighed, rolling his shoulders to dispel the notion that he should have tried a little harder to convince her to spend the day with him. "It's...a woman."

"It always is." The septuagenarian nodded sagely. "The secret is not to try to understand them." He chuckled when his wife nudged him with her elbow. "It'll just drive you crazy."

With a wink at Dylan, the old guy moved off with his wife, leaving him to watch as he laughed and lifted their clasped hands to his lips for a sweet kiss.

Yeah. He wanted *that*. What they had. What his parents and grandparents had. The trick was to find the right woman. One who wanted *him* and not his family's money. One who wouldn't drive him crazy with the conflicting messages she sent out. Not one whose body language said one thing and whose eyes couldn't decide *what* they were saying.

Scrubbing his hands over his face, Dylan dug his hand in his pocket for his keys and headed for his Jeep, ignoring the little voice in his head that told him he was already crazy.

Crazy about a sweet little mess with big stormy eyes and a sexy smile. One who made him want to drag her into his cave and slay all her dragons. Crazy enough to want to change her mind about falling off the wagon with him.

And if that wasn't crazy enough, he thought with a shaky laugh, Dylan St. James—hotshot surgeon and heir to the St. James fortune—was feeling like a pimply-faced nerd with his first crush.

CHAPTER FIVE

A WEEK LATER Dani was awakened by the raucous sound of squabbling seagulls. Muttering about the ungodly hour on her first weekend off in over a month, she slapped a pillow over her head, determined to go back to sleep.

Five minutes later, however, she flung the pillow aside and rolled over to scowl at the ceiling. *Dammit*. Now that she was awake she'd never be able to go back to sleep. Certainly not with that racket on her deck.

She flung an arm over her eyes and sighed. Okay, so maybe the deck wasn't *hers* but since she was paying the monthly docking fees she guessed it was—temporarily, at least. Her landlord—a friend's brother—was currently living in a fancy penthouse in downtown Vancouver, because his current girlfriend hated the inconvenience of the marina and the neighborhood of floating homes.

At the time Dani had moved in she hadn't been able to afford to be choosy. And Cole let her stay free as long as she paid the berth rates—which was *way* cheaper than any apartment within the city limits.

Now she couldn't imagine living anywhere else.

Besides, she still had a ton of student loans to pay off and she'd left her marriage with nothing. Not any of the fancy clothes Richard had paid for and none of the jewelry—except her engagement and wedding rings, which she'd sold to buy a car and pay off some of the loans. She hadn't wanted anything that would remind her of how gullible and stupid she'd been.

Her lawyer had said she was entitled to a settlement but Dani had refused. The relief of being out of that vipers' pit had been settlement enough. The fact that she still had her student loans was *her* cross to bear and no one else's. A cross she gladly carried because it meant she was free and independent.

Shoving aside memories best left in the past, she rolled to the edge of the bed, wondering what the heck was going on outside. She tossed the comforter aside and sat up, scowling as the early-morning sun—and she meant *early*—streamed through the French doors that opened onto the upper deck.

A dozen seagulls wheeled noisily in the air, while even more lifted off and then landed on the deck railing like restless spectators at a hockey match. Shoving the wild tangle of hair out of her eyes, Dani marched across the room. She'd always liked the sound of seagulls in the morning but this was ridiculous.

The instant she unlocked and pushed open the door, the air exploded with panicked squawks, beating wings and flying feathers as the birds took to the air. Stepping out, she padded over to the railing to peer down, unsurprised to see her neighbor's cat sitting statue-still, guarding something.

Axel had a habit of treating her deck like his personal hunting ground—which accounted for the regular remains of his meals. He often left gifts in front of the upper and lower French doors or, if she was careless and left a window open, either on or at the foot of her bed.

Once he'd even left a mangled lizard in her shoe. He

probably thought she was a bad hunter and was providing her with food.

"Axel, shoo!"

Except for the barest tail-twitch, the black cat ignored her, his bright green eyes locked on a nearby seagull. Probably he was waiting for the birdbrain to venture closer so he could pounce.

She gave a couple of sharp claps with her hands but the bird was in a stare-down with the hefty feline, ignoring the fact that he was about to become kitty chow.

Dani took a closer look at what he was guarding and winced when she recognized a lump of downy feathers. "Dammit, Axel!" she cried, running down the stairs and across the deck.

Her sudden move caused the remaining seagulls to take flight, their raucous complaints filling the early morning. Ignoring them, she dropped to her knees and gently nudged the cat aside. He rose fluidly and head-butted her arm with rare affection, as though to say *Look what I brought you.*

"I thought I told you no more gifts?" she muttered but he turned to rub his body against her, playfully batting her hand with one heavy paw. "You're going to explode if you eat any more," she groused, gagging when she saw the pile of fuzz. "What the heck am I supposed to do with—?" She sucked in a sharp breath. "No, no, *no*. You brought me a baby seagull? How *could* you?"

His ears twitched but he continued to wash himself, studiously ignoring her.

"Fine—ignore me," she muttered, throwing up her hands. "You're just like every other male in my life anyway."

Behind her she heard a low chuckle that had her rising and spinning around at the same time—because, one, it was coming from a neighboring floating home that was supposedly empty, two, she was standing there in an oversized T-shirt and panties and, three, it sounded awfully like—

Pain lanced through her foot as it snagged on a broken plank, throwing her off balance. She caught a fleeting glimpse of bare masculine feet, long legs encased in faded denim, a set of ripped tanned abs, sculpted pecs and rounded biceps before she lost her footing and, with a shriek, made a graceless splash into the icy water behind her.

Just before the water closed over her head she saw a black streak disappearing around the side of her houseboat—of course Axel had left. Then the frigid temperature stole her thoughts as well as her breath and she gasped, getting a lungful of icy bay water. For a moment she panicked but the next thing she was breaking the surface, spluttering and coughing up water.

She tried to suck in sweet early-morning air and got a mouthful of hair instead. Treading water and shoving wet hanks out of her mouth while coughing up a lung seemed too much for her sleep-befuddled brain to handle and she found herself going under again. This time she had the presence of mind to close her mouth.

She broke the surface a second time to find those long denim-clad legs a couple of feet away…on her deck.

"You okay?"

Coughing, she peered up—*way* up—and, blinking water out of her eyes, wondered if she was seeing things or if her sleep-starved mind had conjured up the star of her most recent fantasies.

Her bleary gaze rose up those long muscular columns to the large bulge beneath a half-buttoned fly—as though he'd pulled the jeans on in a hurry—and up a happy trail to his innie, smack-dab in the middle of a taut, tanned belly.

Yum.

He dropped to his haunches. "Need a hand?"

The amusement in that deep bedroom voice had her nipples tightening into little buds of aching need that— *Oh, wait!* That was surely because she was up to her neck in freezing water. Maybe…no, *definitely.*

Dani stared blankly up into his darkly handsome face, scarcely aware that she was gaping at him as if he'd stripped naked and was doing the hula. A little voice in her head snickered, *You wish,* and *her* voice when it emerged was a panicked squawk. "What—what are you *doing* here?"

After a long moment he jerked his head, indicating the supposedly empty houseboat behind him. The one she was meant to be keeping an eye on because its owner was somewhere in Africa.

The sliding doors were open and the deck furniture was on display. A kayak rested on a stand along with a paddle board and oars. Several colorful towels were draped over deckchairs beside a wetsuit and a white T-shirt.

She blinked at the sight of all those guy toys, wondering when the heck they'd appeared. Her voice was a shocked splutter. "You live…here…*there*?"

For a long moment he silently contemplated her question, finally asking mildly, "Is that a problem, Dr. Stevens?"

She swallowed the news like a mouthful of ground glass. How had she not been aware of it until now?

"You're C-Cole's friend? The one who's been in Africa f-for two years?"

One dark brow rose up his forehead at the dismay she hadn't successfully hidden. With a chiding look he rose to his feet and shoved a hand through his hair, leaving the overlong strands sticking up and giving him a sexy rumpled look. She was simply *not* going to mention all that rippling anatomy displayed like eye-candy.

She gave a mental *eek* and tried to look away, because she was imagining *her* fingers running through those dark silky strands while she licked his abs right down to his open jeans.

"Why haven't I seen you?" she demanded, treading water, completely forgetting about the cold. "I mean, we share a dock. My bedroom faces out onto your deck and—"

Why hadn't she known he lived right next door? Surely she should have…*felt* something?

"I didn't know the owner was back. I've been keeping an eye on things."

His arched brow said she hadn't been doing a very good job if she hadn't noticed someone had been living there for the past few weeks.

"I've been wondering that myself," he said, studying her with amused green eyes. "The best that I can come up with is that I work days and you work nights. By the time I leave the hospital you're already at work, and when you come home I'm gone."

She thought about that for a moment and decided it made sense—especially as she'd worked the past four weekends and hadn't been home much. But that didn't mean she wanted him on her doorstep. Avoiding him at the hospital hadn't been all that difficult but with him living right next door… Well, her chances of avoiding him—and ignoring him—had just got a whole lot worse.

With his arms folded across his wide muscular chest and his legs planted apart as if he was on the deck of a rolling ship, Dylan St. James looked like a modern-day pirate…or maybe as if he belonged on the cover of a raunchy romance novel.

She hadn't realized she'd spoken out loud until his eyes filled with amusement and he tilted his head to study her. "Raunchy romance novel?" he drawled.

A tidal wave of embarrassment banished the hypothermia creeping up on her and she groaned, briefly considering drowning herself. But, since her problems couldn't be solved so easily, she swam the short distance to the deck and planted her hands on the wooden planks.

Before she could pull herself up, long masculine fingers wrapped around her wrists and hauled her out of the water. Surprise had her stumbling against him, her hands coming up against warm tanned skin to steady herself. And staying there when he sucked in a sharp breath because it was *his* fault she'd taken an early-morning swim.

She considered plastering her icy body against the front of him, then decided it would be safer—*much* safer—to beat a hasty and dignified retreat.

Before she could, he shifted his big hands to her upper arms and eased her away from him, a grin of pure masculine appreciation lighting his handsome features when he looked her over.

Realizing she looked like something Axel had dragged in from the bay, she shoved him back and instantly missed his heat.

"Shut it," she growled, squeezing water out of her hair. "I *know* I look like a drowned rat." Her tone dared him to disagree. He lifted a hand to scratch his jaw and she knew by the amused gleam in his green eyes that he was fighting a smile.

Then his eyes slid over her and his smile became positively wicked. "Not really."

Dani looked down at herself and saw what had caused

the scorching look. She gave a frantic yelp and wrapped her arms around her body to hide the way the sheer white material of her T-shirt had been suctioned against her skin like cling wrap and now exposed—well, *everything*.

Forget the wet T-shirt look—it was as if she was naked.

"Ohmigod! Stop looking!"

One dark brow rose. "Babe…" he drawled, his bed-room baritone sending heat prickling beneath her icy skin. After a moment of heated silence he shook his head and swallowed, his voice dropping to a deep rasp like the rustle of velvet against intimate skin. "I'm a man, not a saint."

Dani's body reacted as if she'd inhaled a giant cloud of pheromones. Her head swam, her heart pounded, her ears buzzed and her skin felt as if she'd been zapped by a hundred thousand watts. She wondered if steam was rising off her skin in a cloud of vapor.

Yikes.

"This is *your* fault," she said, and scowled, attempting to pull the material away from her skin, hoping it would allow some much needed air back into her lungs—or turn the fabric opaque.

His eyes flickered and darkened even more. With her knees wobbling alarmingly, she took a step backwards, crying out as pain shot up through her foot like a bolt of lightning.

The next thing, she was yanked against a hard body.

"What's wrong? Jeez, woman, you're like ice," he cursed, his arm an iron band at her back.

"Th—that's wh-what happens when you s-swim before the sun is even up," she stuttered, wondering why her foot was throbbing like an open wound.

Her left hand slid low on his abdomen while her right gripped the waistband of his jeans, low on his hips, to help with her balance. It was only when his belly clenched beneath her icy palm that she realized exactly where her hand was. She gulped and tried to put a little distance between them but he tightened his arm and craned his neck as though he was trying to see her butt.

"What are you *doing*?" she squeaked, trying to wriggle away. "Keep your eyes *off* my backside."

"Stop squirming or I'll be seeing a lot more than damp pink panties."

She froze, her eyes wide as she recalled she was practically naked.

He dropped to his haunches, one hand sliding down her leg to her ankle. "Lift your foot."

She tried to wriggle away but his grip tightened.

"Lift."

"What? No— I— Ouch!" She sucked in a sharp breath and tried to twist around to see. "*Damn*, that hurts."

With a muttered curse, Dylan rose fluidly and swung her into his arms before she could utter a surprised squeak.

Shocked by the lack of warning—and the ease with which he'd lifted her against his chest—Dani immediately wrapped an arm around his neck and demanded, "What—what are you doing? P-put me down!"

His grunt sounded a little disgruntled, as if she'd insulted his manhood or something, and without even so much as a glance her way, he strode across the deck. Not toward *her* houseboat but his.

"Hey! Where—?" When he didn't slow down, she gasped. *"No!"*

Her eyes widened as she realized that he was going to jump the distance between the decks.

Stiffening, she yelped, "Are you *crazy*?" just as he leapt across the distance.

She tightened her stranglehold and pressed her face

into his neck, giving a panicked squawk when he landed and pretended to stumble.

She rewarded the laugh rumbling through him with a punch as he strode through the open sliding doors into his sitting room. Instead of putting her down, he headed for the stairs with confident strides.

Realizing where he was going, she widened her eyes even more and stiffened again in his arms. "Dylan—"

"Relax." His growl stirred the drying curls at her temple. "I promise not to ravish you. Unless you beg me to."

"Wha—?" She whacked him again. "For God's sake, Dylan. Put me *down*."

He deposited her on the bathroom counter and reached behind him to grab a towel from heated rods. He wrapped her in its fluffy warmth.

"I need to check that foot."

Reminded of the throbbing pain, Dani pulled the thick terrycloth closer and looked down, surprised to see blood dripping onto the pristine tiles. She followed the trail across the floor and through the door into his bedroom... and beyond.

"I'm sorry." She winced apologetically. "I'll clean it up later."

His brief look said she was an idiot, and then he transferred his attention back to her foot. "You've cut yourself," he murmured, wrapping long fingers around her ankle in a way that had a shiver working its way up the back of her leg into forbidden territory.

Dani sucked in a sharp breath, and when he looked up she winced, hoping he'd mistake her shiver for pain and not—*oh, boy*.

"There's something inside..." he murmured as he probed the area gently. "I'll have to remove it." His grip gentled even as his eyes sharpened on her face. "How bad is the pain?"

She bit her lip to prevent a whimper, because it wasn't pain she was feeling. Or rather not *just* pain, she admitted, avoiding his gaze to frown down at her foot. With him so close it was hard to remember that she'd given up men. So close she could see the fine lines at the corners of his eyes and each individual eyelash. So close she got a little dizzy recalling the graphic dreams she'd had since the day she'd all but swooned at his feet.

"About a...a f-four."

His gaze traveled up her long bare legs and lingered for one heart-stopping instant at the apex of her thighs before he abruptly straightened and yanked another towel off the rail behind him, practically tossing it in her face.

Shocked by the abruptness of his action, Dani widened her eyes, her fascinated gaze locked on to the muscle twitching in his jaw. "What?" she asked, and then a little more testily, *"What?"* when his only reply was a grunt that she had no way of interpreting as he reached for her foot again.

Annoyed, she pulled away and narrowed her eyes, tempted to kick him for being annoyingly male.

"What?"

He just looked at her, his gaze heavy-lidded and unreadable. After a long silence his poet's mouth began to curl in a smile so wicked her breath backed up in her throat and sweat broke out behind her knees.

"Dylan—" *Yikes.* She'd never experienced a look that could make the backs of her knees sweat.

"I'm a little...uh...distracted." That was what she thought he murmured but it was difficult to hear anything over the thundering of her pulse.

Her fingers tightened spasmodically on the towel. "B-by what?"

For long moments he stared at her, then he stepped back and scrubbed his hands over his face. "Nothing," he said, clearly deciding a change of subject was needed. "Back to your foot. Do you have any allergies I need to know about?"

Feeling off-balance, Dani shook her head and twisted to examine the jagged cut. She pressed the area around the injury, promptly inhaling at the sharp pain.

"Stop that," he ordered, his body moving closer and blocking out the light.

She stilled, the breath catching in her throat as she waited for his next move. Just when she thought he'd kiss her he reached up to rummage in the cabinet behind her.

"You don't know what is in there."

Her breath escaped in a silent rush that she told herself *wasn't* disappointment.

"I can fix it myself," she argued, determined to ignore the delicious masculine heat surrounding her, making her excruciatingly aware that she only had to turn her head and her mouth would brush that taut tanned skin. Her traitorous lips tingled as though she'd already done just that. "I do this stuff all the time."

He turned his head and she became distracted by the sculpted lines of his mouth, by the almost overwhelming need to press her lips to his. When he didn't move or respond, she lifted her eyes—and everything in her stilled.

His gaze was intense, searching, as though he was looking for something; searching for answers. To what? Her heart gave a little bump and every hair on her body rose—not in fear, as she'd initially thought but because it suddenly seemed as though all her life she'd been waiting for just this moment.

The air in the bathroom abruptly vanished, sucked out by—heck, whatever *this* was that had her body simultaneously melting and tightening—leaving just the two of them in a vacuum of heat that hummed and vibrated in time to the thundering of her pulse. For long moments they stared at each other.

Dani was all but drowning in his darkening eyes as reality shifted and narrowed. It left her reeling, feeling exposed and abruptly adrift in a spiral that threatened to send her spinning into dangerous, unknown territory.

A low moan emerged from her throat, jolting her back from that dark, dangerous edge. She quickly turned away, noting that Dylan was slower to react, looking as if she'd punched him in the head.

Oh God. She knew just how that felt.

"Fortunately," he rasped, closing the cabinet door with a snap and putting a couple of feet between them, "you don't have to."

The abrupt shift from heightened sensual awareness to embarrassment was disorienting. "D-don't have to w-what?" she stammered, pretending to dry her dripping hair with one corner of the towel as she hid her hot face.

Oh God, could she be any more obvious?

"Treat it yourself," he growled.

Dani peeked up in time to see him leave the bathroom. She stared at the empty doorway, wondering what the heck had happened and terrified that she knew.

Oh God, they'd had a *moment*. A sexually charged moment. One that had left her weak and breathless and way too turned on.

Fortunately his abrupt departure was helping to clear her head. Probably from pheromone withdrawal, she thought a little hysterically and took advantage of his absence to gulp in air and will her pulse to slow down from near-coronary levels.

Maybe this wasn't such a good idea. Maybe she should just sneak out while his back was turned. Because she had good reasons for her man embargo. *Very* good reasons.

Reasons that she suddenly couldn't quite recall. Because the longer she was around Dylan, the more difficult it was to think. And therein lay the problem. He made her forget that she wasn't cut out for relationships because she didn't measure up to a man's expectations—especially in the bedroom.

She'd made herself vulnerable once before and it had nearly ended in tragedy. But she'd managed to survive, to build a life for herself. She was stronger, sure but she didn't think she could survive another blow. Especially not from Dylan, because—she shivered—because he was the first man in years to make her feel.

If she let him.

Which meant she had to leave. *Now.* Clear out while the coast was clear.

No sooner had she made up her mind to get out of Dodge and hopped down from the counter, wincing as her foot hit the floor, than he reappeared, a mug of steaming coffee in one hand—*Oh God, she needed that*—and a medical emergency duffel slung over his shoulder.

One look at her guilty expression had a dark brow arching up his forehead. "Going somewhere?"

Flushing, she shook her head and hopped back onto the counter. She fumbled with the towel before taking the mug he offered, hugely relieved to have something to occupy her cold hands—something to hide behind as she met his hooded gaze head-on.

She hoped she was a picture of innocence but feared she looked guilty as hell. Finally he shook his head and dropped to his haunches to rummage through the duffel at his feet.

He was a big man, and his hands, broad-palmed and long-fingered, drew her fascinated gaze. She'd always been conscious of hands, of the harm they were capable of if the person they belonged to was careless. Or cruel. But she'd never been so riveted by the size or shape of a man's before.

Dylan's were big and tanned, graceful as he pulled out supplies and tossed them onto the counter. His thick wrists—well, they were thicker than hers—led to forearms that were strong with bone, muscle and sinew, the veins running beneath the skin looking both tough and fragile.

Her gaze roamed up over his powerful arm to the ball of his shoulder, admiring the play and shift of muscles beneath acres of tanned skin. Their definition was so clear that she was tempted to reach out and test the way they bunched and flexed for herself.

She could name each muscle: deltoid, pectoral, trapezius, bicep and tricep. They were common—everyone had them—but Dylan's fascinated her, drew her, because it was like looking at a work of art. Warm, satin-smooth, living art.

Drawing the towel closer, Dani frowned and thought *Holy cow—the man's lethal*. He made her want things she'd told herself were long dead. Made her want to get her hands on him when just the thought of it would have had her bolting for the door just a couple weeks ago.

"You okay?" he murmured, bent over her foot.

She gave a distracted nod and ignored the multitude of sensations bombarding her. Okay, *tried* to ignore the way her flesh buzzed and the muscles deep in her core clenched and released…then clenched spasmodically again.

Startled by the strength of the sensation—almost as if he'd actually touched her secret flesh—Dani jolted upright, her sharply indrawn breath overly loud in the silence. And when his gaze jumped to hers all she could think was, *Oh God, please let him think that was from pain and not—Oh God, not that!*

CHAPTER SIX

LOOKING UP INTO those heavily lashed gray eyes, Dylan promptly forgot everything. The expression in them—wide and a little wild—reminded him vividly of the dreams he'd battled this past week. Dreams that had left him irritable when he woke drenched in sweat, his heart beating like a runaway horse while his muscles quivered with unfulfilled lust.

Annoyed that she'd had the nerve to invade his dreams when she was so determined to avoid him during waking hours, he'd buried himself in work and deliberately avoided thinking about her. And then, just when he'd thought he might be succeeding, he'd looked up from his contemplation of the morning to see her striding across the neighboring deck, dressed in nothing but a baggy T-shirt that drooped off one shoulder and left her long, slender legs naked to mid-thigh.

At first he'd been too busy admiring the flash of those long legs to recognize her. Until her husky voice had slid across his skin like a secret wish and he'd realized his elusive neighbor was the very woman he couldn't stop thinking about.

And then, alarmed, she'd spun around and with a shocked squeak lost her balance and taken an unexpected morning dip. For one instant he'd worried that she couldn't swim but she'd surfaced looking so adorably annoyed that he hadn't been able to help laughing.

His laughter had faded when he'd hauled her out of the drink and caught a good look at the body she'd been hiding beneath her baggy scrubs. With her T-shirt clinging wetly to all those sweet curves and long slender limbs, she'd looked like any red-blooded man's wildest fantasy.

And while he'd been swallowing his tongue she'd been telling him—no, *ordering* him—to stop looking. She might as well have ordered the sun to stop shining, because he hadn't been able to. Hadn't wanted to, if he was honest. He'd liked what he'd seen—and not just a soaking wet armful of curvy contradictions.

"Dylan?"

He looked up in time to see her tongue dart out to wet her soft lips and the tension that was already setting his teeth on edge soared until the air literally crackled with it.

Blinking away the grinding lust, he inhaled, then exhaled and shifted to relax muscles he hadn't even realized had hardened. *Get a grip, man*, he ordered himself, frowning down at his hand gripping her foot. *The woman is only here because you practically shanghaied her.*

Consciously relaxing his fingers, he said, almost casually, "We're going to have to deal with this."

A tremor moved through her and he heard the click of her throat as she swallowed. She was nervous. Of him or of the sexual tension simmering between them?

Her long dark lashes fluttered against her flushed cheek and the breathy little gasp that filled the heated silence answered at least part of his question. It also shot his blood pressure to hell and it was only when she shuddered again that he realized he'd been caressing her instep with his thumb.

Shifting restlessly, she let her gaze briefly touch his

before sliding away. She was trying to appear unaffected and failing miserably. It was only fair, he thought with dark amusement. Why should he be the only one struggling to keep his mind off her long naked legs and on her injured foot?

"I...um... I thought we were?"

"I'm talking about this thing between us, Dani," he pointed out mildly.

A tiny frown marred the smooth skin between her brows. "Thing?" she asked cautiously.

Despite himself, he felt a low rumble resound through his chest. He wasn't entirely sure if it was amusement, impatience or the sound of a male animal preparing to pounce.

"For lack of a better word," he drawled, and turned his attention to disinfecting her foot, willing his hard-on to fade before she got an eyeful because he'd pulled his jeans on this morning without bothering to button them.

If she was uncomfortable discussing the chemistry that practically exploded the instant they came within twenty feet of each other, he could only imagine what the sight of his erection would do. No doubt she'd run screaming from the house to jump voluntarily into the bay, he thought with amusement.

Yep. And maybe he'd join her, because he suddenly needed an icy dip himself. It surprised him because it had been a long time since he'd felt the need for cold showers as a way to control himself around women.

Finding comfort in familiar tasks, Dylan prepared a local anesthetic and cleaned a small area of skin with an alcohol swab. He removed the needle cap with his teeth.

"You'll feel a small pinch," he murmured, immediately soothing her with his free hand when she gave an involuntary little jolt as the needle pierced her skin.

Cold fingers brushed his lips when she reached up to take the cap, sending hot, achy need spiraling downwards to his gut and digging sharp claws of need into his groin. Jeez, he was in a bad way.

It was humiliating to discover that Dylan St. James, head orthopedic reconstruction surgeon at St. Mary's, only son of Vivian and Ruben St. James and experienced man about town was being bewitched by a stormy-eyed mermaid he'd rescued from the bay. A mermaid, moreover, who'd been doing her best to run in the opposite direction ever since she'd practically fallen at his feet.

Dylan swallowed his dignity along with his ego—which was something she appeared to deflate with annoying regularity. And if he wasn't mistaken she didn't have a clue.

It wasn't a mystery why his heart pounded and his skin itched as though something alive moved through him. What surprised him was the raw intensity of the need twisting him up inside and messing with his head.

To give himself a moment, he turned away to scrub his hands and pat them dry on a clean towel, hoping like hell she couldn't see the way they shook.

He doused them with alcohol and studied her bent head. It made him feel marginally better knowing that she wasn't as unaffected as she wanted him to believe. It was there in her parted lips, in the rapid-fire pulse at the base of her throat, and when she looked up she couldn't hide her dilated pupils or the wild flush ebbing and flowing beneath her creamy skin.

He might have put it down to embarrassment or discomfort but she couldn't hide those sexy little hitches of breath. The ones that twisted his insides like a torquing machine.

Amused at both of them, Dylan selected a pair of tweezers and got to work. He murmured an apology when she flinched and had to bite back a chuckle when she bent her head close to his and demanded, "Is it all out?" and then *"What?"* a little huffily, at the sound of frustration he made in the back of his throat.

"I'm *working* here."

She sniffed haughtily. "And how many splinters do you remove on a daily basis, Dr. Sawbones?"

"Enough to know what I'm doing, Dr. Sassy," he retorted with a chuckle. "I regularly get to remove bone splinters from bits of mangled flesh. So, yes, I've got this."

She made a skeptical noise in the back of her throat and Dylan had to restrain himself from kissing her sulky mouth. The woman was a contradiction who alternately fascinated, exasperated and amused him. She was in turn remote and cool, brisk and efficient, wary and elusive. And then there was the awkward, easily flustered woman he found incredibly appealing.

Despite the *I'm-taking-a-break-from-men* attitude, he was experienced enough to know when a woman wanted him. She either didn't trust her feelings or didn't want them. And, although it was kind of humbling to discover that the woman he was attracted to didn't want anything to do with him, he could be patient.

He could wait.

He hoped.

After satisfying himself that he'd removed all the wood slivers, Dylan irrigated and disinfected the wound before laying out the suture kit. He ignored her assurances that she didn't need stitches, shaking his head at himself when he realized he was trying to impress her with his skills.

If that didn't tell him he was losing it, nothing would.

Once he'd applied a waterproof dressing he left her muttering to herself about overkill and reached into the shower. He punched a few buttons on the console and then, before she could grasp his intentions he'd whipped off her towel, scooped her off the vanity counter and deposited her in the shower.

Her shocked gasp became a shriek of outrage as icy water rained down on her. *"Wha—what the heck are you d-doing?"* she spluttered, leaping for the opening and trying to squirm past him.

He caught her with an arm around her waist, grinning down into her indignant face. "Just relax—it'll warm up. Just takes a few seconds."

"Relax?" she gasped, yanking him inside the cubicle and trying to use his body to shield her from the spray. "How c-can anyone relax in minus twenty d-degrees w-water?"

Trying to get a grip on her slick, squirming body, Dylan didn't feel the blast of icy water cascading over his heated flesh. Probably because all those sweet curves were sliding over him. Pulling her closer, he enjoyed the way she burrowed close and pressed her face into his throat. Although he knew it was mostly to escape the icy blast that was finally heating up. Her cool lips brushed his hot skin but his satisfaction turned into a yelp when she opened her mouth and…*bit him*.

The erotic pain sent instant lust clawing at his self-restraint, digging deep and snapping the last of his control. He couldn't have stopped what happened next to save himself.

In an instant he'd pushed her up against the tiles, his body a hard weight against hers. A startled squeak had barely left her lips when he caught her mouth in a kiss so hot and hungry it rivaled the steam filling the cubicle. He took a moment to acknowledge that he should probably get the hell away from her but he hadn't ever felt this kind of desperation to touch, to taste, to feel a woman before.

Needing to get closer, he pushed one thigh between hers, at the same time thrusting his tongue into her mouth. She made little mewling sounds and slid her hands up his arms to clutch at his shoulders. He distantly comprehended that although she wasn't shoving him away, she wasn't pulling him closer either.

It was as though she'd been stunned by the heat and ferocity of his mouth. He was kind of surprised himself, since he'd never before grabbed a woman and practically inhaled her in one swoop. At the realization he abruptly gentled the kiss, corralling the wild hunger gripping him to slide his mouth temptingly along the length of hers.

This, he thought sampling the subtle flavors of her mouth, the texture of her skin, was worth the time he'd waited—was worth reining in the need pounding through him.

He tormented her with little nibbles that gradually softened her mouth and coaxed a trembling response. God, she tasted good, he thought, sliding his tongue against hers. Like deep, wet kisses on hot silky nights; like cool fresh water after being out in the African sun all day; like some delicate new flavor that burst on his tongue and left him wanting, *needing* more.

Then she moaned—a low, husky sound that had him breaking off the kiss to drop his forehead to the tiles while he struggled to get his lust under control.

What the hell was he doing? he asked himself, trying to ignore the soft, sexy curves pressed against him until not even an idea could pass between their bodies. And what must she think of him, turning all wild and savage on her?

He knew he should move but he couldn't make himself. He'd wanted the feel of her against him for too long. It made him shudder when he'd never shuddered for a woman before.

Unable to keep his hands off her, he moved back a couple of inches and curled one hand around the back of her neck. Nudging up her chin with his thumb, he rasped, "Tell me."

As though coming out of a trance, Dani blinked up at him. She looked as stunned and aroused as he felt, and so damn beautiful his chest and gut tightened.

Her mouth trembled as it opened and closed before she managed a croaked, "Wha—what?"

Dropping his gaze to her mouth, he couldn't resist swiping his thumb across that plump bottom lip. "Tell me to go, Dani," he murmured, leaning forward to nibble on that soft pillow of flesh. "And I will." He didn't want to but he would. "Say the word and I'm gone."

Dazed eyes stared into his as though she wasn't quite certain what he was asking her. "I…uh…"

Then her gaze dropped to his mouth and got stuck there for a couple of beats before she made an unconscious move, her body drawn to his in spite of herself.

Her hands relaxed on his shoulders, drawing her gaze, as though she'd only just become aware that her fingers were digging into his flesh. She gave a soft murmured apology and smoothed the marks her nails had made before trailing heat across his deltoids and pecs with her fingertips.

Her hands halted just below his nipples, then slowly spread wide, the tips of her fingers brushing each tight bud. Her tongue sneaked between her lips and he jolted, as though she'd leaned forward and swiped her tongue across his flesh.

He briefly closed his eyes and prayed for control, because the sight of those pale, elegant hands on his tanned skin and the way she was looking at him, as if he was a decadent dessert, unraveled him faster than a tumble down a flight of stairs.

It was the first time she'd touched him voluntarily and he couldn't stop his flesh from rippling—couldn't prevent the shudder that began at the nape of his neck and buried itself in the base of his spine.

The sight of those delicate hands also forced him to acknowledge just how small she was, how fragile she looked against his bulk.

And how perfectly she fitted him.

He'd never been aggressive with women, either sexually or physically, preferring to coax and charm rather than to bully. And because his instinct now was to conquer and slay he forced himself to wait and watch, while she studied the contrast between her pale hands and his tanned skin.

He wanted her to make the next move—felt *compelled* to let her make it without overt pressure from him. Because he knew instinctively that she needed to feel she had a choice, that she had control when control was an illusion for both of them.

A wild flush bloomed beneath her skin and her breath hitched in her throat before she leaned forward and pressed her mouth to his hot skin. "Stay," she murmured, her tongue emerging to flick delicately against his nipple. "I want you to stay."

He felt that teasing touch like the flick of a whip and a growl of pure need rumbled through his chest. Spearing his fingers in her wet hair, he tilted her face to his. Her lashes lifted and her gaze was dark and turbulent and sweetly seductive.

And he was lost.

Before Dani could grasp that she'd made the decision for him to stay Dylan was kissing her with such heat and hunger she felt her toes curl. She'd never had a toe-curling kiss before—one that drew her in, lifted her up on her toes and pulled a line of fire right through the center of her body, as if he was drawing out her soul along with the air in her lungs.

Her skin, exquisitely and almost painfully sensitive, prickled at the wet scrape of denim between her thighs and made her moan. She shifted restlessly, moaning inside his mouth as muscles deep in her core clenched spasmodically.

He was fully aroused, his erection a huge bulge behind his zipper, hard and insistent as it pressed into her belly. It made her hollow places clench with a need she'd never felt before. She wanted him—wanted the momentary madness that he offered, a madness that would end her four-year drought.

Tugging on his lip with her teeth, she shivered with excitement. She could finally taste him and touch him all over. She could have him thrust into her body and take care of all those pesky needs that made her so miserably aware of just what she was missing by being on the wagon. Needs she hadn't felt in more than four long years.

She could have him. And then she'd be good for another four years.

The heavy ache that settled at the apex of her thighs had her defenseless against the sensations pouring through her. *Oh God*, she thought, sliding her hands up to his solid shoulders. All she could think was *I want*.

He was everywhere—a solid heated package of muscle and testosterone that filled her head with the warm damp smell of aroused man and her body with a sudden and pounding need. His surgeon's hands slid down her arms until they engulfed hers. Palms sliding against hers, he laced their fingers and pinned her hands to the tiles beside her head. The long, hard muscles in his thigh flexed, nearly melting her hair.

Damn, she thought faintly. He knew exactly how to make her blood heat and her mind scatter. It was there in the wicked gleam of his eyes, the sinful curve of his smile. He knew exactly where she ached, exactly where she needed him.

And he wasn't above using the knowledge to make her burn.

Her arms were pinned beside her head and the position arched her back, thrusting out her breasts like a sensual offering. She wanted him to touch her, yearned for that clever mouth to close over her aching flesh.

Frustrated by his barely there caresses, Dani shifted restlessly. She writhed against the long, thick hardness pressed to her belly, hoping to shred his control as he was shredding hers. The wanting was too painful, slicing deep and stripping away her inhibitions.

Ignoring her frustrated moans, Dylan laid a trail of kisses, sending lush sensations rolling through her as he embarked on a meandering path down her throat. He paused to suck sections of skin into his hot mouth before moving on, leaving behind a prickly, slow-spreading heat.

Despite her huffing pants, her restless movements and murmured demands, he refused to be rushed, moving from one erogenous zone to the next, ratcheting up her frustration levels until she wanted to scream.

Pinned against the wall, with solid muscle preventing her movements, Dani panted and shuddered, helpless against the onslaught of his lips and tongue and teeth. The melting eroticism left her weak, left her breath sighing between her parted lips as he thrust her into a firestorm of sensations, a world of kisses, taunting touches and a desperate burn.

Her resistance—had she really thought she had any against him?—lay in tatters, swirling down the drain along with the silky slide of water. She wanted... Her breathing quickened as she admitted to herself that she wanted *this*. Wanted *him*. Here. *Now*. Up against the wall.

She wanted fast and furious, and then she wanted slow and deep and languorous. And then maybe she'd be able to walk away.

"Dani..." The sound of her name—deep and thrillingly rough—pulled her from her lovely sensual haze. Skin buzzing, she lifted lazy lashes to find him barely an inch away, his green eyes stark and heavy-lidded with a look she barely recognized.

"Tell me this is what you want," he ordered in a voice rough with lust.

She blinked water from her eyes and opened her mouth but nothing emerged—even though the voice inside her head was screaming, *Yes, dammit! Don't stop now!*

Arching her back, she pressed her full length against him but he held himself rigidly away from her and his voice, when it came, was laced with utter steel. "In two seconds I am going to strip you naked," he growled. "I'm going to lick every inch—and I mean *every* inch—of your body." He swooped down to score his teeth along the tendon in her neck. "And then," he murmured, sliding his tongue along the same path, "I'm going to take you to bed and rock your world so hard you're going to forget about your man embargo and fall off the wagon with me."

His words sent a shudder through her. "I... I..." She swallowed back the embarrassing stutter and gasped. "Don't..." she panted, her hands curling into fists in his grip as muscles deep in her core pulsed. "Don't stop."

With a low laugh and a rough curse Dylan dragged the wet T-shirt over her head. Even before the sodden fabric hit the floor his mouth closed over her breast with thrilling possession. She yelped at the rough scrape of his teeth on her nipple, arching into the wet heat of his mouth.

Sensation rolled through her like a hurricane and something unfamiliar, hidden deep, unfurled, stretched and tautened. For one shocking instant she thought she would climax. But that was impossible. She'd never...couldn't...

Oh God!

As though sensing her impending release, Dylan immediately backed off, his soothing hand smoothing up her thigh to cup her bottom. His fingers dug in, gripped, kneaded, the rough jerky movements revealing his rising agitation.

He released her wrists, rasping, "God, you're sweet," against her mouth before dropping to his knees, chasing the goose bumps his words sent skittering across her skin with his mouth.

Weak and dizzy, Dani clutched at him, the only solid presence in a world that dipped and tilted beneath her feet. His tongue took a fiery path between her heaving breasts and across her belly where he lingered to circle her shallow belly button before dipping beneath the narrow band of her damp panties.

Eyes glowing like emeralds in his darkly sensual face, he looked up the length of her body, making Dani's heart give a spasmodic jerk. With his mouth an inch away from her liquid heat she had a blinding epiphany that this might not be something she would recover from—that it might not be easily extinguished, easily forgotten.

Then her head dropped back against the tiles with a muffled *thunk*...and she surrendered.

From his position at her feet, Dylan took in her unconscious eroticism. With her body arched, her head thrown back and a look of intense pleasure transforming her flushed face she looked startlingly beautiful. And impossibly aroused.

He reveled in the knowledge that *he* had brought her to this point. That just a touch of his mouth—right there between her legs—would send her flying off the edge. And in that instant he felt the earth rock beneath him because despite her natural sensuality it was as though she was discovering pleasure for the first time. *With him.*

His hands shook and he forced himself to slow down. He wanted to give more—wanted to make her yearn as well as burn. He wanted to hear her cry out and then he wanted to watch her shatter.

Curling his shaking fingers in the narrow pink band at her hips, Dylan slowly drew her panties down her long legs, fighting against the need to rush. Once he'd tossed them aside he lifted one slender leg over his shoulder, gripped her thighs, and put his mouth on her—right where she was hot and wet and needy.

At the touch of his mouth Dani gave a strangled yelp and felt his lips curl against her. His mouth. *Oh God, his mouth...* Stroking, kissing, licking, nibbling every inch of her until she thought she would go up in flames.

She fisted his hair, anchoring herself even as she rocked against his mouth. "Dylan..." she gasped, her need abruptly flaming out of control, shoving her rudely to the edge before she was ready. "I... I'm going to— *Oh!*"

Pleasure burst out of her with shocking ease as he sent her hurtling off the edge. Her knees gave way and she might have slithered into a boneless heap if he hadn't risen to his feet and crushed her against him. Dazed and languid by the force of her climax, Dani could only shudder helplessly and cling.

That had been...it had been... Well, she didn't have words. Only feelings. Feelings that were still rippling through her body like aftershocks.

When she could finally feel her feet she shifted languorously, rubbing her body restlessly against his—because, as amazing as it had been, she wanted *more*. She wanted it all.

Lifting her head, she caught a flash of white teeth that was smug and sexy as hell and told her more clearly than words that he'd watched her lose it. All that masculine satisfaction had a fiery blush working its way up her neck because he'd had his mouth on her, he'd watched her...

Oh boy.

Abruptly needing to turn the tables on all that male arrogance, she reached between them to cup the large bulge straining the placket of his soaked jeans and was gratified by the sharp breath he sucked in. His flesh grew and hardened beneath her hand, sending a feminine thrill surging through her.

It was a rush to feel how her touch affected him.

"Not here," he rasped, covering her hand with his larger one and pressing hard before gently pulling away.

It was the last thing Dani wanted. "But..." she protested, curling her fingers around the buttons. "I've never had shower sex before."

He gave a rough laugh and captured her hand, lifting it to press a kiss in the center of her palm. "What do you call what just happened?"

Surprised by the gesture, she found her hand curling around the hard line of his jaw. The rasp of his beard-roughened jaw against her skin sent heat flashing right between her legs. "But you—"

"Can wait," he interrupted, stepping back to fumble at his jeans with shaking hands.

"But—"

"No condom," he panted, shoving his jeans down his legs.

And then all Dani could do was stare. Because he was gorgeous. And—she shivered—and he'd been walking around commando...

With the water flowing over him he looked like an ancient warrior, big and bad and just a little bit dangerous as he rose, lifting his hands to wipe his face. Not knowing where to look first, because there was just so much to see and touch, Dani reached out blindly, her hand curling around the huge erection jutting between them.

He inhaled harshly, his eyes blazing heat as they caught hers. The message in them was plain: his control was hanging by a thread and she was playing a dangerous game.

Excitement shuddered through her and she tightened her grip. His eyes darkened and dropped to watch her slender fingers wrap around his bulky girth and test his heft.

It was no wonder women sighed when he walked past. Fascinated with the feel of him in her hands, Dani licked her lips. Because more than anything she wanted to taste him as he had tasted her.

Then he staggered and with a rough curse braced himself against the wall behind her. Tipping back his head, he closed his eyes. And in that moment, as Dani watched, a dull flush stained the hard slash of his cheekbones and she understood sexual power. She held it in her hands. It was there in the stark need that tightened his features.

The breath sawing from his lungs, Dylan thrust slowly into her hand before finally pulling back.

She made a sound of protest and tightened her grip. "No, I—"

Roughly turning her to face the wall, he lifted her

hands to press her palms against the tiles. And just like that once again the balance shifted.

"Soon," he promised, opening his mouth against her neck to suck a patch of skin into his mouth. "I want to be deep inside you when I come."

His words made her shiver in anticipation and dread—because this was where she felt inadequate. But then he smoothed his hand from the nape of her neck to the dip in her spine and everything but the need to feel him thrusting into her body slid away.

Thinking he meant to take her from behind, Dani braced herself and waited with bated breath, groaning in disappointment and startled pleasure when his fingers dug into her scalp instead.

With slow, massaging hands he washed her hair and then her body, making her sigh with pleasure, tremble with renewed arousal and cry out when he cupped her breasts or slid long, talented fingers between her legs.

When she was a quivering mass of unfulfilled longing he drew her from the shower and wrapped her in a large bath towel. Floating on a cloud of exquisite arousal, she felt him swing her up into his arms, feeling too wonderful to do more than hook a limp arm around his neck and sink her teeth into the ball of his shoulder.

What *was* it about him that made her want to bite him?

He deposited her gently on his bed and she roused herself briefly—only to clutch him and utter a low moan when his big, hard body followed, pressing her into the mattress with his delicious weight and inserting one hard, hair-roughened thigh between hers.

Arching her back and rocking languorously, she hummed in pleasure. It took an inordinate effort to lift her lashes. Barely an inch away, his handsome face was etched in stark lines of need, his gaze as fiercely intense as it was possessive.

"Now…" he murmured, dipping his head to nip her chin, the gentle curve between her neck and shoulder and then to swipe his tongue along her clavicle. "Now I can taste you everywhere."

Then he closed his mouth over the tip of one breast and flung her abruptly back into mindless pleasure.

Clutching the sides of his head, Dani struggled to remember why she'd thought this was a bad idea. It was wonderful, and so amazingly intense that she wanted to sink under the weight of it. Give herself to it. Let herself go. Take him with her.

But just when she felt herself sliding under his sensual spell panic, greasy and insistent, fought its way to her consciousness. Because now that they were here, on his bed, they were heading in an irrevocable direction. A direction that usually ended in disappointment.

Her heart clutched—and not in a good way. She stiffened. She had to tell him…had to stop him.

"Dylan."

CHAPTER SEVEN

TRANSFERRING HIS ATTENTION to her other breast, Dylan slid his hand up the smooth length of Dani's slender leg. He loved her little gasps and mewls, the helpless little hums of pleasure that burst from her. He'd never *needed* to hear a woman's soft sighs in response to his touch before, never craved the sight of her arching helplessly and demanding more.

Her fingers slid into his hair and clenched against his scalp but he welcomed the pain. It helped steady him as he palmed her crotch, sliding a finger between the hot glistening folds. And, God, he loved the way her body quivered and melted.

She rocked against his hand. "Dylan!" The word emerged as a strangled plea. "I… *I-don't-want-you-to-be-disappointed*," she said on a rush.

Even as her thighs tightened around his hand something in her voice alerted him and he lifted his head and stared into her flushed face. She bit her lip and avoided his gaze, shifting restlessly beneath him as though at any second now she would bolt.

When he blinked and focused everything in him stilled. "What are you talking about?"

"I… I… I'm sorry," she stammered, blushing hotly.

"I'm no good at th—this part..." Her lips trembled and she pressed them together as her eyes swam. "I'm s-sorry."

For Dylan it was a defining moment. Despite the haze of lust clouding his brain, he knew instinctively that if he handled the next few seconds badly she would retreat into herself and he'd never get another chance.

The last thing he wanted between them—especially like *this*—was the specter of another man. A man who'd made her doubt herself, draw into herself. A man who'd put that guarded look in her eyes and had her stiffening whenever Dylan touched her.

But if he wasn't patient—if he didn't show her how good it could be—it would be all over before it could begin. Before *they* could begin. More than anything Dylan wanted that beginning with her, despite her fears. And he couldn't work out why she should think she'd disappoint him when she was so lushly generous with her responses.

Eyes locked on hers, he dipped his head to place a gentle kiss on her lips. And then another. "You couldn't disappoint me, babe," he murmured, stringing damp kisses along her jaw and across the elegant cheekbone to place a brief kiss on the tip of her nose. "Trust me."

When she just looked at him, it occurred to Dylan that she didn't trust easily. She kept her emotions locked up tight and it would take a lot of patience to find the key. The guy who'd hurt her had a lot to answer for.

Gently brushing damp curls off her face, he murmured, "I won't hurt you, Dani. I couldn't. Not you."

She bit her lip, looking tempted but undecided even when it was clear she yearned to believe him. She didn't trust her own judgment. Didn't trust her own body.

He would just have to show her.

Rocking his hips gently against hers, he watched as her eyes darkened and her lashes fluttered as his shaft slid against her tender flesh. Then she sighed, a sound of such sensuality that he wanted to catch it in his mouth before it escaped.

Her eyes dropped to his mouth and she lifted a hand to trace a fingertip along the line of his bottom lip. Giving in to the urge, he parted his lips and drew her finger into his mouth.

"Just relax and let me make it good."

"It's just this," she murmured, sliding her finger free to cup his face, her palm warm and soft against his rough cheek. "This is all I can offer. Once. Here with you."

Covering her hand with his, he turned to press his lips against the soft skin of her wrist. He wanted to argue because he had a bad feeling that once wouldn't be enough—wouldn't be *nearly* enough.

"Yeah…" he rasped, pressing his hips closer and nudging her with his erection. "And then we'll do it again and again…until we're done."

Wild color rushed into her face and she snorted. "I meant—"

"I know," he promised with a wicked grin. "I know exactly what you meant. But just so you know," he added, his gaze and his voice softening, "you couldn't disappoint me if you tried."

And then, because he had only one chance to convince her that once would never be enough, Dylan set his mind to seducing her. Despite his own impatience, the pounding of his blood, he began with hot drugging kisses that swept away her tension and replaced it with another kind of tension. Until she was moaning and rocking into his teasing touches with an eagerness he'd never encountered.

God, she was sweet. And she'd thought she wasn't enough…

He ruthlessly overwhelmed her with sensation until

she was writhing beneath him, teetering on the edge of another orgasm as she begged him to take her. And when he finally rolled a condom down the length of his shaft, captured her mouth and thrust into her body, he felt as though he'd come home.

She was tight, incredibly tight, and he had to resist the urge to bury himself deep. But the moment he breeched her entrance her body clamped down on his invasion like a velvet vice.

Pausing to tangle his hands in her damp hair, Dylan shuddered and breathed through his lust. He gritted his teeth and pressed in another inch, scattering desperate little kisses down her neck and across her shoulder to her breast.

"Relax," he rasped, his voice strained as he carefully drew back an inch, then eased forward again.

He smoothed his palm down her thigh to her knee, enjoying the feel of the long slender muscles flexing beneath silky skin. Curling his hand beneath her knee, he lifted her leg to ease his entrance, watching each expression as it flittered across her beautiful face.

She might lock down her emotions, he thought, gritting his teeth but she couldn't keep her thoughts from showing on her face. It fascinated him to see discomfort at war with desire, excitement and a growing sensual impatience.

She shifted restlessly beneath him as he smoothed damp hair off her forehead with shaking fingers. "You okay?"

God. A woman had never made him shake before.

"I'm f-fine," she gasped, a flush rushing across her chest and up her neck into her face. Clutching at his shoulders, she wrapped her legs around him and arched up into his embrace. "Oh God, it feels so…*good.*"

And, with his gaze locked on hers, Dylan pulled back

again and slowly thrust in deep, drawing a low moan of pleasure from her throat. Muscles burning with effort and eyes fierce, he captured her hands and laced their fingers tightly together.

"Keep your eyes on mine, babe," he huffed out with effort. "And hang on. I'm going to rock your world."

I'm going to rock your world.

Dani bit her lip as heat gathered between her legs and spread across her belly. Her foundations were already shuddering and she wondered if she would survive this sensual attack.

With him filling her completely, stretching her inner muscles, she could almost believe that she wouldn't disappoint him. Almost believe that she could be what he needed, what she desperately wanted to be. For him.

But that wasn't going to happen, she admitted with regret, because she knew from experience that once a guy got to this point he lost the plot along with his control and she always needed more time. More time to get into the mood, to strain for that moment of glory.

Dylan hadn't wanted to listen, so all she could do now was try to make it as good for him as possible and hope he didn't notice her lack of…well, *finishing*.

He was the first man in a long while to make her feel like a woman—the first man to make her feel as though this amazing feeling was possible, that she could let herself go long enough to be swept away. It was an amazing feeling. Almost as amazing as the feel of him inside her, surrounding her, the scent of him in her lungs as he moved over her, thrusting deep over and over and over.

Her inner muscles quivered. Heat was building, spreading. *Oh God, had it ever felt this good?*

Keeping his strokes ruthlessly slow and deep, Dylan

stared into her eyes until the thread deep inside her belly drew tight. She trembled, finding the way he looked at her more intimate than his possession. She wanted to look away, to shut her eyes and lose herself in physical sensation. Maybe then she could—

She jolted when he nipped at her lip. "Stay with me," he growled, and her eyes flew open to that fiercely intense gaze as he thrust long and hard and deep.

She rocked against him more frantically. "Please…" she gasped, clutching at him, desperate to hang on to the only stable thing in her wildly spinning world.

His slick muscles rippled beneath her fingers, oiled steel straining with the effort to keep his rhythm slow and deep as he ruthlessly drove her toward something as tantalizing as it was elusive.

"Please…" she sobbed again, unsure whether she was asking him to stop or to take his pleasure, because she wouldn't…*couldn't* come. Not like this.

Ignoring her pleas, Dylan kept his eyes on hers, kept her hovering on the edge as that thread tightened, building… building…until one hard downward thrust drew her completely under.

Her body arched up as she came, his name a hoarse cry of stunned pleasure bursting from her lips. She clung to him, the walls of her body clenching and pulsing around him as his thrusts increased in tempo and strength, sweeping her away into another helpless orgasm even more intense than the first.

Breath rasping like bellows, he finally slammed into her one last time, driving her up the bed with the force of his own climax. His muscles turned to stone and his eyes were a fierce green blaze in his tight face. Then the breath whooshed from his lungs as though he'd slammed into a wall, and he threw back his head and emptied himself into her.

Finally he gave a rough groan and collapsed over her, buried his face in her neck, his arms bands of iron as he held her to him. And all Dani could do was cling on and drift on a cloud of sensual delight.

She might have been stunned by what had happened if she'd been able to think. Locked to him, around him, her body pulsing with little aftershocks, all she could do was feel.

And she felt fantastic—so fantastic that all she could think of was that she wanted to hold it to her for just a little while longer.

She didn't know how long they lay like that but when her heart-rate slowed to just under stroke level she became aware that she was wrapped around him as though she was terrified he would vanish.

Embarrassed to be caught clinging, she quickly released him and tried to push him off.

Lost in the hazy aftermath of spectacular sex, Dylan felt her pulling away and instantly tightened his arms. He didn't want to move; he wanted to keep them joined, keep this incredible feeling just a little longer.

He flexed his hips and smiled at the odd little sound she made in the back of her throat—kind of a mix between a squeak and a wheeze as her body rippled around his shaft.

And then she gave another little shove.

Groaning, Dylan managed to get his elbows under him. He didn't want to move. He liked being this close to her, their bodies still intimately joined. He liked the feeling of their sweat-slicked skin fused together and the way their combined scent filled the air.

He looked at her. Really looked. And he was pleased

to see the rosy glow flushing her skin even as she evaded his gaze. He continued to study her, smug in the knowledge that he'd made her come not once but twice. All while buried so deep inside her he hadn't known where he ended and she began.

His grin widened. So much for disappointing him.

The rosy glow deepened. "Stop that," she muttered, giving him another little shove.

"Stop...?" He chuckled, dipping his head to taste the pulse thundering at the base of her throat. Her muscles quivered as he slid a broad palm down her back to the base of her spine, where he pressed, keeping them connected.

It was when he rolled them over that he realized why he'd never felt anything so good.

The condom had broken.

The knowledge was like an icy slap in the face.

As carefully as he could, he lifted her off him and slid off the bed, heading for the bathroom as reality hit him like a blow to the head. No wonder sex had been better with her than with any other woman. No wonder being inside her had felt like being wrapped in hot wet silk.

His breath escaped in a whoosh but this time he really *had* hit a brick wall... Because right now his little swimmers were heading for Ground Zero.

Cursing, he quickly disposed of the condom and cleaned up before grabbing the edge of the counter to steady himself. He closed his eyes and dropped his head between his shoulders as reality washed over him. For the first time in twenty years he was facing the possibility of an unplanned pregnancy and...

Abruptly he pushed himself upright and caught sight of his reflection. *Hell.* He looked like hell.

He froze and took another look. Actually, no, he decided, he looked as if he'd just had the most spectacular sex of his life.

Cursing again, he turned and grabbed a pair of jeans that were draped over the laundry basket, pulling them on with jerky movements. In seconds he was yanking at the zipper with unsteady hands, telling himself that they would face it when—*if*—it happened.

He took a moment to splash his face with cold water and then he caught movement out of the corner of his eye. Face dripping, he turned to see her standing a couple of feet from the deck doors, wrapped in his sheet, her eyes wide and distressed in her pale face.

He grabbed a towel and dragged it over his face to give himself a minute. It wouldn't do to lose it now—not with that look on her face.

When he looked again she was still exactly as she'd been, frozen like a deer scenting danger.

With the morning light pouring in through the doors she looked like a young Eve, wildly beautiful and thoroughly ravished. Her pale neck and shoulders rose above the sheet, and even from here he could see the reddened patches of whisker burn and hickeys beginning to darken her creamy skin.

She was poised to run, and something...*something* in her eyes...warned him to be careful how he handled the next few minutes—warned him that she was bracing herself for... What? Movement? Violence? Anger?

Despite his inner turmoil, the panic in her eyes made him feel sick inside—because a woman didn't look like that for no reason. It steadied him as nothing else could have.

Tossing the towel aside, Dylan took a step—and stilled when her eyes widened and she stumbled back. For a long tense moment he watched her nibble nervously on her lip, swallowing the words that sprang to his lips.

"I told you, I'm no good at…at that." She gulped, struggling for composure as she went red, then white, then red again. "I tried to tell you but—"

"I'm not *disappointed*, Dani," he interrupted, aghast that she could think so.

But clearly she did, because the wariness was back and she looked ready to bolt at the first move from him.

Sucking in a steadying breath, he said quietly, "You felt it as much as I did."

Her posture relaxed slightly but her eyes remained locked warily on him, as though waiting for him to attack. *What the hell?*

He shoved impatient fingers through his hair, furious with himself for the fine tremor in them. Dammit, if there was ever a time he needed control it was now. Unfortunately it felt as though she'd wrested his control from him with that first look into her soft gray eyes.

"Tell me you're on the pill."

A quick frown drew her brows together. "What?"

"Birth control," he rasped, cursing himself when she flinched. Exhaling carefully, he said more quietly, "The condom broke."

For long moments she stared at him, confusion swirling in that stormy gray gaze. Then abruptly her eyes cleared, her brows drawing together as his meaning became clear.

Her breath escaped in a quiet whoosh. "Oh."

When she looked neither pleased nor distressed by the news, it was up to Dylan to repeat, "*Are* you?" his fingers tightening painfully on the door frame.

Expression carefully neutral, she said, "No,"—so softly he almost didn't hear it above the pounding of his heart.

He let out a soft curse, his fingers white-knuckling the doorjamb. "So you could get pregnant?"

Her gaze instantly shuttering, she turned and moved to the open deck doors, drawing Dylan's gaze from the long, elegant line of her naked back to the twin dimples at the base of her spine.

The urge to drop to his knees and put his lips there rattled him and he crossed the carpet on silent feet, telling himself it was to keep her from bolting down the stairs.

"No, I can't," she said in a low voice when he came to a stop behind her.

"How can you be so sure?" He wanted to put his hands on her, to soothe the tension pumping from her in almost visible waves.

She gave a ragged laugh and lifted shaking fingers to shove wild, tousled curls off her face. "Because it's impossible."

Studying her delicate profile, the tense set of her shoulders, Dylan thought back to when she'd been flushed and sated. He wished he could turn the clock back five minutes.

"What do you mean, 'impossible'?"

For long moments she didn't speak, and then her jaw hardened. She turned to lean back against the open French door and her gaze was coolly amused. "I mean I have Asherman's syndrome," she drawled. "So I guess that lets you off a very unpleasant hook, Dr. St. James."

Ignoring the subtle bite in her tone, Dylan's eyes narrowed, dropped to her belly where he'd seen and traced those thin silvery scars with his tongue. "Asherman's?"

"I had an accident...years ago," she said with careful neutrality, as though they were discussing a patient. But Dylan caught the convulsive movement of her throat as she swallowed. "A bad one."

Her fingers tightened almost imperceptibly as she dragged the sheet closer. As though to protect herself from the words, from *him*.

"There…um…there was a lot of internal scarring and—" Her delicate brows drew together and she hitched a bare shoulder, the movement jerky and filled with a roiling tension. "The gynecologist said my chances of ever conceiving were negligible." She spun away and sent him a mocking glance over her shoulder. "So you see why this is just a one-time thing?" She looked away. "Men want certain…things. Things I can't give them."

Dylan took the step that separated them and wrapped his arms around her resistant body, drawing her back against his chest. She didn't pull away but stood rigidly in his embrace, tension vibrating through her like a tuning fork.

"You have no idea what I want, Dani," he said deeply, pressing a kiss to her naked shoulder. "But I think we can safely say that I'd be an idiot if I didn't want more of what just happened."

She jerked her shoulder irritably. "That's just *sex*, Dylan," she scoffed, and he fought not to feel offended by her quick dismissal of what had been the best sex of his life.

"Pretty spectacular sex," he reminded her with a trace of humor, smug satisfaction rising in him when she gave a helpless little shiver at the reminder.

Damn, he wanted her again, he admitted silently. She was soft and warm and, despite the driving need to toss her back onto that bed and remind her just how spectacular it had been, more than anything he wanted her trust. He wanted her to relax, to laugh. He wanted her to open herself to him, to turn to *him* when demons kept her awake at night.

Discovering a yearning inside him for all that left him reeling. They'd only just met, he told himself. It would be insane to think this was anything more than what it was: two sexually compatible people having spectacular sex.

Dylan tightened his arms and inhaled the scent of warm, sexy woman. If this was all she would take from him, he decided, then he'd focus on giving it to her. *For now.*

He continued to nuzzle her neck until his patience was rewarded. Her body slowly relaxed against him, although she didn't turn and she didn't try to touch him. Relieved, he brushed a kiss against the tender curve between her neck and shoulder.

Beneath the scent of his soap he could smell both of them. He could smell a unique fragrance that was all her, and the discovery made him want to imprint his scent on her as much as he feared hers was imprinted on him.

Hungry for more, he licked her skin, enjoying the taste of warm freshness overlaid with the faint saltiness of exertion.

A shiver moved through her. She tilted her head to one side to give him more room to run his mouth up to nibble on the tender skin beneath her ear. Mouth curving against her skin, he buried his face in the soft cloud of dark curls, tenderly running his hands up and down her arms, warming her chilled skin.

Finally she gave a ragged sigh and turned to him, her hands leaving a line of fire across his pecs and down his abdomen. She brushed her mouth across his nipple, small white teeth emerging to nip at the tight bud.

He shuddered. The feel of her mouth on him ratcheted up his hunger until he felt as if he hadn't recently experienced that explosive, bone-melting orgasm. And, with his legs threatening to buckle, he swung her into his arms, determined this time to taste the long elegant line of her spine down to those sexy little dimples. He would taste her secret places and watch her face as he thrust into her body.

He wanted to be staring into her soul when she shattered.

It was just sex, Dani told herself for the hundredth time. Incredible, mind-blowing sex it was true but just sex. And now it was over. She could go back to being on the wagon and enjoy being alone.

And maybe if she repeated that to herself enough she might begin to believe it. She might feel amazingly alive for the first time in her life—alive, consumed and possessed—but that didn't mean he wanted anything more than she did.

He lived in his world; she lived in hers.

But if it was difficult to forget the incredible sex—an amazing first for her—what had come after was even harder. He'd teased and cajoled her to spend the day with him, and before she knew it, it was two on Monday morning and she was limp as a rag doll from yet another mind-blowing orgasm.

She'd lost track of how many she'd had—a miracle in itself, considering she'd believed herself incapable. As she'd lain there, boneless and mindless, it had dawned on her that anything that came after would be anti-climactic.

He'd been wonderful, so sexy and romantic, and he'd made her *laugh*. It was the first time anyone had made her laugh as well as sigh while he was buried deep inside her body.

Nothing had ever come close to this intense feeling of rightness, and she was afraid that if she stayed she would start thinking that it was more than just sex. Because, despite her determination to keep it simple, she'd found herself sharing stuff about her family, about growing up geeky and nerdy and largely ignored by boys because she was shy and smart.

When he'd said *he* wouldn't have ignored her, she'd scoffed. "Girls like me are invisible to boys like you."

"Boys like me are idiots," he'd said, and when she'd rolled her eyes he'd gone on to tell her about why he'd needed to get away after losing his grandfather and a close childhood friend so close together. Working aboard the Mercy Ship, he'd admitted, had opened his eyes to the plight of children in war-torn countries and he was determined to do something to help.

How could she not be swept away when he was so darn likeable? Not just wickedly funny but dry and insightful. And then there was that incredibly sweet streak.

He'd likely be horrified that she thought him sweet but what else could she think when a man made time for a lonely neighbor on the houseboat moored at the next berth? Or answered the endless questions Hilda Frauenbach peppered him with about poisons found in Africa and whether the African pygmy was hostile?

She'd found herself watching, waiting for the mask to crack and the impatience to show but it hadn't. Either he was better at hiding his emotions than most people, or he really was what he seemed.

How did a woman resist a man who was amazingly patient and affectionate outside of bed and so thrillingly impatient in it? A man who spoke of his family in a way that told her of the deep love and respect he had for them. A man who didn't ridicule her opinions or force his on her. A man who respected her reticence even as he tempted her to throw caution to the wind.

He'd told her about the woman he'd met on the Mercy Ship and how she'd tried to pass off another man's baby as his, laughing when Dani expressed her outrage.

"I'm lucky," he'd said, smiling sleepily down at her. "If I hadn't overheard Simone bragging to that nurse I might not have been there to rescue you from that killer puddle."

She'd rolled her eyes but her belly had jittered nervously at the implication that he was glad he'd been there that night when she didn't know *how* she felt. She'd told him how she'd met Richard and hinted at bits of her marriage but she couldn't—wouldn't *ever*—tell him about the bad stuff because it was her shameful secret.

And if something inside her had trembled in envy when he'd talked about wanting the kind of relationship his parents and grandparents had, Dani ignored it and allowed him to sweep her up into a fantasy of shared laughter, hot glances and mind-blowing sex.

With him wrapped around her, his deep, even breathing disturbing tendrils of damp hair at her temple, she tried to ignore the panic that had crept up on her until she couldn't breathe.

Old insecurities came flooding back, until it was all she could do not to run screaming into the night. She waited until his hold loosened and then she slid quietly away. Like a memory.

Because that was all their weekend could ever be: a time out of time. She was back on the wagon and they were back to being just neighbors and colleagues.

Yep. Neighbors and colleagues. Exactly as it was supposed to be.

Now all she had to do was convince herself that was what she wanted. She was back on the wagon and… Well, memories—the kind they'd made these past two days— were better than regrets.

CHAPTER EIGHT

DYLAN HADN'T BEEN surprised when he'd awakened on Monday morning to find himself alone and the bed beside him cold.

For just a moment he'd thought he'd imagined the whole weekend. Then he told himself he'd go and find her in the kitchen, brewing coffee and burning eggs. She'd be dressed in nothing but his T-shirt, looking adorably rumpled as she frowned down at the scrambled mess she'd made of breakfast.

He'd pull her back against his chest and slide his hands beneath the baggy shirt where he'd find warm, supple curves and soft, slender woman. Then he'd kiss her neck and inhale the fragrance of heated feminine skin. At his touch she'd give a delicious shiver, before turning to lift her mouth to his. Then he'd kiss her, lift her onto the counter and press his morning erection between her open thighs.

But even as the image appeared he knew without being told that the houseboat was empty of her. Empty and quiet. And the prospect of long, languid kisses and lazy morning sex became nothing but a fantasy.

He'd think their whole *weekend* nothing but a fantasy if not for the scent of her on his sheets—and on his skin, he thought, sniffing his arm. She'd burrowed beneath it, dug sharp claws into his gut and chest and left without a thought.

Anger moved through him as it dawned on him just how empty his life was when he'd thought himself content. He had an amazing family who loved him and a career on the fast track. His professional life was busy and fulfilling and—he cursed and shoved a shaky hand through his hair—his personal life sucked.

Damn. He should have known yesterday, when she'd become more and more distant, that she'd been subtly pulling away even as he'd tried to bind her more tightly to him—to seduce her with pieces of his life, with laughter over his fumbled ten-year-old attempts at being a cool man about town and shared intimacies.

Perhaps that had been what had spooked her. Dani was afraid of being truly intimate.

With him? Or with any man?

Not the intimacy of sex, he mused, stomping around his houseboat in a rare flash of masculine pique. Once she'd overcome her initial fear of disappointing him she'd been generous and wildly passionate. But she'd shared very little of her emotions or the real reason her marriage had failed. And it was there he knew he would find the answers to the mystery that was Danielle Stevens.

Her ex had certainly done a number on her, he thought with growing anger. He'd made her believe she wasn't good enough, that she had little to offer a man. He'd all but stripped a vibrant, generous woman of her confidence in her own femininity and convinced her that she was better off alone.

Dylan had grown up in a house full of women. He didn't consider himself a particularly sensitive man—he had too much testosterone for that—but he couldn't understand the need some men had to break a woman down.

Strip her of everything that made her such a delightful bundle of contradictions.

He wasn't stupid. He knew such men existed. But he'd never understood them. Never understood their need to belittle, to grind away at someone's confidence in themselves.

And Dani…? He recalled the sound of her laughter and the way it had made him feel the first time it had bubbled from her throat. That irrepressible gurgle of mirth had made him feel ten feet tall, because *he'd* been the one to draw it out of her.

Then she'd slipped away without a word, and left him feeling as though she'd taken all the sunshine, all the warmth with her. It made him angry. More with himself because he'd slipped under her spell as easily as she'd burrowed beneath his skin.

In one weekend, damn it.

But Dylan wasn't a St. James for nothing. He wasn't about to give up and he'd be damned if he'd allow anyone to come between him and the woman he wanted. Even the woman herself. And if he wanted Danielle Stevens, in his bed and in his life, more than he'd ever wanted anything— *any woman*—before, all he had to do was convince her to fall off the wagon with him again.

Piece of cake.

If only he could get her to answer her phone or return his damn messages.

Dani had taken to hiding in the ER supply room. She knew it was a cowardly thing to do but she couldn't face Dylan until she had her feelings firmly locked down or people would take one look at her and know that she'd had wild, uninhibited sex with the hot-shot surgeon.

Heat swept through her body and burned in her cheeks.

Oh boy. If just the memory had her sweating in indecent places, she could imagine what would happen if she found herself face to face with him in company.

She'd never met a man who could so easily make her forget that she had good reason to avoid relationships. Or one who refused to acknowledge their very temporary arrangement.

Besides, he had dozens of women calling him, "accidentally" bumping into him wherever he went—even when she'd been with him, for heck's sake. Granted, he hadn't seemed to notice or care, she recalled with a secret thrill. Instead he'd focused all his attention on her, which made him either very well brought up or very, very sneaky. What woman *wouldn't* find all that attention flattering and just a little bit intoxicating?

She certainly had.

But it would be really stupid to think it meant anything more—that he wanted anything more. And Dani had already used up her quota of stupid for one lifetime. She couldn't—*wouldn't*—let herself forget that it hadn't meant anything more than a weekend of fun.

So she'd ignored his calls and texts, hoping he'd get the message, give up and spare her the humiliation when he eventually moved on. Because that was what guys like him did. They moved on.

Unfortunately her heart and her body didn't get the message, and kept insisting that she answer his calls. Fortunately she'd been swamped with work whenever he came around and when she hadn't been she'd managed quite neatly to avoid him.

Even as she'd congratulated herself for handling the weekend with such modern sophistication she'd struggled with the emotional fall-out. She was, she discovered, entirely unsuited for one-night stands—one-weekend stands.

What she *was* suited for, however, didn't matter, because she'd been the one to insist on a one-time thing and she always tried to keep her word.

Besides, she reminded herself, she had very little to offer a man like Dylan, and thinking that she might be falling for him was dangerous and stupid.

So stupid that she was hiding out in the supply room, trying to convince herself that everything was back to normal. She rolled her eyes. If you could call sneaking in and out of her own home the past ten days normal. Or letting his calls go to voicemail. She couldn't even think how his number had got onto her phone.

She was back on the wagon, she told herself firmly, back to living like a nun and loving every minute of it. *Really*. She could do whatever she liked, whenever she liked, and there was no one to distract her from doing it. Things like her laundry. Things like cleaning out the refrigerator, giving herself a homemade facial or scrubbing her bathroom to within an inch of its life…for the third time in less than two weeks.

And she'd spent a delightful, if unplanned weekend with her parents on Vancouver Island, telling herself that she wasn't running away. She wasn't falling for him and she wasn't avoiding him.

The only reason she hadn't deleted his voice messages was because she'd been too busy. And if she listened again to the sound of his voice, especially late at night, it wasn't because she was reliving the weekend like a giddy adolescent with her first crush.

It *certainly* wasn't because she was crushing on Dylan St. James just like every other woman at St. Mary's. That would be beyond embarrassing. Not to mention really stupid. She was a mature, professional physician who could have a brief, steamy affair with a hot guy without getting her emotions or her heart involved.

That particular organ had been killed off by her marriage and it wasn't likely ever to be resuscitated. And certainly not for a pair of wicked green eyes, a deep bedroom voice that slid into her secret places and a mouth that could tempt an angel to fall from grace.

Nope. Nuh-uh. Not likely.

Besides, how could an intelligent woman possibly fall for a man she'd known less than two months? It was impossible—not to mention ridiculous. Despite all signs to the contrary and despite her friends' and colleagues' concern at her distraction.

An ER doctor couldn't afford to be distracted, even during the graveyard shift on a night so slow that she'd checked her phone no less than forty-six times—apparently Amy had counted—for new messages, before escaping to the storeroom.

But, then again, Dylan hadn't called or texted her for three days.

Fine, she admitted, frowning at the packages of wet dressings on the shelf. Three days, seventeen hours and fifty-two minutes. Clearly he'd moved on. *The jerk.*

Pressing a hand to her queasy stomach, she rearranged the packages and counted them—for the third or was it the fourth time? She was muttering to herself when she heard the door open and close. Thinking that Amy—the woman gave *determined* and *obstinate* a bad name—had resorted to cornering her there, Dani sighed.

"Amy, I'm *fine*," she growled with extreme exasperation, glad she was hidden amongst the rows of shelving. "For the ten millionth time, *I am fine.* I'm a little under the weather but I do not have any dreadful disease that requires a visit to a physician." She sucked in an irritated breath. "I *don't* have a brain tumor and I am *not* pining away for any Y-chromosome with hot green eyes *and a sexy butt*!"

She paused in her rant to scowl at the tablet she was checking against the supplies. She ground her teeth together when she caught movement out the corner of her eye.

"You need to get laid," she said irascibly, turning to face Amy. "Focus on your own sex life and not— *Dylan*!"

To say she was surprised to see him propped up against the end of the row of shelves in his scrubs was an understatement.

She gave a shocked shriek and tumbled backward, her scrabbling fingers missing the wooden shelving completely and sweeping several boxes of syringes and surgical gloves onto the floor, along with half the neatly arranged wet dressing packages.

She slapped the hand clutching the tablet against her tachycardic heart and gasped. "What the—? You scared me!"

He folded his arms across his wide chest—and she *wasn't* noticing the way his biceps, triceps and all those flexor and extensor muscles bulged at the movement. She *wasn't* recalling every detail of their weekend together.

His unreadable eyes studied the way she was clutching the tablet to her chest as though it could protect her from him. After what seemed like a millennium his eyes took on a twinkle and his mouth began to twitch. "You think I have a sexy ass?"

"Wha—? *No. Yes*… I mean… *That's* what you got from all that?"

"No." He chuckled, pushing away from the shelving. "I also got that you've been pining for my wicked green eyes. But I agree about needing to get laid. In fact—"

She hastily backed up a half-dozen steps, her eyes widening as he kept coming. "Don't flatter yourself… What are you *doing*?" she yelped when he backed her against the wall and dipped his head to nip her throat then soothe the hurt with his tongue.

"You can't tell?" His drawl was a rough growl of temptation against her flesh and in two seconds she was breathing hard—from annoyance, she told herself. Her knees *weren't* wobbling and that *wasn't* her moaning.

Oh God, it was. How embarrassing!

Her hands clutched at him—when had she reached out?—and she angled her head to one side so he could slide his lips up to the soft spot beneath her ear.

She shivered. "Dylan?"

"Mmm…?" He hummed against her ear, sending an armada of goose bumps sailing across her flesh.

Ooh. Not good…or maybe *too* good.

"What…what are you doing?" she squeaked as he nipped her earlobe.

"I'm saying hello…and punishing you."

Her nipples peaked and her breasts tightened. "What?" she gasped, trying to push him away and finding to her horror that she couldn't. Her fingers had curled into his shirt and they were holding on. "Why?"

"For ignoring me the past ten days," he murmured taking a little bite out of her lip. "Ten days, seventeen hours and thirty-eight minutes."

"But we…you… I…" Disbelief moved through her. *He'd also been counting?*

He ignored her breathy protest. "For leaving me alone in my bed," he murmured against the corner of her mouth when her breath escaped in a shuddery gasp. "For turning my bed into a cold, barren wasteland."

"But I…you…we—"

"You already said that." He chuckled softly, sliding his hands beneath her scrubs top and palming her breasts, satisfaction lighting his dark eyes when she moaned. "Only the other way round."

"I…um…" She licked her lips and dug her fingers into his biceps, her body already arching into his big warm hands.

How was she supposed to talk, let alone think when he was brushing his thumbs over her aching nipples?

"I'm back on the wagon," she managed to get out on a rush of air, before he rendered her speechless.

He paused and lifted his head from where he'd been tasting the hollow in her throat—right where her pulse flopped like a fish out of water. His eyes were dark and heavy with lust as they stared into hers.

"I missed you," he murmured, tugging her closer. "I didn't expect to miss you so much."

Terrified of what he might see there—the little smile she couldn't quite prevent at his words—Dani quickly looked down to see his hands moving beneath her top, sliding away from her breasts.

She bit her lip against the automatic protest that rose but instead of removing his hands he was smoothing them around her back and sliding them beneath the elastic waist of her scrubs pants—and *her panties*—to cup her bottom as he pressed one hard thigh between hers.

"Is that why you're undressing me?" she squeaked breathlessly.

"I like *your* bottom too," he whispered, dragging his lips across her cheekbone to her ear. "It's soft and sexy and it fits perfectly in my hands."

His fingers clenched and unclenched on her bottom until she mewled at the heat gathering between her legs.

"Are you saying I have a…a big *butt*?" She gasped, blinking rapidly to clear the lustful haze from her brain.

He paused in the process of swiping his tongue across her clavicle before moving back an inch so he could stare down into her face. At her aroused, outraged expression, he chuckled. "Seriously?" His fingers clenched again, drawing a little squeak from her throat. "Here I am, waxing lyrical about how I feel about your body, and all you can think is that I mean your butt is big?"

"You have big hands," she pointed out.

"All the better to do this…" he murmured wickedly, and slid two fingers into her.

The surprise invasion drew a shocked squeak from her lips that he captured with his mouth.

"Shh…" he warned against her lips. "We don't want anyone storming in here thinking you're being ravished… or do we?"

Dani shook her head, too far gone to object to what she could only think of as an ambush—if she'd been able to think, that was.

She wasn't.

Every thought save the one telling her she needed to remain standing slipped away under the onslaught of his hot, hungry kiss and the long, flexible fingers between her legs.

His mouth caught her shocked and aroused moan and all she could do was clutch at him and move against his fingers. Just before her eyes rolled back in her head he ended the kiss and removed his hand, leaving her weak-kneed, gasping for breath and on a very fine edge.

Her legs gave way and the next thing she knew she was sprawled in his lap while he held her against him, his arms two bands of iron across her back. She sucked in ragged breaths redolent of warm, delicious man and realized her face was pressed against his throat. After a couple of beats she opened her mouth—to say what, she had no idea—but all that emerged was a death rattle.

"You okay?" Dylan growled, his breath stirring the soft curls at her temple.

"I think…" she gasped "… I th—think someone stole my b-bones."

"That would be me."

He sounded way too smug for Dani's liking but she was too stunned by the force—and speed—with which he'd whipped her up to object.

Sighing, she snuggled closer and licked his throat. "I want them back."

"Not yet."

It took her a full minute to realize that she was draped over him like a tablecloth in the supply room, where anyone might find them. It would take about five minutes for the gossip to reach Oncology, which was over in the East Wing.

The thought was enough for her to recover her bones, if not her mind.

"Ohmigod!" She gasped, scrambling to her feet in horror. "Are you *insane*? I can't believe you just did that. I can't believe I *let* you do that."

"I didn't do anything…yet," Dylan drawled, leaning back against the wall, a satisfied grin pulling at his mouth.

"Stop that," she ordered as she tried to find her balance. "I don't know what you're looking so smug about. It's not like you…" She gestured to the erection tenting his scrubs pants and blushed. "Dealt with *that*," she ended on a half-hysterical laugh.

"You going to take care of it for me?"

"No!" She gasped again, laughter bubbling up from a

place deep in her chest. "It serves you right for ambushing me when I'm so busy."

He looked at the supplies scattered across the floor. "Busy, huh?"

She smoothed her hair off her face with shaking hands and turned away to begin collecting boxes and packages. "Yes. Now, go away—aren't you off duty?"

He rose lithely to his feet, snatching up a few boxes as he did so. "I had a late surgery on an accident victim. And, since you've been avoiding me, I—"

"I have not," she interrupted quickly, careful to keep her face averted lest he see her guilty expression. "I've been busy. *Really* busy."

He was quiet for a few beats before saying mildly, "So you said. But, contrary to what you think, I didn't come here for the express purpose of ravishing you. Delightful though it's been."

She sent him a quick glare before turning away to hide her hot cheeks. "Then why *did* you come?"

"I need a date."

She stumbled and grabbed hold of the shelf at her elbow. "A *date*?" Why she was surprised and disappointed, Dani didn't know. She was back on the wagon, after all. "Dr. Sexy needs a *date*?"

His mouth twisted wryly. "My mother has forced me to buy a couple of tickets to a charity dinner tomorrow night and I need a partner."

"So...*any* woman will do?" she asked, casually pretending to count bags of Ringer's lactate when her brain was still stuck on the fact that all he wanted was a date.

When he didn't reply she peeked at him over her shoulder. He was leaning casually against the opposite shelves, watching her with an exasperated expression.

"Actually, no," he drawled dryly. "I want to take *you*—

although I'm not sure why, especially as you've been ignoring me."

She blinked at him and tried to deny that his words had sent pleasure rushing through her. She couldn't. "But what about my embargo?"

His sigh suggested she was an idiot, because anyone could see she'd fallen off the wagon a second time. With *him*. In record time, too.

His voice dropped a couple of octaves. "Come with me."

A small frown creased the area between her brows even as a shiver eased down her spine. She ignored the unpleasant lurching of her stomach. "I…uh… I don't know, Dylan. Those dinners aren't really my thing." Mostly because it was a world she'd run from and had no desire to re-enter.

His eyes darkened. "Please?"

And suddenly, queasy stomach aside, Dani realized she couldn't resist a pleading Dylan. "All right," she muttered, folding like a cheap suitcase. "I suppose it's a formal dinner?"

"Very." A smile bloomed across his handsome face as he leaned forward to drop a quick kiss on her startled mouth. "I'll pick you up at seven."

CHAPTER NINE

THE ORCHESTRA HIRED for the charity event segued into a waltz as Dylan pushed his way through Vancouver's social elite. He'd left Dani with Cole's sister Maddie and her date, to find some champagne, and he was in a hurry to get back.

His afternoon surgery had run late and to save time he'd had his mother book a suite at the Regency, where the event was taking place. He'd sent word to Dani to make use of the facility and by the time he'd emerged from the adjoining room, white tie stuffed in his pocket and struggling with his cufflinks, she'd been ready and waiting.

Dylan couldn't ever remember feeling as if he'd been hit on the head with a brick at the sight of a woman in an evening gown before. But, dressed in a long sheath of silvery stretch lace and beaded flower work, she'd literally taken his breath away.

In the sleeveless dress, its scalloped neckline molding perfectly to her full breasts and slender curvy body, she'd looked both elegant and so enormously desirable that his only thought had been to strip her out of it and miss the dinner entirely.

Her dark hair was swept up into some kind of complicated style that left tiny spiral curls framing her face, softening the delicate lines of her jaw. She'd applied make-up with a light hand but the effect was stunning, rendering him speechless as he'd stared into deep gray eyes that were wide and smokily seductive.

He'd felt as though the earth had given way beneath his feet and he'd been left free-falling through an alien universe. It had been all he could do not to stammer like a fool.

"You look…*stunning*," he'd murmured when she'd taken over the task of fitting his cufflinks.

The flush creeping up her chest and neck had tempted him to trace its origins, past the scalloped neckline to the full swells of her breasts.

Leaning closer, he'd buried his nose in her throat. "And you smell even better."

"Not as good as you," she'd muttered, her quick smile turning her eyes silver as she'd slipped his white tie from his pocket to fit it around his neck.

"No," he'd grumbled, yanking at the white waistcoat of the black penguin suit his mother had had delivered to the suite. "I look like a damn waiter."

"A very classy one," she'd agreed with a giggle, ducking away when he'd reached for her.

Thinking his unscheduled surgery a convenient excuse for the fact that they were going to be *very* late, he'd caught her at the door and kissed her until she was flushed and dazed. After the way she'd ignored him these past couple of weeks, it had been very gratifying to have her melting into him.

"What's that wicked smile for, darling?"

A husky feminine voice interrupted his musings and Dylan turned to see his mother, bearing down on him with a determined gleam in her green eyes.

"It's the same one you used to wear when you were plotting mischief as a boy."

"I'm just thinking of all the lovely zeroes you're going to add to your foundation's coffers," he drawled, thinking there were some things a mother didn't need to know.

"I know," she said happily, reaching up to kiss his cheek. "Isn't it wonderful? I have a long list of recipients we can help with the proceeds."

He dropped an affectionate kiss on her brow before looking around for his father. "Where's Dad?"

"Oh, talking to some crony or another. I gave him strict instructions to badger them all for large donations this year."

"I'm sure you did." He chuckled, imagining his father—owner and CEO of the largest shipping company in the Pacific North-West—meekly listening while his wife of thirty six years rapped out orders. "And I'm just as sure he's doing exactly what you told him to."

"Of course he is," Vivian St. James said archly. "If he knows what's good for him—which is more than I can say for my children."

He sent his mother a dry look, knowing what she was doing but pretending otherwise. "What have the girls done now?"

"I'm talking about my *son*," she retorted, slipping her hand through his arm and smiling a greeting to nearby acquaintances. Her gaze was direct and slightly narrowed when she looked up at him. "Please tell me you didn't come alone like last time."

His mouth twisted wryly as he admitted, "I didn't come alone."

Her face instantly broke into a pleased smile. "Ooh! And I suppose *she's* responsible for that wicked smile I caught on your handsome face?"

"Mom…" he began, horrified to discover his face heating beneath her dancing gaze.

"She *is*!" She laughed at his discomfort and nudged him with her shoulder, her eyes sparkling with delight. "And…? When are you going to introduce me?"

"I'll do it now, if you promise not to embarrass her or start planning the wedding."

"Oh, silly boy!" She chortled scornfully. "When will you learn? I've already planned your wedding. I'm just waiting for you to meet the right woman."

"Behave," he warned her, finally catching sight of Dani and Maddie talking to— *"Damn."* He scowled, recognizing the man as the son of one of the partners at the law firm his father used.

He knew Richard Ashton-Hall from school but they'd never run in the same crowd. The spiteful, opinionated boy had grown into a condescending egotistical man, who used his social status as a member of one of the leading legal families in Vancouver to lord it over what he called "the peasants." He liked getting what he wanted and bullied people until he did.

Dylan had heard enough unsavory rumors about the man to know that he wouldn't want him dating his sisters. There was something unpleasant in the way he looked at a woman—as though he was stripping her naked with one arrogant glance and finding her either wanting or the perfect candidate as his new plaything.

And he *really* didn't like the way he was looking at Dani now. It roused primitive emotions he'd have sworn he didn't possess.

Chief among them was the urge to smash his fist into that smirking salon-tanned face. His fingers curled into tight fists, because he absolutely did not like the shocked, furious expression on Maddie's face or the rigid line of Dani's spine.

"What is it, darling?" Vivian James asked in concern, no doubt feeling the abrupt tension in the arm she was holding. She looked around in alarm and said, "Oh, look, there's Madeleine... My goodness." Her eyes widened. "She looks quite fierce, doesn't she? Frankly, I'm not surprised. Not with that dreadful man looking at her companion like that—" She stopped abruptly, her gaze snapping from the unfolding drama to her son's face. "It's her, isn't it?"

He nodded. "Yes, that's Dani."

"Well then," his mother urged. "What are you waiting for?" She gave his arm a firm yank. "Go and rescue her from that awful boy."

In seconds he was striding up behind Dani, not realizing that he'd practically shoved people out of the way in his haste to get to her. He was still a short distance away when he heard Maddie snarl, "Why don't you crawl back under the rock you emerged from, you slimy toad?"

Ashton-Hall, looking like a blond male model, dismissed Maddie with a flick of one perfectly manicured hand, his ice-blue eyes never leaving Dani's face.

"Get lost, Madeleine. I'm trying to have a conversation with my...*wife*."

His eyes were sliding over Dani's body with a knowing predatory light and it had a snarl rising in Dylan's throat. His words—and Dani's visible flinch—shocked him into halting a few feet from the group. He could only blink back the red tide of rage rising up inside his head.

What?

"Ex!" Maddie yelped, bristling with fury and looking as if she wanted to strike him. "*Ex*-wife, you mean."

Dylan didn't realize he'd taken another step until his mother's hand closed around his fist. "No fighting, darling," she murmured in his ear. "Even if I'd be cheering you on from the sidelines."

The words and the supportive squeeze settled him, and he stepped up behind Dani with amazing casualness to slide his palm up her back. She jolted at his touch, a quiver racing through her tense body.

Deliberately ignoring the other man, he dipped his head when she looked up. He caught a brief impression of her eyes as he touched his mouth to hers. Her lips quivered and he sank into the kiss as though they didn't have an audience.

"Sorry I took so long," he said, when he finally lifted his head. "The bar's busy."

He was pleased to see his very public display of affection had wild color replacing her pale distress. He took his time to look around at the group watching them with varying expressions—Ashton-Hall showed shock mixed with fury at having his prey snatched away, the lawyer's date was looking wide-eyed at the simmering undercurrents, and Maddie... Well, she'd never looked more gleefully triumphant.

"You know Dr. St. James, don't you?" Maddie said, so sweetly that Dylan felt his blood sugar rise. "He's the leading reconstruction orthopedic surgeon at St. Mary's. Oh, yes—and I'm sure you know his *father*: Ruben James, CEO and owner of—"

"Ashton-Hall," Dylan interrupted with a curt nod, his hand sliding down Dani's trembling arm to link with her fingers. He lifted their clasped hands to brush his lips across her icy-cold knuckles, his hard eyes taking in the way the other man's narrowed gaze took in the intimate gesture.

Her fingers jerked convulsively in his.

"Well, well..." Ashton-Hall drawled softly, his golden good looks hardening into something unpleasant. "My dear, lovely wife...*ex*-wife," he corrected, with a patently false smile of apology in Maddie's direction, "has managed to land herself a bigger, fatter, juicier fish after all." He turned to Dylan. "My…uh…congratulations."

His voice suggested otherwise as he flicked her a contemptuous glance and Dylan bit back a snarl, because beneath the contempt was an unhealthy possessiveness that made his skin crawl.

"I wonder what he would say if he knew about what a disappointment you were in…" He paused for dramatic effect, his ice-blue eyes gleaming with malice at the sound of Dani's abruptly indrawn breath, audible in the tense silence.

"I suggest you stop right there," Dylan warned softly.

"In our marriage." He blinked at Dylan, as though surprised. "What did you *think* I was going to say?"

"Nothing I'd want to hear from a man who likes to hit women," he said smoothly, and felt a savage satisfaction when the man's unnatural tan reddened, then paled.

"How did you—? She *told* you that?"

"No," Dylan drawled smoothly, despite the fury sweeping through him. "*You* just did."

Ashton-Hall's hands curled into fists and his mouth twisted into something ugly as his gaze zeroed in on Dani. Dylan felt her stiffen beside him, as though she was bracing herself.

Then Richard suddenly laughed, all suave urbanity that invited everyone to see the irony of the situation. His eyebrows rose arrogantly. "Maybe," he said to Dylan, "when you're done slumming with the Ice Princess we can compare notes."

Dylan heard his mother's outraged inhalation through a red mist, and before he could think he'd drawn back his arm and punched Ashton-Hall in his smug, sneering face.

The crunch of the man's nose beneath his fist was the most satisfying moment of Dylan's life, dulling the pain radiating up his arm.

The shocked gasps of the people around them snapped Dani out of her misery. Ignoring the man lying on the hotel foyer floor, she grabbed Dylan's arm and held on as he took another step forward. Fury blasted from him like a nuclear explosion, the force of it vibrating through the steely muscles beneath her hand.

"Dylan." Her horrified gaze took in the attention they were attracting. *"Stop!* It doesn't matter."

He was breathing hard, his green eyes a blaze of fury in his stony face. "Doesn't *matter*?" he snarled, taking another step toward Richard. *"He* was the one—" He inhaled sharply and practically ground his next words into pieces as he stared at the other man, menace pumping off him in great billowing clouds. "I'm going to kill him."

Her face flamed with mortification, and quick tears blurred her vision because she would give anything— *anything*—for him not to know. "Dylan, *please*," she urged, her voice low and urgent. "Let it go. It doesn't matter."

"He put his hands on you in *anger*," he snarled, his jaw practically popping with fury. "Of *course* it matters."

"No. It doesn't," she argued gently. "Not anymore. Because *he* doesn't matter."

She closed her hands over his clenched fist, hoping to dispel the violence pounding through him and caught the wince he couldn't quite prevent. Frowning, she looked down at his hand and sucked in a shocked breath when she saw the damaged, swelling knuckles.

"Look what you've done to your hand. How can you—?"

He caught her shaking fingers and waited until her distraught gaze met his. "It was worth it."

"I hope you still think so when I sue the pants off you," the man on the floor snarled, drawing everyone's attention. They'd all but forgotten him. Flushing with embarrassed fury at the curious stares they were receiving, he lurched to his feet and spat out. "I'll sue you until even your grandchildren are paying through the nose. I'll ruin you. I'll—"

"Oh, be quiet, Richard," snapped Dani, suddenly furious with both of them for causing a scene with their masculine posturing. "You're an ass."

She shoved at Dylan while her ex-husband mopped the blood from his nose with a pristine handkerchief.

"And as for *you*—" She probed his hand gently. "You need ice and maybe a lobotomy."

Black spots hovered at the edge of her vision and she sucked in a shaky breath to dispel the odd dizziness and shaky stomach.

"He'll do it," she said in urgent undertones. "I know he will. It's happened before."

"Let him try," Dylan said, unconcerned, wrapping his free hand around her neck and nudging her chin up with his thumb. His expression was concerned as he studied her face. "You're pale."

She wrapped her fingers around his wrist, the feel of his warm skin and steady pulse beneath her fingers stabilizing her. "I'm fine. Which is more than I can say for your hand. Let me get you some ice."

"This is all very sweet and sickening," Richard snarled furiously. "But what about *me*? He broke my nose."

"You should thank him," Maddie snorted unsympathetically. "It'll give your face character. Something the rest of you lacks."

Richard ignored her. "Expect to hear from me next week," he said.

He stepped close in a move Dani recognized from her marriage. It was one that had never failed to make her knees quake.

He smirked at her instinctive retreat before she ordered her feet to stop. "It's going to be fun watching you squirm."

Dani ignored the threat. "Try it and I'll expose you *and* your sleazy club," she said softly.

Richard froze, his eyes narrowing. "What club?" he lied smoothly, grimacing with distaste as blood continued to flow from his nose.

"Your little swingers'—"

"You wouldn't," he interrupted, with an unconcerned scoff that couldn't quite mask the panic in his eyes as he sent a quick glance around to see if anyone had heard.

It was in that moment she realized that he was nothing but a spoilt bully who used his family's legal reputation as a tool to intimidate and scare. Standing up to him suddenly seemed like the most natural thing in the world. Because he couldn't hurt her. Not anymore.

"You're forgetting the non-disclosure agreement," he reminded her coolly as he straightened his tie and brushed off his jacket.

"If you recall," she reminded him quietly, refusing to be cowed, "I declined to sign it."

Conscious of her trembling knees, she turned away. But his hand shot out, his grip cruel as he yanked her against him.

"And *you*," he warned silkily, "might recall what happened then."

Dylan's fingers immediately clamped down on Richard's wrist and with a girlish squeak he loosened his grip immediately.

Dani stilled, a frown pulling at her brows as she resisted Dylan's efforts to pull her away. "What are you talking about?"

His gaze turned malicious. "That drunk driver who drove you off the road?" His lips curled into a hard, cruel smile as he mouthed, *That was me*, before sauntering off.

Oblivious to warm hands settling on her arms, Dani felt the words rushing over her like a swarm of bees. They pierced her skin, leaving their poison to tear through her fragile armor, leaving her with a sick certainty that dispelled any doubts she might have had about that night.

The blood drained abruptly from her head and her knees sagged. She heard Maddie's startled yelp even as Dylan caught her against himself.

"Dani!" he rasped, his deep voice laced with a concern that battered at her, tightening her chest until she couldn't breathe.

Her heart swelled, desperate to pump blood to her numbed limbs. Her ears buzzed and her fingers tingled as the ballroom receded. Unaware of the wounded moan rising up her throat, Dani pressed a shaking hand to her breastbone, hoping to keep her pounding heart from exploding through her ribs. Keep it from leaving a gaping hole in her chest.

She sucked in a tortured breath. She had to get away. She had to—

Nausea burned her throat like acid, and with a desperate cry she shoved herself free, lurching away from him as she frantically searched for the nearest exit. She felt Dylan's hand on her arm, heard him say…*something*. But she slapped a hand over her mouth, snatched up her long skirt and ran toward the ladies' restroom.

She heard Dylan's stunned curse as the door swung shut behind her, barely making it into an open stall before her stomach emptied violently. Collapsing to the floor, Dani hung over the toilet as her stomach continued to heave, as though to dispel the awful truth swamping her.

Richard… *Richard* was responsible for the accident that had taken her baby and left her uterus scarred. A sob caught in her throat.

Through the roaring in her ears she vaguely heard voices behind her—a woman's voice urgently calling, "*Dani!* Dani, where are you?" But she couldn't, *couldn't* respond. She was too busy retching, devastated by the knowledge that the man who'd once promised to love and protect her had—

She was barely aware that she was sobbing, her chest heaving as she wished…no, *prayed*…the floor would open and swallow her whole.

Then frantic hands were reaching for her. Hands that shook as Maddie murmured brokenly, "I had a feeling this would happen one day. This city isn't big enough that you can avoid him forever."

"*Richard…*" Dani rasped, grabbing Maddie's arm in a shaky grip.

"Yeah, he's a colossal ass—what's new?" her friend snapped, gently wiping Dani's mouth even as someone else pressed a cold cloth to her burning forehead.

Eyes huge and dark with shock, Dani whispered, "It was *him*."

"Yeah, I wish he'd drop dead too… Wait!" Maddie frowned, her eyes confused as she crouched at Dani's side. "*What* was him?"

"He… He…" Dani swallowed past the burning ball of glass shards in her throat. "That night… *He* was the drunk driver."

For a moment Maddie stared at her uncomprehendingly, then she sucked in a shocked breath. "Are you saying…?" Her eyes widened. "*That's crazy!* He wouldn't— He— Dani, that's *insane*."

A sob rose in Dani's throat as she gave a jerky nod. "He told me…just now," she said, feeling the shock of it swamp her. "It was *him* that night—*he* caused the accident." She shivered, recalling it. "He was so f-furious with me for embarrassing him in front of his friends. But I didn't think he could—could he?" She sucked in a shaky breath and felt the walls closing in on her. "C-could he really be capable of th—that?"

A snarl of fury burst from her friend's lips as she lurched to her feet. "I'm going to kill him," she vowed, looking murderous. "I'm going to make him wish he'd never been born. I'm going to—"

"Maddie, darling." A low, soothing voice interrupted from somewhere close. "Can you put a hold on those bloodthirsty plans long enough to get Dani out of here?"

Maddie blinked rapidly before sucking in a steadying breath. They were attracting unwanted attention. "Oh, right…" she said, bending to wrap an arm around Dani and pull her to her feet.

But Dani's legs weren't working properly and she swayed dizzily, the blood draining from her head as prickly heat washed over her. She gave a low moan and thrust out a hand to grab the doorframe but the floor dipped and rolled and the walls melted away.

Then firm, warm fingers closed around hers and she blinked up into concerned green eyes that even in her shocked state reminded her of Dylan's. Green eyes set in the beautiful face of an older woman.

"Come on, darling," she said, gently but firmly pulling Dani from the cubicle. "We left Dylan outside, and if I know my son he'll come barging in here if we don't walk out in under a minute."

Dani's eyes widened and she gasped. "You're Dylan's—?"

"Mother," the older woman finished.

"Oh God," she whimpered. She sucked in a fortifying breath and managed to get out, "You…you *saw* all that?"

Her words sounded tinny to her own ears, and even as she saw compassion filling those green eyes a great wave of prickling heat swamped her.

With a mortified moan, she slid to the floor.

CHAPTER TEN

DANI SURFACED TO find herself lying on something soft. Somewhere close, people spoke in hushed tones. She strained her ears but couldn't make out anything other than suppressed fury and concern.

For a couple of beats she wondered why there were people in her bedroom and tried to turn over, to block out the noise but a soft hand held her still as a cold cloth was pressed against her forehead.

Brow wrinkling in confusion, she reached up to swipe at the annoyance but warm fingers trapped hers.

"It's all right, Dani," a gentle, feminine voice soothed. "Take it easy. I *can* call you Dani, can't I?" The low voice quivered with amusement. "Anyone who can turn my son into an avenging pugilist one minute and a panicked wreck the next is someone I'd very much like to meet."

Something brushed her cheek.

"Come on, sweetheart, open your eyes before he calls an ambulance."

Memory returned with the speed of a freight train and she lurched upward, her eyes flying open to see— *Oh God*—Dylan's mother, her green eyes filled with maternal concern and curiosity. A few feet away Dylan paced, his body vibrating with fury as Maddie spoke in urgent undertones.

Panic rose up to blot out everything, because she knew—just *knew*—what Maddie was telling Dylan. All the sordid details of her marriage.

Her stomach roiled in greasy protest. *"Nooo!"* she moaned, trying to scramble off the sofa, as though she could physically stop the words from emerging.

Seeing the direction of her panicked gaze, Dylan's mother caught her, calling out, *"Children!"* in a firm voice that children everywhere recognized and instantly obeyed. "You're upsetting Dani."

As one, they spun around. Within two strides Dylan was at her side, one large hand engulfing hers as he dropped down beside her. Intense green eyes swept over her, cataloging her condition.

"You're looking a little better," he rasped, his fingers lacing convulsively through hers. His dark gaze caught and held hers as though he could see through to her soul. "How do you feel?"

"F-fine," she stammered, trying to disengage her hand from his and put a little distance between them. She needed to leave before she made a bigger spectacle of herself than she already had. And in front of his *mother*!

His fingers tightened. "You're lying."

She froze and blinked her surprise, her gaze flying to his mother, who was watching them with wide, curious eyes and a strange little smile on her face.

"What a terrible thing to say," she accused in a low voice, pulling unsuccessfully at her hand. "And let go— you're embarrassing me."

"And *you're* making me look bad in front of my mother and Maddie." He lifted his free hand to cup her chin but Dani grabbed it, wincing at the sight of his bruised, swollen knuckles.

"Why haven't you iced this?"

"I had other things on my mind," he growled. "Like you fainting in the women's restroom."

He shoved impatient fingers through his hair. Dani was shocked at the pallor beneath his skin and the perceptible tremor in his fingers.

"You have no idea how I felt when I saw you passed out on the floor."

She rolled her eyes and distracted herself by taking his hand and gently probing his injury. An injury sustained on *her* behalf.

"It's probably just a little virus, that's all," she assured him, looking up to see Maddie and Dylan's mother watching them with wide, fascinated eyes. Because she was angry with Maddie, for spilling her secrets, she said coolly, "Dylan needs an ice pack."

Maddie's gaze narrowed at the silent rebuke but didn't look too disturbed when she gave a nod and left the room.

"Don't blame Maddie. She was just trying to help—" Dylan began.

He was cut off when Dani hissed, "*Help?* How can airing my disaster of a marriage be helping?"

Clearly taken aback by her vehemence, Dylan hardened his jaw. "You should have told me yourself."

"Why? Because we slept together?" She abruptly cut off the rest of her words because they still had an audience. *Oh God*—his mother was listening with rapt attention to their exchange.

Face flaming, Dani rose unsteadily to her feet but when she took a step away from him Dylan grabbed her hand and yanked her back to the sofa.

"Dylan!"

"Sit," he ordered, pressing his fingers to her pulse. "I'm worried about you. When last did you eat?"

Her tongue snaked out to dampen her dry lips and instantly the older woman was there, offering a glass of water. "I'm fine," she repeated, taking the glass. "But thank you," she said quietly. "For your concern."

"Yes, Mom, thanks—but you really should get back to the ball. Aren't you in charge of proceedings?"

"Oh, don't worry about me, darling," the older woman said, brushing aside his concern. "Janice Hetherington will take over."

"No, please," Dani said, her fingers tightening around the glass. "Mrs. St. James, I insist. I'm just sorry you had to witness—" She licked her lips nervously and slid her gaze sideways to include the man at her side. "Well...*that*. I'm sorry I ruined your function."

"Call me Vivian, dear. And you haven't ruined anything. Besides, *you* have nothing to apologize for," Dylan's mother declared firmly. "It was all Richard." Her eyes went to her son. "And maybe Dylan too. *But*," she added, when Dani opened her mouth to leap to his defense, "if *he* hadn't punched him, *I* would have."

To say Dani was shocked by the swift rejoinder was an understatement but the glint in the older woman's eye told her she would have done it if her son hadn't beat her to it.

Vivian St. James' eyes bounced between Dylan and Dani for a couple of beats before she sighed. "Fine, I know when to make a graceful exit. *But*," she said, pointing a slender finger at Dylan, "I expect you to bring Dani to meet your father."

And with that she dropped a gentle kiss on Dani's up-turned cheek, arched a peremptory brow at her son and left the room in a swish of skirts.

For several moments Dani stared at the closed door, before turning to see Dylan watching her with an odd combination of concern, satisfaction and amusement.

She narrowed her eyes. "What?"

"My mother likes you."

She puffed out her red cheeks. "I have no idea why—I embarrassed her."

He chuckled. "No, *I* did. But since I brought you along she'll forgive me." His hand was warm and gentle as he cupped her chin and tilted it up. "You're still looking a little pale. What's up, Dani? Talk to me."

Unable to handle the gentle concern and the look in his eyes, Dani pulled away and rose. She needed to put a little distance between them before she forgot they were only having a wild affair.

She inhaled carefully. "Like I said, it's probably just a virus or something." She smoothed unsteady hands down her dress and aimed a shaky smile in his direction. "I like your mother." She bit her lip and pressed a hand against her stomach. "But maybe it would be better if I left."

With a muffled curse Dylan surged to his feet and took a step toward her, coming to an abrupt halt when she sucked in a startled breath and stumbled backward into a nearby chair. She threw out a hand to catch herself before she took another tumble and added to the evening's humiliation.

"Why do you *do* that?" he demanded. "Why do you pull away just when I think we're getting somewhere?" He knew he sounded frustrated and bewildered.

She licked her lips nervously and edged toward the door. "Dylan—"

Dylan shoved his hands in his pockets, the abrupt movement filled with frustration. "I'd never lift my hand to a woman, so you can just stop right there. I'm not like your ex."

Dani's spine snapped straight. "I didn't say you were," she shot back.

Dylan was pleased to see angry color flood her pale cheeks, a sparkle replacing the remoteness in her eyes.

"Don't put words in my mouth."

Anger, he decided, was preferable to that wounded wariness that made him want to find her ex and break his nose all over again. And maybe a few other bones as well.

"It's hard not to when you seldom put any there yourself."

She sucked in a harsh breath. "What's that supposed to mean?"

"Nothing." He sighed, turning away. It wasn't her fault that he wanted more than she was prepared to give, and beating at her with his exasperation would only cause her to withdraw even more. "I'm just wondering why you never told me what he did."

"You expect me to spill my guts just because we *s-slept* together?"

Annoyed, Dylan shoved a hand through his hair, wincing when his swollen knuckles protested. "No…" He sighed again. "But I might have handled the situation better, handled *you* better, if I'd known."

"What makes you think I need you—or anyone—to 'handle' me?" she demanded. "I can handle myself, Dylan. I'm an adult. I don't *need* you to fight my battles for me. I don't need *anyone* to fight my battles for me."

Her unspoken words, *I don't need anyone*, hung in the air between them and he wondered if she really believed it. If she did, he'd have a hard time convincing her to trust him.

Frustrated, he flung words over his shoulder. "I couldn't just stand by and let him slash at you like that, Dani." He faced her and demanded, "What kind of man would do that?"

Her body slowly lost its rigidity and she had the grace

to grimace in apology. "I'm embarrassed," she muttered, wrapping her arms around her torso as her gaze slid away. "I humiliated myself." Her chin lifted. "I embarrassed your mother and now you…you—" She pressed her lips together.

"And now I what?"

She spun away, the rigid lines of her body radiating new tension. "Richard isn't the kind of man who handles humiliation well," she snapped over her shoulder. "He'll—"

"I know exactly what kind of man he is," he interrupted smoothly, annoyed that she would think the lawyer had intimidated him.

"He'll do what he says," she added, as though he hadn't spoken. "He'll pad the truth and come up with a dozen witnesses to corroborate his lies."

"I don't care about him, Dani. I care about *you*. And I care about what he said that had you fainting in the bathroom, that upset you so much that you're repairing those walls around you faster than I can tear them down."

His hands settled on her shoulders. He felt the bones delicate and fragile beneath his hands. He wanted to wrap his arms around her and wished she would lean on him, take what he offered.

"What hold does he have on you?"

Dylan's hands were warm, firm and gentle as they cupped her shoulders. His touch, the deep tone of his voice, made her eyes sting with longing. It would be so easy to lean on him, to take what he offered.

But she couldn't. Didn't dare. Because…because she wanted it too much. And wanting things too much was a sure-fire way to get her heart broken. But he was there, so steady and strong that she couldn't resist turning into him.

"He doesn't," she murmured, sliding her hands up to

his shoulders to tunnel unsteady fingers through his hair. "Not anymore."

With her eyes on his she lifted onto her toes, her body sliding against his as she pressed a soft, tentative kiss to the corner of his mouth. For just an instant he resisted. She could see in his eyes that he wanted to argue but then he gave a low, agonized groan and wrapped his arms around her in one jerky movement. His mouth, hard and seeking, closed over hers in a searing kiss that belied the abrupt strength in his arms, the tension in his body.

This, she thought with a shiver of excitement, was all she could give him.

"Come home with me," he said, and groaned, his hands urging her closer, as though she was infinitely precious and fragile, smoothing a path up the length of her back, his body vibrating with heat and urgency.

She could feel his heart pounding beneath her palm and wondered if he felt what she did—a sense of rightness that scared her even as it made her yearn for what could never be.

With a rough growl he dragged his lips along the line of her jaw. "No...upstairs. I...can't wait."

Dani, lost in the pleasure of his mouth, fought with the buttons of his waistcoat and then his shirt. "Here," she demanded, shoving her hands between the plackets to slide them over his hot skin. *"Now."*

With a savage curse he swept her off her feet, and together they dropped onto the sofa against the wall. He shoved a thigh between hers.

"God, I've missed you," he rasped against her lips, before taking her mouth in a kiss that was abruptly impatient. "I want this...*you*."

And, thrilled by this new dark edginess, Dani lifted her mouth to his and gave him everything.

* * *

Sagging against the bathroom wall, Dani swiped the back of her shaky hand across her mouth. It was the second time she'd lost the contents of her stomach in the past twenty-four hours, and she couldn't remember how often she'd lost them over the past few weeks.

Maybe it was time to admit it probably *wasn't* a virus, or even stress. Maybe it *could* still be stress, she admitted with a grimace. They hadn't yet heard from Richard, and that usually wasn't a good thing. But, although the waiting was exhausting, it wasn't nearly as terrifying as waiting for Dylan to lose interest and dump her for someone more suitable. Someone more beautiful, more exciting, more…*everything*.

Someone not likely to embarrass him in public.

Although, she admitted reluctantly, he seemed to be showing no signs of losing interest. Instead, every day he seemed to be…*more*. More patient, more passionate, more… *God*…more tender, she thought with a delicious shiver. He touched her more often—and not just during sex—as though he wanted her to know he was there. Wanted her to get used to the weight of his hand, the heat of his body, even in a crowd of people.

And he'd made her crave him, she admitted with a touch of panic. Crave the way she'd awake locked in his arms. Crave *being* with him. And if that didn't scare her enough, the way he kept hijacking her thoughts did. She thought about him at the most inconvenient times and she hated it. Hated it that he'd come to mean so much…

Oh God, she was in trouble. The kind that could break a girl's heart if she wasn't careful.

But Dani had learned the hard way to be very careful. Careful not to let the expression in his eyes and the touch of his hand as it smoothed the length of her spine affect anything more than her senses. And she was being extra careful with her heart, which was locked up tight and safe.

And that was a good thing. A very good thing. Or she'd be—

"So…" An annoyed voice interrupted her panicked thoughts. "When are you going to stop hiding in the supply room or the bathroom and tell me what's going on?"

Dani opened her eyes to see two sneakers beneath the stall door—one propped over the other as though their owner leaned casually against the wall. She groaned. Amy gave new meaning to the word *persistent*.

She rolled her head against the wall, too exhausted to shove at the damp hair that had fallen into her face. "I'm fine," she rasped through her burning throat.

The nurse muttered a succinct curse. "You're still sick, aren't you?"

Yeah, a little voice answered, *love-sick.*

No, no, no! she denied, aghast. *Nothing of the sort.* She was just a little stressed. Waiting for Richard to strike *always* made her tense.

"Of course I'm not sick," Dani scoffed weakly because it was patently obvious to everyone that she hadn't been herself lately. "I'm just hoping to escape your endless questions. I'm fit as a fiddle."

Her friend made a rude sound in the back of her throat. "Then you won't mind getting checked out by Rachel."

Rachel, an ER physician in her fifties, was the shift supervisor.

"Don't be ridiculous, Amy."

Dani impatiently brushed her suggestion aside and pushed to her feet. Cursing the exhaustion that made her want to lie down and sleep for a week, she opened the door.

"I don't need to see Rachel or anyone else. I'm just feeling a little under the weather, that's all."

"Okay," the nurse said.

She sounded so agreeable that Dani relaxed as she headed for the row of basins to wash her hands and rinse her mouth. Too soon it seemed, because then came Amy's next words.

"If you won't see Rachel, then I want you to use this. Right now."

Dani sent a frowning look over her shoulder, her eyes widening as she saw the slender box her friend held out.

"Seriously?" she demanded with a snort. "You want me to pee on a stick?"

Blue eyes stared back, level and serious. "Yes."

Dani rolled her eyes and pulled off a strip of paper toweling to dab her face. "You know that's not possible."

"Because you have Asherman's?" Amy asked mildly. "Or because you haven't been getting any with a certain gorgeous orthopedic surgeon?"

Dani quickly looked around the bathroom, relieved to see it was empty. "Well, because… Because…" she stuttered, then snapped her mouth closed when she couldn't think of a single reply other than *You know why*.

She turned away, pretending she was on top of things when the truth was she felt as though she was going down for the third time.

"Unprotected sex?" Amy yelped.

Dani gave a guilty start. A quick look over her shoulder showed her friend staring at her with open-mouthed shock.

"Seriously?" She shook her head as though to dispel the image. "Are you *insane*?"

Face flaming, Dani squawked, "A condom broke and then…and then we didn't…um…" She rolled her eyes and snickered, because she couldn't help feeling like a teenager facing her mother after being caught having sex in the sitting room. "We...um...didn't bother after that. *Mom.*"

Amy snorted. "Let's forget the safety issues for just a moment, shall we?" Grabbing Dani's wrist, she pulled her back toward the stall she'd just vacated.

Resisting, Dani huffed out an exasperated laugh. "Amy—"

The nurse stopped and spun around so suddenly that Dani plowed into her.

"I care about you."

The hitch in her friend's voice, the concern, silenced any retort she might have made.

"You've lost weight, you're pale and you have dark circles under your eyes. You're a mess and I'm worried about you."

After a couple dozen heartbeats Dani sighed and surrendered. She didn't want to tell her friend that she was afraid she was in love with a man who was way out of her league—a man who was a member of a social class she could never belong to. Didn't *want* to belong to, she reminded herself.

"All right," she growled, grabbing the pregnancy test and stomping into the stall. She turned and jabbed it into the air. "If only to prove that your theory is totally off the wall. I'm a little run-down and I can't shake this virus. That's all."

Secure in the knowledge that she was right, she shut the door smartly in her friend's face. *She* was the doctor, wasn't she? Surely she'd be able to tell the difference between a virus and early pregnancy? Even if it was possible.

Which it wasn't.

Ten minutes later, however, she was staring in shock at the twin pink stripes in the results window. Her knees wobbled, her ears buzzed and her head felt as if it was two feet above the rest of her body.

"But… But that's—"

"Impossible?" Amy demanded, her face alternating between delight and shock that probably mirrored Dani's.

"But…but… Dr. Cartwright said… He said—"

"Well, clearly he was wrong," Amy interrupted, practically shoving the stick under Dani's nose. "Doctors sometimes are, you know. They aren't infallible and they aren't God."

Dani refused to believe it. "These things aren't definitive either, Amy," she said briskly, grabbing the box to check the use-by date. "They're often defective and give false positives. I have Asherman's."

"Well, clearly you don't," Amy retorted smartly. "And to make certain, why don't you schedule an appointment with Dr. Dawson? Getting a second opinion won't hurt." Her eyebrows arched challengingly. "*Will* it?"

Yes, dammit, it *would* hurt. Especially if she got her hopes up and it turned out to be a faulty test. It would… She'd be devastated.

"Fine," she said calmly. "But I'm telling you it's a false positive. I'm not pregnant."

She shook her head firmly and for an instant wondered who she was trying to convince. Herself or Amy.

"I *can't* be pregnant. It's just not possible."

She was pregnant.

Fierce joy warred with disbelief and panic as Dani gripped the steering wheel until her fingers ached. Driving off the ferry at Departure Bay, Nanaimo, she was scarcely aware of the stream of cars and throng of people around her.

For God's sake, she lectured herself silently as her heart pounded and her vision wavered. *Get a grip.* She was pregnant, not dying. But *damn* if she wasn't hyperventilating—in a good way—at the notion of life growing in her belly. And hyperventilating—*not* in a good way—at the thought of telling Dylan.

A keening moan escaped before she could shove it back. It was the very last conversation she wanted to have. Not after assuring him they were safe. Not after the best month of her life. And like an idiot, she even found herself dreaming of a future with Dylan—which was ridiculous, especially as she'd been the one to insist they were temporary. He'd think she was trying to trap him and he'd be furious. She couldn't blame him but it would be the end of anything good between them.

Her belly clenched, then rolled greasily with panic. Could it really be true? Perhaps what she and Nicole Dawson had seen was a cyst…or a tumor? She couldn't be so lucky as to be pregnant, could she? Not after the past few years of hell. Not after that devastating diagnosis.

Maybe she should have another scan to be sure. Maybe the sonar had been faulty and maybe—

A bubble of hysterical laughter popped, loud enough to startle her. *She was losing it.* Maybe she should just book herself into the psych ward because she was clearly having a mental breakdown.

There was no mistake.

She'd seen that little blob on the sonar herself, heard the unmistakable sound of a fetal heartbeat through the roar of blood in her ears. And, despite the shock, she'd distinctly heard the gynecologist say, "Congratulations, Dani, you're pregnant."

Nicole had laughed and pointed to the monitor, where the tiny buds attached to the blob were moving like crazy, as if Dani's child was waving at her and saying, *Hey, Mom, look at me. I'm here.*

"Look at that," Nicole had said, moving closer to the monitor. "I've never seen anything like it in such a young fetus." She'd grinned as she'd tapped a few commands into her computer. "This little one's already a fighter."

And in that instant Dani had fallen completely in love.

The baby she'd never thought she'd have was already more than a heartbeat, already more than a dream. In a shocked daze she'd barely heard the specialist promise to send her a video of the scan. She didn't recall heading down to the ER, clutching her prenatal prescription, to arrange a couple of weeks off before getting into her car and driving with no real destination in mind.

She'd found herself at the Horseshoe Bay ferry terminal and had purchased a ticket to Vancouver Island before she'd even known that she was heading home.

Pressing a shaky hand to her belly, where a miracle bloomed, where life blazed defiantly despite the odds, Dani wondered how her parents would react to the news that their divorced daughter was pregnant. How they would feel about her bringing up her child alone.

They loved her and would support her no matter what—she knew that. It wasn't like a hundred years ago, or even fifty, when women had been ostracized for having children out of wedlock. She'd be fine. *They'd* be fine. Lots of women brought up children alone and they turned out great. It wasn't as if she *needed* a man. She didn't. She had a great support system who would only be too happy to help.

The last thing she wanted was a man around just for the sake of his child. Not that she would keep the child from Dylan, Dani mused but that kind of relationship was doomed to fail from the start. Considering her one and only attempt at marriage had been such a disaster, there was no way she'd attempt another.

Besides, Dylan didn't love her. How could he? They'd only known each other a short time—although it seemed much longer. He liked the sex they were having but he didn't love her and probably never would. What they had was explosive chemistry, and even explosions eventually lost energy and petered out.

Would he think she'd lied? *Probably.* Would he think she'd deliberately tried to trap him? *Definitely.*

Oh God, she thought with a shudder, he was going to be furious. He'd demand she get rid of it and then he'd make sure she lost her job, and—

No, she chastised herself. That was Richard—not Dylan. But that didn't mean he'd want to be tied to her because of an unplanned pregnancy. She knew how he felt about that. About that woman in West Africa.

It might be the worst possible time to discover that her scarring had healed but she couldn't—*wouldn't*—be sorry. Not when she so desperately wanted this baby. *Her* baby.

A little thrill worked its way past the panic. Her little miracle. Hers and Dylan's.

Dylan. Panic replaced the thrill until her chest ached and her vision swam. What would she say? What *could* she say?

Oh, by the way, remember I told you I have Asherman's? Well...funny story...seems like the doctor was wrong. And not only was he wrong but I guess he miscalculated the possibility of me falling pregnant too. So how do you feel about being called Daddy?

Sure—she could just imagine how well *that* would go down.

Not.

He deserved to know—he *was* going to be a father, after all—but not yet. Not until she'd had time to get used to the idea herself—time to accept that a miracle had touched her life. And time, she thought fatalistically, to brace herself for the fallout.

For the seventh time in less than two minutes Dylan checked the address Maddie had given him and tried to ignore the annoying GPS voice telling him he'd reached his destination.

That was really great, he thought dryly as he studied the neat house overlooking the Georgia Strait, where Dani had supposedly grown up. But what it *didn't* tell him was why she'd come here when her life and her job were in Vancouver.

He'd had no idea that she'd even been *thinking* of leaving the city. Leaving *him.* Early Wednesday morning, when he'd gone to the ER in search of her, he'd been missing her and planning a romantic weekend away. He'd found her curled up on the sofa in the break room and something powerful had moved through him as he'd dropped to his haunches and smoothed the messy curls off her face.

He'd kissed her soft sleepy mouth, his body tightening when she'd hummed in the back of her throat and slid languid fingers through his hair. He'd left her looking flushed and aroused, as though she'd been missing him too.

By the next day she was gone.

For almost forty-eight hours she hadn't answered her phone or returned any text messages. He'd been frantic, thinking something bad had happened to her, and had called every hospital in the city to find out if she'd had an accident and wasn't able to call him. For God's sake, she'd been dizzy and nauseous for weeks—she could have passed out behind the wheel of her car.

When he'd finally heard from her it had been a hurried voice message saying that something had come up and she'd be out of town for a while.

That had been a week ago—which was how long it had taken him to clear his schedule and, more importantly, track her down.

The ball of slow-burning anger that had lodged in his chest right beside fear and concern flared brighter. She'd kissed him as though she couldn't get enough—as though he was more to her than a colleague and neighbor with benefits—and then she'd just walked away.

He hadn't heard anything from her since that cryptic message five days ago that had made his gut clench with fear and his chest tighten.

"Hi, it's Dani," she'd said, sounding shaky. "I'm… Uh… Something came up and I'll be out of town…a while." She'd paused and exhaled noisily before continuing. "Look, Dylan, I…we…" She'd cleared her throat. *"Oh boy,"* she'd muttered. "This is hard. There's just a few…um…*things* I need to take care of. I'll… I'll call you, okay? Soon…later. Um…bye."

It was obvious even to a blind man that she was either in some kind of trouble or she was dumping him. And if she was in trouble why hadn't she come to him? Surely she knew he'd be there for her? Surely she had to know that he was falling for her?

Hell, he'd done everything but give her the words.

Was that why she'd run? Why she wasn't answering or returning his calls? Had she realized that he'd ignored their "temporary" rule and started thinking long-term? Had she panicked because she wasn't feeling the same?

Neither her friends in the ER nor Maddie knew any-thing—or if they did they weren't talking.

When he'd called Cole's sister to find out if she knew where Dani had gone, and why, the first words out of her mouth had been, "What have you done?"

Maybe he was a clueless male but he had absolutely no idea. And if he listened to her voice message over and over—more to hear her voice than to figure out what she *wasn't* saying—no one had to know but him.

Her disappearance had hit him hard, left him reel-ing. He'd sat on his empty houseboat feeling as though someone had ripped open his chest and stuck a jagged stake through his heart. Unable to stand his bed with-out her in it, he'd crashed on the sofa, only to stare at the roof all night.

It was during those dark hours that he'd finally admit-ted the sobering truth. He wasn't falling for Dani. He'd already fallen—with a rude jolt. And, lying there, all he'd been able to think about was how bleak the future would be without her in it.

He was crazy in love—the can't eat, can't sleep, can't think kind of insanity—with a woman who gave *covert ops* a bad name. Hell, special forces could learn a thing or two about escape-and-evade tactics from one sweet and frustratingly elusive ER doctor with big gray eyes and a husky laugh.

But, then again, Dylan hadn't become the best re-construction ortho surgeon in British Columbia by sit-ting back and letting success come to him. And he'd be damned if he'd meekly wait around for Dani to get around to dumping him in person.

He knew about her marriage and he understood why she was wary of men and commitment. But she hadn't really given them a chance. The entire time they'd been together she'd had one foot out the door, despite all his efforts to lure her all the way in.

Now, clenching his jaw, he shoved open the Jeep's door and slid out, slamming it behind him, ignoring the fear edging his frustration. He *had* to get her back, he admitted to himself. Life just wasn't the same without her.

Looking forward to the coming confrontation, he started down the driveway to the house and took the steps in a single bound. Dani's battered sedan was the only car out front, so he was confident he had the right address. But after five minutes of punching the doorbell he was still outside, cooling his jets.

After a brief battle with himself he set off around the house, beginning to panic because she might be lying injured somewhere. Maybe she was still dizzy and had fallen and hit her head. Maybe she was bleeding out and needed an ambulance. Maybe… Yeah, he thought with a disgusted snort. And maybe he needed to get a damn grip.

She could be out shopping or… Or out with another man, he thought darkly. Maybe this wasn't her parents' house but the home of an old lover—or maybe a new lover. Maybe she'd met someone else and didn't know how to tell him.

Battling his visions of her lying helpless and unconscious—or laughing with another man—he headed around the house, passing flowerbeds in a profusion of colors and a neat vegetable garden that looked well-tended, reaching a sprawling deck overlooking the strait. Although it was obvious by the empty glass and abandoned book that someone had recently been sitting there, it was now deserted. The sliding doors were locked and the house appeared empty.

He was just about to return to his car and wait for someone to show up when he noticed an open gate at the end of the landscaped garden. Realizing it opened onto some steps that led to the beach, he followed his instincts and found himself on a sweep of forest-ringed sand littered with rocks, driftwood and beach debris.

A visual sweep told him it was deserted, except for a single figure about a quarter-mile away. He knew instinctively that it was Dani, sitting hunched on the sand while a dog played in the nearby surf, barking at the seagulls and chasing the crabs.

At the sight of her something in his chest expanded and squeezed with a painful clench. Anger flared, and even if it hid an all-encompassing relief that she was okay he wasn't about to let it distract him from his purpose. He was going to get answers and he was done with playing her games.

Flexing his jaw, Dylan took off down the beach toward the only person in the world who could make him crazy. The one woman, he'd realized this past week, he could not—*would* not—live without. She'd sneaked past his defenses, burrowed under his skin and dug deep furrows into his soul, filling them with her sweetness, her surprisingly wicked sense of humor and with the quiet gray eyes that could look into him and see everything.

She'd teased him with something he never thought he'd find.

A future.

Now all he needed was to get her to accept that he could be *her* future too.

CHAPTER ELEVEN

WHEN THE TONE of Polo's bark changed, Dani turned to see what had disturbed him and froze at the sight of the figure walking along the beach toward her.

No, she amended, her heart fluttering with both excitement and apprehension. *Stalking* toward her. Like a large hungry predator with his unsuspecting prey in sight.

Dylan.

Hands jammed deep in his jeans pockets, he radiated a kind of masculine intent that sent exhilaration shooting up her spine along with a healthy dose of wariness. It was there in the set of his wide shoulders, in the deceptively lazy movement of his long muscular legs, and it was all she could do not to bolt to her feet and take off in the opposite direction.

Oh God, she thought, her belly cramping with nerves. He'd found her before she was ready. Found her before she could shore up her shaky defenses.

With determination in every line of his big, tough body he closed the distance and she knew there was no escaping what was to come. No escaping *him*.

But then again, she thought, swallowing past the lump of emotion forming in her throat, maybe she'd never really had a chance. Maybe her fate had been sealed the moment they'd met—the moment she'd looked up into those moss-green eyes and heard him ask if she was okay.

She wasn't okay. She'd *never* be okay again. And waiting for him to cross those last hundred yards left her jittery and excited.

This is it, she thought as resignation filled her. *Time's just run out.*

And yet she couldn't stop her gaze from clinging, filing away the image of him as he came toward her, so big and safe and familiar. Familiar and yet there was something new…something just a little bit dangerous in the way he'd locked onto her like a heat-seeking missile.

His mouth and his shadowed jaw were set in grim lines, exaggerated by the dark aviator wraparounds that hid his eyes from view. He looked both familiar and foreign. It was that foreignness that had Dani inhaling shakily and drawing her knees to her chest.

Wrapping her arms around her shins, she waited.

Sensing her distress, Polo trotted over, whining and pressing his body against hers. Glad of his comforting presence, she slung an arm around him and hugged him close as Dylan came up behind her.

For long moments he said nothing. The air seemed to prickle with awareness, and the heavy silence frayed her already ragged nerves.

Finally, he said quietly, "You're a difficult woman to find."

There was no sign in his deep voice of the tension she could feel blasting off him in waves.

Feeling unbearably drained—inexplicably miserable—she dropped her forehead to her knees. "What are you doing here, Dylan?"

"The bigger question," he drawled roughly, "is what are *you* doing here, when your life, your job, your *friends* are in Vancouver?" He didn't have to say that *he* was in Vancouver but it hung in the air between them like an unspoken challenge.

Feeling at a disadvantage, she sighed and rose to her feet, staggering when the abrupt change in elevation had her blood pressure plummeting.

He cursed and snatched her against him before she could face-plant in the sand at his feet. "You're still sick? Have you seen a physician?"

The urge to cling was too great to ignore and she found herself clutching his shirt, her body taking advantage of his heat and strength. She felt weak as a kitten, so tempted to just lay her head against his chest and close her eyes.

She shook her head to clear it. God, she was so tired. She just wanted to slide into sleep but she needed all her wits about her.

"You haven't?" he demanded softly, his long surgeon's fingers digging into the flesh of her upper arms as though he was fighting a battle within himself as to whether he would shake her or pull her close. "This has gone on long enough."

She heard him through the roar of blood in her ears and could only shake her head.

"Let me take you back. I'll examine you myself."

Her throat unlocked enough for her to croak, "No." She shoved at him and stood swaying for a moment while her head cleared. "You won't."

She made herself move away when all she wanted to do was sink into him and take a nap. But she couldn't—didn't have the right. Not with what she was keeping from him.

"I'm fine."

"You're clearly not," he countered, frustration and concern making him scowl at her. "Not when just rising to your feet leaves you shaky and pale."

He cursed when she blew out a gusty breath.

"Fine," he said curtly, pulling out his phone. "I'm calling an ambulance. Once you're at a hospital I'll order a batch of tests and find out what's wrong."

Shoving her tangled hair off her face, she gave a laugh as shaky as her legs. "That's ridiculous."

She sighed and rubbed her face, hoping to get some feeling back into her numb cheeks while he just narrowed his eyes.

"I don't need an ambulance. I just need a week, that's all. *A week*. I told you I need to sort out some…uh…stuff." She pressed her fingers against her pounding temples and wished they wouldn't throb in counterpoint to her racing pulse. "Go home, Dylan. *Please*. I'm fine. It's nothing a week being fussed over by my mother won't cure."

Nothing seven months won't cure, a voice in her head reminded her.

"And then I'll be back. I promise."

"You've had a week," he pointed out curtly, studying her with narrow-eyed intensity. "And I'm here because you haven't told me *anything*. How can you when you won't answer my damn texts or return my calls."

"I did call. I left a message."

"That garbled confusion? It told me *nothing*, Dani, and it scared me more than if you'd just told me to get lost."

"Is…is that what you thought?" Noisily, she expelled the breath she was holding. Bending, she scratched Polo's ear—to soothe herself as much as the dog. Voice low, she said, "That's not what this is about."

His sigh had her straightening, facing him warily.

"Then why don't you tell me what it *is* about?"

She opened her mouth to tell him but chickened out. "I'm…uh…how did you find me?"

One dark eyebrow rose mockingly up his forehead.

She sighed. "Maddie."

"Don't blame Maddie," he said roughly. "She's worried about you—*everyone's* worried about you. Besides, I shouldn't have had to hear about it from someone else."

She froze. *It?*

His words sent a shudder of panic through her, because it appeared her nightmare was coming true. He… he *knew*? Knew and was furious?

Of course he'd be furious, she chided herself. After another woman had tried to trap him with an unplanned pregnancy how did she *think* he'd feel?

Heart pounding, she searched his expression for any hint of knowledge that she was pregnant but his face was unreadable, giving nothing away. For a moment she wished he'd remove his sunglasses but she was terrified of what she'd see if he did.

But…*how* could he know? She hadn't told *anyone*. Not even her boss. The only reason Amy knew was because she'd insisted on Dani taking the test and seen her after the gyno appointment had confirmed it.

She felt her face drain of color and locked her shaking knees. "She t-told you?" she asked faintly, ignoring the odd searching look he sent her.

"Of course she told me. She's worried—*I'm* worried." He folded his arms across his chest. "Didn't you think I'd want to know?" he demanded. "Didn't you think I *deserved* to know?"

Her eyes widened. Panicked, she swallowed and took a hasty step backward, murmuring an absent apology when she bumped into Polo. "I…uh—"

He interrupted her with a rough laugh and spun away to thrust impatient hands through his tousled hair. "Yeah, I can see it didn't even cross your mind."

The muscle jumping in his tight jaw drew Dani's fascinated gaze.

"For God's sake, Dani," he rasped. "What the *hell's* the matter with you?"

Rattled, filled with guilt, she burst out with, "I'm s-sorry. I didn't know, Dylan, I *swear*. I thought…"

Tears pricked her eyes and she blinked rapidly before they could fall and complete her humiliation.

"I thought—" She bit her lip and wrapped her arms around herself in an effort to keep from falling apart. "I thought I c-couldn't, you know… Well, the doctor said it was impossible… I just took his word for it and…well, after that first time we…you… Well, we didn't. And… and then Amy insisted… And it was p-positive…which I didn't believe…"

She was aware she was babbling incoherently but she couldn't seem to stop. Her teeth had begun to chatter and she'd balled her hands into fists beneath her armpits.

"Because it was im-impossible, right?" She broke off to suck in a couple of shallow breaths, knowing she was hyperventilating. "B-besides, you *know* those th-things aren't always reliable. Well, anyway, I made an…an appointment and… I'm sorry."

Her voice cracked and she struggled for a moment to regain control of it.

"I didn't tell you, Dylan, and I'm sorry. But I… I couldn't… I just *couldn't*. I know you're angry but—"

The sob she'd been holding in burst out before she could push it back. Spinning away, she pressed the heels of her hands to her burning eyes. The last thing she wanted was for him to see her fall apart like this.

"You're angry, and I don't blame you… *God*, I'm sorry. But I *couldn't*—" Overcome, she covered her face with her hands and struggled to get her emotions under control. "I couldn't tell you," she said, hoping she could make him understand. "I was in shock and I just… I just had to get away."

For the next few moments the only sounds were her ragged breathing and the gentle shushing of the water as it ebbed and flowed against the sand. How could it be so peaceful when her life was falling apart?

Finally, she could stand the silence no longer. Shoving her hair off her hot face, she chanced a glance over her shoulder and saw that he was staring at her as though she'd babbled state secrets in a foreign language.

"What the *hell* are you talking about?"

He sounded so baffled that for a moment she could only stare at him, wondering if she'd crash-landed in an alternate universe. *Okay*, she thought, so maybe he *doesn't* know. Maybe he's talking about something else…

Licking her lips, she shifted her feet, nervously brushing at the sand clinging to her jeans. "What…what do you…um…*think* I'm talking about?" she asked casually.

For about five seconds he stared at her silently, before abruptly shaking his head as if to clear it. "Oh, no," he muttered, yanking his sunglasses off and tossing them onto the sand. "No more evasions, dammit. No more evasions and no more lies. Just tell me the *truth*."

Her heart jolted in her chest as her spine snapped straight. "I never lied to you."

She'd kept things from him maybe, but she'd never lied.

His turbulent green eyes were laser-sharp and she wished for just an instant that they were still hidden behind those dark frames. They made her a little nervous, because he seemed to see right into her soul, to root out all her secrets, all her irrational fears and all her tentative dreams.

"Maybe not," he conceded slowly, "but you haven't been honest with me either. You've kept parts of yourself locked away. You've shared your body but not your mind—and certainly not your emotions."

Her denial was swift and heated. "That's not true. I—"

"*Isn't* it?" he interrupted smoothly. "Isn't that what you're doing right now? Isn't that what you've been doing the past ten days by disappearing without a word? By not returning my calls?"

Dani opened her mouth to hotly deny it, then snapped it shut. What could she say? He was right. She *hadn't* shared herself with him when he'd been generous to a fault.

Blinking rapidly at the realization that she'd selfishly held herself back, Dani could only manage, "I—"

"What do I have to do to prove I'm not like your ex?"

Furious with herself—with him—Dani snapped out, "I never said you were!"

Realizing she was all but shouting, she inhaled to steady herself before lowering her voice.

"I never *thought* you were, Dylan. Not once."

"Maybe," he agreed wearily. "But you can't deny you've been waiting for an opportunity to bolt, Dani. Waiting for me to turn into a lying, cheating bastard."

The truth of it burned a path down her throat. "I'm not. I *haven't*—"

"Haven't you?" he challenged tiredly. "You think I don't see it in your eyes sometimes? Like right now? For just an instant you freeze, and it's like you're bracing yourself for me to turn into some kind of monster who slaps women around."

"I don't think that, Dylan," she assured him, her voice low, intense. "If I'm waiting…" She swallowed convulsively. "If I've *been* waiting, it's for you to get tired of me."

He blinked in surprise. "Tired? What do you mean, tired?"

"As in lose interest in me," she snapped, rubbing her

hands down her arms to ward off a chill that had nothing to do with the breeze that had kicked up. "Get bored. Move on. D-dump me."

He stared at her as though she'd lost her mind, which she very likely had.

"Dump you? You think I'm *dumping* you?"

He shook his head as though he couldn't believe what he was hearing. When she said nothing he inhaled, as if searching for patience.

"What is this really about, Dani? And don't give me that garbage about waiting for me to get bored. If anything, I've been thinking—" He broke off. "Yeah, well, clearly I've been an idiot."

"Dylan…?"

Ignoring her soft, hesitant query, he asked, "Did I really give you the impression that I was getting bored?"

When she said nothing, he sighed and scrubbed his hands over his face, as he sometimes did when he was frustrated. *"Oh."* He gave a rusty laugh. "I get it. Guess I'm a little slow on the uptake, huh? Because I have to tell you I didn't see this coming."

"What—?"

"Is *that* what this is about?" he asked. "You're telling me that *you're* bored? With us? With me?"

She couldn't prevent her shocked denial from emerging any more than he could prevent his shoulders hunching and another ragged laugh bursting out.

"Okay." He sucked in air, let it out again. "Okay…" he said again, dropping his hands on her shoulders and tugging her closer. "So if you haven't found someone else, and you aren't dumping me…what's really the problem?"

Tears filled her eyes and she dropped her forehead wearily against his chest, loving the scent of him, the heat of his body that seeped into hers. Inhaling it because it might be her last opportunity to do so.

She bit her lip and rolled her forehead in denial. If only she could just sink against him and let him take care of everything. She was so tired. Tired of being alone, of being strong and handling stuff alone because she didn't want to worry the people who loved her.

Swallowing a sob, she pressed her face into his warm throat. "It…it wasn't on purpose, Dylan," she murmured tightly. "You have to believe me."

He rubbed a couple of circles on her shoulders before wrapping his hand around her neck and nudging her chin up with his thumb. "*What*, babe?" he asked gently. "What wasn't on purpose?"

Because she couldn't bear to see those beautiful green eyes turn hard as emeralds she dropped her gaze to the soft cotton stretched across his heated flesh and absently realized that her fingers were wrapped tightly in the warm fabric, clinging.

Consciously relaxing, she smoothed out the wrinkles. His deep voice rumbled beneath her palms.

"Dani?"

Before she could chicken out she took a deep breath and got it out quickly, breathlessly. "I'm pregnant."

For a couple dozen heartbeats there was absolutely no reaction except for a reflexive tightening of his fingers. Then he sucked in a harsh breath and, because she couldn't stand not knowing, she quickly looked into his face. Then promptly wished she hadn't.

Oh boy. He looked as though she'd punched him in the head.

Okay, not exactly the reaction she'd hoped to see but better than anger, right? Frazzled by his speechless shock, she shoved away from him and before he could recover filled the silence.

"Don't worry," she assured him quickly. "This is my problem and I'll deal with it. There's no need for you to concern yourself. I'll… I'll handle everything. We'll be fine."

When she paused to suck in a frantic breath, Dylan lifted a hand to silence her. "Hold on," he ordered hoarsely. "Just hold the damn *on*. You're not ill? You haven't been diagnosed with cancer or…or something else?" He shook his head. "You're…*pregnant*?"

"I…uh…yes," she said baldly. "I'm p-pregnant."

The hands he shoved through his hair shook. "You're pregnant and you let me think you were…?" He broke off, swore. "You let me think you were ill and didn't want to tell me?"

She was shocked at the harsh emotion in his voice. "I did not… I wouldn't! I'm not sick!"

He swore again. "Do you have *any* idea what I've been going through? Thinking…thinking the worst, when all this time—?"

"I *told* you," she babbled, horrified by what he'd been thinking. "I told you I was f-fine."

"No, you told me 'something came up,'" he snapped, storming away a short distance before rounding on her. "Something came up and you had some *things* to sort out and— *Oh*." He staggered back a couple of steps, his gaze dropping to her still flat belly. His mouth fell open. He lifted dazed eyes. "You're…*pregnant*?"

Her lips pressed together. "Yes. And, before you ask, it's yours."

He sent her a searing look. "Don't insult me. Of course it's mine. But—" His expression darkened with concern.

"Are…are you sure? What about the Asherman's? Are you okay? Maybe you should be resting?"

Tears filled her eyes and, misunderstanding, he grabbed her and jerked her into his arms.

"There's something wrong, isn't there?" he demanded shakily. "Please tell me there isn't anything wrong with the baby. With you."

She gave a ragged watery laugh and shook her head. "No," she soothed, unconsciously stroking unsteady fingers over his pounding heart. "There's nothing wrong. I'm fine and yes, I'm sure."

She sucked in a wobbly breath, letting her tears dampen his throat as her heart beat in rhythm with his.

"I saw the scan. I have a picture. And Nicole Dawson sent me a video. It's…*amazing*." She sniffed inelegantly. "Anyway, she says the scarring must not have been as severe as Dr. Cartwright thought, or maybe I just healed better than expected."

She exhaled shakily before sucking in another breath.

"I'm okay. Still in shock, I think. But I've been resting. And my mother's enjoyed pampering me. Me and the baby, we're both fine…or *will* be the further along we get. As long as I don't overdo things."

"It's settled, then," Dylan said, wrapping her close and pressing his lips to her temple. "After we're married you can cut down on your hours or even stop working until after the baby is born. You can move in with me immediately and— What?"

Dani had stilled and was easing out of his arms. She backed off a couple of steps, more to resist temptation than to stop his words. "We're not getting married, Dylan," she said flatly, rubbing at the pinch in her chest. Pinch? Hell, it was like a mortal wound that bled at the expression on his face.

He was staring at her as though she'd pulled back and slugged him in the mouth. "Of course we're getting married," he countered. "As soon as we can arrange it—"

"No, we're not," she interrupted furiously. "I've *been* married. I'm already a statistic and I'm not going there again. Not just because I'm pregnant. Marriage should be for people who love each other—like my parents, *your* parents. Besides," she continued frantically when his expression hardened, became blank, as though she'd hurt him somehow when that was impossible, "this isn't the nineteenth century. A woman doesn't *have* to get married anymore just because she's pregnant. Don't forget what you told me about that woman in West Africa. You wouldn't marry Simone just because she was pregnant."

"Forget Simone," he growled, clearly furious that she was using his own words against him. "I wasn't in love with her."

She stilled, her gaze searching. "What are you saying?"

"I'm saying I'm in *love* with you, dammit," he snapped. "I've been in love with you for days…weeks…maybe from the first."

Her eyes widened and she jerked back, a host of expressions tripping over each other as they crossed her face: shock, fear, hurt…denial.

"Yeah, I can see that thrills the hell out of you." He spun away. "Surely you're not surprised?" he demanded. "An intelligent woman like you? How could you not know when it's been there every time I've looked at you? Every time I've touched you, kissed you? Every time we've made love?"

Her throat closed and it felt as if she was trying to push her words through jagged glass shards. "Don't…" she gasped, pressing a tight fist against the pain in her chest. "Don't you *dare* p-pretend something you don't feel just because you think it's…it's what I want to hear. I'm not your responsibility, Dylan. Besides, it's not like I'm expecting anything from you. I told you—I'll handle it myself."

He muttered a few choice curses. "I've just told you I'm in love with you and all you can say is you're not my responsibility? Of *course* you are. You weren't alone in that bed, Dani and I'll be damned if you shut me out because you're afraid of your emotions. Heck, *look* at you—you're terrified of *mine*."

"Don't—don't do this to me, Dylan, please," she sobbed, swiping angrily at the tears that rolled down her cheeks. "I'm trying to be strong here because I can't… I c-couldn't…stand it if…if we got married and one day you m-met someone more suitable and…and then hated me." She gulped and wrapped her arms protectively around her belly, where their child grew. "Hated *us* for being there, for standing in your way. You'd hate that, Dylan, and you'd hate *me*."

Dylan rocked back on his heels, studying her as though he'd never seen her before. "You really have a low opinion of me, don't you?"

Dani blinked. "What? No!" she denied hotly. "I think the world of you. If I didn't I wouldn't be in l—"

"Wouldn't be what?" he demanded when she stopped abruptly and just stared at him, as though she'd admitted to a deadly sin. "Throwing my feelings in my face?"

"I—"

"Give me a chance, Dani," he urged quietly, stepping closer to brush a tangled curl off her forehead with gentle fingers. "I've showed you in a thousand ways just how much you suit me…how much we suit each other."

Dani couldn't resist turning her face into his caress,

stepping into his big hard body. "I… I'm scared," she admitted in a quiet rush. "I'm scared I'll disappoint you. I couldn't bear that."

Wrapping her close, Dylan dropped his cheek to the dark tangle of wind-tossed curls. "You couldn't," he murmured. "Don't you know by now that the only way you could ever disappoint me is by cutting me out of your life?"

He smoothed a hand down her back, over her hip to her belly, so he could press his palm where his child grew.

"Let me love you—both of you. I know you don't—perhaps can't—feel the same but I love you enough for both of us."

Her body jolted against his. "Dylan…?" she murmured, lifting her head. Huge gray eyes swirled with fierce emotion as they tentatively met his.

"Let's make a future," he urged quietly, dropping a gentle kiss on her soft mouth. "Together."

For a moment her mouth remained passive and he felt his heart sink, quietly break. Then her lips trembled and she gave a ragged moan. Her hand stole to his, pressed it where it lay against her belly.

"You…*love* me?"

"Can't you feel it?" he murmured against her mouth. "Can't you feel it every time I touch you? Every time we're together?"

She pressed closer, her mouth curving against his. "I thought we just had really great chemistry."

He chuckled and pushed her away so he could see her face, no longer pale and unhappy but flushed, glowing, beautiful. "We do. But it's more than that, Dani. It's… *more*."

"I…"

He watched her dark lashes sweep down to cover her

gaze. When they lifted, the emotion burning in the silvery depths staggered him.

"I love you, Dylan." She lifted his hand to her face, pressed it against her cheek. "I didn't want to but I couldn't help myself."

"I know," he murmured, his thumb soothing her cheekbone. "I'm irresistible."

She gave a laughing snort and turned, biting his thumb. "Yeah, lucky for you. Because it's not like you have anything *else* going for you."

He chuckled but soon sobered. "I *am* lucky," he agreed softly, fiercely. "Make me even luckier by setting a date."

And because he was holding her he felt the tremor go through her. Her gaze turned wary and he could feel her pulling away. Even though she hadn't moved.

"Date?"

"Our wedding—"

She quickly slid one slender finger over his lips before replacing it with her mouth. "Not now," she murmured against his lips. "Ask me again. If you still want to get ma—" She stopped and cleared her throat. She huffed out a shaky laugh. "If you still want to do…um…*that* by the time our baby is born, ask me again then."

"Wow," he said, amused. "You can't even *say* it, can you?"

"Of course I can," she spluttered, going red. "It's just… it's such a big step, Dylan, a huge…*thing*. I don't want to mess up again."

"You won't," he said, with a conviction she didn't seem to share. "But, hypothetically speaking," he added casually, "if I asked you again, when our baby is born, you'd say yes?"

Her arms slipped around him, and with her face pressed

into his neck she hugged him hard. "Yes," she murmured. "I might just say yes."

Knowing he'd pushed her as far as he could for now, Dylan snatched her off her feet and cupped the back of her head. Pressing a kiss to her laughing mouth, he knew he'd won the war.

EPILOGUE

Six months later

"GOOD JOB, PEOPLE!" Dylan called out, pulling off his mask and cap with one hand while stripping off his gown with the other. Surgery had gone overtime and he was eager to head down to the ER to see how Dani was doing.

She'd been a little pale and tired this morning but had insisted that she was fine. *Soon*, he thought, tossing the soiled garments in the laundry bin and heading for the basins to wash up. Soon he'd insist on her taking maternity leave and he wasn't taking no for an answer.

The past six months had been the happiest of his life, he mused, reaching for the soap and nudging the tap open with his elbow. And even though he hadn't yet managed to tempt her down the aisle he'd made it a habit to sneak a proposal in regularly. Like when she was soft and drowsy and sated, her barriers down.

Just this morning he'd kissed her soft mouth and gently rubbed her growing belly, chuckling when the baby moved beneath his hand. Dani's lips had smiled against his and she'd snuggled closer, making his heart clench with love.

"Soon," she'd murmured, smoothing her hand down over his chest, when he'd asked her again when she'd make an honest man of him. With a contented sigh, she'd pressed her lips to his left pec—right over his heart—and told him she loved him.

Full of her, he'd let it go, even though he wanted to tie her to him so tightly that she'd never get away. Never *want* to get away.

But his mother had warned him to be patient, so he'd be patient.

Even if it killed him.

He was grabbing a handful of paper towels when the outer door slammed open and a nurse burst in, red-faced and out of breath. It looked as if she'd been running. "Dr. St. James?" she demanded, her gaze frantically racing over the remaining surgical staff milling around. *"Where's Dr. St. James?* We've been trying to get hold of h—"

"Here," he interrupted, even as her gaze zeroed in on him. "What's wrong?"

"It's Dani," the woman gasped. "The baby's coming. You have to come quickly."

He was at her side in an instant. "What? It's too soon. Tell me what happened."

"No time," she yelped, shoving him toward the outer doors. "Obstetrics Wing—surgery. They've called Dr. Dawson. *Hurry.*"

Dylan didn't recall tearing through the hospital to the East Wing. Nor did he remember taking the three flights of stairs at a dead run. He was a doctor, *dammit*, a surgeon. He'd been trained to maintain a level head in a crisis. But panic ripped at him as he hit the obstetrics wing and tore through the swing doors with his lungs burning.

Just as he shoved his way into the room he heard a thin wail break through the silence.

Nicole Dawson looked up. "Congratulations, Dad, it's a girl!"

* * *

Dani floated lazily up through layers of sleep to hear the steady beeping of machines. It was a familiar sound that comforted her and for a moment—just a split second— she thought she was back on surgical rotation.

Then she remembered seeing the flashing lights, feeling the jostle of the gurney racing down brightly lit passages. And then Dylan's face, his eyes dark and filled with love and concern. She remembered telling him she loved him and then… Nothing.

Her eyes flew open as she tried to heave her body upright. *"Dylan—?"* It was a gasp on her lips, emerging as a kind of gurgling rasp.

She was barely aware of a groggy, "Wha—?" cutting through her panic. But it brought her head around as a disheveled Dylan lurched up from the chair beside the bed, his frantic gaze sweeping the room.

On their return sweep his eyes locked with hers. "What's wrong?" he rasped, his eyes suddenly wide awake and intense. "Are you in pain? Can I get you anything?"

Dani stared at him, vaguely aware of the sound of approaching footsteps.

A young nurse skidded into the doorway, her eyes wide in her pale face. "Is…is everything all right, Dr. St. James?" she demanded.

Clearly realizing that he'd been almost shouting, Dylan cleared his throat. "Everything's fine, thank you," he said quickly.

"Dr. Stevens?" the nurse asked quietly, moving into the room to check the IV cannulas.

"I'd like some iced water, please," Dani said, wanting to buy them some privacy. She waited until the nurse had left before meeting Dylan's gaze. "What's going on?"

He collapsed back into the chair. He looked exhausted. His jaw was rough and dark, his eyes deep pools of some fierce emotion that stole her breath. She couldn't remember ever seeing him look so rattled.

"How are you feeling?" he asked.

"Tired."

His laugh emerged roughly before he leveled a crooked smile at her and reached for her hand, sliding their palms together, lacing their fingers. His were warm and solid, familiar.

Lifting her cold hand, he pressed a kiss to her knuckles. "You couldn't wait, could you?" His fingers tightened around hers. "I sprinted all the way from the West Wing to get here, just in time for Nicole to congratulate me."

She licked dry lips. "What happened? I remember sudden cramps," she admitted. "And then you... Wait... You were holding—"

"Yeah, our daughter," he said, with such pride that Dani blinked. He kissed her knuckles, his eyes warm with love as they clung to hers. "She's beautiful—just like her mother."

A little thrill moved through her. "Where is she?" she demanded urgently, struggling to sit up. "I want to meet her."

"In a minute," he soothed as the nurse hurried in with a glass of iced water. "Let's get you some water first. You have a lot of fluid to replace." He gave the nurse a brief glance as he took the glass in his free hand. "You can bring our daughter now," he said.

"Of course, Dr. St. James."

Watching the departing nurse, Dani gripped his hand. "She's...okay?"

His grin was a white flash in the dim room. "She's

better than okay," he said with satisfaction, and dropped a quick kiss on her mouth.

It was a kiss that instantly gentled, clung and after a long sweet moment ended on a sigh. Hers *and* his.

His forehead touched hers. "She's a fighter—like her mom," he murmured, moving back a couple of inches to look into her eyes.

His gaze, soft and endlessly green, had something tight inside her melting, unfurling.

"She came into the world shaking her fists and bellowing!"

He straightened as the nurse reappeared, pushing a neonatal bassinet into the room.

"Thank you, Nurse Richards, I can take it from here."

Dani's eyes remained locked on Dylan as he gently scooped up the tiny bundle in his big, capable hands.

"Hey, sweetheart," he crooned softly, drawing a sigh from the nurse, who was now checking Dani's vitals. "You're awake. Can't wait to meet your mom, can you?"

He dropped a tender kiss on the infant's forehead, giving Dani a quick glimpse of huge dark eyes, a wealth of dark hair fluffed around a delicate pink face and a tiny rosebud mouth.

"Well, she can't wait to meet *you*." He lifted the swaddled infant as though they shared a secret. "You won't tell her about you know what, will you? She doesn't need to know your dad completely embarrassed himself back there. She doesn't need to know he went a little crazy."

The nurse gave a short chuckle.

Dani arched a brow at him. "If he knows what's good for him," she announced primly, "he'll stop talking and let me meet you."

Grinning, Dylan gently tucked the pink bundle into

her arms and pressed a kiss to her temple. But she could only stare down in amazement at her baby.

Their daughter.

Their miracle.

She looked into the perfect little face for the first time—into those slate-gray eyes that looked far too large and wise for such a tiny face—and felt tears spring into her own.

"Oh…" Her breath caught on a huge ball of emotion, because it was like holding a priceless gift—one she'd never expected to receive. "L-look at her, Dylan. She's so perfect and tiny."

Just then the infant opened that delicate rosebud mouth and yawned, making Dani laugh and cry as love burst through her like a shaft of golden light through heavy cloud.

With her free hand she brushed tender fingers across a delicate pink cheek and the little face turned toward the touch, rooting hungrily.

Dylan laced his fingers with hers and eased down behind her on the bed, cradling them both—Dani *and* their daughter—against his chest.

Snuggling in, she realized her heart was filled with a fierce kind of joy—joy and gratitude and a new hope for the future.

"She's wonderful, Dylan." She tilted her head back, her eyes meeting his, filled with the staggering thrill of the miracle they had made together and the life that loomed ahead. "And so are you."

Lifting her mouth, she accepted his slow, gentle kiss. A kiss that stirred as it soothed so that even when he slowly ended it her lips clung, not ready—not *nearly* ready—to let go.

It was in that moment she realized with blinding clarity that she didn't have to let go—didn't ever have to. Because she loved him enough to take a chance.

"I don't know what we'd do without you," she murmured, her throat tight with the terrifying emotion that had banished all her fears and uncertainty in one blinding instant.

"It's a good thing you didn't see me last night, then." His chuckle was a deep and wonderful sound. "You might rethink the whole 'wonderful' thing. You might change your mind about making us a family."

She shook her head. "No," she said firmly. "Sophie deserves two people who love her."

For a moment she felt him tense but he must have seen something in her eyes because his gaze turned intense, searching. "And *do* you?" he asked quietly.

Distracted by the overwhelming feelings filling her for this man—this amazingly tender and wonderful man—who'd come to her rescue one rainy night, Dani blinked. "Do I what?"

"Love me?"

Her breath escaped on a soundless sigh because she'd never been more sure of anything. "You know I do."

His hand brushed over the wild fluff of dark hair covering the tiny head of their daughter. "Then say yes," he urged. "Say you'll marry me and make us a family."

With fierce joy bursting through her, Dani turned and smiled up at him. "We're already a family," she murmured, and slid the fingers of her free hand into his hair. She pulled him closer, held him where she knew he belonged. "But, yes," she murmured. "I'll marry you."

And with a softly muttered, "Finally…" Dylan laughed and kissed his future.

* * * * *

MILLS & BOON

Coming next month

MENDING THE SINGLE DAD'S HEART
Susanne Hampton

Harrison's head was telling him to pull back but his heart was saying something very different.

They were two professional people who had spent time getting to know each other outside of work and he had allowed it to go too far. Now he needed to take her cue and set boundaries. Jessica had been upfront about her intentions. Stay six weeks and leave town. There had been no deceit, no false promises. He had to try and colleague zone Jessica immediately and put some distance between them. He had no choice, for his own sake. But he doubted how successful it would be after the kiss they'd shared.

'I can assist with that...'

'You've done enough.' Enough to unsettle him. Enough to even at that moment make him want to pull her close again. Enough to make him kiss her again. He was so confused, and she had made him think clearly when he'd felt her pull away. Now he had to do it too. 'I'll email hospital admin when I get home and let them know to roster cover for you until eleven. It's not the entire day off, but it's a few extra hours' sleep. I arranged the same for the other staff before I left. And the neuro-surgeon is flying in from Sydney mid-morning, to consult on the two suspected spinal cord injury patients.'

'You certainly have everything under control.'

'It's best for everyone that way.' Though Harrison knew he was losing control with Jessica. And that was not the best option for a man who had finally gained control of his life.

His tone had changed and he could see it hadn't gone unnoticed by Jessica. Torn best described how he felt. He didn't understand what he had seen in her eyes only moments before. It confused him. Her gorgeously messy blonde hair fell around her beautiful face and she looked less like an accomplished temporary Paediatric Consultant from a large city hospital and more like a fresh-faced country girl. She was so close he could reach out and cup her beautiful face in his hands and kiss her again.

He had to leave before he went mad with the gamut of emotions he was feeling.

Opening the door, he walked into the icy night air without stopping to put on his jacket.

Or say goodnight.

Continue reading
MENDING THE SINGLE DAD'S HEART
Susanne Hampton

Available next month
www.millsandboon.co.uk

COMING SOON!

We really hope you enjoyed reading this book. If you're looking for more romance, be sure to head to the shops when new books are available on

Thursday 2nd May

To see which titles are coming soon, please visit

millsandboon.co.uk/nextmonth

LET'S TALK

Romance

For exclusive extracts, competitions
and special offers, find us online:

Get in touch on 01413 063232

For all the latest titles coming soon, visit
millsandboon.co.uk/nextmonth